D0173184

Contents

BOOKS BY LOREN D. ESTLEMAN

*Published by Tom Doherty Associates

CAPE HELL

⇌ AND ⇌

THE BOOK OF MURDOCK

Loren D. Estleman

FORGE®

A TOM DOHERTY ASSOCIATES BOOK / NEW YORK

CAPE HELL AND THE BOOK OF MURDOCK

Cape Hell copyright © 2016 by Loren D. Estleman

The Book of Murdock copyright © 2010 by Loren D. Estleman

A Forge Book
Published by Tom Doherty Associates
175 Fifth Avenue
New York, NY 10010

www.tor-forge.com

Forge® is a registered trademark of Macmillan Publishing Group, LLC.

ISBN 978-0-7653-9302-9

Our books may be purchased in bulk for promotional, educational, or business use. Please contact your local bookseller or the Macmillan Corporate and Premium Sales Department at 1-800-221-7945, extension 5442, or by e-mail at MacmillanSpecialMarkets@macmillan.com.

First Edition: February 2017

Printed in the United States of America

0 9 8 7 6 5 4 3 2 1

CAPE HELL

Robert J. Conley, in memoriam:
Heaven needed the entertainment.

"And this also," Marlow said suddenly, "has been one of the dark places of the earth."

—JOSEPH CONRAD, *Heart of Darkness*

I

The Ghost

ONE

Halfway back to civilization, Lefty Dugan began to smell.

It was my own fault, partly; I'd stopped on the north bank of the Milk River like some tenderheel fresh out of Boston instead of crossing and pitching camp on the other side. I was worn down to my ankles, and the sorry buckskin I was riding sprouted roots on the spot and refused to swim. The pack horse was game enough; either that, or it was too old to care if it was lugging a dead man or a month's worth of Arbuckle's. But it couldn't carry two, especially when one was as limp as a sack of stove-bolts and just as heavy. I was getting on myself and in no mood to argue, so I unpacked my bedroll.

A gully-washer square out of Genesis soaked my slicker clear through and swelled the river overnight. I rode three days upstream before I found a place to ford, by which time even the plucky pack horse was breathing through its mouth. In Chinook I hired a buckboard and put in to the mercantile for salt to pack the carcass, but the pirate who owned the store mistook me for Vanderbilt, and then the Swede who ran the livery refused to refund the deposit I'd made on the wagon. So I buried Lefty in the shadow of the Bearpaws and rode away from five hundred cartwheel dollars on a mount I should have shot and left to feed what the locals call Montana swallows: magpies, buzzards, and carrion crows.

The thing was, I'd liked Lefty. We'd ridden together for Ford Harper before herding cattle lost its charm, and he was always good for the latest joke from the bawdy houses in St. Louis; back then he wasn't Lefty, just plain Tom. Then he took a part-time job in the off-season blasting a tunnel through the Bitterroots for the Northern Pacific, and incidentally two fingers off his right hand.

Drunk, he was a different man. He'd had a bellyful of Old Rocking Chair when he stuck up a mail train outside Butte and was still on the same extended drunk when he drew down on me not six miles away from the spot. I aimed low, but the fool fell on his face and took the slug through the top of his skull.

Making friends has seldom worked to my advantage. They always seem to wind up on the other side of my best interests.

It was a filthy shame. Judge Blackthorne had a rule against letting his deputies claim rewards—something about keeping the body count inside respectable limits—but made an exception in some cases in return for past loyalty and present reliability, and I was one. It served me right for not allowing for Lefty's unsteady condition when I tried for his kneecap instead of his hat rack. The money was the same, vertical or horizontal.

To cut my losses, I lopped off his mutilated right hand so I could at least claim the pittance the U.S. Marshal's office paid for delivering fugitives from federal justice. I packed it in my last half-pound of bacon, making do for breakfast with a scrawny prairie hen I shot east of Sulphur Springs. I picked gristle out of my teeth for fifty miles.

The money from Washington would almost cover what I'd spent to feed that bag of hay I was using for transportation. After I sold it back to the rancher I'd bought it from just outside Helena, I was a nickel to the good. I rode the pack horse in town until it rolled over and died. I wished I'd known the beast when it was a two-year-old, and that's as much good as I've ever had to say about anything with four legs that didn't bark and fetch birds.

I spent the nickel and a lot more in Chicago Joe's Saloon, picked a fight with the faro dealer—won that one—and another with the city marshal—lost that one—and would have slept out my time in peace if the Judge himself hadn't come down personally to spring me.

"You'd better still be alive," he greeted me from the other side of the bars. "This establishment doesn't give refunds for bailing out damaged goods."

I pushed back my hat to take him in. He had on his judicial robes, but the sober official black only heightened his resemblance to Lucifer in a children's book illustration. I think he tacked the tearsheet up beside his shaving mirror so he could get the chin-whiskers just right. His dentures were in place. They'd been carved from the keyboard of a piano abandoned along the Oregon Trail, and he wore the uncomfortable things only when required by the dignity of the office. It was unlike him to go anywhere straight from session without stopping to change, especially the hoosegow. I was in for either a promotion or the sack.

"How's Ed?" I asked. The city marshal's name was Edgar Whitsunday, but only part of his first name ever made it off the door of his office. He'd been named after a dead poet, but being illiterate he sloughed off the accusation whenever it arose. He was a Pentecostal, and amused his acquaintances with his imperfect memorization of Scripture as drilled into him by a spinster aunt: I think my favorite was "I am the excrement of the Lord."

"He's two teeth short of a full house," Blackthorne said. "I told his dentist to bill Grover Cleveland."

"That's extravagant. What did you do with the rest of the piano?"

He scowled. The Judge had a sense of his own humor, but no one else's. "You realize I could declare court in session right here and find you in contempt."

"And what, put me in jail?" I looked at my swollen right hand. "At least I used my fists. Ed took the top off my head with the butt of his ten-gauge."

"You should be grateful he didn't use the other end." He sighed down to his belt buckle; it was fashioned from a medal of valor. Just what he'd done to earn it, I never knew. Even scraping forty years off his hide I couldn't picture him scaling a stockade or leading a charge up any but Capitol Hill. Probably he'd helped deliver the Democratic vote in Baltimore. "You cost me more trouble than half the men who ride for me. A wise man would let you rot."

"You make rotting sound bad." I slid my hat back down over my eyes. "Find somewhere else to distribute your largesse. This ticky cot is the closest thing I've had to a hotel bed since I rode out after Lefty."

"You can't refuse bail. Marshal Whitsunday needs this cell. The Montana Stock-Growers Association is in town, and you know as well as I those carpetbaggers will drink the place dry and shoot it to pieces."

"Good. I was getting lonesome."

"Shake a leg, Deputy. You're needed."

That made me sit up and push back my hat. He wouldn't admit needing a drink of water in the desert.

He said, "I'm short-handed. Jack Sweeney, your immediate superior, went over my head to Washington and commandeered all my best men to bring the rest of Sitting Bull's band back from Canada to face justice for Custer."

"They gave that bloody dandy justice at the Little Big Horn nine years ago. What's the rush?"

"Sweeney's contract runs out in September, and there's a Democrat in the White House." He held up a key ring the size of Tom Thumb's head and stuck one in the lock. "Go back to your hotel, clean up, and report to my chambers at six sharp."

"Since when do you adjourn before dark?"

"I swung the gavel on the Bohannen Brothers at four. You've got forty-five minutes to clean up and shave. You look like the Wild Man of Borneo and smell like a pile of uncured hides."

"How'd you convict the Bohannens without my testimony? I brought them in."

"They tried to break jail and killed the captain of the guard. That bought them fifty feet of good North Carolina hemp without your help."

"Bill Greene's dead?"

"I'm sorry. I didn't know you were close."

"He owed me ten dollars on the Fitzgerald fight. I don't guess he mentioned me in his will."

His big silver watch popped open and snapped shut. "Forty-four minutes. If I catch so much as a whiff of stallion sweat in my chambers, I'll fine you twenty-five dollars for contempt of court."

"Collect it from the stallion."

"That's twenty-five dollars you owe the United States."

I swung my feet to the floor, stood, wrestled for balance, and found it with my fists around the bars. "What's so urgent? Did we declare war on Mexico again?"

He looked as grim as ever he had during damning evidence. "What have you heard?"

TWO

When the Judge and I entered Whitsunday's office from the cells, the marshal was sitting in a captain's chair on a swivel with a pitcher of chipped ice at his elbow to ease the pain of his missing teeth. His big face behind its waxed moustaches looked like raw meat; but that was a chronic condition, having nothing to do with our recent difference of opinion.

"I'm sorry," I said, when he got up to fetch my gunbelt. "I only wanted to break your nose." It had already been twisted into so many configurations I didn't think one more would offend him; in another incarnation he'd tried his hand at prizefighting under the company name Paddy O'Reilly, and displayed with pride a rotogravure of himself in tights on the wall next to the gun rack. It had been my hard luck, when it came down to cases, to choose fists over firearms; although the butt of his shotgun had seemed too much in his favor. But then the Marquess of Queensbury couldn't pass a bank draught in the territories.

"Your aim hasn't improved since Butte, I guess," Whitsunday said.

I'd nothing to offer for that. Even in this age of telegraphy I'll never understand how news travels faster than a man on horseback; I'd thought my arrangement with Lefty Dugan less important than the cost of a wire. But a tale's a tale, which is how history gets written. I spend my leisure time reading Scripture instead. No one can argue with the Word and win.

I stopped at my hotel only long enough to grab my town clothes. At the Cathay Gardens I soaked off the sweat of two horses seasoned with forty miles of tableland and caught a shave in the King Alexander Tonsorial Parlor, making use of Minos Tetrakokis, the Judge's personal barber; charging both bills to the court, with a nickel tip. Evidently I was still employed.

The room Blackthorne used for his chambers was a stuffy varnished-oak box with a tattered Mexican flag tacked to the back wall, a large-scale map of the territory plastering the one adjacent, and the cracked and thumb-worn legal books he'd carried on his back over the Divide piled on his leather blotter. He scowled when he smelled the Parisian soap they used at the Gardens, and at the evidence of Tetrakokis' art on my pink cheeks; but he took his revenge.

"I understand they never found your bullet," he said. "It passed through his brain, down the alimentary canal, and out through the seat of his trousers, true as the Katy Flyer."

I worked the mechanism of his mahogany-paneled cabinet—a Chinese box it had taken me a year to figure out—and poured us each a tumbler of the twelve-year-old whisky he imported from San Francisco by way of Aberdeen. I handed him his and put down half my portion in a gulp. "I killed a man. A friend. He pulled me out from under a mare in the Yellowstone and pumped a half-gallon of river water out of my lungs. You came that close to losing the best deputy marshal you ever signed on."

"That would be Cocker Flynn; but point taken. I always wondered just where you developed your antipathy to our noblest beast of burden. Now I know."

"You're thinking of those civilized geldings tied up to that circus wagon you ride here in town. You can't know how it feels to be outsmarted by a creature with a pecan-size brain and a heart like stove black. That damn buckskin cheated me out of half a year's wages."

He sipped from his glass, carving deep hollows in his cheeks; the Steinway-ivory choppers were stored securely in the iron safe in the corner.

"With one breath you eulogize a friend, and with the next you complain about losing the bounty on his head. Have you any code of behavior, apart from your continued survival?"

I slid the travel-weary pocket Bible from inside my frock coat and laid my palm on the limp leather cover.

"That's your fault, your honor. You sent me to Texas in a clerical collar, purely as a pose, but it got under my skin. I had to read the book to quote from it."

He switched subjects like a yard engine.

"Are you aware of the name Oscar Childress?"

"'Women and Children' Childress?"

"An unfortunate sobriquet, possibly unearned. However, he'll most likely bear it to the grave, alongside the innocents slaughtered in Springfield, Missouri."

Legend said Childress—who'd given up a colonelship with the United States Army in order to serve as a captain under Jefferson Davis—had stopped a trainload of civilians just outside Springfield and ordered his men to shoot them all as enemies of the Confederacy. After the war he'd led a company of volunteers into Mexico to fight alongside Juarez. This time he won. But instead of being named to high office, he'd dropped out of sight. Some said *El Presidente* himself had had him executed as a threat to his own job.

"He's resurfaced," I said then.

For the second time in an hour I'd made the old man jump. "In the Sierras," he said; "an almost impenetrable place. Once again I ask, what have you heard?"

I savored the Judge's fine whisky, knowing how bitter the chaser was bound to be. He saved the best for the men he wanted to seduce into something they'd never agree to sober.

"I've been six weeks breathing nothing but Montana topsoil," I said, "and hearing no news, short of how the wheat crop's doing. I made a joke about Mexico, which put your bowels on edge, and figured out Childress is back among the living, because you brought him up. Why bother otherwise? With respect, your honor, I'd admire to get you in a hand of poker."

He drained his glass and set it down with a thump.

"I find it interesting you should bring up the game," he said. "It's a form of war, purer than chess because of the element of chance involved."

"Not the way I play it."

"Precisely. The expedition I've in mind has no place for straight shooting and fair play. War is what I said, and war is what we're looking at if Oscar Childress and our invidious State Department has their way. He's raising an army to capture Mexico City."

"Again? That country changes hands like a Yankee dollar."

"This time he's doing it for himself. Once he has

control, he intends to add the Mexican Army to his band of irregulars and rekindle the Civil War."

"Oh, that." I drank.

"Pardon me, Deputy Murdock, but am I boring you with this latest threat to the union?"

"We don't know if it's the latest until tomorrow morning. Every time I open a newspaper, someone's fixing to bring back Fort Sumter. John Wilkes Booth was seen riding a cable car in San Francisco just last week. I read about it in the barbershop."

"Some important people are taking this one seriously. I've had wires from the District, each one a brighter shade of yellow than the last. I can only assume the authorities in the border states receive them in greater frequency; however, I take it a compliment to my record that I'm included at all. No doubt there's an ambassadorship for me, in some Godforsaken country on the other side of the world, if I capture Childress."

"You mean if *I* do."

He unstopped the bell jar containing the bullet-shaped cigars he ordered from Cuba for six bits apiece and set one afire.

"How's your Spanish?"

"Better than my Greek. I picked up some French on the Barbary Coast, but all that did was snarl up what little Mexican I had."

He blew a smoke ring. "You're trying to talk yourself out of an assignment."

"Without success." I finished my whisky and got up to pour myself another. It was clear I wouldn't be drinking anything but tequila for a long time.

THREE

"Childress is an enigma," Blackthorne said. "Graduated West Point at the top of his class, and in the meanwhile published a slim volume of poetry that drew the attention of the eastern elite; not the helmet-headed, wing-sprouting type of epic you might expect of a warrior, but rather a deep thinker on the order of Emerson. I don't expect you to grasp the meaning of all these names."

"I read *The Conduct of Life* in a lineshack one long winter. Half of it, anyway. The hand who left it used it to start fires."

"Indeed. I can't imagine you got much out of it."

I let him have his head there. The truth was Emerson might have been writing in Chinese.

He sat back and contributed to the nicotine stain on the ceiling. "To the men who rode down there with Childress, and to not a few of the locals, he's something of a god; a man you listen to rather than discourse with, and feel yourself the better for the exchange, however you come away unenlightened by it. Before the war, there was talk of running him for the U.S. Senate.

"He's a savant, of sorts; we're just not sure what: martial, literary, political, or scientific: I'm told he submitted a treatise on galvanization to one of those boards that finds such things of interest. After Juarez's victory, he sent a letter to the U.S. State Department, recommending we exploit the peons' near-worship of our civilization to annex Mexico."

"No wonder he went underground."

"No doubt his comments led to the assumption he'd been executed. He was already under suspicion for switching his allegiance from Emperor Maximilian to the revolutionists. His success in the field spared him punishment, but once he was no longer needed—"

"That's the problem with being a born general," I said. "There isn't much call for it once peace breaks out."

"Evidently he agrees. He appears to have spent the last eighteen years assembling his own private army, comprised of former revolutionists, the remnants of his original rebel force, and the Indians who inhabit the Sierra Madre Mountains twenty miles south of the Arizona border. That's the report, in any case."

"Who wrote it?"

"A Pinkerton operative, posing as an aimless drifter. He sent a long coded wire to the agency's headquarters in Chicago and hasn't been heard from since. Numerous attempts to make contact through pre-arranged channels have failed."

"That's two Americans that country's misplaced. I didn't know it was so careless."

He picked up the bottle, frowned, then set it back down and rammed in the cork. "The obvious answer is he was found out and eliminated. Now it's up to us to confirm or disprove the report."

"Why us?"

"I volunteered the services of this court, and Washington has generously accepted."

"That was white of them. How many men did Sweeney leave us with?"

"Irrelevant. One man may succeed where a regiment would not."

"I'm supposed to comb all of Mexico looking for one Pinkerton?"

"Just the Sierras; and that isn't the mission. You're to infiltrate Childress' command and find out if there's anything to the report. If it's mistaken, or Childress is a harmless charlatan, or there's no truth to it at all, come back and report to me in person."

"And if it turns out to be right?"

"Must I express the obvious?"

"You must. It might spare me from a firing squad if I can tell the federales I killed him on your orders."

"Very well. He committed high treason the moment he offered his services to a foreign power. The penalty is death. Especially if any part of that report can be verified. The part that concerns me most is the arms he's supposed to have stockpiled: Gatlings, Napoleons, and a dozen cases of carbines. A shipment of that very number was reported missing from Winchester's warehouse in Boston. Wars have been won with less."

I uncorked the bottle and refilled my glass without asking permission.

"If I'm to start one all by myself, I'll need some things up front, starting with a decent horse."

"Black Dan Stuart is holding a bay thoroughbred for you. I made the arrangements when I heard you were back."

"A good long-distance rifle."

"Draw one from the arsenal. The deputy in charge has all the paperwork."

"Two hundred dollars in gold."

"Absolutely not. Your salary covers all your responsibilities."

"I can't bribe my way across Mexico on twenty a month."

"In lieu of receipts, I'll need a detailed record of your expenses. It will be checked."

"And a case of this Scot's courage." I lifted my glass.

"More bribery?"

"I get thirsty in the desert."

"Anything else?"

"If I think of it I'll let you know."

"Aren't you forgetting transportation?"

"You said I had a horse coming."

"You'll need it when the tracks end, but until then I'm giving you a train."

He puffed his cigar, pleased at my uncharacteristic silence.

"We don't know Childress' timetable," he said, "or even if he has one. In any case we can't risk his plans going into effect while you're crawling your way across the Sonoran Desert on horseback."

"Won't he wonder how I got my hands on a train?"

"You stole it, naturally. It's your ticket into his camp. The revolutions travel by rail down there; no self-respecting insurgent would be caught dead without one.

"Just return it when you're through playing with it," he said. "It's on loan from President Diaz, Juarez's successor. He has as much riding on this mission as we do. It's waiting for you in the railyard."

It was a smart plan. I wouldn't say it to his face. "Do I get to blow the whistle?"

"That's up to the engineer. It has a name, even if he doesn't." Blackthorne slid a fold of foolscap from an inside pocket and snapped it open. "*El Espanto.* I'm told it means 'The Ghost'; 'The Terror'; something along those lines. In some remote regions it makes sense to strike fear into the savages who'd oppose progress."

"All right," I said.

"I felt certain you'd assent eventually. I was prepared to offer to stock the saloon car with my entire cellar, had you demurred. You should have held out for more than just one case."

"I don't mind. I want to talk to Childress. He promises better conversation than I've had in a spell."

He screwed out his cigar in a heavy brass tray. "From what I've heard, he'll do all the talking."

"That's grand, too. I never learned anything listening to myself."

Which was one thing I'd said that turned out to be truer than I knew; and something I'd have torn out along with my tongue when I got the truth of it.

"Is there a settlement where I'm headed? The Sierras cover a lot of ground."

He hauled an atlas the size of a dining table from the slots where he kept his ledgers and made room to spread it on the desk.

"The map is centuries out of date. We have the pillaging Spaniards to thank for its existence at all; but nothing's come along to supplant it, and I doubt little has changed there since the death of Columbus. It's the last wild place in North America."

He ran a finger down the coast to a ragged hangnail sticking into the Gulf of California across from the mountain range.

"'Cabo Falso,'" I read.

"'The Cape of Lies.' It's home to an anonymous fishing village, the only source of communication with the outside world for a hundred miles. Even a traitor needs a conduit: That's where his alleged weaponry would have landed. If you should need to get in touch with this court, it's two weeks in the saddle from his base of operations. There's no railway spur. The only line crawls through the foothills of the Sierras; the blankest space on the map this side of darkest Africa, all craggy peaks, deep abyss, and dense jungle, teeming with mosquitoes, venomous snakes, and leeches the size of trout in Montana. I exaggerate, possibly; but better that than to underestimate the hazards. It's a pity our modern cartographers have grown too sophisticated to make allowances for dragons. If the mystical beasts were to thrive anywhere, that would be the place."

"What about women?"

"Savages, who'd mate with you and cut your throat in the moment of ecstasy; so I'm told." He flushed a little, although over the bloodshed or the carnal implication, I couldn't tell.

"I could get the same at Chicago Joe's, and save the expense of travel. Why Cape of Lies?"

Here he was on more comfortable ground.

"Legend says Cortes promised to deliver Montezuma to the natives who were rebelling against him, in return for directions to all the gold mines in the region. They delivered, he didn't. You won't find its other name on any map: Cabo Infierno; lyrical, don't you agree?"

"Cape Hell. It's practically a sonnet."

"In 1519, the disgruntled Aztecs captured several Conquistadors there and put them to death by pouring molten gold down their throats. Clearly, the concept of irony is as indigenous to the New World as the potato."

"Let's hope it hasn't survived as well. I can't swallow even a jalapeno without regret."

"I rather think Captain Childress is at least partially responsible for the endurance of the name. The Pinkerton's report cites rumors of soldiers beheaded for desertion and their bodies turned over to cannibals."

"He got into the tequila. Indians aren't man-eaters."

"I suspect Childress circulated the stories himself. He's established in the local cane sugar trade—that's public record—and when it comes to discouraging competition there's nothing quite as effective as tales of massacre."

"Planting sugar for profit makes sense, if he is raising an army. The kind of men he needs don't fight for love of country."

"That isn't all," he said, helping himself to an unprecedented third helping of spirits; his Presbyterian leanings counseled against them, and he wasn't a hypocrite in practice. "The federales say he grows poppies between the rows."

"Opium."

"The climate is ideal."

I emptied my glass a second time. "The Civil War's starting to be the least interesting part of his biography."

FOUR

The cashier in the Miner's Bank read the draught signed by Judge Blackthorne, then rolled mud-colored eyes above his pinch-glasses to see if I wore a bandanna over my face. I got out the badge I carried in a pocket, showed him my appointment papers signed by U.S. Marshal J. S. Sweeney, waited while he retired behind a door with PRESIDENT painted in black letters on the pebbled glass, pasted on an angelic expression when the man who belonged to the office stuck his head out and studied me head to foot, and walked out a half-hour later, leaving behind my signature on a receipt and carrying two hundred dollars in double-eagles in a canvas sack. I could have robbed the place in half the time and gone off with ten times as much.

Black Dan Stuart ran a stagecoach stop on the Bozeman, supplying the horses himself from his small (five hundred acres) ranch a mile outside Helena. He wasn't any more black than I was: He claimed service with the Scots Highlanders, also called the Black Watch, in the Crimea. I had my doubts, and they were shared; but when he took it into his head to man the way station personally, he greeted dusty travelers in a kilt and tam-o'-shanter, warping their eardrums with a set of bagpipes.

The costume wasn't suited to the local climate in summer, and Marshal Whitsunday had offered to fine him the next time he squeezed his bag of wind within earshot of Helena, so I found him in ordinary canvas and blue flannel and the straw planter's hat he wore when the sun hammered down. He had a mouth somewhere, but the only evidence of it was the almost unintelligible brogue that came out from behind his red muttonchop whiskers, stirring the silvered tips.

"What's that you're r-r-r-riding, lad?" He stood on his rickrack porch, thumbs hooked inside the cinch he used to hold up his trousers. "It's too big for a sporting girl and too pr-r-r-retty for a horse."

I stepped out of leather and smacked the pinto mare's neck. It rolled an angry eye my way; I'd yet to make a good first impression on anything that burns hay. "It belongs to Judge Blackthorne's wife. She's too fat to ride it anymore, and too stubborn to sell it. It's a loan until I take possession of that thoroughbred he says you're holding."

"I hesitate to let go of it; but he pr-r-r-romised to let me play at the Independence Day dance."

I thanked God I'd be a thousand miles away by the Fourth.

It was a sound enough beast, a bay with one white stocking and a crescent-shaped blaze. He'd named it after a character he said was in *The Arabian Nights,* but there were a lot of *r*'s in it and he was still rolling them when I left, leading the pinto. Chances were I'd have to shoot it sooner or later and I wasn't about to take time to carve its name on a cross. I swear it: As I topped the first hill, I heard the old fraud serenading me with a wheezy interpretation of "Amazing Grace."

My next stop was the Montana Central yard, and my home-on-rails for the foreseeable future.

At first glance, *El Espanto* disappointed; on a siding near one of Broadwater and Hills' two-story-high locomotives, the engine looked small and quaint, although shiny as bootblack with red trim and its name painted in italics on the wooden cab just beneath the opening where the engineer propped his elbow. It hauled four cars only: the tender heaped with wood, a Pullman parlor car, a stock car, and caboose. No sign of the saloon car Blackthorne had teased me with; he jibed as he ruled in court, without fear of consequences.

At second glance the outfit passed muster. It was short but sturdy, mounted on wheels disproportionate to its size, built to churn their way through floods of muck and mud and blizzards above the tree line, with wicked-looking iron spikes on the cowcatcher, stout enough to impale a buffalo bull and carry it along with all the ease of blown chaff. The *Ghost* it was called, but the name was the only ethereal thing about that outfit.

A caterpillar scampered up my spine then. I was riding the rails into a place called Cape Hell, aboard a train equipped to enter the original.

A squat Indian sat on the edge of the cab with his feet dangling, eating a sandwich and washing it down with something from a canteen; I'll call it water. His hair was cut short, mission-style, and he wore overalls and a checked shirt with a filthy bandanna around his neck, but there was nothing European about his black eyes or blunt features, which looked as if they'd been hacked out by a sculptor who hadn't gotten around to smoothing the edges. I never saw him wear a hat, come driving rain or pounding sun, in all the time I knew him; and as it turned out, I knew him longer than most of the men I called my friends.

"Your pardon, Chief," I said. "Where's the fellow who runs this train?"

"I'm not a chief, Chief. Just the fireman." His English was as good as anyone's, drenched though it was in Spanish pronunciation. "He's in town, getting drunk on anything but mescal, and a bite if there's time."

"I'm your next passenger." I showed him the scrap of tin, which based on his expression had all the effect of Monday turning into Tuesday. "Mind if I look around inside?"

"I'm not paid to mind anything but the firebox."

"Page Murdock," I said, since it looked as if we'd be in close association for a while. "What should I call you?"

He showed me his eyeteeth. "Call me your next of kin."

His name, as it happened, was Joseph. He said he'd

snatched it at random from an open book of Scripture when he'd been asked to sign it to a manifest.

The parlor car was as plush as the bedrooms in Chicago Joe's, paneled in sweet-scented cedar (I can't abide the smell to this day) with lace curtains on the windows and armchairs upholstered in supple pigskin. You could lose a boot in the figured carpet. Just for safety's sake I moved the most inviting chair out from under a crystal chandelier, but decided not to get used to it until we were under way; I had enemies in town, and too much comfort tended to dull the fine edge. Behind a gnurled cabinet door I found a dozen bottles of Blackthorne's own label secured by leather straps, with all the accouterments in leaded glass; the old man could be as hard to take as Dr. Pfister's Spirits of Castor Bean, but he was as good as his word.

A dry-sink mounted a mahogany pedestal, lined in mother-of-pearl, equipped with a badger brush, pink Parisian soap, and a pearl-handed razor with a Sheffield-steel blade. Bay Rum to lay the skin to rest. I pulled the cork from the bottle. The contents smelled like an explosion in a field of lime; my eyes watered.

It was my brand, to take the edge off the trail. The Judge had done his homework. In any other case I'd have been flattered.

Another cabinet contained a gun rack stocked with a .45-70 Whitney rifle, a British Bulldog revolver, and a Springfield trap-door shotgun. The first was a dandy long-range weapon, and the belly gun sufficient for close-up work when my Deane-Adams wasn't handy, but the Springfield was available only in 20 gauge, enough to annihilate a jackrabbit but not enough to stop a determined man beyond a hundred feet. I saw Ed Whitsunday's hand in that; town law seldom had to engage the enemy more than the length of a barroom.

Worse, the scattergun had only one barrel, which doubled the odds against the man behind it. But since I hadn't even brought up the subject of a scattergun, I didn't plan to kick.

A drawer contained all the ammo I'd need to conquer Mexico, for whatever that was worth. Every time we took it, we seemed compelled to give it back.

Not that I cared for the food. You can do only so much with beans and ground corn, and I'd sampled it all a hundred times over before I traded my lariat for the badge in my pocket.

With that in mind, I flipped up the lid on the zinc larder, and looked at tins of tomatoes, peaches, shredded beef, sweet peas, and baby potatoes. I saw Mrs. Blackthorne's hand in *that*. She was a good enough cook to recognize that importing beans to the Halls of Montezuma was like shipping Studebaker wagons to Detroit. She didn't care for me any more than she did the rest of her husband's crazy-quilt crew, but she was as good a Christian as they came.

More tins, big square ones of coal-oil, lashed inside a cabinet lined in lead. They'd have lit the lamps of China through the next dynasty.

I snatched open other doors. Dozens of jugs of water, drawn from Montana wells, proof against parasites; laudanum, in quantities that would ease the pain of hundreds; yards of gauze, enough to patch the wounds of a regiment; a gallon of iodine, another of alcohol. A leather case, glittering with scalpels, forceps, syringes, and bone saws: *bone saws*. Cold Harbor had been less prepared for casualties. I'd been there, and seen the tent.

I looked, but found no sign of a surgeon packed in salt. Blackthorne had missed a step there.

A pattern was emerging; one I didn't like half so

much as the one in the carpet, which had come halfway across the world to settle on a portable floor in
Old Mexico.

I investigated further. The stock car had straw and
sacks of oats sufficient to feed a string, let alone one
thoroughbred. The caboose was a cozy affair, equipped
with a bentwood rocker, a ticking mattress on an iron
frame, and a rolltop desk, with several decks of cards
and a bandbox-new checker set in the drawers.

From food to artillery to medical supplies to diver-
sions, the train was stocked halfway toward the twentieth century.

I made a mental note to bring along *The Odyssey*
for entertainment; it might last me to the last stop, if
I read it in the original Greek and played a few thousand games of checkers.

I thought I'd snookered the old man out of a case
of Scotch whisky and two hundred dollars in gold,
but by the time the thing was through I figured I'd be
lucky to clear a nickel an hour, not counting doctor's
bills, with nothing left to drink but warm beer distilled through the bowels of a burro.

The Honorable Harlan Blackthorne always had the
last word. I fancy I hear it whenever I lay flowers on
his grave.

FIVE

I f I'd learned nothing else during my time with him, I knew better than to expect explanations once I'd accepted an assignment. He'd only give me one of those toothless tight-lipped cat's smiles and say no intelligence was as useful as the kind I found out on my own; Washington jargon for what I didn't know couldn't hurt me. Which was a bald-faced lie, as I'd found out on my own more times than I could count.

So I went over his head, literally: straight to the attic.

Blackthorne had lost patience while the local, territorial, and federal authorities were arguing the details of constructing a courthouse, and had set up shop in the headquarters of the *Herald* building, arranging recesses to coincide with when the presses in the basement began their daily rumble. He'd had the attic cleared of stacks of old numbers of the newspaper to make room for records and evidence, turning it into a combination file room and Black Museum. Trial transcripts rolled and bound with cord stuck out like ancient scrolls from floor-to-ceiling pigeonholes, clamshell boxes stood cheek-by-jowl on freestanding shelves open on both sides, and wooden cases contained case files in leather folders amidst a thicket of edged and percussion weapons hung up like heraldic arms. The collection bore nightmare tales of beheadings, back-shootings, and duels fought at such close range the combatants' shirts caught fire; these, too, dangled from pegs, singed and stiff with old blood, reeking of stale smoke and charred flesh. It all added up to some ten thousand years at hard labor and a potters' field of necks broken on the scaffold.

The curator and headmistress of all this sat at a student desk, her erect back supported by whalebone wrapped in black bombazine and a rimless monocle behind which swam a brown eye swollen all out of proportion, like a fish in a bowl. Just where Electra Highbinder spent the hours of darkness added color to the conversation in Chicago Joe's. Depending on which story you bought, she slept on a cot among the stained broadaxes and jars of poisoned livers or sipped green tea from a translucent cup in a room above the Gans and Klein Clothing Store at Main and Broadway furnished in the Federal style, all carved mahogany eagles and rich leather bindings inside blown-glass presses; this on the authority of the man who'd delivered her four-poster bed from Montgomery Ward.

I followed protocol: Took off my hat, called her Mrs. Highbinder, and stated my request. I had no evidence that she actually refused access to those who got it out of sequence, but the ghost of a husband last seen at the bottom of a shaft in Last Chance Gulch hung about her like tuberose and there was nothing to be gained by stirring him.

"Childress?" She off-loaded one of her plat-book-size ledgers from the stack on the floor by her knee onto the desk, splayed it open, and ran the fletch of her old-fashioned quill down the crowded columns, stopping near the bottom of the page. The quill rose from the sheet, pointing across the room. "CH-17."

I found it among the clamshell boxes on a shelf and started to leave with it tucked under my arm. A rapid clicking noise brought me back around to where she sat tapping the nib of her pen against tea-stained teeth.

Again she reversed the quill, lining it up with a writing table standing in a pool of milky sunlight leaking through a fan-shaped window across from her station. The meaning was clear: I could leave, but the box stayed.

The split-bottom chair found every saddlesore I'd accumulated since I'd left Helena the last time, but I opened the box and spilled its contents onto the table. They were in a bundle, tied with more cord. I tugged loose the knot, set aside a ragged stack of newspaper clippings, and began reading a neat clerkly hand on foolscap sheets, identified at the top as a transcription from the decoded report wired by the Pinkerton who'd vanished in Mexico.

His name was DeBeauclair, but he'd walked the length of the Sierra Madre posing as a Portuguese sailor who called himself Salazar, and who'd had his fill of the sea and had pledged to hike through all the uncivilized places of the earth until some vision told him what direction his life should take.

The story was just lunatic enough to satisfy the most suspicious observer. In reality, DeBeauclair/Salazar was working for U.S. banking interests, tracking bandits who'd been raiding the border for months, looking for names and evidence for warrants to extradite. Along the way, he'd picked up on the rumors of Oscar Childress' activities in the interior.

The agent had been sufficiently intrigued to take time out from his original assignment and report what he'd heard through the Western Union office in the anonymous fishing village in Cabo Falso, but according to a letter accompanying the notes, all attempts to reach him afterward had failed. That letter, written on heavy rag bond and addressed to U.S. Attorney General Augustus Garland, bore the disturbing all-seeing eye and "We Never Sleep" pledge of the Pinkerton National Detective Agency, and the signature of Robert A. Pinkerton himself, son of its legendary founder, and every bit the miserable son of a bitch his father had been. He demanded federal intervention. An addendum scribbled in a different hand suggested that the matter "be taken under advisement."

Which explained the letter's presence in Judge Blackthorne's files.

It was dated five months ago, which was standard procedure regarding stories of conspiracy against the Union. They were as cyclical as the tides, and few of them attracted more notice than it took to file them away; but whenever one managed to creep so far north from its origin, the president had to be consulted, and Grover Cleveland was not a man to dismiss such things lightly only four years after the Garfield assassination.

DeBeauclair's report, if it had been disencrypted faithfully, was practical, offering no assumptions beyond what he'd overheard in cantinas and peso-a-week flophouses in coastal villages and witnessed firsthand. The rumors passed without comment; some of them were fantastic on their face, stories of cannibalism and human sacrifice. But he'd read flyers offering top wages for experienced soldiers, preferably without family, seen wagonloads of grim-faced men bound for the Sierras wearing bandoleers of ammunition, rifles and carbines slung from their shoulders, and while passing through a filthy storeroom on his way to an outhouse, staggering convincingly, had lifted the canvas cover off a stack of crates stenciled CUIDADO, and leant down far enough to catch a whiff of sulphur and potassium, the principal ingredients of dynamite. As there was no mining or railroad-building taking place within a hundred miles of the ginhouse, he'd seen fit to include the discovery in his report. Under all these eavesdroppings and observations had run a theme, whispered in disease-ridden brothels, sung in urine-soaked alleys, and spoken in opium trances: "*El General* Childress."

It had taken him almost a quarter-century to overcome his demotion from Union colonel to captain of the Confederacy and promote himself to general.

I turned from the report to the yellowed cuttings, sliced from crumbling copies of *The Charleston Mercury* and *The New York Times*, the leading journalistic voices of the War Between the States. The *Mercury*, a rebel sheet, trumpeted the victories of Childress' volunteers at First and Second Manassas, Chickamauga, and Cold Harbor, while the *Times* made scant reference to an obscure band of southern mercenaries until its commander leapt into its lead column in April 1863:

ATROCITY IN SPRINGFIELD.
Rebel Guerrillas Stop Civilian Train.
Open Fire on Defenseless Passengers.
Eighteen, Including Women and Children, Blasted into
Eternity in as Many Seconds.

Accompanying it was a woodcut illustration of a uniformed firing squad with rifles raised, spitting smoke and lead at a reeling line of men in bowlers, women in ankle-length dresses, and children in hair bows and knickers withering before the blast.

Ten minutes later I found a corresponding report in the Charleston rag, headed SKIRMISH IN SPRING-FIELD. This was a brief account of a battle involving Childress' volunteers and passengers aboard a federal troop train, who had opened fire on the Confederates from onboard. The editors had not elected to provide an illustration.

I'd fought in that war, and had learned, when newspapers were available (usually wrapped around a slab of greasy catfish), that what I'd experienced and what I read about later might have been separate engagements. Throw the *Times*'s massacre and the *Mercury*'s armed encounter into a bushel basket, shake it, draw out your own interpretation, and you might have something approaching the truth. Personally I had trouble singling out a specific act of malice from the general hell of war: The worse it got, the better, if anyone who might wind up in charge had learned anything from it. I was more interested in Cold Harbor, and whether one of the faces I'd looked into across the crossroads that long day, black with powder and striped from sweat, had belonged to Oscar Childress. By that fourth year of fighting, officers' insignia were practically nonexistent among the gray and butternut; their uniforms had gone the way of all shoddy, replaced by Union castoff and motley snatched off clotheslines. I remembered a burly party in a dirty lace camisole and a raddled straw hat with holes cut for an ass's ears, turning back a flank attack with a saber stained crimson to the hilt. He might have been a general.

Cold Harbor, Virginia: Fifteen thousand dead or wounded on the side of the Army of the Potomac, as opposed to two thousand on the other. Of all the forgotten battlefields I had no intention of revisiting, that intersection of twin ruts leading nowhere in particular came in dead last.

The *Mercury* ceased publication when Charleston fell in February 1865, and no mention of Childress had been preserved from the *Times* after Crook's cavalry set fire to a barn his men had deserted during the retreat from Winchester; two hogs and a goat lost their lives in that action, and their affiliation remained undetermined. The last item, therefore, belonged to a publication with a different typeface whose name wasn't included with the clipping. It was two inches only, and read:

Readers of this journal will be relieved to learn that Captain O. Childress, author of the infamous slaughter at Springfield, Missouri, has decamped to Mexico with the remains of his command, and is believed to have thrown in with Emperor Maximilian in defense against revolutionists loyal to former President Benito Juarez. May God in His mercy protect the women and children of New Spain.

Unless the reporter got things backward, Childress had started out hoping to change his luck by siding with established authority, then turned coat and fought once again with the rebels, this time with better results. If so, his mental prowess lived up to its reputation; but it hadn't outlived the nickname he'd acquired during those eighteen seconds in Missouri.

SIX

Something slid out as I was sorting what I'd read from what I hadn't into separate bundles and landed on the table with a plink. Electra Highbinder glanced up, then returned to the column she was filling in one of her ledgers.

I looked at the wrinkled orange tintype of a callow youth in the tunic of a West Point plebe, fastened at the throat: Faded ink on the back identified the model as Cadet O. Childress. Useless to compare that face, unstamped by time and experience, with the man I'd been sent to investigate, and possibly to eliminate: eyes slightly wolfish over a nose thin as crystal and prim slit of a mouth, the whole supporting a bulbous cranium already pushing through the fine pale hairs that covered it. He'd be bald by now, and an ideal specimen for phrenology considering the size of his brain case. I put the image on the pile of deadwood.

I finished the rest of the material and started packing it up to return to the box. A sheet of onionskin was stuck to the back of one clipping. I peeled it away carefully; it was as thin as a postage stamp and as fragile as a butterfly's wing.

The text started in the middle of a sentence; clearly it belonged to a longer tract. The script was written in red ink, the hand coarse, like something in an exercise book kept by someone who was learning his letters, but the language was fine, as if it had been transcribed into formal English from classical Latin, with the occasional foray into the local dialect; a symptom common to an extended stay in a foreign land. The phrasing was elegant, but by the time I came to the end of each carefully crafted sentence I knew no more about its meaning than I had at the beginning. Like Emerson, it fascinated and at the same time left me lost.

A technical term here and there suggested this was a leaf from Childress' own notes, laying out his theories on exploiting Mexican peasants' awe of us *Norteamericanos* in the national interest: The existing seeds had only to be planted, was what I made of it. In a less distracted frame of mind, I might have been persuaded to accept his argument, except for the cold finger that touched my spine when I took a closer look at *matear* (to plant seeds) and realized what he'd actually written was *matar* (to kill).

I wasn't the only one who'd been taken in by the scrawled Spanish: Judge Blackthorne had said the authorities had been impressed with the proposal to turn the peons' awe of our civilization to national advantage, never suspecting he was recommending their extermination. The word, it was true, was all jagged angles, the *t* uncrossed and the *a*'s open at the top, and smudged by too much handling. It was easy to imagine some bureaucrat, inclined to hope for the best, interpreting it as a harmless reference to growth. For all I knew it was just that, and my own traffic with brutish humanity had tainted my outlook; but I'd never gotten in trouble for thinking the worst.

That brought me to Blackthorne's motive. Had he removed the report from the file in order not to alarm me, and overlooked the last page? He overlooked nothing. Had he left it, probably the most revealing passage of all, as a warning to take care? Not for concerns about myself. He was possessive in regard to all the tools at his disposal, and loath to train a replacement.

The paper smelled of pinon smoke and something bittersweet I could place only by bringing it close to my face and breathing deep: nightshade. Childress had picked berries and crushed them to make the ink.

That provided a picture more vivid than the outdated tintype. I saw him sitting cross-legged in a mud hut, filling page upon page with his fevered scratches, pausing only to dip his pen—a cactus needle or a porcupine quill—in scarlet paste in an earthenware dish. He wore only a loincloth, native headdress, and a snailshell necklace. He'd have gone heathen.

How else explain a man who proposed wholesale massacre as a step toward progress? I had to meet him.

You needed to run a thousand head of cattle minimum to qualify for membership in the Montana Stock-Growers Association, but Harlan A. Blackthorne had never gotten closer than a rare steak in the dining room of the Magnolia Hotel. He'd been granted honorary standing for his legal efforts to defend the open range from an army of lawyers determined to cut it up for the real estate interests back East. Although he had no love for cattle barons, nor they for him—he often ruled in favor of small ranchers in disputes over property lines—he agreed that the grassland was designed by God for grazing and that to plow it under would expose the subsoil to harsh winds and brutal sun, inviting drought. No less an authority than Chester Alan Arthur had tried to intervene on behalf of the

New York lobbyists who had kept him in the White House, but like several presidents before him he'd dashed himself to splinters against that rocky shore.

The house had been built by a silver magnate who'd put a ball through his head when his wife left him, taking their daughter and son with her back to New Hampshire. Its turrets and gables, copied from a castle in Sweden, had appealed to another sort of pioneer, and the molded plaster ceilings and cedar paneling were dark with old cigar exhaust and soaked with the sickly sweet stench of Levi Garrett's. The association's founders had turned the old ballroom into a gallery of Remington prints, bought the works of Shakespeare and De Quincey by the pound, and interred them in glazed presses that were opened only by the servants who dusted the uncracked leather spines: The slyest man under that roof could cheat a Vanderbilt, but he couldn't read or write his own name.

The doddering veteran of the War of 1812 who'd kept the registration book in the pink marble lobby had passed finally, and been replaced by an erect young Negro with a British accent and a white eye, who informed me that the Judge was in the gymnasium.

"The bar, you mean," I said.

"No, sir. End of the hall."

I studied his face, planed flat at every angle like the head atop a totem pole. "Didn't you cost me a bundle in the Blessing fight?"

"Blessing made it back. He bet against himself. Not that he didn't try to lose it." He touched the corner of the dead eye.

The gymnasium smelled of good spirits squeezed through sweaty pores. A pair of swollen bellies in padded gear was fencing in the middle of the floor, but neither of them belonged to the Judge. He watched the battle from an oaken bench, both hands wrapped around a silver-plated flask.

I sat down beside him. "Impressive," I said. "Do you think they'll ever replace stone axes?"

"That jackanapes Roosevelt has taken over upstairs, gassing about the strenuous life on his spread in Dakota. While he was about it I watched him polish off two plates of lobsters he had packed in dry ice and shipped all the way from Maine. Then I came down here to watch two old fools play at pirates. You found all the appointments satisfactory?" He waggled the flask, but I held up a palm and handed him the onionskin sheet I'd folded and put in a pocket. He glanced at it and gave it back.

"Ghastly hand; not that it signifies. Graphology is based on the naïve assumption that when the tail of the *g* sweeps too low and the crown of the *d* climbs too high, the one represents melancholy, the other monomania; as if north is up and south is down anywhere but on a map. Poor illumination and haste are discounted."

"You've seen it."

"It was in the envelope with the letter from the attorney general. I haven't decided whether that was deliberate."

"Me, neither. I thought it was you. How's your Spanish?"

"Rusty, same as my skills with a saber; although I flatter myself I could show these moo-cow millionaires a trick or two. You can ask Childress himself if he was referring to gardening or genocide."

"I think you know."

He unstopped the flask and sipped, swallowed.

"Great men are seldom good. Andrew Jackson murdered a man, ostensibly over an affair of honor, turned his back on the Constitution he swore to uphold, and sentenced a peaceful and assimilated tribe of Indians to an eternity in the desert; yet he's celebrated as our greatest president since Washington."

"Jackson never called for wholesale slaughter."

"Didn't he? Two thousand British dead in New Orleans might argue the point. The war had been over for two weeks."

"He didn't know that at the time."

"Perhaps not. I wonder if it would have made a difference if he had. As a general he invaded Florida against direct orders from Washington."

"You're not making much of a case against Childress."

"That's your job. Or *for* him, if the rumors prove false. I asked you if you had everything you needed."

"I inspected the train. You left out cannon."

"Are you complaining that you're overequipped?"

"Undermanned. According to Agent DeBeauclair, he's got dynamite. I don't think he's blasting stumps."

"If you're asking how to do your job, I'm fresh out of ideas."

"I would be, if you meant what you said about investigating the rumors. You'd send Dick Button for that. He worked undercover for Wells Fargo three years. I'm not a detective; I'm a hired gun. I just can't figure out why you don't have Childress brought back and do the thing proper with a rope."

"He'd take the stand in his own defense. You know his reputation. By the time he was through testifying, the jury would nominate him for territorial governor."

"How do you want him?" I asked. "Nailed to the

wall of the president's mansion in Mexico City or dumped down a mineshaft in Chiapas?"

"It won't matter either way." He looked at me for the first time since I sat down. "It's Mexico, Page. No one cares what happens down there."

SEVEN

I packed my biggest valise for a long stay, with plenty of changes and books for every mood, beginning with my Bible, looked around my room as if I'd never see it again—not for the first time—and rode the bay down to the railyard, where I gave a pair of roustabouts a quarter apiece to back it into a stall in the stock car and hobble it. I put my saddle and bridle, my two most valuable possessions, in the private coach with the valise. That made it seem a little more like me.

Back outside I found Joseph the fireman hurling chunks of wood from a wheelbarrow into the tender. I asked him if the engineer was back from town. He jerked his chin toward the locomotive.

A man built nearly as close to the ground, but just as wide, leapt down from inside, wiping his broad broken-nailed hands on a rag and transferring as much grease to his palms as it removed from them. I shook his hand, making sure to give as good as I got; men who spent most of their time gripping steel levers seldom throttled back for flesh and bone.

"Hector Cansado." He had one of those deep, burring voices that came from shouting over a chugging engine. His accent was unconventional, neither Spanish nor Indian; it seemed to have been dropped by accident, borne by some strange bird from terra incognita. He wore the ticking-striped cap, faded red kerchief, and brass-studded overalls of his profession, the heavy denim pitted all over with burns from flying sparks. His broad face, similarly scarred, had a bloated quality, the skin stretched to its limit, like an India rubber balloon, and yellow-green in complexion. Mahogany-colored eyes tilted away from a flat nose, creating an impression of desperate fatigue. Even his name translated as "tired."

He was dying; his coloring suggested advanced jaundice. That cold finger touched my spine again. I was in the hands of a fireman whose ancestors had known nothing but tragedy at the hands of the white race and an engineer who had nothing to lose by piloting a train through darkest Mexico.

His breath stank of sour mash. I asked him if he'd succeeded in finding anything to drink besides mescal and something to eat. The tight face registered annoyance. The weary eyes slid toward the Indian.

"That savage has been carrying tales. What a man does on his own time is his business."

"I guess. I haven't had my own time in ten years. There's good Scotch in the parlor car and not a grain of cornmeal in sight."

"Is this an invitation?"

"We've got a thousand miles to cover. I don't want to lose my company manners out of habit."

He leaned forward and dropped his voice to a murmur. "Don't tell Joseph. The only time you can trust him is when he is drunk, and then you can trust him to cut your throat."

I glanced at the man throwing wood. "Why do you keep him on?"

"I would rather have him aboard than wonder about him outside in the dark."

"You know where we're headed?"

"Cabo Infierno, *sí.*"

"Does Joseph?"

"Not from me, but he has ears to hear and eyes to see, and *El Espanto* is not your ordinary train. I would not put it past him to throw in with that devil."

Under some circumstances I might have considered that a good beginning. Tragedies always start out bright, comedies grim. But life isn't the theater.

Cansado left Joseph to his labor on the pretext of showing me features of the train I'd already seen and joined me in the coach. I tugged the cork out of one of Blackthorne's bottles and poured two inches into each of a pair of cut-crystal glasses and we settled ourselves into the pigskin chairs. He looked around, at the paneling and the rich rugs, shook his head.

"In the village where I was born, the cost of this coach would keep us in meat for a year; beef, I mean. I have eaten so many chickens it is a wonder I do not lay eggs. I have heard they serve tortillas as far north as Santa Fe. I cannot believe this."

"It's worse than that. You can order green chiles in Portland, Oregon."

"Myself, I would travel twice that far to escape them. Someday I shall don a serape and hike toward Canada, and when I meet the first person who asks me what it is I am wearing, there is the place I will settle."

"Strange talk for a Mexican."

Tired eyes glared at me over the top of his glass. "I am Basque. My people owe loyalty to no one but themselves."

"It sounds lonely."

He drank, wobbled it around his mouth, and swallowed. The played-out gaze remained steady. "I think you know this feeling."

"I travel with friends." I set down my drink, got up, unstrapped the valise, and took out the Bible. "Mark, Matthew, Luke, Ezekiel. I call them by their first names. They go where I go."

"And should the book be lost or stolen?"

I tapped my chest with a corner. He shrugged.

"Myself, I have no friends, dead, canonized, or other. It is why I took this job. No other would accept it, once they heard where this train was bound."

"Are all your colleagues so superstitious?"

"Demons are easy. There are spells, talismans. It is not so with men. I see you know nothing of the Mother Range."

"I've climbed the Bitterroots and crossed the Divide. One set of mountains is much like all the rest."

He drew a jagged line through the condensation on his glass with a forefinger. "You have heard the story of how Cabo Infierno got its name?"

"I have. The Spanish demanded gold; they forgot to say how they wanted it delivered. I don't fear places named for hell or the devil or death. It's men who named them."

"You talk as one who never laid eyes on the devil."

I resumed my seat, the Bible in my lap, and picked up my glass. "I suppose you're going to tell me you have."

"Not I. But then I have not had the privilege of

meeting Oscar Childress. Have you angered your superiors, that you should be sent to the Sierras?"

"I volunteered."

"You seek your death willingly?"

"No one has ever done that. Even men who jump off bridges must have second thoughts just before the end. Everything I hear about Childress convinces me I'd be missing something if I passed up the chance to meet him face-to-face."

"I am certain that is what Montezuma said about Cortes."

He doubled over suddenly, hugging himself; then just as quickly recovered, sat back, and resumed drinking. I realized then that he'd been in constant pain, and that the spasm had only been the worst in an unbroken line.

I felt a sudden rush of pity; it was probably the whisky. "What is your affliction, my friend?"

"My liver. Too much tequila and mescal, not enough grapefruit and apples. The doctor in Durango allowed me a year, the shaman in Quezalcoatl three months. I should have quit after the first." He raised his glass. "I drink to my liver, for bringing me this far. I have never been north of La Junta." He emptied it and stood. "Thank you for the excellent spirits. We must be on our way. I am told an express is coming through."

"It's not due until four o'clock. There's time for another. Unless—" I made a gesture in the direction of his misery; or where I thought it might be. I knew next to nothing of the bodies I'd sent to the grave.

"The damage is done; I speak not of that nor of the hour. I must ask you to take care that one of us remain sober at all times."

"We're a long way from the Sierras."

"We shall speak again of that subject, when I explain to you the rules. Meanwhile I cannot predict what Joseph would do if he found both of us *borracho*. I trust him no more than my liver." He left me to my drink and my Holy Writ.

EIGHT

Working up a head of steam, the boiler sent a pulse the length of the train, like a horse bunching its muscles for a long gallop. The delay between the pull of the tender and the reaction by the coach was like a gasp for breath. In the weeks ahead I would come to regard that arrangement of bolts, plates, pistons, and couplers as a living thing, and when I slept—which is how I recommend traveling through most of Utah and Arizona—to fancy that I was an extension of it, my veins and arteries connected with it the way Barnum's Siamese twins were each physically dependent on the other; the churning of the drive-rods melded with the beating of my heart, the rhythmic wheezing of steam and smoke with the function of my lungs. When Hector Cansado blew the whistle at crossings, I felt its hoarse shrill bellow in my testicles. We were one and the same, the *Ghost* and I.

From Great Falls to Tucson, we stopped at the same place to take on water and wood: the long low frame station, the loafers holding up its porch roof with their shoulder blades, the slouch-hatted driver handling the reins of the team hitched to a dray carrying its cargo of barrels down a cross street strung together with all the others. I manufactured names for all of them, man and beast, the closest friends I'd had in a long while. I ate chicken and dumplings twenty times in the Bluebell Café, served by a substantially built woman named Martha, drank coffee that had been boiling since dawn. One tree had provided all the apple pies, the crusts burnt in a black crescent. In each place, the talk was of a farmer kicked by a mule, a little girl drowned in a well, a midwife hacked to pieces and distributed alongside a mile of county road. The victims were interchangeable, but the mayhem followed the theme as before. A man named Gus would hang a hundred times.

I don't know when the engineer slept, or if he did at all; maybe, aware of how little time he had left, he'd decided not to waste any of it insensible, dozing in snatches at the throttle, close enough to the surface to react to sharp bends, steep plunges, and obstacles on the tracks. Apart from that—if even that—he took his rest with me in the private car while Joseph tended the boiler at rest, drinking a hole in Judge Blackthorne's private stock, sometimes joining me in a hand of poker, playing with matchsticks and swapping biographies.

He was the eldest of eleven, not counting one miscarriage, two stillbirths, and a sister who died of diphtheria at the age of two weeks. His mother took in washing, and his father had spent a total of six hours with his children, leaving their one-room hut before sunup and chipping bits of color out of granite until the coal-oil ran out around midnight.

"We had a good working system," he said. "Mama would take a turtle from a trap in the river and I would stand on its shell while Felipe applied pliers to its jaw, pulling out its head, Alessandro chopped it off, and Delores snatched it by its tail and threw it into a boiling kettle. You know turtle soup?"

I nodded. "In San Francisco. They called it terrapin in the Bella Union."

"Snapper, we. I learned to avoid the severed head at an early age, when a hen pecked at it out of curiosity and it locked onto the bird's throat. They will hold on, you know, until sundown, or until the brain gets the message that it is no longer connected to the body. Pass the bottle, *senor, por favor.*

"Ah! To have discovered such nectar years ago would have been worth my liver. It was an important moment in my passage when I was declared old enough, first to use the pliers, then to swing the axe. What I would not give to eat turtle soup once again. The river was fished out long ago."

"And what of Felipe, Delores, and the rest?" I asked.

He set a matchstick to use, igniting a cigarette he rolled himself in brown paper. The smoke from the scorched grain made me lightheaded, an argument in its favor; liquor benefited no one but the drinker.

"*Quien sabe?* The soldiers came for Alessandro to help them fight for Maximilian; we never heard from him again. Then more soldiers came for Felipe to help them fight for Juarez. We heard he was shot for desertion. Delores became pregnant by the son of a don and was sold to a brothel. I do not know what became of the child. The *rurales* arrested me when I trespassed upon the don's ranch. They took away my rifle, which was fifty years old and did not work anyway, and I was sentenced to labor in the same mine that claimed my father's life when it fell in, along with those of a dozen others.

"I served with the crew that excavated it. I do not know which of the skeletons we uncovered belonged to my father. I would be working there still if a man representing railway interests in *Los Estados Unidos* hadn't come looking for a fireman to replace the one he'd lost when a boiler exploded near Chihuahua; he was blasting tunnels for a line to be owned jointly by the Oklahoma, Texas, and Missouri Railroad and the government in Mexico City. I had just started as an engineer when *El Presidente* Diaz nationalized the railway in the interest of the Republic. *Lo mismo, senor, por favor.*"

I refilled his glass. He'd drunk half a bottle to two drinks on my part without affecting either his speech or his reflexes.

He sipped, sighed. "When we were grading track not far from my old village I chanced to look in upon the home where I grew up. Strangers were living there, and knew nothing of the former occupants. It is a trial, *Senor* Deputy, to visit a bordello and not know if one is lying with one's own niece."

I had nothing to offer in comparison with his experiences. I'd been shot, almost burned to death, lured into traps by evil women, and spent a season as a slave with Cheyenne renegades, but I had nothing to match his loss.

That is, if he was telling the truth. If I had a cartwheel dollar for every Mexican whose sister had been raped by a Spanish don, I could have spent my life traversing the continent in a private railway car.

Joseph was a puzzle of another sort. I doubt we exchanged more than fifty words total, most of them monosyllabic and unrevealing, but even before we left Montana Territory I was convinced he was some kind of Judas goat, leading us toward a slaughterhouse. He spent all his time in the locomotive when he wasn't foraging for fuel—not overlooking the merest scrap of driftwood on the shore of the Great Salt Lake or mesquite twig in the Painted Desert—crunched down cracked corn by the handful, chasing it with water from a goatskin bag, and crossed himself before he ate, clutching the carved-stone crucifix suspended from the rosary around his neck. For all his show of Christian conversion, I pictured him more easily offering morsels to a beast-headed god squatting in some undiscovered ruin, praying for our destruction.

The *Ghost* passed through city and plain, leaving no more evidence of its passage than would its namesake. Most unscheduled journeys by rail fostered a host of gossip, and questions at every stop. The endless chain of Marthas set before me bowl after bowl of chicken and dumplings—scrawny prairie hen, and blobs of mealy flour swimming in grease—with only the usual tinned cheer and no apparent curiosity as to where I was bound and why. There was nothing furtive about it, only a complacency I'd never witnessed before. No one asked me about the news from up north, yet I sensed no hostility, no reticence. I was a piece of furniture, and nothing so interesting as a piano or a new kind of plow.

Out of duty I put in to post offices along the way, in case Blackthorne had wired further instructions or calling for a progress report, only to meet blank faces and shaking heads. Either I'd been forgotten—written off, as a bad debt—or the Judge was laying the groundwork for a plea of ignorance when the mission went sour. I was as much an orphan as Hector Cansado, whose brothers and sisters had been taken from him as by the unfeeling wind.

No, nothing so substantial as an orphan. I was a phantom, like the train I rode, drifting through human bodies, constructions of wood, brick, and adobe, like a mist, only without the chill that came with it. There was no evidence that I existed. Outside Yuma, an antelope grazing next to the cinderbed didn't raise its head as the train swept past within inches. As the animal dissolved in a wave of heat I put my hand to my mouth and bit hard into the tender flesh between my thumb and forefinger, and waited for the blood to come to the surface. When it did, proving something, I knew not what, I cracked open my Bible and read:

> Yet he shall perish forever like his own dung; they which have seen him shall say, Where is he?
> He shall fly away as a dream, and shall not be found; yea, he shall be chased away as a vision of the night.

I slammed the book shut. Who wrote this thing, anyway?

I worked my way back to the stock car, bracing myself against the arid wind that struck me like a sheet of superheated iron on the verandah; it stood my skin-cells on end and crackled the hairs in my nose. The wheatgrass stretching to the horizon laid down in the opposite direction the train was headed, making me dizzy. The world was spinning away from me, the ultimate rejection.

The bay lifted its wedge-shaped head when I came through the door, studying me first with one eye, then turning to confirm what it had seen with the left, like a bird on a perch. I strapped on its feedbag and stroked its neck; it lunged, trying to bite me through the canvas. I found that reassuring. Horses still hated me; proof that I was flesh and not air.

I had a strange sensation—a waking dream, like the wisp of unreality that told you you'd been dozing, even when you were struggling with sleeplessness— that I was looking at Lefty Dugan, the friend I'd killed in Butte.

Is that what you thought? he seemed to be saying. *It's the other way around, Page. I killed you.*

Nothing had changed: Shoot one old partner to death and he never let you forget it.

NINE

"T he time has come," the walrus said, "to speak of rules."

The walrus in this case being Hector Cansado. I'd drunk myself into an Aberdeen stupor, with *Alice in Wonderland* splayed facedown on my chest and a touch of malaria, and awoke to a visage that lacked only whiskers and tusks to fulfill the dream.

"*Senor,*" the engineer said, "we are in Mexico. But where we go, there are no *fiestas,* no *pinatas,* no pretty *senoritas* dancing barefoot upon tables. Nothing you have learned from the past applies to the place we are bound."

"I've been to Mexico before."

"I am sure you had your picture struck in Mexico City, wearing a sombrero and sitting upon a stuffed burro. Where we go, they know nothing of cameras or the telegraph. Men have been slain there for their watches; not to sell, but to take apart and see how they work. They mark the passage of time by the sun and the seasons. The sun sets early in the mountains and rises late, and what happens in between wears the cloak of night. It is no mystery how grotesque stories flourish there.

"Trust no one, least of all your friends. That is rule number one.

"Trust not yourself. Reason and insanity are not so easy to separate in the Mother Mountains: Down is up, dark is light, crooked straight. That is rule number two."

"How many more are they?" I asked. "Should I take notes?"

"Ignore all rules. That is rule number three, and the last I shall give you."

"Was this conversation necessary at all?"

He shrugged. His people were experts at that. "Perhaps not. *Mi madre,* rest her soul"—he crossed himself—"said you cannot know a man until you have seen him in his nightshirt."

I sat up in my berth. "Where are we now?"

"The village of Alamos, in the Sonoran Desert. I suggest you take it in. It is the last civilization we shall encounter this side of Cabo Falso."

I dressed and went outside. The *Ghost* snorted rhythmically, pausing between exhalations, like a stallion bred for racing champing before the gate. Joseph sat as I had first seen him, feet dangling outside the cab, foraging in his sack of corn. His black eyes were more opaque than usual, like wax drippings; either he was relieved to be back on home ground or he'd sweetened his meal with leaves from the plants that grew in lush patches on the sides of the foothills beginning just steps from the train, their distinctive five-leaf clusters stirring in the slight breeze. I remembered what Blackthorne had said about Childress and his poppies growing between rows of sugar cane. They would thrive in that climate, like the marijuana. No country was better suited for cultivating human vice.

The village, as old as any in North America, sprawled at the very foot of the Sierra Madres. It was as if one of the ancient gods had tilted the earth at a seventy-degree angle, and everything on it had slid into a jumble at the bottom. Some of the adobe structures were the oldest in appearance, the original surfaces beaten hard as concrete and covered with patches on patches, each smear a darker shade than its predecessor. The territorial movement had modified later constructions, the windows framed with piñon wood and roof poles extending two feet beyond the walls, looking like elephants' tusks sawn off blunt. Signs identifying the businesses—CORREO, HERRERIA, CARNICERIA—were painted directly on the adobe. More recent buildings were built of pine carted down from just below the tree line and put up green, a blessing during the hot months, when cross-breezes swept through the spaces between the boards, but a curse in monsoon season; inside they would smell of moss and mold and breed mosquitoes the size of sparrows.

A priest leaned in the doorway of the chapel, which although built of the inevitable adobe sported an outer shell of polished limestone, a gleaming white phantom in a world of brown earth. Although he wore the surplice and robes of his calling, his attitude, anticipating something he dared not hope for, a soul saved or a miracle granted, put me in mind of a butcher awaiting his next customer. His gray face brightened as I drew near, only to settle into resignation as I passed, smiling with my lips tight. His faith wasn't mine; I felt no need for an intermediary between myself and my God.

Drinking locally brewed beer in the cantina, dark and damp as a grotto, I heard a loud plop and rescued a woolly caterpillar from drowning among the hops floating in my glass.

I didn't tarry. In winter, gringos would migrate to
that climate like swallows, but with the heat rising in
twisting ribbons from the beaten earth of the street,
mine was the whitest face in the room, and I was still
burned as dark as cherry from riding the width of
Montana Territory and back. The bartender—a full-
blooded Yaqui, judging by his flat features and eyes
like shards of polished coal—kept a machete slung by
a sinew thong from the wall above the taps, and it
didn't strike me as just a decoration.

I tossed some change on the bar, but as I made my
way out I saw a rectangular sheet posted next to the
door, as brown and wrinkled as cigarette paper, with a
woodcut reproduced in black ink of a man in the uniform of a Mexican *federale*: khakis, Sam Browne belt,
knee-length boots, schoolboy cap with its shiny leather
visor, tearing the clothing from a terrified-looking *se-
norita,* and a legend I preferred to translate into English when I wasn't among witnesses. I pretended to
stumble, bumping against the wall, and held up a hand
to my audience, reassuring them of my welfare, as
with the other I tore the sheet off its nail and stuffed it
into a pocket.

VOLUNTEERS WANTED! [It read]
TOP WAGES!
FIGHT FOR FREEDOM, FAMILY, LAND
SEE PROPRIETOR FOR DETAILS
OSCAR CHILDRESS, MAJOR,
THE ARMY OF LIBERTY

I showed it to Cansado when he reported to the
coach for his regular session with Scottish skullbender.
He stared at it, said:

"This same picture accompanied *El Presidente*

Juarez's leaflets at the time of the revolution. Alas, I was pressed into service before I learned my letters."

I made him a beneficiary of my incomplete Spanish. He nodded.

"Ah. No monetary inducements were offered then. Had they been, it may not have been necessary to recruit my brother at the point of a bayonet."

"Correct me if things have changed since my last visit, but isn't this evidence in favor of a firing squad?"

"It is, perforce. But we are many miles from the capital, with many more to travel, most of them vertical, and steep canyons whose floors the sun has never reached. Many things lurk there, *Senor* Deputy, some with a hundred legs, and poison enough to paralyze a regiment. However, it is my observation that the danger increases as the number of legs wane, until one is left with but two, that march to the beat of General Childress' drum."

I tilted my glass, pointing its rim at my companion. "Don't be insulted, but you're a liar. No illiterate can spout such poetry merely from the hearing."

The yellow bloated face showed no offense. "Is it not wise, sometimes, to feign ignorance, in order to barter time while your foe seeks to educate you?"

"I don't know what you're talking about."

He hesitated, turning over the words; then grinned for the first time, looking like a jack-o'lantern on November first. He handed back the flyer.

"I fail to see that this is of use. You knew of this already, from the American detective's report. Surely you did not doubt its existence."

"He neglected to include a point of contact. Have you tried the local beer? The caterpillar I fished out of it seemed none the worse for swimming in it."

"Why drink that swill when you have—?" He paused with his glass half-raised. He set it down gently, his eyes fixed on mine. They had a strange quality, like the brother's I'd never had.

"This bartender," he said, "will direct you to a lonely spot, where you will be assassinated, stripped of your clothes and skin, and dragged still living behind an oxcart, and then they will fry your entrails and serve them up with the local beer."

"The hell you say. Indians don't eat human flesh."

"Did I say anything about Indians?"

He was difficult to fathom. How did a man, whose entire life had been lived south of La Junta, know so much about the depths to which humans could sink? Just seeing his family decimated by continuous revolution didn't answer. Some men are born already old in the ways of the wicked world.

"You're forgetting what I have to offer," I said.

"*Dinero?*" He drank, snorted Scotch out his nose, wiped his face on his sleeve. "*Banditti* apprehended with American gold coins are shot without trial, the gold divided among the arresting officers; these brigands would sooner handle a rattlesnake. Weapons? They will raid this car upon your death and confiscate them all."

He shook his head. "You *Norteamericanos* are all the same. You think what you own is what you are. You can take nothing from these people that they haven't lost already, including their lives."

"I have one thing they can't have, without the skills to use it," I said, "and that, my friend, is your own ticket to life."

He drank, swallowed. "Now it is you who spouts poetry. What can you possibly give them that they cannot take?"

I settled back in soft pigskin and gestured with my glass, taking in the coach, and by extension the *Ghost* itself.

"As a wise man once said, no revolutionist would be caught dead without a train."

He set down the rest of his drink, rose, smoothed his overalls with all the care of a New York robber baron tugging down his white waistcoat.

"I am not a slave, *senor,* to be sold with the machine I am employed to operate. You may make your terms with Joseph; but he knows little more about the whims of this particular conveyance than you."

"You picked a hell of a time to quit."

"No more so than the time you chose to tell me of your plan. You knew of this in Montana?"

"I did. I had no way of knowing you weren't aware of it yourself."

He sighed; he did it as well as he shrugged.

"It is ever thus. The peon need not be consulted as to his fate."

I drained my glass, filled it again, and tipped the rest of the bottle into his.

"I'm consulting you now. If you refuse, I have no choice but to turn back. A train's no good without the man who knows how to run it."

"What is that to me? Your people are amateurs at war. My country has been at it since Cortes. Should I care whether Chester Cleveland or Oscar Childress is in charge of *Los Estados Unidos*? I have seen emperors and presidents rise and fall, and I am not yet forty years of age. I shall see many more, and yet my people will remain in the same sorry state as they were at the beginning." He spread his palms. "What have I to gain?"

"You've mixed up Chester Arthur with Grover Cleveland."

"No more so than those who have the privilege of voting."

"You're going about it all wrong," I said. "What more have you to lose?"

"My life."

"Spent doing what? Carrying passengers from here to there and back? I saw cable cars doing just that in San Francisco. Where do you end? Where you started."

I stirred my drink with a finger. "Cape Hell, they call the place we're headed. I should have asked you about that back in Helena, as an expert. I can't think of any kind of damnation that didn't put you back where you were in the beginning."

He picked up his glass, swirled the contents, looked into them, like a gypsy reading leaves in an empty teacup.

"You make an interesting point, *Senor*. I cannot help but think that one way or the other leads to death."

I raised my glass. "To death. It's the debt all men must pay."

"*Por que no?*" He raised his. "I for one always feel relieved once I have settled a bill."

TEN

The door at the front of the car opened. Joseph in his overalls stood silhouetted dimly against the rear of the black tender, the white rectangle in his hand startlingly bright in the light of the lamps. It was a recent arrival, obviously. Nothing in his world of smoke, cinders, and grease remained unstained for more than a few minutes.

"For him." He pointed a corner of the envelope at me. "It came just now by a messenger."

He stepped forward to hand it to me. An awkward moment passed during which the engineer and I sat unmoving, waiting. Presently the fireman withdrew, drawing the door shut behind him.

The envelope, in silk bond, was addressed to me in neat copperplate, sealed with a blob of black wax and the letters K.G.C. pressed into it, probably by a signet ring, in the center of an oak-leaf cluster. I showed it to Cansado.

"I do not know these initials," he said.

"Knights of the Golden Circle. They spied in the North for the Confederacy during the war." I broke the seal, and read, in the same tidy hand on matching stationery:

Dear Mr. Murdock:
I represent the legal interests of General Oscar Childress, and would consider it a great favour if you would honor me with your presence in my quarters this evening.

A card engraved on heavier stock of the same quality was clipped to the page, replicating the name the writer had signed and his address:

Felix Bonaparte, Esq.
No. 9 Calle Santa Anna
Alamos, Mexico

"This name is French, is it not?"

"It might explain his connection with the K.G.C.," I said. "France sided with the rebels."

"It may be a trap."

"Probably." I rose, rummaged among the artillery in the drawer of the gun rack, and buckled on the Deane-Adams.

"Shall I go with you?"

"No. The only thing I brought of any value is this train. If I gave them the man who knows how to run it, I'd be hailed as a hero of the Confederacy."

"I keep a pistol in the cab. Not even Joseph knows about it."

I got out the Springfield shotgun, laid it across his lap, and handed him a box of shells. "There's no telling how many might come. If you let them get close enough, you can take out several at a time. Do you know—?"

Before I could finish, he opened the trap-door action, poked a shell into the chamber, and slammed it shut. He smiled at my expression. "No, *senor*, I have never held this weapon. It is a poor engineer who can examine a piece of machinery and fail to determine how it works."

I spread my hands. "Then I'm away."

"*Senor* Deputy. Page." He stood, foraged in a pocket

of his overalls, and came up with an image of St. Christopher embossed in bronze at the end of a chain. "This was a gift of my grandmother, the day I left the village in which I was born. It has seen me through these many years."

I reached to take it. He snatched it back against his breast. His lips twisted.

"Do you think, upon the basis of some nights spent in drink, I would give this to you?—this, of all things? I wished merely to say that I hoped you owned something in which you found the same measure of protection."

I grinned. "You son of a bitch."

"*Sí.*" He returned the token to its pocket. "I have this same information from the man I called my father, on his deathbed, where lies are useless. The knowledge of my bastardy by nature gives me a certain advantage over those who must earn the distinction by conduct."

I unholstered the English revolver, spun the cylinder, twirled it back into leather, patted my Bible, and put it in the side pocket of the frock coat I wore in civilization with the same flourish. "What the one cannot deliver, so the other shall."

Something approaching a wrinkle creased the tight expanse of his forehead. "Mark? Matthew?"

"Murdock."

"Ah. A book yet to be written; had I but my letters." He refilled his glass.

A hag draped in tatters, with a tin tiara gleaming in the rats of her hair, knew El Calle Santa Anna, and offered to take me there for the price of an American dollar. She'd have known me for what I was even if I'd worn a filthy serape and a tattered sombrero; they can smell it. A year saturated in fried peppers, cornmeal, and rapid immersions in leechy creeks would hardly have been enough to wash away the gringo. When, nearing the corner, she backed into a dark doorway and raised her skirts, hoping to raise the ante, I thanked Christ for the darkness, slipped another half-dollar into her crusted palm, and shoved away from her. Her parting cackle interrupted itself long enough only to bite into the coin. I'd have trusted her rotting incisors over any assayer's scale when it came to separating silver from lead.

The street had been laid out under the early Spanish colonists, with no thought of anything broader than a dogcart passing through. At times the way was so narrow I couldn't have stumbled over one of the many uneven stones and fallen as far as the ground; a scraped shoulder was as much as I'd get, and the devil of a time prying myself loose to proceed. As the way grew darker and tighter, I had to concentrate to avoid confusing horizontal with vertical, and thinking I was climbing the inside of a chimney. The soot was as thick, and the path as black.

Not all of the buildings bore numbers. I had to strike a match to read the addresses that existed, some painted directly on the lintels above the sunken doors, others, harkening back to a more genteel past, enameled in flaked paint on the pebbled-glass panels of coach lamps, most of them dark and colonized by wasps, sleeping in their paper cells. A rat crossing the alley paused on my instep, its eyes glowing red by matchlight, then humped along the rest of its way. I was the trespasser, but not one worth challenging.

No. 9, when it revealed itself, was something apart from its surroundings. The street broadened just before I came upon it, like a forest clearing in a fairy tale, with the witch's house nestling quietly in its center, all brown sugar and molasses with a roof made of short-bread.

It wasn't quite that; two stories built in the Tudor style, mortar and timber, oak shutters pierced with holes just wide enough to expel and repel bullets. It was of more recent construction than the rest of the village, but created the impression of something older, harkening back to a time of medieval siege. The prosaic sign stretching the length of the street front belonged to a time neither of the building's inspiration nor of its surroundings:

BONAPARTE & SONS
SOLICITORS

A large bronze bust of Napoleon in his cocked hat shared a plate-glass window with a group photograph on a small easel of the justices of the U.S. Supreme Court, embalmed in stiff collars and moustache wax. A lamp burning deep in the interior shone through the picture, making the judicial branch of the federal government appear transparent.

The door swung open away from my raised knuckles, framing a small man in a black cutaway and a white cutthroat collar. My other hand tightened on the butt of the revolver, but his hands were empty and he was alone in the room. I relaxed my grip.

His clean-shaven face was as brown as a bottle. I assumed at first that it was the contrast that made his linen seem spotless, but as he pivoted in the direction of the door, beckoning me past him with a dusky palm sticking out of four inches of starched cuff, the inside light fell full upon him and revealed a coat brushed to a bright sheen, a copper-colored necktie snugged tight without a dimple or a scrap of lint, square-toed boots like polished obsidian, and a shirt that would pass muster at a White House state dinner.

He did not shake my hand, but when the door was shut behind him snapped a bow, exposing a round patch of pink scalp in the middle of close-cropped hair, with his thumbs parallel to the seams of his trousers. "Felix Bonaparte, *Monsieur,* and your servant."

His voice was a mild tenor, touched with an accent I associated with the French Quarter of New Orleans. How a Creole had come to light in a village perched on the ankles of the Sierra Madre was as much a mystery as how he managed to support such linen in that climate. The first was none of my business, but I couldn't resist asking about the second.

"The widow two streets over was born in Shanghai, of a Spanish missionary and a *fille de joie.* An aunt shipped her to the New World at the time of the 1864 rebellion, for her safety. San Francisco was the destination, but the navigator was blown overboard in the same typhoon that altered the vessel's course. I can but assume that God intended for me to keep up appearances in this barbaric country. My credentials, you see, are not honored north of the border."

He'd managed to satisfy my curiosity in less than a hundred words. If he could settle all my questions in such short order, the American Bar Association had missed its bet in denying him permission to practice law.

He circled the room, turning up other lamps until the walls were visible, wainscoted halfway to the ceiling, with more pictures leaning out from the walls, suspended by wires to a rail. They were the usual three-quarter portraits of men in fierce whiskers and black broadcloth, one-eared representatives of eastern schools and northern authority, glowering down on the usual office furniture of oak and maple and over-stuffed leather. A plate of beans and a half-eaten tortilla occupied the copper-cornered blotter on the desk.

Bonaparte caught the direction of my gaze. "Have you dined?"

It struck me just then that I hadn't. I was hungry enough to sample the local fare, but wasn't sure how well it would sit on a reservoir of beer and Scotch. I said I was fine.

"You will pardon me, then. I received a packet of material by the morning train, and at such times I frequently work straight through breakfast and dinner. I am anemic, you see. The head, it spins." He gestured toward one of his temples, sat behind the desk, tucked a napkin the size of a tablecloth under his excellent collar, and began scooping beans into his mouth with the skill of someone born to the process without utensils. "I must ask your pardon as well for the lateness of the hour. That same work prevented me from issuing the invitation sooner."

I sat in a tufted love seat facing him. "I don't work by the clock myself. I can't imagine what business you and I have to discuss. I haven't come all this way to enter into any legal agreement."

"Your business is decidedly not legal." He chewed, swallowed, touched a corner of the napkin to each lip-corner, and chased the mouthful with water from a glass goblet. "Everyone in Alamos knows you have come to kill General Childress. It is my responsibility to turn you from this path."

II

The Mother Mountains

ELEVEN

Do not insult us both by denying the fact," Bonaparte said; although if he was any kind of lawyer he wouldn't know by my reaction that I had any such intention. I'd spent too much time in Judge Blackthorne's courtroom, being turned on the spit by defense attorneys, to change expressions. "A stranger cannot cross the border unnoticed, dragging his mission behind him as clearly as smoke from the stack of your splendid train. I myself have lived here nearly twenty years, and when someday I am found extinct at this desk, the publisher of the village newspaper, who is my oldest friend, will write a stellar account of my life, adding that this late arrival will be missed in this village."

I watched him scoop the last of the beans into his mouth, repeating the ritual with his napkin and glass of water. *Joseph*, I thought. The messenger who had brought Bonaparte's invitation was a phantom; the fireman had lost no time reporting to Childress' representative, and been asked—politely, of course—to wait while the lawyer drafted his note. Even George Pullman's superior standards couldn't construct a private parlor coach with walls so thick they'd foil a determined eavesdropper. Had he tried, no less than three locomotives would be needed to pull it.

"You've heard the rumors," I said.

"General Childress would not be the extraordinary man he is if legends did not grow up round him like desert flowers after a spring rain. As with all great men, it is necessary to discount a third of them as invention, another third as either exaggeration or monstrous distortion, and to assign truth to the rest.

"That he intends to liberate this country at last, most definitely. That he is a traitor"—thin shoulders rose above his pristine collar—"must be left to history. Washington and Jefferson were both marked for the gibbet had they failed to repel the British from their shores."

"Since you know so much about me, you must know also that I'm not interested in history lessons."

He sat motionless; but whether he was turning over what I'd said or planning his next move didn't make it as far as his bland placid face. He knew his own way around a courtroom, it seemed.

At length he stirred; I flexed the knuckles of the hand resting on the thigh nearest the Deane-Adams. But all he did was lift a small copper bell from the desk and shake it once. The tinkle was discreet, like everything else about him.

A door opened at the back of the room. I gripped the butt of the revolver; only to relax once again when a boy entered in white cotton peasant dress and sandals. He couldn't have been older than ten, with straight black hair cut square across his brows. Bonaparte spoke to him in clipped tones, in Spanish so rapid I couldn't catch it. The boy withdrew, to return a moment later carrying a leather folder bound with a cord and placed it on the desk. He was dismissed with a snap of the hand.

Bonaparte went on in his pleasant company voice, as if there'd been no interruption, untying the cord as he spoke.

"Do not think that I shall warn the General of your coming. There is no telegraph to his plantation, and the bandit situation is such at present that no mounted messenger would accept the commission. At all events he is prepared perpetually for contingencies of every sort. It is you who should be warned."

"*Merci, Monsieur.*"

"Ah! *Parlez-vous?*"

"*Un petit.* I spent a season in San Francisco."

"A cosmopolitan city, I am told." He removed a bundle of paper from the folder and sorted it into stacks on the desk. His fingers were long, spatulated at the tips, and moved with the swift grace of a skilled faro dealer. "Yes, a most extraordinary man, the General; though he himself prefers the humbler rank of major. These are his papers, which I hope someday to donate to your Library of Congress, and ask no more than a footnote identifying myself as the contributor. Men such as I can hardly expect glory beyond that reflected from the blaze of the truly great."

I watched mesmerized as he placed portions of Childress' meteoric life into prosaic piles, according to his file-clerk's sense of order.

"Your client conducts most of his affairs with the outside world through Cabo Falso," I said. "How can you represent him from five hundred miles away?"

"I agree the situation has difficulties. That I remain alive is not one of them." He continued his activity, cutting no-doubt revealing documents like a deck of cards. "I am not courageous, like you. It is a failing, yes, but one over which I have no control. Would you condemn me if I were born without an arm or with my heart on the wrong side of my chest? It is the same, an unintentional omission on the part of our Lord. Cabo Falso is a nest of pirates and worse. A man of my sort would not survive a week. The General understands this, and thinks no less of me, because I am so much better equipped to deal with paperwork quite as crucial as fertilizer and harvesting equipment. It requires a measure of courage, I assure you, to take a dispatcher to task for a serious error in shipment."

He described his situation so practically I felt ashamed of my own lack of cowardice.

I reflected on what he'd said about fertilizers and harvesting equipment. "He's keeping up the pretense of producing sugar?"

"There is no pretense about it; quite the reverse. He produces more sugar than his five closest competitors combined. You are aware of the importance of bones in the refining process?"

"I hunted buffalo, and saw pickers collecting the bones. They sold them to manufacturers in Detroit, who ground them into powder and ran raw sugar through them to take out the impurities. The bottom fell out of that market with the buffalo."

"He's found a substitute; or another method every bit as good. His merchandise is sought after in all the best restaurants in *Los Estados Unidos* and as far away as Paris, France, so I am told. It is nearly as fine as flour, but superior in granule texture, refusing to clump under the most humid conditions. Master chefs in the tropical colonies have threatened to resign if their employers will not agree to pay thrice as much for what Childress produces. You have seen his label, perhaps? The armored head of a knight circumscribed by gold laurels?"

Whereupon the son of a bitch turned his lapel, showing me a pin bearing the embossed emblem of the Knights of the Golden Circle. I kept my temper.

"And his opium? Is the quality as good?"

If I'd disappointed him by failing to rise to the bait, he didn't show it; I'd have been disappointed myself if he had. He dropped the lapel back into place and continued sorting, calm as a stone in moonlight. I had his measure now. A poker face is only so good as the amount of pressure you applied to it. When it blew, it would shake the earth.

"I, too, have heard this canard. It is without foundation; and even if it were, where is the crime? One can purchase it in any chemist's shop, diluted with grain alcohol and labeled laudanum; good for the miseries of the lumbago and all other manner of complaint. Had I been born to a caste lower than my own, I'd have hired a wagon and gone town to town peddling it by the quart."

A lawyer to the bone, *Monsieur* Bonaparte. A client is always innocent; but if guilty, then of nothing unlawful.

At length he squared away his stacks, palming the edges as even as bricks, and lifted one.

"Since, as I believe, you insist upon pressing forward despite my friendly advice, perhaps you will be so kind as to deliver these to your proposed victim."

Given the cordiality of the exchange so far, it seemed bad manners to leave him holding the bundle he offered. I turned it over, reading the delicate script on the top envelope. Like the rest, it was pressed from pale rose deckle-edged vellum, the whole bound with matching ribbon. It was addressed to "*O. Childress*."

"They were sent by his fiancée in Virginia, an estimable woman by all accounts, and upon the evidence of her choice of husband, certainly. She has been waiting months for a reply."

"Childress has a fiancée?"

"Is it so strange a great man may love in the corporeal sense?"

"He hasn't been to Virginia in twenty years."

"The relationship is all the sweeter for the absence. Had the women I married respected my privacy to such an extent, I should not be alone this day."

I brought the bundle to my nose, but whatever scent she might have sprinkled on the envelopes had long since evaporated in that climate. "I'll do my best." I slid the letters into a side pocket.

"When you have finished reading them, please reseal them as well as you can. He will not be fooled, but he will appreciate the gesture."

It was as bizarre a meeting as I'd attended, and I'd sat in on Indian tribal councils and armed truces during range wars in Wyoming. "Is that why you called me here, to tell me I'm a suicidal fool and ask me to deliver mail?"

"Not entirely." Felix Bonaparte returned the rest of the material to the folder and tied it securely. I wondered what it contained that he'd held back. "I doubt you welcome death, or you would not attend so to the weapon you carry. A man who ignores this precaution would ignore others, and not survive. The odds— odds; this is the word, *oui*?"

"*A* word, yes." His relentless courtesy had begun to stand my nerves on edge.

"Thank you; it's a hazard of my background and circumstances that I sometimes am not sure whether I am conversing in English, Spanish, or French. The *odds,* you must see, are decidedly in General Childress' favor. He would consider me small in the light of his own chivalrous nature if I did not attempt to bring them closer to even."

He pointed. He grew his nails long, but as round as coins.

"On that wall, *monsieur,* is a map more current than any you have seen. It was drawn by a German cartographer named Muehlig, who took it upon himself to chart all the impenetrable regions of the earth, and thus leave his footprint on the path of the great explorers. The dream ended when he was beheaded by *banditti* for the value of the surveying equipment he packed upon his burro; but not before he drew this. The *rurales* who apprehended and shot the brigands found it of no value compared to the other items they confiscated, and so were generous enough to offer it to me. It is less than ten years old, and thus three hundred years more current than any you may have seen. I cannot part with it, but I suggest you commit as much as you can of it to memory. It may mean your life—for a while.

"At the very least you will go to your grave knowing a bit more of where your bones will rest until trumpet's blow. To die is one thing, but to die lost—" Again he shrugged.

The map, framed in black walnut without glass, hung in gloom. I lifted the milk-glass shade off the nearest lamp and carried it over. The names of various peaks and canyons were in German; I ignored them, not because they were foreign but because they'd been named by men, and of no use to the man who roamed among them. Muehlig, using the inks and paints he'd carried, had washed the whole of the eastern coast of the Gulf of California in pale blue, but tinted the jagged bumpy region of the Sierra Madre a bilious shade that in the flickering flame inside the soot-smeared glass chimney seemed to throb, as if it had a pulse of its own, sickly green, like the discharge from an infected wound.

"The Mother Mountains, *monsieur*," said the lawyer. "There the bones of the *Conquistadores* lay mingled with those of their predecessors, whose civilizations have been forgotten by time, buried by the very riches they sought. They died wealthy. If you will be so kind as to give me the name and address of your closest relation, I shall do my best to report where you were last seen alive."

I turned his way, and made as much of a bow as I could. It wasn't a patch on his, but he seemed to appreciate the effort. My last image of Felix Bonaparte, Esq., was of an arrangement of patches of light on a stoic face hovering above the lamp on his desk. If it weren't for the bundle of letters in my pocket, I'd have thought I'd dreamt the whole thing.

I passed back up the narrow alley, groping my way along the walls, which seemed closer together now, then farther apart, a vast expanse; I couldn't see as far as the one opposite. The adobe was hot to the touch. I snatched my palm away. I wondered if a fire was gutting the building. The heat followed me, coursed up my arm, across my chest, and down the other arm, passing out the ends of my fingers like electrical current. Raw cold rushed in to fill the void. I shivered. By the time I emerged from those thousand yards of darkness I was staggering.

The *Ghost* stood on its siding, inhaling flame and exhaling steam, its headlamp plowing a pale shaft through vapors as thick as churned butter. Hector Cansado, ghostlike himself, stood with his back to it, a moderate wind fluttering the end of the bandanna tied around his neck. He had the shotgun clamped to his right hip with the muzzle pointed at me.

I spread my hands. "It's Murdock."

"I know this." He didn't lower the weapon. "Stop walking, and keep your hands as they are."

I stopped. Of a sudden I felt no chills, no fever.

"I wondered how long it would take you to come around to that," I said.

"It requires no genius. There is the train, and here is the man who knows how to run it. Where, *Senor* Deputy, does that leave you?"

His image swam, shifted right and left, refusing to stay in one spot. I thought it was a distortion caused by the steam. I jerked my right arm, sliding the Bull-dog revolver out of my sleeve into my hand. I leveled it and fired.

Missed.

I actually saw the slug float past him, riding the steam like flotsam on the ocean. I saw nothing after that but steam. It thickened, drifted around me, clung to my body, filled my eyes and nose, stung my nostrils. I was drowning in it. I clawed for the surface, lost my grip on the little belly gun. An hour passed before I heard it strike earth with a dull thump, as remote as at the bottom of a well two hundred feet deep.

By then I was falling, too, plummeting through the chill air of the well. I heard the roar of the shotgun, dull also, as if it were swaddled in the same steam that pulled me down and down and shut out the rest of my senses.

TWELVE

I was adrift on a calm ocean, jammed into a tight berth with the sun nailed to the sky like a cartwheel dollar, blinding me with its brilliance and draining all the moisture from my body, drying me out like a dead fly on a sill. The surface of the water was as flat as a sheet of iron. Then a great toboggan-shaped bank of blue-black cloud slid across my vision, blanking out the light and drenching me in icy cold. The wind came up, turning the surface of the ocean on end, the ship sliding down one wave and climbing another, dizzying me so I couldn't tell up from down. I gripped the edges of my berth so tightly I knew my fingers would never come unclamped; when the inevitable came, someone would have to break them to get me loose to throw over the side.

An angel came for me, or rather tried to reach me, but it never got close enough so that I could make out its features. All I saw was a white blur, always the same distance away, a bright star obscured by haze. That was the sum total of my life: help on the horizon, always just beyond arm's length.

Where there are angels, devils can't be far behind. Mine looked like Hector Cansado. His face was as big as the *Ghost*'s boiler, each of his nostrils like the bore of the Springfield shotgun whose stock he had braced against his shoulder, taking aim at me. Time and again I saw smoke erupting from the muzzle, the lead pellets coming my way, spreading as they went, the pattern the size of the mortar-and-timber wall of the building where Felix Bonaparte practiced law on behalf of Oscar Childress. When they struck, with the force of ten locomotives, I jerked out of my nightmare with a tongueless shout, but not into reality, only into another dream as bad. Every fugitive I had ever killed ran hot on my heels, Lefty Dugan foremost, bent double as he closed the distance so that I could see clear down inside the hole I'd bored in his head, the sides sleek and shining like the piston rods that propelled the train.

Then something broke, and I lay in a pool of cold sweat, my vision clear. I stared at the convex coffered ceiling of the parlor car, secure in the berth that folded up into the wall when it wasn't in use. I was alert, but weak to the point of death; when Joseph pulled me by my arms into a sitting position, then laid me back down to lift my legs, stripping away the sodden sheet, and repeated the process in reverse to replace it with fresh linen, I was as limp as a marionette in a medicine show. He had to raise my arms and brace them with one shoulder to change my nightshirt.

I slept then, without dreaming, or with no memory later of what I had dreamt, beyond the blazing coin nailed to the sky and the engineer and his shotgun and the icy rise and fall of the ship tossed by the sea.

"He can speak?"

A new voice, this, resonant, not loud, like the echo of cannonfire in the ears after a period of constant bombardment: a low rumble with a distinct Spanish accent.

"I am not a doctor, *Jefe*. The danger is past. I can say no more."

This voice was familiar. Joseph, the fireman I'd been too smart to trust; the one who'd saved my life, possibly twice. With Cansado gone to the other side there was none else to have gotten me into bed and seen me through the fever.

I raised my head, and thought at first I'd slipped back into delusion: The star burning brightly through haze was back, but with a difference. This time it managed to approach me, and as it drew near the blurred outlines became distinct, so that when it stopped at the edge of the berth and looked down at me I saw it was a man.

He was dressed in white, but not the shapeless dress of a peon; more like the sugar-cane barons one saw smoking cigars and reading newspapers in the lobby of the best hotel in El Paso, in a pressed linen suit and narrow-brimmed straw hat, squared across straight strong brows. The white was interrupted only by tobacco-brown skin, a parti-colored hatband, a thin black knitted necktie, and highly polished black boots, as small as a boy's. Everything about him, in fact, was small, but he was built perfectly to scale, so that you didn't realize he was anything less than normal stature until you had something to compare him to; in this case one of the overstuffed chairs, the nearest arm of which reached above his waist. I knew, had we stood face-to-face, he wouldn't tip back his head to look up, forcing me to tip mine forward if I wanted to meet his gaze. I would want to, rather than guess where he might be looking if not at me. To this day when I think of him I don't see him as small; and I do think of him.

He wore no emblem of office, and no weapon as far as I could tell. The suit was cut so carefully to his measure it didn't seem as if a pistol or knife could be concealed on his person. He introduced himself as Vigía Férreo, "Chief of police on approval."

I tried to wet my lips, but my tongue was as dry as a dead leaf. "On whose approval?" It came out in a croak. Immediately Joseph placed a hand against the back of my head, supporting it as he trickled water into my mouth from a gourd. Most of it splashed down my chin, but it tasted cool and mossy, as if it had been cranked up from the same deep well I'd fallen into when Cansado had leveled the shotgun at me. It seemed a hundred years ago. I wondered what had happened to him.

"The citizens of Alamos have granted me the honor. My predecessor was appointed by *El Presidente* Diaz. He died last month, and the city fathers are awaiting word from Mexico City regarding his replacement; but *los bandidos, senor,* they await nothing."

"Were you his deputy?"

"His mathematics tutor. He hoped for an accounting position in the state house in Hermosilla, but our merciful Lord had other plans for him." He crossed himself.

"Since when is long division a requirement for law enforcement?"

"None that I am aware of; but I was the only one he trusted with the key to the office, and the city fathers respected his judgment."

"What did he die of?"

"Yellow fever. It stalks this place like an old puma. You are the very first person I have spoken to who survived it."

"I've had practice in survival."

"So it would seem. Whom shall we bill for your engineer's burial?"

Now I knew the report I'd heard was the shotgun going off in some harmless direction, diverted by Joseph with whatever weapon he'd had at hand. "You might try *El Presidente,* who loaned the train and its crew to the federal seat in Montana Territory. Failing that, try Judge Harlan A. Blackthorne in Helena."

Férreo wrote the information on a starched cuff with a short stub of orange pencil. He seemed to make use of the same half-breed Chinese laundress as Bonaparte. I asked how the engineer had met his end.

"At the head of an axe."

I glanced at Joseph, whose face registered nothing. The fireman would be an artist with that tool.

Férreo seemed to have read my thoughts. "Our little village has witnessed much that it would perhaps be best to forget—it is, you see, the path of revolution and raids across the border—but I have never before seen a man cloven from the crown of his head to his waist. This man"—his eyes slid briefly to Joseph— "has provided me with an account of what took place three days ago. I should like to hear yours."

Three days? I thought it had been three hours. "He threatened me with a shotgun. That's the last thing I remember. If Joseph told you he killed Cansado in my defense, I'd take him at his word."

"I fear the word of an Indian does not travel as far as that of a white man."

"Then that's what happened. I'll sign an affidavit if you want."

"We are not so formal here. Can you enlighten me as to *Senor* Cansado's motives?"

"I can only think that he wanted to take over the train and sell it in the Sierras, along with his services as operator."

"*Senor* Bonaparte has informed me of your meeting in his office. You are still determined to press on with your mission?"

"I don't see how I can do that without an engineer."

"Nor without a train. In the name of the citizens

of Alamos I am taking possession of it until further notice."

"What gives you that authority?"

He smiled, teeth blue-white against brown skin. "You may have three more days to regain your strength. Then you must make arrangements for other shelter or to return home. I shall hold the train until Mexico City sends someone to claim it.

"We live in a wilderness, *Americano*; wilder than anything in your frontier. A *bandido* with such transport as this is a dangerous animal. Moreover, to do other than I have chosen would be to countenance an act of murder. I do not believe that my predecessor would have done otherwise." He touched his hat. "*Buenos dias, Senor* Deputy. If you require anything that will make your stay more pleasant, please feel free to send me a message by way of the guards. The men I trust with such duty fought alongside Juarez. Juanito will be only too happy to show you his collection of gold teeth. You have but to ask."

After he left, I signaled to Joseph for another drink. The water tasted better than Blackthorne's Scotch whisky. I drank greedily, and would have gone on if he hadn't snatched the gourd away. "Why?"

"Lest you founder, like a horse."

"Not that. Why'd you take my side against Cansado?"

He lifted his shoulders and let them fall. "Perhaps I wished to be an engineer."

"You know how to run this train?"

"Stoking the fire is not the distraction you might think. I have had much time to watch and to remember what I have seen. All I need is someone to tend the boiler." A sly look crossed his hacked-out features. "I am afraid your days of riding in ease are at an end."

"Don't apologize. I was getting soft." I swung my feet to the floor. My head struck an invisible wall. I settled back onto the mattress. "I'd better rest," I said, when the car stopped spinning. "Stealing a train is a two-man job."

THIRTEEN

If I'd harbored any hope that the guards Férreo stationed to watch the *Ghost* were local amateurs pressed into service, it washed away when I alighted and saw them, one in front, one in the rear, and one on either side of the coach: slit-eyed Yaqui half-breeds with brown gnurled faces, carrying Mexican Winchesters at parade rest, bone-handled pistols in holsters with the flaps cut off attached to Sam Browne belts, short-bladed machetes balancing them out on the other side. A series of civil wars had provided them with surplus uniforms: riding breeches, knee-high boots and epaulets. They held their heads at the same ten-degree tilt to keep the smoke of their smoldering cheroots from collecting under the brims of their sombreros. They might all have been related, which was more than just a possibility: There were villages throughout that peninsula whose populations had bred among themselves for centuries, normally a recipe for weakness, but not in this case. Each generation appeared to have doubled the hardness of the last, like lichens forming additional inches to shelves growing on rock.

"Veterans of the revolution." Joseph spat and rubbed

his spittle into the rug at his feet. "Bandits. *Tio* Benito could hardly pick and choose when killers were required." I couldn't tell if the avuncular reference to Juarez was genuine or marinated in sarcasm.

"My horse needs exercise." I shook my head when he stirred himself. "As do I."

He noted the wobble when I rose from the chair where I'd been resting, excused himself, and returned to the car a moment later carrying a crooked stick. "I was told to tap the wheels with it whenever we stop."

"Why?"

"*Quien sabe?* Cansado I think did not know either."

I took the stick. "What was the tribal remedy you treated me with?"

"The powder of the cinchona bark. This area is rich in the tree."

"I did you a disservice. Cansado said I couldn't trust you and I believed him."

"I trusted neither of you until he showed his hand. I am Aztec, after all, born with the earned wisdom of those who passed before. One traitor is to be expected. Two, they—" He faltered, made a gesture with his fists together, the thumbs turned away from each other.

"Cancel each other out."

"*Sí.* A double betrayal leads to faith."

The statement made as much sense to me as that entire business. I never did trust him entirely. It was like taking up with the woman who'd thrown one man over to take up with you.

The guards stood motionless, their eyes alone following me as I led the bay by its bit, as long as my steps took me no closer to the locomotive. Neither Joseph nor I was a prisoner, but their orders would be to prevent us from moving the train at any cost. Pressure was up; the fireman had seen to that while he nursed me, but every moment he stayed away from the tender was a loss of steam. Soon, keeping the train where it was would be no more than a formality. Without fire and water it was so much dead metal.

I walked alongside the tracks toward the caboose, then back, as much to restore strength to my muscles as to stretch the horse's sinews, supporting myself on the stick. Just for diversion I tapped a couple of wheels with the end, but if there was a crack in one it didn't sing out. In time that stick came to sum up the whole of my use to the federal court in Montana Territory. Judge Blackthorne abhorred the thought of any of his pistoleers lying idle. If not a Childress, then something else would have had to be trumped up to justify my time. The whole Mexican affair was nothing more than tapping a stick against an endless succession of wheels.

"Why not?" I said aloud.

"*Senor?*" The guard nearest me sent a blank expression my way.

"When was the last time you ate?" I asked.

"*Que?*"

I made a scooping motion toward my mouth. He shrugged. In all the years since I left Mexico I've never tried to imitate that gesture. Mexicans alone are educated in communicating through body movements; the roll of a shoulder, the lifting of an eyebrow, can out-debate William Jennings Bryan in the full cry of his eloquence.

I jerked my chin toward the parlor car. Not a muscle moved in his face, but after a glance forward and back he took a step that direction. I hung back to let him board first, but he planted his boots in the cinderbed and motioned with his carbine's barrel. I mounted the steps and turned to clear the doorway. He had one foot on the plush rug when something moved in a swift blur. There was a thump and the guard teetered backward, falling away from his sombrero. Moving from instinct I caught him before he fell outside the train, swiveled my hips, and let him slide to the floor, snatching hold of the Winchester on the way.

Joseph stood on the other side of the open door, still holding the Springfield shotgun, butt foremost. The curtains across from me were drawn, blocking the view from the guard posted on that side. The Indian read my expression.

"This was your intention, no?"

"I was going to get him drunk, but I guess this is faster. What now?"

"I at least thought beyond the moment. The man who stands at the front of the train has a bladder the size of a *cucaracha*'s, but has trouble emptying it. He steps to the side every ten minutes and spends five minutes in the effort."

"How do you know?"

He reversed ends on the shotgun. My tin shaving mirror was lashed to the barrel with a bootlace. "I thought it best not to lean out the window."

"When did he make the trip last?"

"I cannot say. I was involved in waiting for this man." He gave him a stiff kick in the ribs. The guard grunted without stirring.

I used our prisoner's machete to cut the plush rope attached to one of the curtains and thrust it at him along with the crooked stick. "Tie him up and make sure he doesn't sing out."

He gave me the shotgun and looked wistfully at the Winchester, but I shook my head and leaned it in a corner. "I said keep him quiet, not silence him forever." He accepted the stick with a sigh. The window nearest the front of the car on the left was open. I poked the barrel outside, turning it until the guard near the locomotive was visible in the mirror. He yawned once, patting his mouth with the back of a hand; apart from that he was as immobile as a carved chief in a tobacco shop.

"Ten minutes, you said?"

A shoulder moved. His eyes remained on the man tied up at his feet, holding the stick in both hands poised to swing. "*Poco más o menos.* I do not own a watch."

"He seems to have cured himself since the last time. How long will that head of steam last?"

"Not long. I stoked the fire as hot as the gauge would stand to give me time to tend to you—as much and then some—but each moment lost—"

"Are you always this cheerful?"

He uncased two rows of tobacco-stained teeth in a ghastly grin.

The air was stifling; in that climate an open window brings no respite from the heat. The shotgun grew slippery in my grasp. I wiped one palm on my shirt, then the other. Steam drifting from the boiler condensed on the mirror in droplets that evaporated one by one before my eyes, and with them the life's-blood that kept the locomotive alive. The man in the glass showed no more life than an image in a tintype. The man on the floor groaned again; clothing rustled as Joseph prepared to silence him with the stick. I was about to put down his report as a beggar's wish when something rippled beneath the parched flesh of the man's face, a distinct surge of discomfort. He lowered his weapon and slid out of the mirror's range, walking rapidly with his toes turned inward, pigeon-fashion.

"Go!" I swept the mirror to the floor and traded the shotgun for the crooked stick. In a flash the Indian was out the door, feet crunching through the cinder-bed as he made a dash for the engine.

Everything was against it, least of all the guard at the rear of the train stepping out far enough to see one of his charges making for the front. One well-placed shot and I'd be that most useless of creatures, a man with a contraption he didn't know how to run. Try selling that to a man like Harlan A. Blackthorne.

The guard he'd struck opened his eyes, saw me standing over him, and dropped his jaw to cry out. I swung the stick, catching him along the temple. His eyes rolled over white and his head fell back to the floor.

In the next moment I nearly fell myself. The floor lurched forward, my ankles turned, and I flung my shoulder hard against the wall, dropping my stick. Then as the train continued to pull, the floor slid the other way, resisting the pull of the hitch, but by then I had a grip on the frame of the door Joseph had left open and kept my footing. I snatched my hand away just as the door swung shut, sparing my fingers. The boiler chuffed steam, a live cinder from the stack flew through the open window, sizzling when it landed on a rug. I stepped over to crush it out with the toe of a boot, then went back to grasp the senseless guard by the collar, swing the door back open, and heave him outside before we reached lethal speed. At that he struck on his hip and shoulder and rolled three times.

As I pulled the door shut, something split the air by

my left ear and knocked a piece out of the mahogany
molding near the ceiling in the far corner, exposing
raw yellow wood. I heard the report a quarter-second
later, a shallow pop in the open air. Another slug
starred a window, but had been fired at too shallow
an angle to penetrate the glass. Through another window I saw Vigía Férreo running our way from the direction of town. He stopped, watching the train pick
up speed. The face under the neat straw hat showed
no emotion. The mathematics tutor–turned-policeman
might have been calculating our rate of travel.

There was a thud overhead. I followed the sound
to the window Joseph had left open, but laid aside the
shotgun in favor of the machete I'd confiscated from
the guard he'd struck. I waited with it raised, staring
at the opening.

It took a week for a bone-handled Colt to come
through it, clenched in the brown corded hand belonging to the man on the roof. I curled both hands
around the machete's handle, hesitated to make sure
of my grip, and swung it down with the force of an
axe. Something hot splashed my cheek. Someone
screamed hoarsely. The revolver, still attached to the
hand, fell to the floor and slid across it, spraying blood
from the stump of the wrist. The trigger finger tensed.
The report was deafening in the enclosed space, but
the bullet plowed a harmless path across the rug, bur-
rowing like a mole. A moment later something flashed
past the window: the rest of the guard I'd crippled,
falling to the earth.

The adobe buildings sped past in a brown swipe.
Just then the whistle brayed: a long and a short, followed by two longs, an impudent farewell. I thought
that unnecessary. Adding train robbery to my employment history seemed enough without Joseph rubbing

salt into an open wound. We were manufacturing enemies the way they cranked out machine parts in Chicago, and we hadn't even begun the climb into the
Sierras.

FOURTEEN

A dead hand would make a fierce opponent at arm-
wrestling. Luckily for me, this one came without
an arm.

I pried the Colt loose, picked the hand and wrist up
by the fingers, and pitched it out the window to re-
join its master in whatever afterlife awaited him. The
fingers were warm and a little moist. They opened as
it fell, like a crumple of paper losing tension or a sup-
plicant asking for mercy.

I see that hand in dreams. At times it pleads, at
others beckons. If the damned thing would just strum
a guitar, or play a few bars of "Old Dan Tucker" on
the piano, I might be rid of it; but it refuses to erase
itself by becoming ludicrous.

I thought about packing the Colt along when I left
the coach, but like the Winchester it was a Mexican
copy of an American original made with inferior parts
and unreliable, so I left them there and balanced myself out with the Deane-Adams and Bulldog revolver.
The shotgun was too unwieldy and might pitch me to
my death, so I left it as well and stepped out onto the
car's verandah.

A steel ladder bolted to the back of the tender led
to the top, but it was open, filled as recently as our

stop in Alamos, rounded over with uneven chunks of mossy-smelling wood, and offered shifting and treacherous footing aboard a moving train. I climbed halfway up, gripped the top with both hands, and made my way around the corner, scrabbling with my feet until they found tenuous purchase on a nearly nonexistent ledge.

The *Ghost* was approaching forty miles an hour, but from where I stood it might have been going a hundred. Hatless, in my shirtsleeves, I clung to the tender, the hot wind buffeting my ears and snapping the ends of the bandanna around my neck. Given the choice I'd have turned around and gone back to the safety of the coach, but a train needs a fireman and the man assigned to that post was busy operating the locomotive.

Inch by inch, my fingers growing numb from the desperate tightness of their grip, I crept forward. I glanced down once, when my boot slipped, and saw the land dropping off nearly vertical to the piles of rocks at a base that seemed a mile below; and these were only the foothills. The mountains themselves shot straight up on the other side of the car, their peaks piercing the clouds like the tines of a fork.

I wasn't so much afraid of losing my grip as I was of surrendering it. In a flash—as if the train had turned a corner square into the sun—burning Mexico became frozen Nebraska, five years ago. I'd been either collecting or dropping off a prisoner, in a city I've forgotten the name of, when the clanging of the bell belonging to the pump-wagon, the town's pride and joy, brought my attention to the half-finished steeple of the Methodist church, where a carpenter clung to the remnants of a scaffold that had collapsed beneath him. The ladder just reached him, but as the volunteer stretched to take his hands, the carpenter let go,

plummeting without a cry to the street below. He
didn't die immediately, but lingered on, succumbing
to pneumonia on his third day on the cot in the doctor's back room. My business was finished, but I
stayed on to hear the end of the story. The Methodist
pastor declared his passing the work of Satan during
his services, but in his quarters later told me that
Death was a siren, whose call was sometimes more
strident than the will to live. At the thought, I felt the
backs of my knees tingle with the thrill of instant
release. That made me tighten my hold. I would not
be ruled by my joints.

I was nearly to the cab when we swung around a
bend, the train seeming to lean out from the shelter of
the hill forty-five degrees. My feet swung clear; I was
like a shirt on a clothesline blown out straight by a
gust of wind. An image flashed into my mind, a photograph I'd seen in a book, of a train lying full on its
side, the hollow V-shaped underside of the cowcatcher
exposed like the tender flesh under a man's chin.

I lost my grip, scrabbled wildly at the smooth side
of the tender, but some infernal force had pulled the
edge of the top beyond my reach; the car seemed to
have increased in height. Groping in panic, I came to
a rod of some kind mounted horizontally, and threw
my other hand up beside the first just as the train entered a bend in the opposite direction. I didn't know
the rod's purpose; probably not to encourage some
reckless fool to suspend himself from it. For what
seemed an hour I hung loose as a broken shutter, my
legs dangling free two hundred feet above an earth
made entirely of broken stones like eggs hatched by
some extinct bird. I hung that way, arms dead to
the shoulders, until we straightened out. A toe found
the ledge. I groped with my other foot, placed it beside

the first, spread my legs, braced myself, released and flexed each hand in turn until circulation came tingling back, grasped the rod again, bounced on my knees three times, counting, and hurled myself forward through the opening at the rear of the cab.

For a third of a second I was airborne, prey to the first crosswind that would hurl me out the side into open air. Then I landed, throwing myself sideways to avoid colliding with Joseph, standing at the front with a hand on the throttle. I came up shoulder-first against something diabolically hard sticking out of the cab's side, bruising the bone and turning my lungs inside out. I feel the tender spot still when the barometer drops; and it's been forty years since I rode outside a train.

The man at the throttle glanced back over his own shoulder. "I gave you up."

"You almost did on that last bend." I rubbed the place where I'd struck, gasping for breath.

"I dared not stop. These hills swarm with bandits who fall upon everything standing still and worry it to the bone."

I nodded. That last effort had exhausted the wind I needed for conversation.

He pointed at the firebox and a pair of sooty leather gloves jammed inside the handle. "We are losing steam."

I nodded again, put on the gloves, and fell upon the woodpile. I wrenched free a squarish chunk, opened the box, and poked the wood inside. It caught like a curl of paper, the flames burning blue along the bottom edge. I repeated the action until there was no more room in the box. The heat drew all the moisture from my pores and baked my face until I was sure it was as dark as the Indian's.

"Take the wood from the bottom. The rest is green."

I was no longer *senor* to him. His promotion to master of the *Ghost* hadn't come so suddenly he'd failed to note the shift in our relationship.

From Alamos we climbed and climbed, the scenery turning from green to near black in its density; my ears popped, and still we were only in the foothills. To our left the country rose in succeeding folds of old-growth wood, the limbs pregnant with leaves, the trunks straight up and down and as close together as ribs of corduroy. They had no place to fall if they fell. It seemed nothing could squeeze between them: yet when I wasn't stoking the fire Joseph kept me entertained with stories of marauding bears, half-human predators, and pumas that pounced without warning.

"We have them up north," I said.

"Not like these cats. They strike with the sun at their backs, making no noise, so that you are aware of one only when it is eating you alive."

"You've seen this?"

"Eben, my sister's husband, died in this way. I could do nothing; so of course I watched."

His family, it turned out, was a wealth of uncles, cousins, and brothers-in-law whose deaths he'd witnessed, or whose remains had been found half-devoured after days of searching. To hear him tell it the local wildlife had been living on the sole diet of his people for generations. I couldn't tell how much of what he said was truth and how much invention, to keep me under his influence; but I found the heft of the two revolvers reassuring.

As I chucked wood, I couldn't stop thinking about the pistol Hector Cansado had told me he had hidden somewhere in the cab, the one he claimed Joseph didn't know existed. Just because the Indian had saved my life didn't mean he wouldn't reclaim it the moment I was no longer needed, and there was no sense in allowing him a weapon beyond the axe he'd used on the engineer. DeBeauclair, the vanished Pinkerton, had reported Oscar Childress' recruitment of Indians into his private army. The promise of plunder would explain why Joseph had chosen to press on rather than turn back.

Every time I pulled something out of the tender I expected the fabled pistol to fall out. There didn't seem to be any other place in those close quarters, crowded as they were with levers, gauges, handles, and every description of cast-iron protuberances, to have concealed it, and I had to be ready to scoop it up when it appeared.

Unless he'd found it already and had it hidden under his overalls.

Up and up we scaled into the black heart of the Mother Mountains, the engine laboring like a broken-winded mount, guided only by a map whose artists were dust and the memory of a fleeting glimpse at the updated chart in Felix Bonaparte's office, with its bilious green blob representing what Blackthorne had called the ideal habitat of dragons.

Thought of the attorney in his modern circumstances brought me back from the medieval nature of our present location.

"Where's the nearest telegraph office after Alamos?" I shouted above the straining of the engine.

"Cabo Falso. Four hundred miles."

"We can expect a welcoming party there. Férreo wouldn't have lost any time wiring the authorities we're on our way."

"There are no authorities in Cabo Falso. It is run by whores and brigands."

"That's a relief. I thought we might be in trouble."

Teeth showed in a face stained permanently by soot. Apart from that, his having taken full possession of the controls, I found it hard to tell him from the slain engineer.

Higher yet, and then we leveled off, chugging along the brawny shoulder of the mountains. The sun blazed red briefly, flickering like wildfire between passing trunks, then vanished, as if snuffed out between a monstrous thumb and forefinger. In the sudden darkness, pairs of eyes glittered green in the reflected light of the lamp mounted on the front of the boiler, like cold jewels strung out raggedly. Absent the pull of gravity, I found time between replacing logs to ask if there was a place where we might put up for the night. I wasn't up to full strength yet, and the trip alongside a speeding train had been no remedy. My muscles burned from tugging loose logs and stooping to pitch them into the firebox. Belatedly, I realized that apart from the inevitable watery broth to keep up my constitution I hadn't eaten in days.

"In ten miles, perhaps," he said, "if there are no rockslides to stop us before then. Pray there are not. If the tracks are blocked, we must reverse directions for as many miles as we have traveled, and since this train does not move as fast backwards, what bandits we have passed would find it a simple thing to board us from above, when we are too busy with the engine to defend ourselves. We must not stop below these rotten shelves of shale." He pointed upward through the cab opening, to ragged escarpments of black against a sky only slightly less dark. Pallid star-light showed through semicircular spaces, like fresh bites taken from a crust of bread.

"Does this country never relent?"

"You have not yet seen her at her worst."

He said it with a kind of pride. Everyone has a pro-prietary interest in the place he calls home. In the ab-sence of anything good to boast of, he'll compete with anyone for the bad.

He wasn't exaggerating, as it turned out. I once sur-vived three days and two nights in a barn stacked with frozen corpses in the comfort of knowing that at least it wasn't the Sierras.

For a long time we traveled in silence. Then he said:

"There is a dugout, carved into the rock by no one knows who, no one knows how long ago, with logs for shelter from monsoons; the originals have rotted away, but those who come there to rest have replaced them from time to time. It has been used by trappers, missionaries, and other wanderers. If it is still there it would be a safe place to spend the night. Such rocks as might fall have fallen already, and one can see all the way to the valley below."

"What about above?"

He tugged on the whistle. A bull elk that had been preparing to cross the tracks swung its great antlered head our way, eyes glowing in the light of the lamp, and backed away into the woods.

"If you seek to be safe from everything, you should never have come to this place."

FIFTEEN

At first I thought the dugout had fallen in, or been carried away by rocks; the Sierras were continually shifting shape, like the beasts in Indian lore. The spot Joseph had pointed out, cleared from forest that had grown right up to the tracks, looked swept clean in the shaft of light from the champing locomotive: A crumb-scraper couldn't have been more thorough. Then the fog and drifting steam parted to expose something black and gaping, as if the mountain had opened its mouth to expel sulphurous smoke from its lungs. It was the entrance to a structure erected in partnership between nature and man.

Joseph busied himself with the engine while I retrieved the Whitney rifle and scouted out the location, gripping the weapon in one hand and a bull's-eye lantern in the other. I tipped open the louvers, directing the beam inside the arrangement of mossy logs with a roof made of rocky outcrop and an extension of poles shingled with bark. Apart from the usual rubbish of temporary habitation and the palpable odor of earth, mildew, and sodden wood-ash, it was unoccupied, at least by humans. I'd half expected to disturb a sow bear sleeping with her cubs or at the very least a nest of rats. A beetle nearly the size of my hand stirred and scaled the Pike's Peak of my toe, that was all. I shook free of it and hung the lantern from the end of a pole by its bail to investigate the rest.

A pile of moldy rags got the attention first of my nose, then my eyes as a likely resting place for rattlers. It lay heaped in the corner where a windscreen of logs

chinked with clay and dead leaves met the side of the
hill, where a previous tenant would have flung it to
lighten his load before venturing back out. I picked up
a stick, poked at the heap, and when nothing issued
forth twisted the stick, winding a bit of rotting cloth
around the end, and tugged it free. Something tumbled out, rattling like hollow wooden flutes; something rolled across the packed clay floor and came to
rest against my foot, leering up at me with the porcelain grin of death.

I started; but I'd seen human skulls before. Stripped
of flesh and gutted of brains, they offered no harm. It
wore a patch of black hair like peat on a rock and two
inches above the right eye-socket a hexagonal hole as
big as my fist. It might have been made by a stone falling, but I doubted it.

"*Que pasa?*" Joseph's call, bent out of shape by
damp and distance. I ignored it, stirring the stick among
the bones. Something crackled; I speared it and brought
it up into the light. It was a scrap of foolscap, as yellow as any of the dead leaves stuck among the chink-
ing between the logs, but marked with script written
in faded ink:

gone up the tracks for help, but

That was it: a journal entry of some kind. Who'd
gone up the tracks for help I might never know, but if
he'd returned with it he'd been too late.

I brought the scrap close to my eyes. It seemed to
be deteriorating as I looked at it, from sudden exposure to the open air, like the mummified remains of an
ancient Incan king disinterred after centuries; but it
was more recent than that. Like Judge Blackthorne, I
had little faith in a man's personality revealing itself

in his hand, but I knew a closed loop from an un-crossed *t*; and I knew as sure as I was a hundred miles from the civilized world that I was reading the last words of Agent DeBeauclair, the Pinkerton operative who'd disappeared after filing his last report on Os-car Childress.

"A friend?"

I jumped again. Joseph stood in the entrance, the light from the lantern lying on his square cheeks and the edge of the axe in his hand.

"DeBeauclair is a French name, *sí*?" The Indian crunched cracked corn. "I would think he would look more foreign."

I sat across the fire from him in the entrance of the dugout, the Whitney across my lap. The fire was of my own making, chunks from the tender chopped into kindling with the axe Joseph had brought. The light of the flames crawled and twitched over the bone face where it had come to rest, changing its expres-sion from amused idiocy to deep contemplation. Out-side, tree frogs, night birds, crickets, and cicadas made a racket, as deafening as in any city. The bay, hobbled just outside the halo of heat, grazed and switched its tail at mosquitoes the size of chimney swifts. I ate beef from the tin with a spoon, washed it down with water, and passed him the canteen. "We're all the same under the skin. What do you think made that hole?"

"A rock from a sling or a stone axe." He drank, his jaws grinding without cease. His molars must have been worn down to stumps.

"Not a ball from a percussion weapon."

"I know of none that would make a wound that size."

"I do. I saw my share of them in the war."

"I cannot think why white people should make war on each other except over horses."

"We can't all be as civilized as Indians. Who do you think he sent for help?"

"Someone unreliable, I should think."

Something cried, sounding close. In town, I would have put it down to a colicky baby. In that country it made the hairs bristle at the top of my spine. "There's your puma. You must have a cousin or two left."

"I think I am that cousin. Perhaps my great-great-grandfather destroyed all the litter-mates of a cat that has sworn not to die until it has done for his family as well."

"It didn't kill the detective, that's plain. There'd be no bones left to tell the tale."

"Bandits. Yellow fever, and the hole came later. The great bird of death swooped down and snatched his soul. Where is the good in guessing? *He* is beyond caring."

"He cared enough to write something, but that scrap is all that's left." I'd found a ball of shredded paper left by a brood of mice. They'd built the nest inside the dead man's rib cage, from the record of his last days. "What was he doing here? It's a long way into the wilderness, even if he rode a horse or took along a pack animal."

He helped himself to another handful of corn. "What are *you* doing here?"

"They say, even his enemies, that Childress is a brilliant man. I came to see what makes him shine."

"You wish to learn from him about horses and making money?"

"If he brings them up; not that I care a shuck about

horses, and money runs out between my fingers like water. I expect to hear about poetry, philosophy, history, governing, science, and religion."

"What will you do with what you learn?"

"Something, possibly. Nothing, maybe. Sometimes knowledge alone is enough."

He shook his head, rooting in his sack for corn. Those loose kernels had reality for him, purpose and meaning.

"And after you have learned these things, you will kill him."

"Those are the orders. The killing, that is. I added the other."

"It is like squeezing all the good out of an orange and throwing away the skin."

"Very like." I scraped up the last of the beef, ate it, and set the tin on the ground.

He turned his face into the wind. It carried the smell of brimstone. "The dry season is early. We must take on water tomorrow. There is a tower twenty miles ahead. Nearer twenty-five. After that we must draw it from the earth."

"A village?"

He shook his head. "Only the tower, and such as gathers there. Good local beer and a woman."

"Just one?"

"I would not say 'just' of this woman."

His face showed no amusement. A man of his kind, in a place like that, didn't leer about such things. They were like water and meat. "What about you?" I asked. "What made you come all this way?"

He spoke without raising his eyes, poking a stick at the fire. They reflected the light like pieces of polished coal.

"I wish to be the first of my people to pilot a train from the top of Mexico to the bottom. Then perhaps I will be made an engineer in truth as well as in name."

"That's important?"

"My father and all my brothers died, either in the mines or from the dirt that filled their lungs. It is not my wish to die as they did."

"They should be grateful."

He looked up at me sharply, his hand still gripping the stick. "Why?"

"The mines got to them before the puma."

He looked down again and resumed stirring the ashes. "I did not think of that."

The noises from outside increased, as if whoever directed them had raised his baton. Further conversation seemed not worth the effort to compete. I mixed water from the canteen with a handful of Arbuckle's and set the pot on a flat rock by the fire, turning it from time to time as the Indian munched.

"Do you think the men who run the railroads will not want to make me an engineer because I killed the one I worked for?"

"Not the railroad men I've met."

He smiled, pieces of corn shell stuck between his teeth. When the coffee was ready I filled two cups and handed him one. He wrapped his hands around the tin as if they needed the heat, but he didn't drink from it at first. "I think they would choose the puma," he said.

"Who?"

"My father and my brothers. It is better to be eaten by an animal than by the dust from a shaft."

"Quicker, anyway."

Outside the dugout the big cat cried.

SIXTEEN

T he hot wind blew perpendicular to the train, booming the side of the stock car where the bay doubtlessly fiddle-footed and tossed its head, trying to crawl out of its hide. My own skin prickled as if I'd fallen into a crock of needles. I was afraid to touch my lips in case they peeled off in paper-thin layers. Every time I stoked the fire I felt like a pig on a spit, my skin turning orange and crackling. Joseph, manning the throttle and leaning out the opening on his side to look ahead for obstructions, showed no reaction other than to take a long draught from the canteen when I handed it to him. A goatskin bag hung inside the cab, pregnant with water, but he told me to resist using it to refill the canteen. He didn't say why.

I looked out at the pinon and fescue flying past. The green seemed to fade as I watched, the grass blades shriveling like dead petals on a fireplace grate. "What about fires?" I asked.

"I brake as little as possible, but one cannot prevent every spark. The thing is to keep the burning country behind us."

"What happens when we stop?"

"Oh, the fires stop too. We have an agreement, this place and I."

They say, the experts back East who know everything, that Indians have no humor in the white man's understanding of the term. I've been the length and breadth of the West looking for one who could answer an honest question with anything but a macabre joke.

When we did stop, to conserve steam for the last run to the water tower, we struck off down the track to confirm his agreement with the wilderness. I carried six pails of sand, strung out three on each side of a yoke across my shoulders, which I used to put out sporadic buds of flame along the cinderbed while Joseph chopped brush with his faithful axe, piled it, and wet it down with water from the goatskin bag to create a firebreak.

"You might have told me what it was for." I tugged my bandanna back down below my chin. The top half of my face would be black.

"Too much talking dries the throat."

I watched the wind baking the wetness from the limbs. I could smell wood still burning a mile or so down the rails, hear the whoosh of flame consuming a parched pinon in one gulp. "I can't claim confidence."

"You expect too much. These forests have burned to the ground many times. They continue to burn until the rains come, or until they reach woods so dense the flames can find no more air to breathe. It has always been so, a thousand times a thousand years before men came with sand and water to put them out, or there would be no trees left to burn. To slow down the fire is as much victory as we can expect."

As we turned back toward the train, something rustled in the undergrowth; a deer or an elk, possibly a bear. The woods were too dense for my eyes to penetrate. I remembered the cry of the puma, and Joseph's constant reference to bandits, and picked up my pace. I'd left the Whitney rifle behind to carry the pails and didn't like the odds of defending myself with hip guns from an enemy I couldn't see. I wasn't sure I could even slow it down.

The *Ghost* labored up a long grade, panting like a stove-in horse. For an hour and a half Joseph had been staring at the gauges with an expression I never want to see on a doctor's face with me as the patient. I had the impression we were running on a teaspoon of water, and asked if what was left in the canteen, the goatskin, and the kegs of fresh drinking water in the parlor car would help.

"A drop in the ocean," he said. "We have fifty gallons in the boiler, and to expect it to take us beyond this grade would be to tempt God."

It was my first intimation that he'd been converted; and my first lesson in just how much even a small engine drank.

Nearing the top we slowed to a crawl. Less than that; it seemed the trees were moving forward rather than backward, and slowly enough at that to count the leaves. If any bandits were close at hand, that would be the time to strike. Over and over again I rehearsed in my mind the move toward the Whitney rifle leaning in the corner, wondering if I'd be better served by the shorter distance to one of the revolvers on my hips. The moment required for the decision alone, in the heat of action, might kill us both.

The boiler wheezed; the stack cried for smoke, I fed the box. The drive-rods that turned the wheels strained agonizingly slow, like a milk-maid churning at the edge of fatigue, rotating stubborn steel against the friction of the rails, steel also: What had been designed as a partnership of identical elements was deteriorating into a contest, Philadelphia versus Detroit, or more internally still, the fraction of temperature between one smelting-vat and another. The slightest variance in joints, a spike driven an eighth of an inch off true, or not driven flush, a tiny flaw in the crucible back at the finery, a bubble formed when a piece was removed from the cast; an indifferent laborer a thousand miles away at the end of his shift, who said good was good enough, and fair fair, had sealed the fates of two men in a place whose name on a map he couldn't pronounce.

What if it wasn't an illusion, and we were rolling back down the grade? Would the brakes hold, or would the natural law of gravity take over where the efforts of man had failed, plummeting us at breakneck speed toward the level, where a sharp curve I remembered would flip us off the rails like an annoying bug, the whole ludicrous link of cars like a string of sausages sent down the steep flanks of the Mother Range into a pile of scrap iron and crushed flesh at the base?

Was I raised in a trapper's shack at the top of the Bitterroots to die in a tangle of metal at the bottom of a pimple of a hill in Mexico?

"There it is," said Joseph.

I started. He'd said it as if we'd come through a light rain into bright sunshine.

It was bright, at that, shining on a squat wooden barrel the size of my furnished room in Helena, mounted on spindly legs of pine bound with thongs with the bark intact. Beads glittered on the staves as on a glass of ice-cold beer.

"I wondered some," he said. "She was working herself that last half-mile."

"'Wondered'?" I wanted to swallow back the word; I knew I'd been had for a fool.

He leaned on the brake, his face grave. "I always worry along this stretch. It asks much of a boiler this size."

It had been an initiation of some kind. I should have recognized it, army and bunkhouse veteran that I was. All that talk of pumas and bandits and relatives done to violent death had lured me into the oldest game of all. He was leaning out the opening on his side. I waited for him to turn away before I struck him between the eyes. I saw his shoulder stiffen; not at the thought of my assault, but by something he'd seen up ahead. By the time he drew himself back inside, my fist was back down at my side. I don't know now if it was his dead-blank expression that made me relax my fingers or the stench prickling the hairs in my nostrils. They'd become inured to the smell of burning, but this one came with the sweet tint of roast pork. I'd come across it before, not at communal events behind a ranch house, but in the heat of battle, with dead men shot at such close range the powder-flare set fire to their flesh.

He alighted; but not before tugging his bandanna up around his nose and mouth. I did the same with mine and stepped down behind him.

There was no smoke; the fires that had caused it had gone out long since. Beyond the water tower, which had remained untouched, a briarpatch of blackened timber poked up at random angles from acres of ash; knee-deep, should one want to wade into it. We didn't. The stench of burnt flesh alone held us back. Such shells of humanity that lay swaddled in those ashes would add nothing to what we already knew.

A white boulder, sunk so far into the earth as to suggest it had tumbled down from the mountains years before, bore a sign, etched likely with a charred stick and pounded pale gray by sporadic rainfall: a reverse crucifix, with the crosspiece at the bottom.

Joseph crossed himself, confirming my suspicions of conversion, and pronounced three syllables that chilled the oven-baked Sierras to the bone:

"Cholera."

I placed my palm against my bandanna, pressing it to my face. "Not yellow fever? You said there's plenty of cinchona in these woods."

"For that, they would not try to burn out the contagion and then flee. There is no medicine for this evil. It kills and kills until it has gorged itself with death."

"Do we turn back?"

He was silent; thinking. After a moment he shook his head.

"No. They have burned it out, the survivors. Their only hope to survive is to press ahead."

"And if they haven't burned it out?"

"Then they carry it with them; or turn back to escape it." He stared at the ground. "I was wrong. I think they have turned back. There is nothing ahead."

"What about the water?"

He was motionless; then shook himself and tilted his chin toward the squat tower.

"The *Ghost* is already dead. No contagion can infect it. We will fill up and move on."

"You're sure they turned back? That they haven't taken the disease into our path?"

Just then something whooshed, a half-mile down track, if that: another stand of trees gone up in flame.

"The fire behind," he said; "the plague ahead. What have we to lose?"

SEVENTEEN

With both hands, Joseph tugged an extra cap down to the bridge of my nose, pulled up my bandanna, and tied it tight around the lower half of my face, with all the firm and caring attention of a mother bundling up her child to go out into a blizzard.

"Shield your eyes with your sleeve when you twist off the top," he said. "We let the pressure drop, but the water's still hot enough to poach a steer."

I climbed the ladder to the boiler, pausing twice to rest; in spite of all the exercise stoking the firebox, I'd yet to retrieve all my strength. The spout attached to the water tower was at the end of my reach. I braced a foot against the brass grab-rail, hooked a hand under the roof of the cab, and leaned out almost perpendicular to the locomotive, snatching the spout by its chain and swiveling it into place. I wore the leather gloves, but wrapped a rag around my hands before I bent to the boiler's cap, which was about the size of the lid of a gallon jar of pickles and took twice as much effort to twist loose even with the aid of a wrench the size of a mule's hind leg. Once it gave enough to do the rest with one hand, I slung my other arm across my eyes, leaned back, and jerked loose the cap, releasing a geyser of white water and steam whose heat I felt through the bandanna, my borrowed overalls, heavy flannel shirt, and long-handles. When it died down I lowered the spout into the opening and tugged on the cable that lifted the gate. Water pulsed through the crimped-together steel tubes like blood through an artery.

Waiting for the boiler to fill, I took in the view. At my back rose the wall of wooded mountains, as black as the hills of Dakota, while in front of me the land sloped down to a green-and-brown shelf stretching for miles to the gulf, which I couldn't quite see but could determine its existence by an open expanse of sky with nothing to obscure it but white clouds that seemed to touch the shore. It seemed to me I could smell the salt water, but that was imagination; miles of desert would have absorbed all the moisture and replaced it with the odor of earth scorched by the sun. Down track I saw the way we'd come, and a smudge of smoke belonging to the still-smoldering fires ignited by sparks from the *Ghost*'s wheels. Up track, their smoke vanished sometime since, piles of ash pierced by gaunt charred timbers marked the graves of the men and women (I thought of Joseph's "I would not say 'just' of this woman") who had lost their fight with cholera. The cleansing flames had spread as far as the rails, but after strolling along them and back, the engineer had reported the steel intact.

"What about the ties?"

"Burned through, a few. We'll go slow and pray for the best."

Back on the ground, the box heating back up, the tender filled with freshly chopped wood and the pressure rising, I gripped the Whitney rifle and scanned the forest for signs of bandits, but Joseph said the miasma of death would likely keep them away. "A clean bullet, or the jerk of a noose, these things hold no terrors for them. They did not take up the work to perish in a wallow of their own sweat and vomit."

I'd begun to wonder if his tales of land-bound pirates hadn't been glossed up a bit, like the stories of mountain lions stalking his family exclusively; but as we pulled forward I continued to divide my attention between the dense growth and the fire, with now the added detail of the burned ties.

We moved at walking pace, the wheels barely turning. As we approached the scorched acre of ground, my belly tightened, jerking itself into a knot when the floor lurched under my feet. Joseph didn't stop, but the long muscle in his jaw stood out like taut cable as he teased the throttle forward. Something crunched: the crushing of the weakened ties under the weight of the train. The earth shifted, like plates sliding; the rails, unsupported, splayed beneath the pressure of the wheels. My hands gripped the edge of the cab's opening and the handle of the brake lever on the other side, anticipating the drop when the wheels slid off the spreading rails. My bunched knuckles seemed to be fraying through the leather gloves. If the left gave way, we'd tilt toward the mountains, and be stranded without the equipment to set the wheels back onto the tracks. If the right, the train would yield to the pull of its own weight, tumbling down the steep hillside like a string of milk cans held together by cord, and us with it if we failed to jump clear. My hands were clamped so tight I couldn't imagine any power that would free them. I thought of some stranger months later coming upon my remains like Agent DeBeauclair's, the bony fingers still hanging on to the crushed cab as if welded.

Another lurch snapped my teeth together. The earth was dropping out from under us. The muscle in Joseph's jaw twitched—he couldn't have prevented it even if all his concentration weren't centered on maintaining pressure on the throttle—but apart from a hissing through his nose he made no sound. Gently he eased the control forward, as if he were urging a skittish horse across a swaying bridge. This drew a noise from the boiler like a sudden intake of breath and then a shorter stroke from the drive-rods that turned the wheels, with an accelerated *huh-huh-huh* from the pistons: The *Ghost* was giving birth.

The panting increased, we picked up speed. The broken ties were behind us.

I let out my breath, pried loose my fingers, and flexed blood back into them. I waited for a flippant remark from Joseph. None came; this time he'd been on the same edge with me.

We'd dodged one disaster, but the place we were in was lush with it.

A cluster of leaves hanging like bunched grapes at the end of a branch stirred sharply, with no such movement among its neighbors to suggest a gust of wind or the draw of the train passing. A bird, possibly, taking flight from its perch, or an elk browsing for fodder. But there was an unnatural abruptness in the motion, as of something invading from outside the wilderness. A week ago I'd have thought nothing of it. I'd developed a connection with all that dense growth almost as close as the one I'd formed with the train itself. It wasn't my first extended stay so far outside civilization, but there was something about the Sierras that was apart from all the untracked places I'd seen, as if they'd been dropped there by something flying from one world to another. If I'd been so deeply absorbed into them in so short a time, how much more difficult must it be to separate Oscar Childress from his place of exile?

The hot wind blew without ceasing, crackling in my ears, standing the hairs on the back of my hand at military attention, extending the nerves beneath the skin to the tips, so that the slightest change in its direction stung them like live sparks; and when it changed, it boomed like Lee's artillery at Cold Harbor. I blinked constantly, to lubricate my eyes; but they sizzled on the instant of drawing open the lids, like side-pork frying in an iron skillet. When the *Ghost* turned a bend into a fresh hot gust, it was as if the desert below had stood on end and smacked me in the face with all the dead dry weight of sand and desiccated skeletons and granite ground down to powder by the hot wind. I drank from the canteen, guzzled from the goatskin bag, and full upon the orgasm of water on my throat came the sensation that it had expelled itself the way it had come, in the form of pure steam; if I dared to exhale, it would come out as smoke. I felt my intestines roasting; I could almost smell them turning into tripe.

When I pushed my face into the slipstream outside the cab, in search of at least the illusion of cool air, I saw always in the next bend of the rails a pool of blue water. I didn't care if mermaids swam in it, or if it was alive with leeches; it was neither hot wind nor dry sand. Men had died crawling toward that illusion. I couldn't help but think that in the last moment before death they'd experienced something close to satisfaction.

They'd triumphed, in their way. What did it matter whether a man withered into the earth like a fallen leaf or rotted at the bottom of a six-foot grave, one with the pine boards that had contained him? The first fed the coyotes and carrion-birds, the second worms, gray slick creatures who laid eggs to make more worms. Birds flew, at least, crossing vast territories in moments, blinking down at trains crawling beneath them at forty miles an hour; coyotes hunted and mated and cried at the moon. It shone back. All it did for me was hang in the sky, drum its fingers, and wait for dawn. We were strangers who passed on the street.

It was the yellow fever talking. The moon was just a hole punched in the sky when you were in the pink of health.

Even as I bent to scoop yet another of the endless chunks of wood into the firebox—the next in line rolled into the former's place with all the inevitability of loose dirt filling a hole—I felt the amputated hand of the man I'd slung the axe at while leaving Alamos, caressing my burning muscles, forgiving in every stroke what I'd done to him and telling me it wasn't so bad on the other side, where all were made whole and the water ran blue and ice-cold, ideal for mixing with Judge Blackthorne's good Scotch whisky.

"To hell with that," I said aloud. "He cut it straight from the Missouri before he sent it aboard. I caught a minnow in my teeth."

"Something?"

Joseph, hand on the throttle as always, turned his graven-idol head thirty degrees in my direction.

I shook myself loose of everything not connected to the cab I was riding in. It was just that, after all: a construction of wood on an iron frame, propelled by fire and water through a landscape carved from common clay.

"Nothing. How far to civilization?"

"Civilization? A thousand miles. Two hundred to Cabo Falso; Cabo Infierno, if you prefer. We should be there by week's end."

Two hundred miles to Cape Hell. It seemed that I'd spent my entire life at that same point.

EIGHTEEN

Nothing changed. We might have been standing still while the trees rolled by on our left and the foothills fell behind on our right, propelled by some cranking mechanism of their own. Even the birds flying from one high branch to the next might have been jerked on invisible wires, their cries made by wooden blocks scraping against each other. The motion of the wheels and the swaying of the locomotive were the only stability I knew; if the train were to stop and I to alight from it, I'd walk with a rolling gait as if the earth itself were in motion, like a sailor cast ashore after months at sea. The *Ghost* was reality, solid ground the phantom. Nothing was unexpected; not even the lump of white-hot lead that sparked off the cab's frame, so close to my face I thought a match had been struck off the tip of my nose.

We'd slowed for a sharp curve, our bodies leaning instinctively toward the mountains, as if our combined weight would have any effect on the pressures pulling tons of iron out into space; whoever had fired the shot had been waiting for that, had probably picked the spot knowing we'd have to reduce speed to make the bend.

Joseph was first to react. He shouted something in a language I'll never know and hurled his upper body out the opening opposite the source of the bullet, placing as much steel between it and himself as he could within the cramped space we shared. I was more sluggish, lulled into a standing doze by the monotonous movement the way I'd slept in the saddle during long drives; but I came around after a beat, snatched up the Whitney rifle, and sent a slug flying into the dense growth. I had no target, only the desperate need to announce to whoever it was we were more than sitting fowl.

Hell came after.

I thought at first we'd hit a section of rough track and were rattling over a series of sharp joints. We were speeding up, trying to outrun the attack, and the chopping noise kept pace. Then a piece of the wooden post holding up the roof came apart and something stung my hand and when I looked at it blood was spreading from a ragged hole shorn through the leather. I'd been grazed by a sliver of iron from the firebox or a shard of shattered lead ricocheting off it. The broken edge of the roof looked as if it had been chewed up by a sawmill blade. A ribbon of shining chips was stitched across the stoveblack surface of the panel where the gauges were mounted; one of the thick glass lenses was starred.

I knew then I'd lost another piece of my innocence. As often as I'd been shot at, this was the first time I'd stood in front of a Gatling gun in operation.

I dove for the floor, snatching hold of Joseph's sleeve and jerking him down alongside me. His face registered surprise and rage, but when he looked down at the offending hand and the dark stuff that was staining his sleeve, he nodded jerkily and rammed the throttle all the way forward. Gifted natural engineer that he was, he hadn't let go of it. The locomotive pounced like a big cat. Hot wind boomed past my ear and the panting of the engine mixed with the chopping sound of the revolving barrels, swallowing it as the reports receded into the distance.

"Bandits!" he shouted.

"Bandits travel light. Would you lug heavy weaponry through the jungle with the authorities on your heels?"

"Who, then?"

I shook my head; but I knew the answer.

The part that concerns me the most is the arms he's supposed to have stockpiled: Gatlings, Napoleons, and a dozen cases of carbines. Judge Blackthorne's words about Oscar Childress, delivered between sips of his quality whisky back in Helena.

We charged full speed for ten more miles before we thought it safe to stop. I'd wound my bandanna around my bleeding hand, and put the throbbing out of my mind as I scouted down the tracks with the rifle to make sure whoever had set up the ambush hadn't stationed more of the same ahead. Back in the coach, Joseph splashed on alcohol from the medical supplies, working so swiftly I was still gasping from the burn when he bound it and tied off the gauze. "There were no doctors in the village where I grew up," he said when I admired the result. "We learned either to tend to ourselves or die from the corruption of the blood."

"Don't forget the pumas."

"I would sooner be eaten by one than by my own rotting flesh."

I couldn't argue with that.

He slid the bottle of alcohol and roll of gauze into the bib of his overalls. "We must sleep in the engine, not here. And one of us must be awake at all times, to mind the gauges and to keep watch." He was silent for a moment. "You are certain about the gun?"

"You saw what it did to the cab."

"Several men with rifles could have done the same."

"On an open firing range. That dense growth would have deflected ordinary rifle rounds. I watched a Gatling demonstration in Fort Benton. Those fifty-caliber slugs took a piece the size of your head out of the stockade wall."

"How could Childress know so soon we were coming?"

"Our friends in Alamos. If what I was told is true, there's no wire service to his plantation. Even if lawyer Bonaparte or Chief Férreo got word to Cabo Falso, no horse and rider could make it back this far in so short an amount a time. One or the other of them must have sent a messenger directly to wherever this band was camped. Is this whole country in cahoots with Childress?"

I tried to open a bottle of Scotch, but I couldn't get a grip with my injured hand. He made a sound of impatience, took the bottle from me, smashed off the neck against the brake handle, and took a swig. Wiping the back of his hand across his lips, he passed it over.

"He is not *El Presidente* Diaz's only enemy. Are you still so interested to hear what this man has to say?"

I drank, swallowed. The spirits crawled up my spine, down my arm, and into the torn heel of my hand, numbing the pain. Up ahead the *Ghost* conserved its strength, its iron heart pumping in measured beats like a lion at rest. "The fire behind, the plague, too, and now a blizzard of bullets. What's a little quiet conversation compared to that?"

He grunted and fisted the bottle. "Here, a man need not burden himself wondering what to do next. The country decides."

We had another bracer apiece, then put the spirits away and got up to leave the coach. It was a relief to get to my feet without dizziness; my strength was back at last, if made a bit more buoyant by alcohol. We filled the canteen from a cask of water, pocketed some tins of food, and requisitioned extra belts of ammunition from the arsenal.

Just before stepping down I turned back and laced my arms through the bails of two buckets of coal oil, and gestured to him to do the same. He did so without question.

We put in another fifteen miles before sundown and pulled onto a siding in a notch that had been blasted into the mountainside to rest. Travel at night was risky, especially with the threat of a tree or a boulder blocking the tracks, either by natural or human design, and Joseph said the line wasn't exclusive to the *Ghost,* for all its loneliness: "The weekly express from Guadalajara is due any month."

Like a garment soaked with sweat in the heat of day, the jungle damp turned clammy after dark. We were warm enough in the blankets we'd brought from the coach, but the cramped quarters of the cab stiffened our muscles and we stirred often, Joseph muttering half-awake oaths in a combination of Spanish and Indian, I more often bumping against something hard and protruding, bruising my scalp, cracking that inconveniently placed knob of bone on the inside of the elbow and sending a wave of pain and nausea all the way up my arm. More than once I thought of stepping down and sleeping on the ground, but I had a horror of cockroaches, so much a part of that country the revolutionists had written them into their anthem. It was no idle fear: When my groin itched I reached down to scratch it, blaming too many days and nights spent in the same clothes, and something the size of a ground squirrel crawled onto the back of my hand. I leapt to my feet, shouting and cracking my skull on the roof of the cab, and shook the thing out into the night.

Joseph opened one eye, the white glistening in ragged moonlight. I told him what had happened.

"You should have waited. He was only looking for a warm place to curl up."

"I'm not in the business of providing shelter for vermin."

"You must learn to accept this country for what it is, and not wish it could be what it is not. Men have gone mad wishing." He turned over and resumed snoring, in that steady, half-pleasant way of the native tribes.

I inspected myself and the blanket for more intruders, gave the blanket a vigorous shake just in case, and lay back down. I didn't know I'd fallen back asleep until I dreamed again of Lefty Dugan. He doffed his hat and bowed his head to show me the hole I'd opened there, shiny as a shotgun bore.

I should of left you to drown in that river, Page.

He wasn't speaking so much as willing the words into my head, where they dropped and lay like dead ash from spent kindling.

My eyes popped open. I'd have slept easier with the roach. I slid out from under the blanket and stepped down, carrying the Whitney rifle. I'd traded the ticking-cap for my hat; the sweatband felt like snail-slime against my forehead. I walked alongside the tracks, paying no attention to things that crunched under my boots. On a cloudless night in the mountains, the stars were as big as Christmas balls, the quarter-moon hanging so close to the earth I could grab its bottom horn with both hands and pull myself up to my chin.

The hours of darkness belonged to the lesser creatures. The din of crickets and tree-frogs was as loud as the Barbary Coast at midnight, with the empty-barrel gulp of the odd bullfrog coming in at intervals so irregular they were impossible to predict; it had waked me every time. In the distance—it might have been my imagination, caused by all our talk—the cry of a hunting cat shredded the heavy overlay of sound like someone tearing canvas.

I don't know how much time I spent walking, but when I stopped and turned back, the train was almost out of sight, its black prow visible only as the silver-blue steam drifted through the slots in the cowcatcher like a phantom passing through solid matter. I trudged back, hoisted myself up by the grab-rail, and wound myself back into the blanket, clutching the rifle as if it would stand off nightmares the way it did men and beasts. The rest of the night was as long as what had come before, and although I slept no more I was glad when first light came. I assumed men who were condemned to hang at dawn welcomed the end of that last night just as much.

NINETEEN

Jesus Dio!" Joseph hauled back on the brake.

The wheels screamed, showering sparks in fan-tails on both sides of the cab; one of them landed square on the back of the hand that was still healing. It stung like a wasp, but I hardly noticed it. I was too busy flying backward.

I was an India-rubber ball attached to an elastic band. I slammed against the stacked wood in the tender, the impact slapping my lungs flat. Then the band contracted, pitching me forward; but I was ready for that. I threw my hands against the cast-iron panel with its goggle-eyed gauges, catching myself before my head could go into the open firebox. There I leaned, pumping air back into my chest. I was a broken bellows sucking up shards of glass.

The rest of my senses blinked back on like bubbles popping in thick soup. My vision cleared, the engine wheezed rhythmically, I smelled the sharp odor of steel on steel, identified the sour-iron aftertaste of fear on my tongue. My ears ached from the shrieking of the wheels.

Every curse my father had taught me came to mind, along with some refinements I'd picked up in battle and on the cattle trail, but I choked them back. I respected Joseph's mastery of his machine. Most times he operated it as if the brakes didn't exist. All I could see was his hunched back, seemingly decapitated; he'd stuck his head that far through the opening on the left, straining to peer up the tracks. The muscles on the hand gripping the brake handle were bunched tight, stretching the glove taut.

I peeled my palms away from the front of the cab. The wound was throbbing now, aggravated by the live spark that had burned a hole through the bandage. "Did we hit something?"

No reply. He pried loose his grasp. The handle looked crimped, as if by a pair of powerful pliers. I couldn't remember if it had been that way before, but I wouldn't have been surprised if he'd done it with his fist alone. He blew out a bellyful of pent-up air and hopped down from the cab.

I followed. I thought of the rifle only when I was

on the ground. I didn't go back for it. Something about the episode told me it wouldn't be useful.

It wasn't. A great dark heap lay across the tracks, not ten feet from where the locomotive had come to rest. I thought at first part of the mountain had fallen away, and felt the full force of the collision we'd narrowly missed.

Then the wind kicked up, clearing away the steam from the pipes and the smoke from the wheels, and I saw it was no rockslide, although the result wouldn't have been different if we had hit it. Coarse black hair stirred in the current of air, the tips glinting, as if they'd been dipped in silver by a smith. A slagheap of muscle beneath. I caught another smell then, of rank sweat and suet and something more visceral, thick and pungent, like musty wine gushing from a shattered barrel; the last expulsion of life, spilling out like—

"Guts." Joseph pointed to a glistening red pile a few feet away from the mound, still steaming even in that torpid climate; the last combative gasp of a life lived on its own terms.

I walked around to the front of the thing, which was pointed in the direction of the mountains, the blunt muzzle with its shotgun-bore nostrils raised slightly; inexorably, the brute had been heading for high ground, nose into the wind. The ears were tiny in comparison to the oven-size head, the open eyes like black shoe-buttons; but the corrugated lips were curled back to expose fangs the length and thickness of a man's thumb, defiant even in death. Extinct, the American Grizzly still boiled with savage hate. The remnants of its breath stank of raw fish and fermented juniper berries. I thought of sardines preserved in gin.

Joseph took its left rear paw with its calliope of razor-sharp black claws and lifted it with both hands. The old fellow still had his lungs; they hadn't got them. A gust passed through the reeds of its throat: more rank air, accompanied by a roar, or rather the ghost of one; a sickly thing, almost a bleat, with only the memory of power behind it, but it was enough to shrink my spine. I sprang back; impossible not to, even knowing the source. I'd heard too many stories of hunters slain by a beast they thought was killed.

"He is warm still," the Indian said. "I should say he has not been dead an hour. But he came here with more inside him." His arm swept across the pile of guts; it was too small to account for the size of the cavity. "He was killed and gutted, but to what purpose? The meat remains."

"One of your pumas, interrupted by the train."

"I have never known one to attack a grizzly, let alone win. Also the cat eats from the outside in, starting with the neck and shoulders, then the buttocks. They have not been touched. Always he saves the insides for dessert." He groped the thick mantle of matted fur encircling the massive neck, stopped, probed, then held up a forefinger, stained purple to the second knuckle. "Gunshot wound. Man is the only animal who slays for anything other than food."

"There's only one reason anyone would shoot down a bear on railroad tracks and not take the skin or meat."

Immediately he straightened and joined me in scanning the forest. Birds perched and nested undisturbed among the branches.

"It is not a good place for an ambush," he said. "The undergrowth is too thick, and a man in a tree presents too good a target. One cannot choose where a bear will decide to cross the rails."

"But why take away the guts?"

"*Quien sabe?* The other thing about man is one can seldom judge his actions until it is too late."

The Indian was getting to be tiresome company. He seemed never to grow weary about being right.

Neither of us was foolish enough to attempt to remove eight hundred lifeless pounds from the tracks without a brace of oxen, but after contemplating the immense mound of hair and flesh and gristle and bone I went back to the locomotive and brought two buckets of coal oil. Joseph, catching the significance, did the same, and we spent ten minutes splashing the contents over the carcass, soaking it to the skin; by the time we finished, our eyes were watering from the fumes. He backed up the train another fifty yards for safety's sake while I wrapped a rag around a branch I broke off a tree and saturated it with what was left in the last bucket. I stepped back and touched a match to the rag. It went up with a sucking sound. I cocked my arm and flung the torch at the bear.

Blue flame traced a narrow path through thick hair toward the hump behind the grizzly's neck, and then the rest of the heap caught with a thud that shook the ground. By then I'd retreated almost as far as the train, but I felt the heat all down my front. The flames leapt sixty feet into the air, gushing black smoke that would continue to stain the blank sky long hours after we'd pulled away. My nostrils shrank from the stench of scorched hair, fumes, and roasting meat.

The long coarse guard hairs, designed to shed water,

went first, flaring yellow and peeling away from the tan downy undergrowth, like yellowed cotton batting, that kept the animal warm when the mercury fell below zero. Next came the flesh, such a bright pink that many hunters would rather take the hide from a skunk than a bear; the naked carcass looked too much like a freshly skinned human being. I turned away at that point.

We lay over for the night while the obstruction smoldered, taking turns carrying the red safety lantern to flag down any other trains that might approach from behind; it was obvious none would be coming from the other direction, with the fire making a beacon visible for miles.

I fed and watered the bay and walked it along the track away from the burning hulk and its sinister stench. The horse placed its hooves carefully; days aboard a moving train had robbed it of its faith in stationary surfaces. I gave it a sympathetic pat, but just one. That breed of creature and I understood each other too well to expect any greater sign of affection.

The fire was still burning at dawn, but by the time the sun cleared the mountains the bear was a pile of charred bones, stubborn clumps of smoking fur, and simmering puddles of grease. If anything it looked more fearsome in that state, like something prehistoric from a time when the earth was no safe place for man. The hooped rib cage, big as it was—a full-size man could have crawled through it on hands and knees without brushing the sides—brought me back to the abandoned dugout where we'd spent a night, and the bones of the murdered Pinkerton detective, like hollow wooden flutes. He'd made a study of Oscar Childress and wound up a skeleton; the grizzly had attracted his attention or that of someone like him, and ended the same way. I'd been sent to kill him. What was to prevent me from leaving my own bones behind in Mexico?

"Nothing," Joseph said.

I jumped; no matter how civilized an Indian, he always managed to come up on a white man noiselessly. "What?"

"There is nothing here that two men cannot now remove; although I wish I'd thought of sparing the heart before we set fire to it. My people say that to eat the heart of a bear is to inherit some of its strength and courage. Why do you laugh?" he asked then.

I stopped. The sound was strange in my own ears. I hadn't heard it since before I'd crossed the border.

"I wish I'd known that before I ate my first chicken liver."

He snorted and tugged on his gloves. No matter how uncivilized a white man, no Indian will ever share his humor.

We wrapped our bandannas around our faces and cleared away what we could of the debris, breaking often when our gloves started to smolder. At last we took hold of the great leering skull and twisted it this way and that, again and again. The half-incinerated tendons fought us with all the determination of the beast in life, and when finally the skull tore loose with a pop, the sudden release nearly threw us to the ground. We hurled it down the slope. It turned end over end, slow as a ballet, its jaws opening in one last silent roar. When it landed at the base of the foothills, it threw up a geyser of dust and ash. We crossed ourselves in unison.

"What about the ties?" Panting, I stared at the still-glowing timbers supporting the rails.

"The *Ghost* laughs at such things, as we well know."

It didn't; but after a few teeth-clenching moments

of wild rocking, the train settled onto the level. Joseph eased the throttle forward and we thundered deeper into the green empty space on the map of the Conquistadors.

III

Cape Hell

TWENTY

We hadn't gone a mile when the sun went out, like a sharp draft blowing out a candle. The sky turned black and the dam broke, simple as that.

We crept through ten miles of rainfall so heavy we might have been rolling along the bottom of the ocean. At noon, the time when under normal circumstances the Mexican sun scoured everything as bright as brass, our headlamp was good for no more than five yards, with the water lancing down through its shaft like silver spikes. The rain was as thick as molasses and nearly as black; Joseph had me light a lantern in order to see the gauges. The air in the cab was so heavy we were breathing each other's exhaust. We took turns leaning out the sides looking for the oncoming lamp of another train or more obstacles on the track, and pulled our heads back in, blinded by water and soaked halfway to the waist; but it was worth it to escape the fug inside.

"The gods have taken a dislike to us," Joseph said, squeezing a puddle onto the floor from his bandanna. "The monsoons are not due for another month."

"The *gods*?" I stressed the plural. Scratch the newly converted and you found a heathen every time.

"Jesus, He is not so *vengativo*; what is the word in English?"

"Vengeful."

"They are weak, the old ones, and so they huddle together in the rain, where the priests cannot ferret them out."

I couldn't argue with his science; but I could inject some of my own. "The same rain is falling on Childress, don't forget."

"We shall see. The seasons are not so *sensato* up here as below."

I saw what he meant an hour later, when we emerged from the deluge as suddenly as if we'd slid through a curtain. Ahead, the sun flashed off the rails and made cracks in the earth on either side of the cinderbed; behind us was a black wall of water. Oven air filled the cab, as stultifying as when we'd been hemmed in by rain.

He leaned forward on the throttle and motioned toward the firebox. I'd just fed it; flames leapt out when I opened the door, heating the space beyond bearing. I looked at him, panting like a parched dog.

"There is a two-mile grade ahead," he said. "Without enough steam we will have to back down to the level and start again."

I poked as many chunks into the box as would fit, the flames licking at my gloves and drawing steam from where I'd stained the left with blood. We swung around a bend—going fast enough, I swore, to lift the landward wheels clear of the track—and began the steady climb; the pistons pumped their elbows, planted their feet, and leaned into the grade. A third of the way up we slowed, slowed some more; the wheels made a noise new to me, a wet sliding sound like a catfish makes when it misgauges a leap, lands on the deck of a boat, and slides across the boards. Just then we stopped moving at all, although I could still hear the wheels turning; in place, with a shrill complaining whine and the drive rods churning—grunting, like an old man grappling with a steep flight of stairs. The cords stood out in Joseph's neck; he had the throttle all the way forward and was still pushing. He wouldn't have shown more strain if he'd loaded the train onto his back and started carrying it himself.

"Grease on the rails," he said through clamped teeth.

I smelled it then, through the wood-smoke and hot oil and steam rolling off scorched metal: a rank stench, as if something had crawled up into the cab and died days before.

The Indian smelled it too. He had both fists on the throttle then, but freed one to touch the four points of his throat, shoulders, and abdomen.

I knew then what he knew: why the grizzly was dead, and what had happened to the rest of its entrails.

They hadn't gotten there on their own. Whoever had gutted the beast had carried them all that way and spread them on the rails where the grade began, to stop the *Ghost* literally in its tracks. My stomach did a slow turn. I forced back bitter bile; and I was ten feet from the source of the reek. I saw in a flash the wretches charged with the task, faces bound and breathing through their mouths.

There came an evil outhouse fetor of boiling offal as the slime reacted to the heat of friction. The wheels spun, but we were stock still.

The trees along this stretch were of much more recent growth than what we'd passed; sometime within the past couple of decades, a fire had cleared several acres, leaving only black earth behind; striplings had sprouted, growing into adolescent trunks spaced far enough apart for a man to squeeze between them on horseback. From the greased grade to the open terrain, the area might have been designed by the patron saint of bushwhackers.

I thrust out a hand and closed it on the engineer's where it gripped the throttle. "Put it in reverse."

He acted without question, hauling the handle back toward his body. The wheels screamed with the sound of metal shearing, the *Ghost* shuddered, violently enough to make me lunge for a handhold; it seemed as if the boiler was about to blow. Then the shaking stopped, steam sighed, and the trees began moving forward. We were backing down the tracks, still slipping a little but moving, if far too slow for comfort.

Then the pounding started again, slugs the size of lumps of coal punching holes in the cab's wooden frame, spanging off steel and iron and kicking up sparks. The bear's carcass had delayed us long enough for the men who'd dropped it there to ride to the spot, measure the range, and set up a nest. This was no catch-as-catch-can operation like the last attack; I ducked just as a shrieking ball of lead passed through the space where my head had been. Thank God I'm not tall.

We were picking up speed. Trains don't go as fast backwards as forward, but gravity was helping out. Joseph left the brake alone. We were doing thirty at least when we hit the level, and when we made it back around the bend he let the throttle out all the way. By then we'd picked up fire from another angle, not as regular as from the Gatling, but from more than a few rifles placed in strategic position. I could picture the snipers arranged in two rows, kneeling in front, standing in the rear, firing in volleys. We crouched below the opening in the cab, I clutching the Whitney across my thighs. It was no good as long as I couldn't risk showing myself long enough to locate a target and take aim from a moving platform, but the solid stock felt good in my hands.

I heard something then, louder than the chugging of the engine: a long shrill splitting noise and a rush of leaves and branches, like a tree lashed by howling wind.

A tree.

Without consulting the engineer I reached up and hauled on the brake handle. Again came the high-pitched cry of locked wheels against the rails, and the sickening lurch of the engine fighting inertia; I'd set my feet so I couldn't be thrown off them in my crouching position, but Joseph had had no warning, and fell back against me; I wobbled, but kept my footing. He fell hard on his buttocks, but his grasp of the throttle prevented him from sprawling all the way onto his back.

A train doesn't stop on the instant, especially with slickum on the wheels. We struck hard enough to shatter branches and send them spinning end over end past the cab, carrying with them the sharp sweet scent of green wood. Another party had stationed itself behind us, and had to have had their axes swinging while we were still slipping on the grade.

I didn't wait for what was coming next. I stuck the muzzle of the rifle through the cab opening on the side of the mountains and squeezed the trigger. Once again I had no hope of hitting anyone or anything; I was gambling for time.

A gamble I lost. When I turned my head to see how Joseph was getting along, the Indian's hand came out of a recess inside the tender on his side of the cab. An ugly pistol pointed at me. The muzzle was as big around as a drainpipe.

I let the rifle fall butt-first to the floor—I'd never clear the barrel through the opening in time—and scooped out the Deane-Adams; but I knew that was just as futile. Long before I could level it, a sheet of white flame blinded me and I fell as hard as the tree and a lot faster.

I keep a pistol in the cab. Not even Joseph knows about it.

Hector Cansado, the dead engineer, hadn't invented the hidden weapon, but he'd misjudged his fireman. He'd thought to keep it secret by concealing it on the side of the tender opposite the Indian's post, but either Joseph had discovered it earlier or stumbled across it after he took Cansado's place at the throttle.

The glimpse I'd had of it before I blacked out had suggested early manufacture, nearly ancient; percussion arms were a scarce commodity in a nation racked with revolution every few years and in the control of nervous governors with seasoned troops and no laws against search and seizure. This one reflected none of the grace of its era. Built simply of thick steel and all of one piece, the frame curved to fit a man's hand, it was equally effective as a firearm or a bludgeon. As I lay in a watery half-world lanced with splinters of white-hot pain, I didn't know whether I'd been shot or struck over the head.

When I came far enough around to choke back a sudden sharp flash of bitter vomit, I felt the earth moving beneath me. This was nothing new since Montana Territory, but the rhythm was different, less regular;

when whatever I was traveling in lurched, sending a burning bolt of agony straight to the top of my skull, I recognized the feel of a wooden wheel plunging into a rut in hard soil. I smelled green wood then, fresh-sawn, heard the hollow plop of shod hooves, and knew I was in a wagon.

And I knew without opening my eyes that I was being watched.

I raised my lids a crack, fighting the urge to flutter them; God alone knew what awaited me when whoever had me realized I was awake. What I saw through a haze of pain and green-tinged sunlight made me think I was still out and dreaming. The face staring into mine was only remotely human. In the shadow of a broad raddled straw brim with green dappling it through the holes, it looked as if someone had gripped it between the jaws of an enormous pair of pliers and squeezed.

I lowered my lids. The eyes in that pinched face, as black and dull as crabapple seeds and nearly as small, seemed to be studying me closely for any sign of awareness. But my sense of smell was more acute than usual. The owner of the face gave off an odor of cedar smoke and something less pleasant: It made me think of the moldy rags swaddling the bones of the Pinkerton in the dank dugout where he'd died. It seemed to have less to do with the clothes the creature wore—shapeless coverings only—than with an inner corruption. It was too strong to have come from just one source. The thing—I supposed it was human— had companions as redolent.

We were moving up, I could tell. My lungs strained to filter oxygen from the thinning air and my head throbbed, partly from the blow, but as much from the pressure of breathing at that altitude. My tongue was wrapped in a cotton stocking. Involuntarily I licked my lips. They were as cracked as dried clay.

A hand made of sinew wrapped around bone slid behind my head and raised it. I gasped in surprise, and before I could close my mouth something splashed into it, tasting of moss and iron and limestone. I nearly choked, but I swallowed. It tasted better than Judge Blackthorne's aged Scotch whisky.

The hand withdrew and my head hit the wagonbed. Light burst again, nausea flashed, and I blacked out a second time. When I felt again the rocking motion of the bed, I suspected I hadn't been out long, but there was no telling how far we were traveling from sea level. A great weight seemed to be pressing against my chest. The air was getting rarer. Only two types of creature lived so high above the earth: One was Joseph's pumas.

The posters offering reward for joining with Childress had gotten to the Indian finally. He'd come to the realization that as the man who knew how to operate the train he was more valuable than his passenger; but why I was still alive and worth the effort of transporting over that steep terrain eluded me.

When at length I grew weary of pretending to be insensate, I opened my eyes and propped myself up on my elbows. My companion in the wagon was no longer staring at me; he was crumpled in the corner opposite me, one arm dangling over the tailgate and his ragged straw hat tipped over his face. I was grateful for that. Something about those squeezed-together features made me think of a photograph of a shrunken head I'd seen in one of the Judge's travel books. The man wore a bandoleer with heavy-caliber brass cartridges in the loops, but no weapon that I could see, possibly because he was guarding a prisoner who might be tempted to try to disarm him.

A few yards behind the wagon, a pair of mules with gray muzzles towed another vehicle, a two-wheeled oxcart piloted by my keeper's twin brother: At least I hoped there wasn't an entire race of such nightmare creatures living in those mountains. (That hope would be dashed quickly enough.) This one had on a pair of bandoleers crossed on his chest and a machete like the one I'd taken off the guard in Alamos in an open sheath on his belt, the abbreviated blade hanging off the edge of his narrow seat and banging against the side of the footboard.

In the bed behind him sat a man with his back to me, wearing a decrepit straw hat like the others and more ammunition. Past his shoulder, Joseph faced forward with a stout pinon limb across his shoulders, his wrists bound to it with thick hemp and his arms stretched out on both sides, a seated Christ figure with his face twisted into an expression of indescribable agony.

TWENTY-ONE

My head hurt worse trying to work it out.

It was like one of those cruel games adults play with children: Is the penny in the right fist or the left? It was in the left last time, but that doesn't mean this time it will be in the right. It might be in the same fist ten times in a row; but wasn't that too much to expect? So you bit your lip and pointed, and you were wrong most of the time because you haven't learned to think outside of a straight line. That came with growing up.

And then there was that rare diabolical adult who pocketed the penny, presenting you with two empty fists.

I'd gone out too abruptly to see where the blow had come from; if it was a blow. I located the pulpy spot on my scalp, but just touching it sent a thrill of pain out in all directions, so I couldn't probe it thoroughly enough to decide if it was a bullet crease or if I'd been struck by a buttstock. Joseph had aimed the pistol in my direction, but whether he pulled the trigger or used it as a bludgeon, or was aiming at something through the opening in the cab—a man trying to board, who managed to shoot or crack me over the head before the Indian fired, if he'd managed to fire at all—was lost.

There were two possible explanations: Either he'd acted in my defense and been taken, or he'd betrayed me and then been betrayed by those he was in league with. Had they, too, decided that a man who would turn against another—Hector Cansado, myself—wasn't worthy of their trust? But in either case, why not kill him outright?

Childress.

I'd said it myself: If the *Ghost* was what he was after, it was useless without a man who knew how to run it. They would have their orders to bring back the engineer alive at whatever cost.

Which left the problem of why they hadn't killed me or left me for dead at the train.

Sitting up enough to look around, I found the craziest theory to be the most plausible. The man guarding me, the man driving the wagon carrying Joseph, and—when he stirred to stretch himself and turned his head my way to work the kinks out of his neck—the man guarding him might have been identical triplets, born to a family of marked ugliness and, if their vapid eyes and slack mouths were any indication of what lay behind, brute stupidity. The same was true of others riding mules and gaunt horses behind and alongside the wagons: two-legged beasts with pinched-in skulls, displaying no more intelligence than the cartridges in their belts. The obvious conclusion chilled me there in the thick, sopping atmosphere of the Sierras. They were all related, or nearly so, bred for generations in the same small community, doubling and redoubling family strengths—force and ruthlessness—and faults—lack of reasoning—until what was left was a race of vicious idiots.

Oscar Childress, it seemed, had given instructions to spare my life as he had with Joseph. Probably he wanted to know what I'd learned and reported home; or—crazy even to consider it—maybe he was as starved for intelligent conversation as I was.

Why wasn't I trussed as well? On the evidence of appearances, our escorts were incapable of deciding I was in too much misery to attempt escape, which I was: Just the thought of crawling over the side of the wagon and taking off on foot through that wild country made the scenery spin around me. More likely it was a tribal thing, and I was immune. There must be Indian blood in anyone living that long so far from villages, but there had been hatred and rivalry between peoples in the New World for hundreds of years before Columbus. With so many guards and in that landscape, the chances of freedom were next to nothing, but it would be only natural to make the journey as painful as possible for a traditional enemy like Joseph.

I didn't ask my throbbing head to explore the situation further just then.

Tethered to the back of the wagon carrying Joseph was my bay. I heard a gurgling, caught a sharp whiff of ferment, and turned to see my driver lowering one of the Judge's bottles, drawing a sleeve across his lips. He hadn't bothered to uncork it, had just knocked off the neck, and a smear of blood on his sleeve told me he hadn't the sense to predict what a jagged shard of glass could do to his mouth. Maybe his brain was too weak to record pain.

Looking around once again, I saw others guzzling from bottles broken the same way, and knew they'd have looted the train of everything they could use: the firearms along with my hip guns, the tins of food, certainly the gold I'd drawn from the bank; but I'd gladly have traded the money to separate these half-humans from the combination of weapons and liquor. They rode spavined, grass-fed mounts with faces as stupid as theirs. Some of the men were singing—humming—moaning—an approximation of some bawdyhouse song or songs, their voices ranging from guttural growls to nasal whines, and the mix of tones, melodies, and off-key renditions of tunes imperfectly remembered fell somewhere between madhouse wails and cats fighting in an alley, or worse: cats and rats tearing at one another for meat. The wheels of the wagons cried out for grease. The din was hellish.

The animals weren't in charge of the zoo, however.

I'd been reluctant to crank my head far enough around to see very much up ahead—it was hurting fine on its own without that, and my guard was still sleeping; passed out, most likely. I didn't want to find out what he was like with a skull full of drunk's regret. But when a rider came trotting back to smack a dozing idiot's thigh with a leather crop, I saw a man with regular features and fierce black muttonchops wearing a campaign hat stained black with sweat and a gray tunic with the cuffs buttoned back to expose a yellow lining: the contrasting colors were faded almost to the same shade, the fabric darned and patched all over, but the stovepipe boots gleamed black above dusty insteps. Gold braid, faded also, made loops on his sleeves, and on his collar glittered the insignia of a captain of the Confederacy, the engraving worn nearly smooth, but the brass highly polished. The left side of his face was white and shiny, in sharp relief to his deep sunburn, cutting a bare patch from his whiskers, and the eye that belonged on that side lay on some old battleground, leaving behind an empty socket, the flesh around it shrunken to the bone.

I remembered that the nucleus of Childress' private army comprised members of his old command. This one, whose burnsides were tipped with gray like the coat of the dead grizzly, drew back his hand with lightning reflexes to avoid being bitten by the man he'd jolted out of sleep, but I heard his teeth snap together inches from the flesh. The captain responded with a backhand swipe, striping the man's face with a red welt. He blinked, but apart from laying his own hand on the machete on his belt showed no other physical reaction. If he'd had a tail (and I wouldn't have bet against it), he'd have tucked it between his legs.

The officer cantered back another hundred yards, casting his one-eyed iron gaze along the procession, then wheeled his mount—a muscular sorrel fattened on grain, unlike the others', with sleek haunches— and galloped the other direction to resume his post in the lead.

The parade wasn't heavily populated, but it was strung out for a quarter-mile. As we climbed, the vehicle bringing up the rear rose into view from below a grade. It rolled on tall, iron-felloed wheels, a bundle of ten blue-steel barrels mounted on a wooden crosspiece. As a weapon of wholesale slaughter the Gatling should have been ugly, but it had been hand-crafted by masters, the weight and balance of its wheels allowing it to roll smoothly, almost gracefully over the rude terrain, its brass fittings flashing in the sun. Some of the deadliest vipers are among the most beautiful things in creation.

Joseph, whose own groans of pain had subsided, swayed and pitched with the motion of his wagon, his eyes closed and his chin on his chest. He'd either passed out or died.

Just then his guard cocked a leg and dealt him a blow that left the clear outline of a bootheel on his temple. He snapped to. Pink-tinged drool dripped off his chin, but the whites of his eyes showed briefly before they closed again.

A toad had climbed into my mouth, bloated and sluggish. It was my tongue. My guard had shifted again in his sleep, exposing the stiletto-sharp neck of a bottle sagging in the side pocket of his threadbare canvas coat. There was no sign of the water vessel he'd let me drink from before. Had I dreamt it? The whole trip, it seemed, had been the product of bad whisky and tainted oysters. But liquid was liquid.

I leaned over until my shoulder touched the wagonbed, stretched my arm across the boards until my fingers just touched the neck. I didn't want to slide closer. Animals have instincts, and what he lacked in brainpower he might make up for in the physical senses. I teased the bottle loose slowly, a fraction of an inch at a time, until I could grasp it firmly and slide it free of the pocket.

As I did so, my shirtcuff snagged something. The guard stirred, whimpered. I caught my breath and held it. He opened his mouth, smacked his lips, and snored so rackingly I felt it in my own torn gullet. I let out a bellyful of air and concentrated my attention on freeing the cuff without dropping the bottle. When I pulled gently, something gave: One of the fifty-caliber Gatling shells had come loose from a loop on his belt. I turned my wrist, still holding the bottle by its neck, and curled my little finger around the flanged receiver. With that grip secure I lifted away bottle and round of ammunition in one movement.

I turned the cartridge around in my fingers. The brass shell alone was four inches long and an inch across the base, with the conical lead bullet adding another two and a half inches to its length. Just holding it made me shudder. One of those slugs had come within a handspan of taking my head off.

I put it in a pocket. I had no idea what I was going to do with it, but its weight was reassuring. It was as heavy as a roll of quarters.

There was only a trickle left in the bottle, and just then I'd have traded a carload of the Judge's aged Scotch for as much water as could be wrung from a sponge; but it was all I had available. I closed my cracked lips gingerly around the broken neck and tipped the contents over my tongue. They burned like acid, but I lapped up every drop, stuck my finger as far inside as I dared, wiped it along the glass, and licked it. I lowered the bottle to the boards and let it roll to a stop against the sleeping guard's hip. I lay back, as exhausted as if I'd been pulling the wagon myself.

I dozed, woke; dozed again, and dreamed I was back in Virginia, desperate for rest but bombarded by mosquitoes the size of gypsy moths, whining like mortar shells and stinging like the dull needles military orderlies used to prevent smallpox, wallowing in a puddle of my own sweat in a tent rank with mildew. We were on our way to a place called Cold Harbor, as poorly named a destination as ever there was. I'd been born in the high chill dry air of the Bitterroots, and would never accustom myself to inhaling oxygen as through a moldy bandanna. I jerked myself awake by sheer will—and started shivering. My teeth chattered so loudly I wanted to clasp my hand over my mouth to avoid drawing the attention of my witless beast of a guard; wanted to, but hadn't the strength to lift my arm from the wagonbed.

That's when I learned what I've known ever since: Once a victim of malaria, always a victim, at intervals no physician could predict, no matter how well-trained.

And higher we climbed. I looked up at the black-winged things wheeling in circles against white sky and felt I could reach out and pluck a feather.

TWENTY-TWO

Time is measured by clocks, calendars, the turning of the earth and the shifting of constellations, none of which was capable of marking our passage up those mountains. I woke abruptly, and lay for a moment wondering what was responsible, until I realized we'd stopped. I'd grown so accustomed to the pitch and sway of the wagon and the shrieking of the ungreased axles that the sudden cessation of noise and motion had come as rudely as a pistol report. Dusk was all about, turning the sky the shade of eggplant, the zigzag treetops flat black, as if they'd been stamped against it with printer's ink. I wondered if we'd stopped to rest the animals. The thought that the ghastly shades who commanded them needed to halt for any human reason was too unlikely to consider.

It was dusk, yes: *A* dusk, anyway. There was no telling how many had come and gone since those two insignificant things, guts from a dead bear and a felled tree, had succeeded where nothing else could, stopping the *Ghost*. Nearer ground level, wriggles of yellow and orange suggested flames, spaced too evenly apart to belong to anything so random as nature. They twisted and snapped atop narrow posts stuck in the ground, illuminating a broad one-story building pale with whitewash, pierced at regular intervals with paned windows, dark shutters folded flat against the walls, and a proper shake roof. Peering over the side of the wagon, I swept the sweat from my eyes with the heels of my hands, but when I looked again it was still there, a cozy domestic arrangement, with bowls of flowers hanging by chains from a long front porch containing a bentwood rocker and a wicker table. All it lacked was a pitcher of lemonade to complete the effect. Between the torches, I identified similar posts supporting pale oblong shapes: gourds, set up possibly for target practice, although they looked too close to the house for safety.

Half of it, of course, was delirium. The building had to be an illusion. Such a house, the grass around it shorn close to the ground, with homey yellow light glowing through the glass and a blue-enamel mounting block resting beside the flagstone walk, had been transported there in my fever from a neighborhood in St. Louis or Denver, within walking distance of a schoolhouse and a church. It no more belonged in that wild place than a hopscotch court on Cemetery Ridge. The gourds were homely enough to be real.

I was wrong about both, as it turned out; but by then I knew I'd been wrong about almost everything connected with Oscar Childress from the start.

As the creatures dismounted and milled about, unhitching harnesses and opening their trousers to spill acrid-smelling water onto the ground—I swore steam rose from it, although the evening was warm—I looked for Joseph, but by then it had grown too dark to see inside the wagon that had been carrying him. Once again my gaze went toward that impossible house. Piled up against a side wall, just visible in the shifting light of the torches, was a pale heap that struck a gong deep in my memory.

In my ranch hand days I'd supported myself winters hunting buffalo, then switched to wolfing and traded the pelts for bounty. The packs had swollen on the easy pickings of the shaggies' abandoned carcasses, and when they'd stripped them to the bone, armies of vagabonds had swarmed in to harvest the skeletons for sale to manufactories back East, which fashioned them into buttons, combs, and handles for knives and chests of drawers and pulverized them to press into china for the table and to filter the impurities from sugar. Within months of the last hunt, the plains were scraped clean of any evidence the beast had ever existed, millions vanished in twenty short years. I'd led pack horses piled with wolf pelts through city streets turned into canyons of bone; but soon even they vanished. Where Childress had managed to find so many to refine his coarse-ground cane was another of the mysteries that piled up around him like—well, the bones themselves.

I heard the *shink* of a pin being drawn from an iron staple, followed by another, and then the tailgate swung down with a rattle and thump of elmwood. A toe struck me in the ribs, shooting a red flare of pain all the way to my torn scalp. My keeper, awake at last, stood stretching, his own bones making as much noise as the tailgate. I pulled myself to my feet before he could aim another kick. I was wearing my old comfortable range Stetson, trained to my head so it wouldn't blow off in a stiff wind, but I held the brim as I made to step down, because the angle I'd chosen to avoid contact with the sticky lump wasn't natural. I steadied myself with the other hand on the side of the wagon as I groped for the ground with one foot. Standing on bare earth I couldn't feel my legs. I took a couple of steps to get the blood flowing, but instead of the pins and needles I expected my knees folded and I pitched straight forward into black.

At first I thought the whole business of the house and the torches and the pile of bones and the stop itself

was a dream, and actually felt the familiar lurching of
the wagon; but there was something different, almost
alien, about the surface where I lay on my back. I
hadn't slept in the upholstered berth aboard the train
in days, and had no idea how long I'd spent stretched
out on the weathered boards of the wagon. My muscles and bones had adapted themselves to unyielding
planks, beginning with the floor of the locomotive's
cab, to the point where the softness of feathers, ticking, and clean linen—it smelled of cornstarch and
fresh air—made them ache. Whoever had carried me
here would have been kinder to have laid me on a floor,
then a stiff bench, and brought me by degrees to occupy a civilized bed.

Just where the bed was I couldn't say, even when I
opened my eyes. Darkness surrounded me, so black it
made my heart clatter. I was sealed inside a padded
coffin; cedar, from the sweet scent. I lay breathing
shallowly, to avoid exhausting what air was left me,
dreading to raise a hand and confirm the tightness of
my confinement. My hand twitched, lifted an inch,
dropped back to my chest. I pressed my lips tight and
willed it to rise again. My arm went up and up and
felt nothing but empty air. I opened my mouth wide,
exhaled in a whoosh, and sucked in, filling my chest
until it ached. I felt as if I'd dived into a thousand-
foot lake, touched the bottom, and clawed my way
back to the surface with my lungs straining through
the last fathom close to bursting. The air was even
sweeter than it smelled.

Gradually—glacially—my eyes adjusted themselves, allowing a gray glimmer of light to measure
the dimensions of the room where I lay and to suggest a shape for the objects that shared it with me. It

was either windowless or the curtains were heavy, because the only source of illumination was a hollow rectangle at the far end where a door didn't fit flush to the frame. I had no idea if it was day or night, or if the space beyond was lit by the sun or a lamp. It reflected on the curvature of a pitcher near my head, and fell from there to the top of a table or a nightstand within reach of where I lay. Through the corner of my eye I made out a bedpost, curved also, but not well enough to decide whether it was wood or metal, only that it, too, was capable of reflecting light.

They fascinated me, those polished surfaces. Apart from the glass-bezeled gauges and steel of the *Ghost* and the rails it rolled on, it had been days since I'd laid eyes on anything that wasn't coarse and light-absorbing; even the lush fittings of the parlor car were a dim memory since I'd decamped to the front of the train.

Something else glittered, as if from its own source of light; the gilded binding of a leather-bound volume lying beside the pitcher on its stand. I brought my face close to the spine and peered, but the room might have been black as pitch for all I could make of the gold-stamped title: It was German. That gave me a good idea of whose bed it was. Two people in that vicinity might understand English and Spanish; it was unlikely more than one would be educated in any other language.

I decided it was night. The air was chill at that altitude without the sun to warm it, and wrapped my face in a cold mask. My arm, cold too, was bare where it lay on a coverlet made from the pelt of some animal and cured to silken softness; doeskin, I thought. Between it and my body was a linen sheet, woven so finely it felt like heavy cream. It covered my other arm. I slid my hand down my body, confirming my suspicion that I was naked.

I felt weak, but my skin was cool and dry. There was no determining how long I'd been there, or how many times I'd been bathed of sweat and the bedding had been changed. Malaria has been with me off and on in all the years since, and the time needed for the fever to break varies. It might have been hours or days.

Carefully, to avoid triggering a relapse, I peeled aside the coverlet and sheet, sat up, gathered energy, and swung my feet to the floor. That amount of effort took as much out of me as I had for the moment; I leaned my shoulder against the bedpost to collect my strength. My bare soles rested on thick wool, a woven rug probably of Indian workmanship. I worked my toes, enjoying its warmth. I'd begun to shiver, and to worry that another attack was on its way.

When the sensation faded, I found the courage to test the extent of my recovery. I shifted my weight forward, grasped the bedpost, and pulled myself upright. The room did a slow turn but ended up stable. I tugged the sheet off the bed, wrapped it around me, closing it at my throat, and went exploring.

Some kind of decoration hung on a wall, a large painting, I thought, but the subject, painted in dark colors and possibly made more murky with age, remained anonymous inside a frame of some dark lustrous wood.

Beyond the edge of the rug the floor was wooden as well, cool and smooth under my unshod feet. There was pine aplenty in the Sierras, and evidently labor sufficient to cut and split and plane and sand it. Such mindless and repetitive work would be ideal for the tiny brains of the men who'd brought me there.

I bumped into something tall and solid. I laid a

palm against the door of a wooden cabinet. The cedar smell increased when I pulled it open. I groped inside, felt fabric. I hadn't been out of my canvas coat in a week, and knew the texture even in the dark. Probing further, my hand found the Gatling cartridge in the pocket where I'd put it. My relief was tinged with revulsion: Who'd be senseless enough to overlook it when he was undressing me, if not one of my doltish escorts? The thought of his hands touching my bare skin made it crawl. It was as if a snake had slithered over me while I slept.

The rest of my clothes, gritty as they felt from constant wearing, were as welcome as the coat with its secret treasure. I let the sheet fall to the floor and stood naked in the stiff Mexican night. I dressed slowly, pacing myself, sitting on the bed to pull on my boots. The effort spent me. I lay back for a few minutes to refuel. I wasn't quite as weak as a kitten, but I fell short of a full-grown tabby.

Whoever had hung up my things hadn't been accommodating enough to leave behind my revolvers; but there was no need to be greedy. The fifty-caliber slug slapped pleasantly against my hip when I put on the coat.

I had a fair notion where I was: the plantation headquarters of Major Oscar Childress, thousands of feet almost straight up from Cape Hell.

TWENTY-THREE

My hat occupied a top shelf of the cabinet, still damp with sweat. That was encouraging; I hadn't been out of my senses more than a day or two or it would be dry. I'd been in that state before, once when a bullet grazed my scalp and a few times when the horse under me decided I didn't belong and pitched me headfirst into the American frontier. It was always like reading a book with pages torn out, and a relief to know it wasn't missing anything beyond a couple of chapters.

The thought of old head injuries reminded me to check my scalp. My temples were throbbing, but that could have been part of the fever. I fingered the tender spot carefully, felt woven cloth, and around it bare skin. Someone had shaved a tonsure some two and a half inches square and patched it with gauze.

I couldn't picture any of Childress' half-animals performing that operation, or bothering to consider it. The image of poor Joseph, traitor or not, crucified in the back of a wagon was as vivid as when I'd first seen it. If the major had added physician to his long list of skilled occupations, he was a da Vinci for the nineteenth century.

I slid a hand inside my pocket and closed it around the Gatling round, purely for security. I still didn't know what to do with it, but it was the only secret I had left.

Approaching the rectangle of light I hesitated, then groped for a handle. It was a knob, engraved bronze or brass from the feel. It would be locked, naturally.

Naturally I paused again when it turned without resistance and a latch slid free with the slight friction of metal scraping metal.

Caution be damned. I'd been carried up the mountain for a purpose, and if it was important I stay in that room the door wouldn't have been left open. I swung it wide and entered a library.

It was rigged out like the shelves in a ship, with wooden lips attached to keep the books from falling. Were earthquakes common at that altitude? The shelves were pine; tiny cones of sawdust had been left by termites, but the books themselves were in good condition, although they showed traces of use. The titles were printed on cloth and stiff paper and stamped in gold leaf into leather old and shabby and oiled and glistening: *The Origin of Species by Means of Natural Selection, Selected Poems of Robert Browning,* odd numbers of the Encyclopedia Britannica, *Frankenstein,* a shelf of Dickens, *The Anatomy of Melancholy,* bound copies of *The Lancet, Principles of Steam, Alice in Wonderland,* Clausewitz, *The Oregon Trail.* I didn't linger over the ones in German, French, Latin, and some hen-scratches that were either Hebrew or Greek, but I'd heard of Nietzche somewhere and knew Julius Caesar had had something to say about how Gaul was divided. There were many more, hundreds more, on adjoining shelves all around the room, but they were lost in gloom. It was a hodge-podge of science, history, fiction, philosophy, and poetry, arranged in no order I could apply, either by author or subject, as if they'd been flung randomly into place after consulting, like oranges squeezed dry.

It wasn't just show. I'd visited the libraries of wealthy self-made men and seen their immaculate sets, the spines uncreased and bought by the yard to impress visitors not observant enough to note the fact they'd arrived unopened from the dealers and stayed that way. Waiting—which is what you spend most of your time doing where important people are involved—I'd taken down dozens of them to kill time, only to find most of the pages uncut. Plainly these books had been opened and shut scores of times, their spines thumb-blurred and the bindings loose. Someone had underscored whole passages of Shakespeare in iron-gall ink. The reader had marked his place in Act IV, Scene II of *Richard III* with a Confederate two-dollar bill. I snapped shut the hefty volume—all tragedies—and slid it back into its slot, not before a tarantula scampered out and vaulted up to the top shelf.

The hour was later than I thought; or earlier. A gap in the heavy curtains covering one of a pair of tall windows let in the tarnished light of either dawn or dusk. I walked up to it, spread the heavy green panels, and looked at a crescent of brilliant orange stuck to the edge of a shadowy mountain. I guessed we were in the middle of the range, and having no other means of sensing direction couldn't determine whether I was looking east or west. I waited. It seemed to me the sun was moving up rather than down. When a yellow ray sprang free I knew it was the former. Dawn comes late in the mountains. That made the time nearer six o'clock than five. I was alone, but wouldn't be for long. In the Sierra Madre, no one sleeps in.

The window was unbarred, but as the land fell straight down from the foundation for several hundred dizzying feet, no bars were necessary. It was a large room, three times as long as it was deep, like the inside of a train station, and must have taken up the entire back half of the house; if it was the house I'd seen when our caravan stopped. A rug of Indian design covered the pine floor to within a foot of the walls, with a thunderbird spreading its square wings in silver-gray on a background of red and black. The wool looked as soft as the one I'd walked on barefoot in the bedroom. Paintings in massive gilt frames leaned out on wires from the walls between bookshelves: Portraits with brass nameplates of Thomas Jefferson, John Marshall, and Robert E. Lee, Virginians all; the *Monitor* and the *Merrimack* chucking smoke and fire at each other at Hampton Roads.

Across from the battle scene, a replica of the Conquistador map I'd seen in the Judge's chambers hung uncovered by glass in a snakewood frame. No, I thought, when I stood close: It was no replica, but an original, drawn on either parchment or the skin of some unborn animal, signed in copperplate by a Spaniard whose name I couldn't pronounce. Ancient silverfish had munched the corners round.

A ton of what were no doubt native elk antlers swung from the ten-foot ceiling on a heavy chain, tangled inextricably, cold tallow candles skewered on their points. Between the windows stood a cherry-wood desk supported by carved gryphons, on it an amethyst-shaded banker's lamp, a green baize blotter, a Bible the size of a Missouri River ferry, cigars in a bell jar, a blobby bronze inkstand, and a tired grapefruit with a bristle of horsehair pens stuck in it like arrows in Custer's corpse. A quilted leather chair with a hickory frame mounted on a swivel stood at attention behind the desk.

The walls not hidden behind books were rush-covered, the material probably harvested from ponds and marshes, laid out to dry, tea-stained, and woven on looms. Everything in the room, except the books and a great glass globe cradled in maple, seemed to have been fashioned from local resources. It seemed familiar, yet remote, like something I'd read in a book. I was illiterate compared to the man who used that room, but when you've spent much of your life snowed in, you're no stranger to reading. I just couldn't remember which book. It hadn't ended well for the hero.

A fire burned—in that climate—behind mica inserts in an enameled parlor stove. If it had been kindled for my benefit, the connecting door should have been open.

I smelled good tobacco. I've never gotten the habit, but I knew the aroma of the cigars Judge Blackthorne had brought in by boat and train from Havana, and the air here smelled even more refined.

"I grow it myself," said a voice behind me. "Just a small patch, for my pipe; I can't spare any more because of the amount of land the cane needs to flourish. The curing is done by one of those revenants you've met. It's ideal work for creatures without wits. Their capacity for undistracted concentration is remarkable."

I turned to look at the man who'd entered through a side door. He was bald, as I'd predicted he'd be, based on his receding hairline in an old tintype; but I'd been wrong about his going native. A man like Oscar Childress, I saw instantly, would expect nature to go his way rather than the other way around.

TWENTY-FOUR

He wore conventional dress, if the conventions of Boston, Denver, and San Francisco were in order: a black morning coat, striped trousers, dove-gray gaiters. He lacked only a cravat, having buttoned his shirt to his throat. As there was some swelling there, the beginnings of a goiter or dropsy, there was no room for it. Beyond that, his skull was obvious beneath a layer of skin no thicker than the sap from a rubber tree, and the skin itself the dead gray of stagnant water. His eyes, glistening plums floating in deep sockets, were brilliant, with the unnatural brightness of a star burning itself out. That explained the stove; it was there for a sick man, after all. Here was a man dying, who would no more conquer Mexico City than a leper groping for alms with a hand without fingers. I smelled the corruption as surely as from the dead grizzly on the rails, but the exact location of the cancer was a mystery, only that it was the cause.

My journey was useless; if killing Childress to prevent a second Civil War had been why I'd undertaken it.

He joined me before the map. At that range the odor was feral.

"It's fashionable to poke fun at those old cartographers who swarmed the uncharted regions with monsters. They didn't believe in them any more than you or I. It was a ruse to frighten others from the treasures they knew were there."

I was about to ask him what he used in place of

monsters when something shook the floor at my feet. The books on the shelves jumped against the strips of wood that restrained them, and I knew then their purpose. A deep bellowing explosion came on the heels of the shake, and something the size and shape of a barrel hoop drifted past the window from which I'd drawn the curtains. I hadn't seen the smoke ring from a discharged cannon since Lee's surrender. The silvery thin strains of a bugle followed, distorted by distance and the irregular topography.

Childress was watching me. His pale eyes were bordered by paler lashes. "I order it fired three times a week. I wanted to conserve powder, but having the brutes practice less often was a mistake. Captain Mc-Cready had to re-teach them the rudiments every time. During reveille is best. It's important to keep the experienced troops on edge, and necessary to pound the lesson into the empty heads of the others."

"McCready's the officer with one eye?"

"He lost it at Petersburg. It's disconcerting, I know. I ordered him to wear a patch, but he said the itching was a distraction. I'd rather not risk it in the heat of battle."

He approached the desk, his back straight as from disciplined effort, and stroked the mirror finish. "I don't expect you to appreciate this item. It belonged to a marshal of France. He brought it with him to New Orleans when he fled the Bourbons. I bought it by telegraphic bid at his estate auction and had it shipped by rail to Cabo Falso and hauled up here by wagon. There was a revolution on at the time, and some men lost their lives in the endeavor. I like to think it a vessel for their wandering souls."

"I'm sure they'd appreciate it." So he was insane as well as physically ill. I'd considered the possibility;

but it's one thing to assume and another to experience it at first-hand.

Someone tapped gently and a woman entered, a Yaqui I thought, wearing a muslin blouse and a flowered skirt, huaraches on her bare feet. She carried a silver decanter and china on a tray, which she set on the desk. Her face and hands were as gnarled as an old root.

"Coffee?" Childress offered. "I'm forced to barter for it in Central America. I tried growing my own, but it won't cooperate at this altitude. I couldn't afford the acreage in any case. Sugar's greedy."

I realized then I wasn't thirsty anymore; someone had seen to that while I was suffering. But just the rich smell seemed to level off the pounding in my head. I accepted a cup and sat balancing it on its saucer in a straight chair facing the desk. The china was paperthin; my fingers made shadows on the other side of the rim. He dismissed the woman, seated himself in the leather chair, rummaged inside the top drawer, and poured white powder from a paper into his cup, stirring it with a tiny spoon. He patted his flat belly.

"A bromide. After all these years I can't get used to the local diet." He sipped the steaming brew. His eyes brightened further. He'd lied; I wondered if he grew his own coca leaves, and if the sugar cane resented them. "You're here to kill me," he said.

If he'd expected to ambush me with that one, I disappointed him. For all I knew his chain of spies extended as far as Helena. I fell back on the original lie.

"I'm not a hired gun. Washington's heard some things, and I was sent to hear them myself, from the horse's mouth if possible, and report back."

"And yet I was told you came to offer me a train in return for a commission with my irregulars."

It came as no shock that Blackthorne had furnished me with two lies of my own, the second to cover the first. An experienced tactician would expect a ruse, and possibly be satisfied once he'd exploded it. It was another example of which fist held the penny.

I sipped from the cup. The coffee was strong but not bitter; he'd made a good trade. "If you found out as much about me as I did about you, you saw through that one right away. What if you succeed in commandeering the Mexican Army and reversing Appomattox? After you conquer a country you have to govern it. What would I be then, attorney general? I've never been comfortable on that side of a desk."

"You can report that everything Washington heard is true. I intend to capture Mexico City, annex the federales, and invade El Paso. Once you control the border, you control international trade. The *Ghost* stays here. It will expedite securing supplies and provisions, and once I've acquired the additional rolling stock, I can have my troops in the capital in half the time—when they're ready."

"Those animals who brought me here never will be."

"I'll lend you my Machiavelli. Cannon fodder wins wars. Once the enemy has spent itself on that carrion, my professionals will be rested and ready to take the field."

"Is this to be a four-year education or a crash course? In other words, how long are you holding me?"

"You've been very ill, and the rainy season is almost upon us. If you set out tomorrow, you'd never make it to Cabo Falso alive."

"What about Joseph? My engineer," I said, when he showed no reaction.

He drew a plain steel watch from his waistcoat, popped the lid, and put it back. The bones of his hands showed through the skin on the backs as clearly as my own fingers through his china; the bright eyes bulged slightly as he pushed himself to his feet. Apart from that he dissembled the expenditure of energy required. "Come with me."

I got up and followed him out the door he'd come in through. A narrow hallway, properly plastered and painted green, led the way to the front of the house between more portraits of prominent Virginians suspended from a picture rail ending in another door. It opened onto one end of the front porch. There hung the flowering plants of my fever-dream; there was the rocking chair and table, and just visible at the opposite end of the porch the curve of the great heap of bones. The torches placed in front, extinguished now, looked like oversize burnt matches, smelling of coal-oil rather than sulphur, and between them the objects I'd thought had been set on their posts to perform as rifle targets. In the light of day they were human skulls.

It was no wonder I'd taken them for gourds. The temples were sunken, as if the meat had been scooped out, and they sloped back shallowly from just above the beetled brows. They were human, but just barely. I'd made the trip up the mountain in the company of their brothers.

Childress saw me looking at them. "I gave up trying to discipline them by rewarding good behavior. The brutes respond only to fear, and while the concept of death itself is beyond their understanding, they share with the rest of us a terror of the unknown."

As he spoke, a pair of his creatures came around the end where the bones were piled with a third between them, his wrists behind his back. Dressed as they all were, in identical shapeless white shirts and trousers, tall boots, bandoleers, and tattered straw sombreros, heads concave on both sides, expressions vapid, I was more convinced than ever that they were related in an unhealthy way.

"What are they?" I asked.

"Revenants. Animated corpses. I rescued them from starvation in an extinct village carved into the side of a mountain by ancient ancestors they don't know ever existed. The women are housed in a building attached to the sugar refinery. They're useless in most of what's required of the sex except the obvious, so I keep them to placate the men. If it weren't for grass and small game slow enough to slay with rocks, they wouldn't have lasted long enough for me to recruit them. They do the sort of work that frees up their betters for more worthy duty.

"I can't tell you what tribe they belong to. I doubt they could themselves, as they're barely capable of speech in any language; everything human has been bred out of them through generations of incest. But they retain all the resentments inherent between the tribes, which is why your man was so mistreated against my orders. That's another reason I keep them around, as subjects of study. Why reasoning should perish and fear and hatred remain as potent as ever is a question no one has answered."

The man with his hands behind his back was forced to kneel in front of the blue enamel mounting block alongside the flagged path. His wrists, I saw then, were bound with a thong. Without protest, he laid his cheek on the block.

"I don't even know if he's the one responsible for that crude punishment," Childress said. "The brutes all look alike, and I suspect they can't tell even one another apart. I gave up having them whipped for their misbehavior; their minds are so weak they are either unable to feel pain or to connect it with their actions. In any case the lesson is lost. So I teach by example."

He thrust two fingers into the corners of his mouth and blew an ear-splitting whistle. Slow as erosion the two men standing turned their heads in the direction of the noise. He jerked a palm up from his waist. Another long pause before one of them separated himself from the others, slouched back around the bonepile, and returned a moment later supporting Joseph's weight on his shoulders. The engineer was hollow-cheeked, his head down and his hair in his eyes. The soles of his boots scraped the earth. He was barely able to lift them.

By then the major's whistle had summoned a crowd. From either end of the house and from below the drop of the mountain, Childress' creatures shambled into a rough formation strung out facing the house. Hoofbeats pounded, and then some stragglers joined it, driven over the incline by Captain McCready aboard his well-fed sorrel, herding them with his head cocked to one side to monitor them with his single eye. The man who'd brought Joseph mounted the steps to the porch, half-carrying his charge. At another signal, he turned him to face the group. Very slowly, Joseph raised his chin. He may have seen me out the corner of his eye, but he showed no recognition.

"They react to sight and sound," Childress said. "Those senses are remarkably acute. Unfortunately, their memories are poor clay. I have to keep repeating examples to refresh their understanding."

I made no answer. He was treating me as some kind of student, perhaps an apprentice.

McCready swung down from the saddle and snapped a hand to the brim of his campaign hat. "Sir."

"Proceed, Captain."

He drew a saber from the scabbard on his belt. The sun, clear now of obstructions, flashed off the gold chasing on the blade. He raised it. The man standing over the man with his head on the mounting block drew his short-bladed machete and lifted it as if in imitation. It may have been just that, an ape's duplication of a gesture by a member of a superior race.

I'd seen hangings, fought hand to hand, slain men, without flinching. When the captain's sword swung down, I turned my head away before the machete followed; but I heard the thump and roll, and a collective gust of air from dozens of primitive throats in response. It sounded exactly like the feeble roar the slain grizzly had made when its remains were disturbed.

I despised myself for looking away. I had no authority in that country, but as Blackthorne had told me often enough I was an agent of justice. If I could stand by while a helpless man was beheaded without trial, I could damn well witness the act.

The body lay without twitching, slumped sideways to the ground, the earth stained around the stump of its neck; there's no violent eruption after the initial severance, despite what they write in sensational fiction. The head, looking hardly less aware than it had in life, lay a few yards away where it had come to rest.

I hadn't seen the worst yet.

Captain McCready pointed his saber at two of the men assembled, who came forward to hoist the corpse by its wrists and ankles and bear it around the far corner of the house. Their vacant faces offered no indication that they connected the burden with anything more than a pile of sod.

The captain mounted, cantered over to the head, leaned down, and skewered it deftly with his saber. The sorrel was a trained warhorse: Apart from distending its nostrils during the grisly operation, it showed no reaction. It wheeled at the kick of a heel and trotted up to the line of skulls on display, where the rider plucked one free and, resting it against his pommel, removed the dripping head from the blade and jammed it onto the sharpened pike. He leaned over again to plunge the point of the weapon into the earth, cleansing it, and returned it to its scabbard.

He rode the length of the porch, the horse stepping high, neck curved in a Grecian arch. There was something obscene even in that, an arrogant coddled mount prancing as in an Independence Day parade. The skull it carried had every reason to leer.

McCready scooped up the skull, tossed it onto the mountain of bones, and swung round to salute the major.

"Muster 'em out, Captain."

The dullards dispersed, feet dragging—another second lost between their brains and their extremities and they'd have toppled forward from the waist—but I paid them small attention.

It wasn't so much the spectacle of that nightmare rider, whose own hollow eye-socket resembled so closely those of the martially aligned skulls, or even the casual disposal of human remains, like slops emptied into an alley. I'd seen as bad in the most vicious war ever fought between man and man. This was more barbaric still. Plainly the dead man's body had been borne no farther than that same pile. And I knew now the source of the bones Childress ground to refine his sugar, and probably shape into the fine china cup I'd sipped from minutes ago.

My stomach did a slow roll, my vision blurred; black petals blossomed in the haze. But I remained upright, either by sheer force of will or because inch by inch I was becoming accustomed to darkness.

TWENTY-FIVE

Joseph's escort turned him toward the front door. The beast-man's strength was ten times his ability to think; he bore 160 inert pounds, inches from the ground, as easily as a sack of grain. I asked Childress where Joseph was being taken.

"To an ambulance, and from there to a fully equipped infirmary. I'd have had you brought there, but you were in worse condition, if you can believe it, and might not have survived the journey. These Indians are hardy. He needs hydration and nourishment administered under close supervision and a dose of cinchona, just in case. The natives have used it to treat malaria for two hundred years, but it's been slow to catch on outside Mexico. I sent a paper to *The American Medical Journal,* but it was ignored, probably because of my affiliations. Medical science should rise above petty politics. As a beneficiary, perhaps you can make the case for the remedy."

"I'll do my best; assuming I don't die of the cure."

"It's not a cure. You'll revisit the symptoms again and again throughout your life, but they'll not be fatal. You came through the first time, thanks to the bark, and the chances are you'll survive the others. Once your friend has recovered, he'll share quarters with you in the barracks. I'm looking forward to having my own room back. Captain McCready is a fine officer, but he snores like a steam shovel. Are you up to a tour of the grounds?"

"Have I a choice?"

I'd transgressed. He looked at me with the expression of a host whose guest had insulted his accommodations. I had to keep reminding myself he was insane.

"You're free to go any time you feel up to the journey. I wouldn't recommend it until I'm satisfied you won't relapse anytime soon. Your horse is in good hands—you may examine it whenever you like, it's a splendid animal—and I'll provide you with directions to Cabo Falso. It would be ungrateful of me to reward you for the gift of the *Ghost* by making you a prisoner."

"And Joseph?"

"He'll follow—once he's instructed my men in the operation of the locomotive."

He read my thoughts. "No, I wouldn't charge these creatures with anything more complex than cutting cane. You've yet to meet the rest of my regulars. McCready trained the men under his direct command, and I trained him.

"You'll find your other things in the cabinet. Ysabel has cleaned and pressed them by now. You'll be more comfortable once you're out of these rags."

As he spoke, he patted the pocket containing the Gatling round.

I left him in his private study, cracking open a book the size and apparent weight of a paving stone, and entered the bedroom, well-lit now with a similar set of heavy green curtains spread on either side of a window as tall as the others. A scuttle-shaped iron bathtub, lined with white porcelain, steamed in the middle of the rug I'd stepped on earlier. If it had been there in the dark I'd have bumped into it, so Ysabel—if that was the Yaqui woman who'd served coffee—would have had to enlist a couple of Childress' trained monkeys to carry it in; those gnarled hands of hers would have found challenge enough lugging in buckets of scalding water. I'd been bathed repeatedly, I supposed, but although the heat was moderate that far above sea level, my skin glistened greasily once I'd stripped. Whatever effect Childress' justice had or hadn't had on its audience, it was enough to break me into a sweat even if I'd been in the midst of a winter in Montana Territory.

I took the cartridge out of the pocket of the coat, hefted it, and tossed it into a corner. I hadn't the slightest idea what use I might make of it, apart from the fact it was the one secret I'd managed to retain. His knowing it robbed it of all value. I'd gone up against men before who were smarter than I was, more ruthless, readier to act when the moment presented itself; this was the first time I found myself face-to-face with a man who embodied all three—

Virtues? Make of it what you like. One or the other or the other yet had seen me to a ripe old age in my work.

The painting I'd glimpsed in the gloom wasn't much less murky in broad daylight. It was smaller than I'd thought—the heavy filigreed frame almost overwhelmed it—and darkened with age and layers of dirt, cheap varnish laid in over dirt, and more dirt laid in over the varnish, but it seemed to show a man bound in the rags of what must once have been grand martial attire, being disemboweled by a band of curly-haired men in some kind of peasant dress. There appeared to be a signature in the lower right-hand corner, illegible under the layers of grime and shellac. A ghastly thing, probably worth a lot of money to people in New York and St. Louis.

The clothes I'd packed, with some exceptions I noted later, were folded and hung in the cedar cabinet, with my range hat and the fawn-colored Montana pinch I wore to special occasions sharing the top shelf. There was no sign of the overalls and flannel shirt I'd borrowed from Joseph to wear while serving as fireman; Childress had been student enough of human behavior to separate them from my personality. He'd studied me as surely as his poets and philosophers. I suspected I had Felix Bonaparte, the Alamos attorney, to thank for supplying him with information. He'd be Childress' conduit to the greater world.

That thought nudged me in the ribs, painfully enough to hurt, but not enough to tell me why. I'd been threatened, shot at, shot almost through, weakened with plague, and stood to witness cold-blooded murder masquerading as execution. You don't count that kind of time in hours or days or weeks or years; centuries hardly answered. I'd forgotten everything about my meeting with Bonaparte apart from the man himself and his oily command of English.

I lowered myself into the tub gingerly, gasping with

each inch, but the sensation of being parboiled melded into a deceptive feeling of well-being as the heat penetrated bruised muscles and strained tendons. Compared to the tarry yellow soap I'd been used to in boarding houses and railroad hotels, the cake in the dish, lavender-scented and impressed with an escutcheon of some kind, wouldn't have turned up the nose of Queen Victoria.

Lathering up, I noted for the first time that my injured hand had been re-bandaged with the same attention paid to my scalp. I attributed that to the woman as well; but I was as wrong about that as I was about the house being an illusion and the gourds that turned out to be skulls. After I'd dried myself with a towel as thick and soft as any to be found in the best hotels in Denver, I picked up the German book on the nightstand and found it dog-eared to a page with pen-and-ink illustrations detailing the process of cleansing and dressing open wounds, with whole paragraphs of text underscored in ink fresh enough to still carry a scent. A Mexican squaw might be able to interpret the drawings, but it seemed unlikely she'd read German, with Latin phrases interlaced, much less select passages for closer study.

Something else shared the nightstand: A sepia photograph in a silver frame of a pleasant-faced woman bombazined to the neck, the collar closed with the standard cameo brooch, with her hair skinned back into what would be a tight bun and—I couldn't shake the certainty—the devil's own time trying to appear grave for the man behind the camera; she seemed about to burst into laughter. This, I thought, would be the fiancée Childress had left in Virginia. Naked as I was, I slapped nonexistent pockets for the packet of letters I'd been given by lawyer Bonaparte.

I had it then, the most important part of our conversation; which is always the first to go under pressure. Bonaparte had given me the packet for delivery, and it had weighed less heavily in my pocket than the useless piece of ammunition Childress had known about all along.

He surely had the letters by now, if the walking corpses who'd brought me up the mountain hadn't burned them for kindling; or used them even less respectably.

I made a decision not to bring up the subject. If the wretches had mistreated the letters in their childish ignorance and he found out, there would be at least one more head on a pole, and another decapitated body on his utilitarian pile.

Why I should think any more of them than of a stag whose head might decorate the wall of some gentlemen's club, or a prize-winning bass mounted on a board in a saloon, eluded me; unless it was the conviction that, generations back, a normal woman had lain with a normal man, with no thought beyond creating a normal family, human at least. What had come from that was no one's fault; unless you embraced the existence of Satan.

Which I surely did. A man could not have seen what I'd seen, met whom I'd met, and still denied it. Tidy dress and a broad knowledge of science, literature, and the arts were cover enough for horns and a tail.

For some reason I couldn't recall, I'd packed a fine linen shirt I'd had made to my measure in San Francisco, and the suit of clothes I wore to make a good impression testifying in Judge Blackthorne's court. Maybe I thought I'd be invited to a state dinner in the governor's palace in Mexico City upon the successful completion of my mission. Someone had brushed the suit to a sheen. That the valise containing this finery had been carried up the mountain with greater care than my engineer, said something about the character of my escort; but I didn't dwell on that. The clothes, and a fresh set of cotton underdrawers, were laid out on the turned-down bed as if by a valet. On the floor at the foot of the bed stood my second-best pair of boots—I'd left the best behind to be resoled—blacked and buffed to a mirror finish. Oscar Childress, it appeared, was gearing up for diplomatic occasions, accustoming himself to entertaining elegant guests.

Well, what was so ludicrous about that? I hadn't much history compared to my host's, but if I'd never read beyond the Bible I'd still know that being mad has never posed much of a drawback to ruling a nation.

TWENTY-SIX

The old Mexican woman knocked at the door while I was putting on my shirt. I let her in carrying a tray containing a pitcher of hot water, a fresh folded white towel, a pearl-handled razor, and another cake of the lavender-scented soap in a silver mug.

A plain tin mirror hung on a nail above a washstand next to the window. Leaving my shirt open, I filled the basin and scraped off the growth of weeks, the Spanish steel blade gliding through the coarse stubble like a scythe through corn silk. After rinsing off, I slapped on bay rum from a flask on the stand and stared at the stranger in the mirror. I'd begun to resemble Childress' creatures, but shiny-faced and clean-smelling in my best clothes I might pass muster in the drawing-room of a Forty-Niner; if he hadn't become so rich he'd forgotten his time grubbing in gulches and riverbeds and sharing his tent with lice and rats the size of cocker spaniels.

I went into the study, but it was deserted. Retracing our path to the front porch, I found my host seated in a spring buggy with a sleek rubber top hitched to a deep-bellied black with one white stocking and blinders, a rig straight out of Montgomery Ward. He wore an ankle-length duster over his indoor clothes and a milk-white straw planter's hat with a wagon-wheel brim and a black silk band. Outside the shelter of the porch roof, his face was dishwater gray, the black's reins wrapped around wrists thin as drawn gold. In those surroundings he might have passed for a missionary with an unmentionable disease, exiled to the wilderness to die.

He'd stopped beside the blue enamel mounting-block, but although it glistened from a fresh scrubbing I avoided it as I stepped aboard and sat beside him on the upholstered leather seat.

"How far are we going?"

"No more than a thousand yards; but as it's all uphill I wouldn't recommend it for strolling. Every month or so one of the poor idiots stumbles and drops off the edge." He shook the reins and we started forward.

A ledge wound around the mountain nearest the house like the screw on a printer's press, railed with stretches of pine on the outside. Where there wasn't a horizontal surface sufficient to support them, the land fell nearly perpendicular from the edge. In places the path was just wide enough for the wheels to maintain a purchase, with pebbles and broken shards squirting out from under them and caroming down the mountainside. It had in the solider patches a finished look of black stone, not at all the rough fluting caused by centuries of erosion. I said it looked like a proper road.

"It's a road; though I'd hesitate to apply the honorific. We started with dynamite, but we had to conserve it for more practical use, as the supply lines are long and the merchants are vultures. Also, there's brittle shale tucked in between the veins of granite. I lost a fine engineer to a landslide. When the creatures came along I was able to free the men of skill for worthier work."

As he said it, we passed a crew of his creatures dismantling a cairn of fallen stone with picks and spades. Stripped to the waist, they were all bunched raw muscle, indistinguishable from the mountain itself until they moved or the sun glistened off their sweat. At sight of the buggy, they shouldered their tools and flattened themselves against the rock while we passed within inches, sending a shower of dislodged mountain tumbling. I gripped the vehicle's white-ash frame tight enough to split the skin of my knuckles, leaning against the driver like an infatuated maiden out for a turn in the park.

"The brutes are good for something," he said. "What they lack in brain power they more than make up for in animal strength, and they can survive for a week trapped under a ton of rubble."

"How frequent are the slides?"

"Constant. Most of them are minor, but there are days when I'm unable to visit the plantation. The Sierras never miss an opportunity to reclaim what's been taken from them."

At length the ground leveled off, until we came to a plane several acres large, so flat it seemed something had lopped off the top of the mountain the way the machete had decapitated the poor creature before the house. Long buildings of log resembled military barracks, and there were two large constructions of stone standing against a curtain of cane, the stalks growing as high as ten feet, with half-naked creatures plowing aisles through the thick growth with truncated blades, swinging them like sickles. Others gathered the mown stalks and threw them into the beds of wagons hitched to mules and oxen. The crunch of the falling cane and the swish of the bundles as they were piled into heaps sounded like an eighty-mile-an-hour wind leveling a forest.

We alighted from the buggy, and Childress' place was taken by a white man in a butternut uniform, patched and darned all over, who saluted him smartly. He was the first probable member of the major's original command I'd seen apart from Captain McCready. He drove the buggy around the corner of one of the stone buildings.

"I was told so many times that sugar won't grow at this altitude I began to believe it." Childress was shouting over the din. "I've since formed the opinion that the big interests had their eye on the place and sought to discourage competition. As a rule, cane grows to eight feet, sometimes nine; but as you can see, the climate and conditions are ideal, and possibly unique. I provide most of the sugar sold in Acapulco, and since I began marketing in Mexico City, the Cuban interests have petitioned the government to enjoin any United States citizen from participating in the trade. Since I'm the only one in the business, I find that complimentary in the extreme."

"Why would a rich man want to conquer a nation?"

When he scowled, the paper-thin skin plastered to his skull broke into a myriad of wrinkles.

"Money is only a means to power. Any man who would settle for the first is no better than a carpet-bagger."

He pulled open a heavy door, gripping the iron handle with both hands, and we entered one of the stone buildings. When he shut the door behind us, the cacophony outside ceased. The interior was as big as a warehouse on the docks of San Francisco, lit by sunlight canting through mullioned windows just under the rafters, fifteen feet above our heads. Plank catwalks suspended by thick ropes circled the walls and bisected one another in tiers, with more laborers stripped to the waist standing and walking along them, supporting themselves on the hemp rails.

The top tier was occupied entirely by men in Confederate uniform carrying rifles. He saw me looking at them.

"No, they're not enforced labor. They're fed, sheltered, and all their medical needs are addressed, far better than when they were trying to survive on their own. Their tempers are quicker than their powers of reason: An accidental collision is seldom shrugged off, and once engaged, they fight to the death unless someone stops them."

"Shoots them, you mean."

"It rarely comes to that. As I said, their senses are unnaturally acute. The report alone is agony to their ears, and a near-miss is sufficient to distract them. Their ability to maintain their purpose is almost nonexistent. They literally forget what sparked the fight, or that they were fighting at all. Repetitive work like cutting cane and pulling ropes is more suited to them than anything they might attempt through any will of their own.

"I won't show you the other building," he said; "to do so would be redundant, and the heat is miserable. There the cane is mashed into a pulp, boiled in copper cauldrons, and distilled. It liquefies at a temperature of one hundred sixty degrees. I don't know how the brutes stand it. Before I discovered them, the men I employed had to work in shifts no longer than fifteen minutes. We lost three in one month when they weakened and fell into the cauldrons, ruining half a day's output. Here is where the final refinement process takes place."

A waterfall of golden syrupy liquid gushed from a wooden vat tilted on ropes and pulleys into a larger container, filled nearly to the top with black ash and erected on a platform in the center of the hardpack floor. A sluice, wooden also, slanted down from the base of the larger vat into another on the floor, where the liquid came out as clear as water. The air was filled with a stench like scorched hair and the heavier, almost seductive smell of molasses.

"Charcoal." Childress pointed to the contents of the larger vat. "We fire it in kilns from bone, grind it fine in revolving barrels, much like gunpowder, and pour the juice through it, leaving the impurities behind."

I made no response, knowing the source of the bone.

"We let the liquid cool and crystallize in clay vessels. What moisture remains is then spun out of it in more rotating barrels by centrifugal force. The pulverizing itself is by mortar and pestle, albeit it on a grander scale than ordinary."

He turned to face me. "And that, Marshal, is how you manage to take the bitterness out of your coffee."

We went back outside, where the noise of cutting and stacking was as loud as before. Strolling toward the stalks of cane, I peered between the rows.

Childress missed nothing. "Don't strain your eyes looking for the poppies. They're indistinguishable from common weeds when they're not in bloom. In any case I'm phasing out the trade in opium. The refining process is even more elaborate than sugar and the market is limited to those who can afford it. I can move the legitimate product in much greater volume, without fear of confiscation except by the locals, who are cheap to bribe.

"You wouldn't credit it," he said, "but the world's addiction to sugar far surpasses all the others. Any country practitioner can furnish you with laudanum, but men have slain each other over a peppermint stick. If I'd never touched a gram of opium, I doubt you'd have been sent here. A rebellion without financing is only the pipe-dream of a lunatic, but more governments have been overturned on traffic in harmless indulgences than drugs; but try running for re-election on bananas and tobacco."

"What's in the other buildings, besides the barracks and infirmary?"

"The women's quarters; brothel, seraglio, call it what you will. Simple creatures require simple pleasures. The brutes fight over them as much as over anything else, but if I'd left them behind they'd be buggering each other all the time, and I can't have that. Whatever else you may think of me, I am a southern gentleman."

Two flags flew atop the nearest barracks, the stars-and-bars of the Confederacy and the other bearing the visored and laurel-encircled head of the Knights of the Golden Circle. A stable had been built onto the end of the structure, as long as the barracks itself and lined with stalls on both sides. Here one of Childress' creatures was at work shoveling manure into a great pile outside the back entrance, and more well-tended mounts, each branded CSA, blew and twitched their tails at flies. My bay occupied a stall at the end, looking no worse the wear for its journey in the stock car.

Childress' horse and buggy waited for us outside the stable, with the soldier who'd driven it holding it by the bit. He saluted as his commander grasped the frame and started to pull himself into the driver's seat.

His hand lost its grip and he folded slowly to the ground, like a barn collapsing. The soldier lunged forward and stooped to help him up, but he was as limp as the dead creature the others had slung onto the bonepile, his face even grayer than before. Major Oscar Childress, the southern gentleman who owned slaves, sold poison, ran whores, and conspired in treason, was close to death.

TWENTY-SEVEN

Childress, I decided, was never far outside the scrutiny of his subordinates. No sooner had the soldier lifted him from the ground than Captain McCready appeared, straddling his fine sorrel, and swung down from the saddle in one fluid movement. He took the fallen man by the shoulders, the other by the ankles, and together they carried him to the next barracks over. I followed, leaving Childress' straw hat where it had landed.

The room they took him to was small and separated from the rest of the building with a pine partition, scoured white and stinking of carbolic. A hospital bed erected on a system of cranks and wheels stood in the center of the room, made up in fresh linen, with two down pillows and a thick cotton blanket rolled up at the foot in a topsheet. In seconds they had the patient laid out with the covers drawn to his chin. Dismissed, the soldier evaporated; there's no better way to describe how quickly he made himself absent.

There was an evil smell about the place I knew all too well, apart from the carbolic: the thick air of ether, old blood, rotting flesh, and alcohol; gallons of the last, splashed about like water on a raging fire, and over it all the gaseous residue of human organs exposed to the air. It brought me back to a place and a time I'd hoped was long behind me; of a mildewed tent in a farmer's decimated field packed with sweating, cursing orderlies, frantic surgeons, and grown men screaming for their mothers. The farther you got away from a thing the closer you came back to it.

"Lift his head."

There being no one else present, I slid a hand behind Childress' head and raised it while the captain opened a shallow drawer in a cabinet with a zinc top and took out a red morocco case the thickness of a deck of cards but twice as long. Tipping back the lid, he drew a steel syringe from its form-fitted depression, a squat brown bottle from another, shook the bottle, drew the cork, and filled the syringe with a sucking sound. He restopped and replaced the bottle, tapped the barrel of the syringe, depressed the plunger, squirting an arc of liquid from the end of the hollow needle, and in a series of deft motions wetted a wad of cotton from another container he'd taken from the drawer, tipped something from another bottle into the wad, and cocked an elbow, pointing at his superior's near arm with an unmistakable gesture.

Unmistakable for only a few.

How he knew I'd filled in for a stricken orderly at Cold Harbor I never learned; either he'd studied my record or expected me to understand what must have been an automatic action. Whichever was the case, he'd judged correctly. I rolled back Childress' sleeve and watched as he daubed the inside of the major's elbow with the cotton swab, filling the room with the sharp stench of alcohol, cast the swab to the floor, pierced the vein he knew was there, and made the injection.

"Opium?" I asked.

"Highly distilled," he said. "One of the major's discoveries. I don't pretend to know how it works, only that it does."

I watched Childress' face, gray as dead clay. He'd been breathing shallowly, in short bursts. As the medicine took hold, his lungs filled, then emptied, and fell afterward into the rhythm of a man in deep slumber.

All the paraphernalia was returned to its place in the same measured order as it had been brought into play. McCready cocked his head to bring his one eye to the operation. I saw then that the dead socket wasn't empty after all: Worm-shaped muscles pulsed as if they were still in charge of a working orb.

"I know a glass-blower in Helena who could fit you with an eye no one would notice," I said. "A U.S.

senator came all the way from Washington on his reputation."

"I tried that. A fellow from someplace called Vienna had one painted from a chip he matched to the eye God gave me. Beautiful thing. I keep it in the case it came with." He shook his head. "Too much time had passed. The skin had shriveled too far to support it. It kept popping out at inopportune times. Better the truth up front than to have the lie exposed over a plate of oysters in champagne sauce."

He smiled then; anyway the wide, thin-lipped mouth in the piebald face twitched at the corners. I felt a twinge of respect, for the soldier if not for the executioner. We might have faced each other across a battlefield strewn with men we'd both murdered for no reason I could remember, but loyalty is rare even in civilization.

"What's his complaint?"

"He's being eaten from inside; it's this blasted climate, and his own genius consuming itself in the company of idiots. It hasn't gotten to his brain, that much is certain. That's the hell of it. Those brutes next door, dying of their own sinful birth, don't know what's happening to them, and are all the better for it."

As if in response, a guttural cry arose from one of the adjacent rooms. If it had been at least half-animal I could have put it aside; that it was more than half-human was impossible to ignore.

McCready was an educated man, that much was certain. The southern universities had it all over the ivy leagues of the North. Their founders had come straight from Oxford and Cambridge.

"How long does he have?" I asked.

"He went to see a specialist in El Paso. Crossing the border could have meant his life, but I suppose he found that preferable to this. The doctor could have practiced in Chicago or Denver, maybe even New York City, but he was loyal to the War for Southern Independence, and couldn't countenance treating Yankees. He estimated six months. That was a year and a half ago. The major rebels against everything." He stuck out his hand. "Eustace McCready, Captain of the Confederacy."

I gripped the hand as firmly as I could. It was like taking hold of a train coupling. "Page Murdock, Corporal of the Union."

The mouth parted, exposing a fine set of coral-colored teeth: He seemed to know his wine. "I started as a corporal with the Chesterfield Volunteers."

A division I was unfamiliar with; but then Childress had assembled his own regiment from among the oldest families in Virginia. "My mistake," I said. "I wasn't aware you'd worked for a living."

He made a sound I took for amusement. We were close comrades, for that moment at least; and in silence agreed how sorry we'd be when one of us killed the other.

He pried apart Childress' eyelids, striking a match off a thumbnail to study the pupils. "He'll rest for a day. With God's good grace he'll come out of it roaring for someone's head. I don't envy the first of these brutes who fall beneath his expectations."

"Well, you need the bones."

McCready straightened to his full height, easily a head above mine, and fixed me with his eye, blue-green and as clear as egg-whites around the irises.

"He doesn't need the excuse. This country is as rich in game as the one you came from, before the blasted federals raped it of buffalo to bring the Indians to their knees. That grizzly the brutes slew and dragged across the tracks will be harvested and put to good use. What does it serve to set aside the bones of these creatures—or you, or me, comes to that—to waste in graves? If we truly believed in life hereafter, there would be no reason to visit a cemetery. I'd rather my remains be put to use than moldering six feet under. The uncivilized peoples of the East believe that death is not final, only rebirth. Who is to say I won't some-day sweeten the tea of a saint?"

"Or of a St. Louis whore; you don't have a vote. You're just coughing up something your worshipful master said over a dinner table."

"And who do you serve, that fat New York Yankee in the White House?"

"Is that who's in? I haven't voted since Abe Lincoln."

"That carpetbagger?"

I looked around the room. Apart from another finely woven rug, it was undecorated except for a small paint-ing in a heavy frame: Another murky representation of coarsely dressed peasants, this time gouging the eyes out of another captive in the rags of a fine uniform. I made some comment about his commander's taste in art.

McCready's eyes jerked toward the painting. "He buys those at auction, by wire. I don't see much dif-ference between them and Antietam."

"He wants to bring it all back," I said. "If you re-ally want to know who I'm serving, it's anyone who stands in front of that."

Just then the soldier he'd dismissed entered. I saw from his unlined face, the chin pale of any trace of shaved whiskers, that he was too young to have served

Childress in combat. The generation that had come up since the war had been all too ready to offer its services to the glamour of a lost cause.

McCready returned his salute. "What?"

"Sir. The men are wondering."

"*Wondering?*" He pronounced the word as if it belonged to a foreign language.

The young man cleared his throat; if anyone had ever wanted to be somewhere else, this was him. "In the absence of the major, are the maneuvers to proceed as always?"

The captain inhaled and exhaled, a mighty gust. "Look you, private. Who is the man in this bed?"

To his credit, the private didn't look. "Major Childress, sir."

"Is he absent?"

"No, sir!" Had the young man straightened further, his spine would have cracked.

"Then go to the devil with you, and look smart during the maneuvers."

"Yes, sir!"

McCready deflated a little after the man's exit. "If this is what we have to work with, so be it. The major will whip them into shape."

Just then the major drew a mighty breath. His eyes opened, exposing the bright orbs, blazing now, like dying suns: the same fierce fire that had come through at Cold Harbor and Bull Run. We both leaned in to hear his gasp:

"God forgive me."

He'd taken in too much breath for the purpose; the rest went out in a gush of air. It was his last.

TWENTY-EIGHT

When great men die, they say, the room in which they expired always seems larger; as if the soul that had passed from it had filled it to the walls.

Oscar Childress' death-room didn't look or feel any different from when he'd been brought there, his heart still beating, feeding that singular brain. The man himself seemed smaller; but even dolts shrivel a bit when the life-force has departed.

He lay with his eyes open—less bright by the moment—and his lips still parted just enough to let his last three words escape. He'd have hated them, I was sure. He had to have known his time was near, and thought to draft a valedictory worthy of a giant; but even a gifted actor can forget his lines in a role more challenging than the rest. *God forgive me*: a plea so banal as to be worthy of any of his brainless creatures.

McCready—inspired, perhaps, by his commander's triteness at the finish—performed the conventional duties, kneading shut his eyes and tipping the jaw closed. Comically, it dropped back open, forcing him to repeat the operation and hold it for a moment like a cabinetmaker clamping two pieces of wood together until the glue set. From Moses to Alexander to Washington, and all the saints and generals who had come before and between and after, the epilogue would have proceeded similarly, with a lesser light sweeping up the ashes of the extinguished blaze. I left then. He'd forgotten about me, and would hold that position until the dead muscles went rigid, if that was what it took.

The infirmary was built on the shotgun plan, with the rooms connected end-to-end like railroad cars. I went through a door, crossed a vacant room with the mattress rolled up against a plain iron headboard, and entered the next. There lay Joseph, on his back with a thin blanket drawn to his bare chest and his hands folded on top of it. I stood watching for several seconds before I confirmed his chest was rising and falling. His eyes didn't open and I chose not to wake him. There was a forest of brown bottles on a plain table beside the bed, some with rubber droppers. The air was strong with a sharp smell I'd grown accustomed to lately: the fumes from the juice distilled from cinchona bark, Mexico's answer to malaria. I took myself back out.

The captain was still standing beside Childress' bed, with his chin on his chest and his hands crossed at his waist. Whether he was praying silently or waiting for his master to rise from the dead I couldn't say; more likely for a military man he was considering the next move. I left, making as little noise as possible. He seemed to have forgotten I existed, which was how I would have had it.

There was no sign of my saddle or bridle in the stables. Likely it had been left aboard the *Ghost* when my bay was hitched to one of the wagons. I outfitted it with the tack available and picked my way back down the trail, dismounting and leading it when the way narrowed and an attack of malaria might throw off my balance at any minute. The creatures clearing away fallen debris went on working as I passed; without Childress along, I might have been a bird pecking for grubs in cracks for all I was visible to them.

Nearing the house I passed the cannon I'd heard earlier, a blue-black six-pounder Napoleon mounted on wheels as tall as a man, stinking, like the dead grizzly, of rancid fat greasing the barrel and also the sulphur stench of burnt cordite, and here and there a soldier on foot or on horseback, their uniforms tidy but as patched and darned as ancient quilts. Once again, I attracted little attention. I could have pranced around in the arrogant scarlet of a Yankee Zouave and drawn no more than a sneer. In an armed camp, much is taken for granted.

"Major Childress is dead."

The captain's drill-trained voice rang without emotion; he must have finished tidying up just after I left and ridden straight back to the barn. A contingent of men wearing uniforms in varying degrees of repair would be gathered in formation before the house, with their immediate commander standing at parade rest on the front porch. There would be a general removal of hats.

Apart from the announcement itself, which reached me in Childress' study, I assumed the scene had played out as described; I'd only heard the bugle call to Assembly and the jingling of raiments and sabers.

The key was missing from the lock, but I rolled the desk chair across the room and tilted it, jamming the back under the knob. I wished it hadn't had casters; a strong shove would clear the path inside, but it would slow an intruder down for a second or two.

The room was as the major had left it, with the enormous book he'd been reading still flayed open on the desk; a thing of stiff heavy leaves unevenly cut and decorated with pen-and-ink illustrations tinted by a hand that had been skeletal for at least two centuries, lettered elaborately in a language I will never know; from the charted coastlines and studies of animals I recognized as pumas and buffalo despite their exaggerated features, it seemed to be a tract on the New World based on early French explorations; in all likelihood his talk of monsters on the map had prompted him to crack it. The pipe he'd smoked while reading, carved from ivory (or what I hoped was ivory) into the likeness of a horned creature with an amber stem, lay still warm in an onyx bowl, permeating the room further with its rich fragrance.

Another smell, coarser and acidic, drew my attention to the parlor stove and to its door, which was slightly ajar. I took it by its dangling coiled handle, tipped it open, drew a short poker from the brass rack beside the stove, and separated the ashes, which had gone out but for a few sparks that erupted into vertical threads of flame when I disturbed them. A bit of charred cloth came apart from a thick sheaf of burned paper, which itself separated in two sections, exposing under it an image impressed on stiff cardboard curved at the corners. A hole had burned through the center, obliterating the face, but the flames had cast a rose hue on what was left of a high-collared dress—bombazine, beyond doubt. I felt no need to go into the room where I'd slept to confirm that he'd taken the photograph from the silver frame on the nightstand and burned it along with the letters the woman had written to him. He hadn't even bothered to untie the ribbon, much less read them. I'd fretted for nothing over whether they'd reached him and what might happen to his creatures if they'd failed to deliver them.

I remembered Childress' notes on his report to the American authorities, and the possibly mistranslated suggestion to "plant seeds" (*matea*) among the unsophisticated natives of Mexico to foster their awestruck regard for their neighbors to the North America: What he'd actually written was *mata*: "kill." The error had not been his. A man who would exterminate the creatures, as he had been doing piecemeal on the pretext of setting an example to the others, would destroy every link to the civilized life he'd known in Virginia.

For months or years, he'd slept beside that likeness, until it occupied his thoughts no more (or not as much) as his paintings of fierce peasants torturing prisoners of war to death, until the letters came to remind him. Then he'd thrown the photograph in the fire with the lot.

I went back to the desk. The belly drawer was unlocked, but there was nothing of interest in it. The same was true of five of the six deeper drawers that flanked the kneehole. The last I tried was locked. I'd seen nothing resembling a key, but took a silver-plated paper knife from the blotter and poked it this way and that inside the keyhole, tugging on the bronze lion's-head knob, until something snapped and the drawer came open.

The first thing that greeted me was my old Deane-Adams in its gun belt. I inspected the cylinder, found all the chambers loaded, and buckled the rig around my waist. I looked for the Bulldog revolver, without success; but I hadn't had it nearly as long and was less familiar with it, so I didn't spend much time regretting the loss.

On the bottom of the drawer lay a black iron strong box edged with gilded oak leaves. It, too, was locked, but I inserted the scratched paper knife under the lid and forced it open.

Some of the papers inside were in Latin. These I set aside. At the bottom was a long parchment envelope sealed with the K.G.C. crest impressed in red wax. I broke it open and unfolded the parchment sheets from inside. It was lettered in copperplate and signed by Childress.

I skimmed through the bequests; for it bore all the highblown obsolete language of a will. There was no mention of his fiancée's name, and I recognized none of the others. Upon the signer's passing, command of the army was to pass to Eustace McCready, Captain (to be promoted to the brevet rank of major upon acceptance). On the fourth page was the passage I'd been looking for:

> Under no circumstances is my death or incapacity to interfere with the purpose of this militia, which is to march upon Mexico City and by military engagement induce the government of Mexico to surrender the command of its forces to Captain McCready, who will annex them to the militia and invade the United States of America.

A sound outside brought me to my feet; it was the clank of a dangling saber in its metal scabbard banging against a boot-top. Either Captain McCready or one of his subordinates was coming to gather the personal effects of their deceased leader or was looking for me.

I refolded the sheets and put them in the inside pocket of my coat.

My way was clear. If my suspicions were right and I had been allowed to live only because Childress wanted fresh conversation, my usefulness was at an end. Unless McCready disobeyed the posthumous command—and if anything the man would be even more fanatically devoted to the major now than when he breathed, he'd be more interested in taking possession of the *Ghost,* in which case Joseph the engineer's existence was more secure than my own. The Indian had saved my life, but he was in no condition to escape that place, and from what I'd seen of the infirmary his chances were better there than anywhere within a hundred miles.

But a hundred miles from where? I had no idea how far I'd been brought from the train, or in which direction other than up. To miss it by fifty yards in either direction would be the same as missing it entirely. I could wander along the rails for days, then blunder into an ambush; or break my neck riding down a grade as steep as a grain elevator in search of a fly-speck on the map called Cabo Falso.

Map.

The saber was jangling down the hallway. I spotted the ancient Spanish wall decoration in its frame. I took along the paper knife and slashed the map all around the inside edge. The doorknob rattled, someone pushed at the door, encountered the resistance of the chair. Whoever it was put his shoulder into it. The chair's wheels skidded out from under it and it fell on its back. It bought me a second.

I bought another. A slug from the Deane-Adams split a heavy panel. I hadn't hoped to hit anything, just play for time. I loped to the connecting door to the bedroom.

The key was in the lock. I turned it and swung open the door just in time to stop a slug from the man who'd pushed in from the hall. Just as I jerked the door shut, I caught a glimpse of a gaping eye socket in a face black with fury.

TWENTY-NINE

The room where I'd recovered was a bedroom once again, with no sign of the bathtub or shaving materials; the late Major Childress had run a tight ship in a country not notorious for its discipline. I'd brought the key inside with me and turned it in the lock just as a hand grasped the knob on the other side, and got away from the door an instant ahead of the next bullet. This one penetrated the thick pine and punched a hole in the tall window across from it.

I didn't waste time returning fire. In another moment the lock would be shot off or the door forced. I snatched up the heavy washstand and flung it that direction, but I didn't look to see if it fell to the floor in a position to slow down pursuit. That kind of time goes for gold double-eagles, and I hadn't a penny to spare. I crumpled up the ancient map and stuffed it into a pocket on the run.

The window was the only other way out. I used the barrel of my revolver to clear away the rest of the glass and got a leg over the sill just as the crash came, accompanied by splintering wood. For good measure I slung another piece of lead that direction and dropped four feet to the ground.

Or to be more exact, onto a pile of skeletons. At that corner of the house they reached to the sill.

There was no getting through that grotesque stack except the long way. The closest end, at the rear of the house, led to a cliff that fell hundreds of feet almost straight down the mountain. I'd climbed and descended as bad in like situations, but not when I was still recovering from serious illness, with the possibility of a fresh attack coming on while I was hanging by my fingers from a slippery shelf of rock. Even if I made it to level ground, I'd be on foot in country I didn't know and easily recaptured. I'd left my bay tethered to the rail of the front porch.

So on I went, stumbling over rib cages, flinging aside skulls and pelvises and arms angled like cranes. Stiff jagged fingers snagged my coat and snatched at my hat as if they were the last to give up. Razor-sharp sternums slashed at my shins. I tripped and fell, shouting, into grisly spirals of bone, struggled in a panic to untangle myself from limbs I swore still had life in them. There was more than dried stalks in that heap; it had been added to as recently as that morning, and I breathed through my mouth to avoid the stench when I wasn't gritting my teeth against the likelihood of sinking my fingers into rotting remains. Flies the size of hummingbirds floated on the foul air, buzzing drunkenly, their abdomens glistening emerald-green. They landed on my face, favoring the moist corners of my mouth and eyes, and quitted with sullen reluctance when I swiped at them. They flew so slowly, fattened on their feast, I caught three of them in mid-air, only half-trying, and batted them to the ground. All around me sections of human jetsam plinked and plunked and clattered like someone striking together hollow sticks for the pure perverse pleasure of making a racket.

The same thing was happening behind me, as McCready came hard on my heels.

A bullet screamed a foot past my ear and crackled to a stop in a nest of bones. I didn't stop, and when he heard the noise he returned to the chase. I'd gained ground while he stopped to level his pistol.

My luck held. I made my way through that charnel yard without encountering putrefying flesh, and stumbled into the open.

My luck didn't hold. My bay wasn't where I'd left it.

No, it still held. When I raced around the end of the porch, it was standing nearer the front door; I'd been careless with the tether, leaving enough slack for the animal to drag it down toward an inviting clump of grass.

That was where my luck gave out. A group of men dressed in rags with pinched-in heads stood at the far end of the house facing me, their eyes dull between sunken temples, but their unsheathed machetes burning bright in the sun.

I didn't want to do it. The wretches were little more than the brutes Childress had called them, but human, and hardly in command of their lives. They existed because of Childress and for Childress; they knew no other god. When the first one lumbered toward me, raising his short-bladed weapon, I shot a fresh hole in the crown of his hat high up, snatching it off his low cranium. I might have been shooting at the house for all the effect it had. He took another stumbling step, swinging the machete back as far as his arm would reach. Cracked lips skinned back from black gums, spittle bubbling in the corners.

I aimed lower and fired. He was still coming when the scarlet stain spread all the way across his belly; then he tripped over his own feet and fell headlong, landing stiff as a plank with his weapon still at arm's length, and lay without jerking so much as a nerve.

By then the others were on the move. If, as the major

had said, they understood only fear and hatred, the second was stronger than the first. I didn't think they mourned their comrade so much as saw me for a member of an alien tribe, where wrath and fear intermingled, like grease and fire, leading to white flame. It hardly seemed possible the news of Childress' death had reached them, but if their instincts were as bestial as he'd made them out to be, they might have smelled it, the way they said some breeds of dog can detect disease before a trained physician can suspect it. In any case his order to spare me from harm was no longer regarded.

I could have shot them all. It was a small group, and their reflexes were so primitive it would have been like picking bottles off a fence rail, but maybe because of that I saw no honor in it, even in defense of my own life. When the first of the rest came within blade's reach I swept the barrel of the revolver against his wrist, where the bone was as obvious as those in the pile I'd struggled my way through, and striking it with a noise that was half-thump, half-crack. He yelped and stumbled, losing his grip on his weapon, and I followed through, shoving him off his feet with my forearm.

By then I had my hand on the bay's reins, but as I jerked them loose of the rail a vise closed on my gun arm just above the elbow. It went dead to the shoulder and I felt the butt slipping through my fingers. The creature could have cracked a cue ball in that fist. Something flashed in the sun; I threw up my other arm, expecting the blade to slash through muscle and tendon as easily as it sliced cane; but something struck with a thud and a third eye opened at the bridge of his nose. The machete spun out of his hand, hitting my shoulder with the flat of the blade and bouncing off.

He fell even faster than his partner; those weak minds had only a tenuous connection to their bodies, and switched off like a telegraph key snatched loose of its wires.

I heard the echo of the shot then, but I didn't sacrifice a second looking over my shoulder to confirm it was McCready who'd fired. I swung the bay between me and his weapon, hooked one foot over the edge of the saddle, and loosed a round close enough to its ear to put it to gallop. We took off toward the mountain trail I'd come up by wagon, I riding Apache fashion, hanging on by a handful of mane with one foot lifted just short of the ground and the horse serving as a moving breastwork shielding me from lead.

Not that it stopped the captain, who seemed to have no more sentiment for the beast than I; a bullet struck the saddlehorn square, gouging the leather and ricocheting off the hickory core, and when I had the opportunity later to examine the bay's hindquarters I saw where another had plowed a furrow a half-inch deep through the flesh behind the cantle.

Which would have been the moment when the animal screamed and took off like Pegasus.

I wouldn't repeat that ride. The way down from the house to where we'd left the train was as steep as the way up from it to the plantation, but I'd made both trips aboard the relative safety of a wheeled vehicle under someone's control. Just galloping on flat ground plugged my throat with my heart, and I don't trust the animal at even a slow walk.

More shots came, rattling and growing fainter. When they stopped—to reload, I thought—I swung my leg across the saddle and pulled myself upright, and almost as an afterthought holstered the Deane-Adams. I'd shifted it to my left hand in order to grasp the bay's mane with the other; the bandage on the bullet-crease in the left had come loose in the meanwhile. I unwound it and threw it away. The wound was still angry red, but it had closed. Taking care to keep it from bleeding again was less of a distraction than the bandage itself.

Distractions I had in plenty. Behind me I heard the pounding of more than one set of hooves. McCready had rallied all the troops handy. Childress had been over-conscientious in writing down his wishes for his campaign against Mexico and the United States to continue after his death. If his captain was this determined to prevent me from reporting back to Washington, he had no intention of abandoning his predecessor's mad dream.

The road narrowed. I slowed my pace, ducking overhanging tree limbs, and took a nearly vertical grade with the reins taut and leaning back parallel with the side of the mountain. The bay picked its way daintily, whistling through its nostrils, eyes rolling over white. That was the test of a good mount; but you never knew how it would measure up until you put your hide on the line. I cursed Judge Blackthorne more often than I praised him, but when it came to outfitting the men he sent into hazard he spent every nickel he kicked and bit the Congress to get, and when it pulled tight its purse strings he chipped in from his own household accounts. This was a good horse.

I found respect then for the creatures who had carried me up that same route by wagon. And I was grateful I'd spent so much of the trip senseless. At times the way was so narrow they had to have rigged ropes to steady the wagons when the outside wheels had no purchase, and just how they'd managed a ton of Gatling has vexed me in all the years since.

The sun was making its rapid descent behind the mountains before I felt secure enough to dismount and lead the bay down the more precarious stretches. After pounding along in the first heat of pursuit, McCready's cavalry had had to slow down, and with darkness piling up the echo of hoofbeats had receded. I didn't dare hope they'd given up, but Childress' insanity hadn't spread so far they'd risk riding that terrain at night. I made a cold camp in the shelter of a shale shelf, sitting up with my back against the Sierras and my revolver in my lap, listening to a healthy set of three-year-old teeth chomping grass and wondering if I'd ever set foot on level ground again.

I dreamed I had, my boots clomping a civilized boardwalk on a street as flat as a lily pond, touching my hat to men and women who'd never heard of Ralph Waldo Emerson and when they spooned sugar into their coffee didn't pause to consider where it had come from and whose bones it had sifted through; and woke in gray light, still a thousand feet above the ocean and Cape Hell.

The birds were awake, singing their sweet melodies of murder. A twig snapped. It was as loud as a pistol report at that empty hour. The birds heard it, too, and went silent. I looked at the bay, standing with its forefeet crossed, eyes shut and breathing evenly; it hadn't stirred in its sleep. I stood and swung the Deane-Adams up the trail, where the danger was greatest. An iron shoe scraped rock. I rolled back the hammer. The crackle echoed among the surrounding peaks, followed by thick silence.

"Do not shoot."

I recognized the voice, the accent. It had been so long since I'd heard it, I couldn't place it at first.

"Come out in the open."

The shoe clanged again, then another and another. I steadied the revolver against my hip, concentrating on the curve of the mountain. Most of a minute passed; I could have measured the time with a calendar. Then a man appeared, leading a gray mule with a rope bridle and only a worn and faded blanket for a saddle.

"It is I, *Senor* Deputy."

I seated the hammer and leathered the pistol. It was the first time Joseph had addressed me as anything more than an equal since he'd promoted himself to engineer.

THIRTY

He wore the white cotton shirt and trousers of Childress' creatures, and sandals in place of his boots. He was pale and gaunt, and when he spoke he broke often to take in air. I took the mule's reins from him, tethered it to a stunted pinon, and helped him into a sitting position under the rock shelf, lowering myself beside him; two pilgrims resting from their travels.

"I didn't think you could make it out of that bed," I said.

"I was awakened by shouting, and guessed the rest. Major Childress—"

"I was there when he died."

"One of those—things was in the room next to mine, with its legs in splints. I took its clothes from a cupboard, and unhitched this animal from a wagon outside."

"How did you get past McCready and the others?"

"I grew up in these mountains. I know a hundred trails to their one."

"You should have stayed where you were. They'd have taken care of you. Without you they can't run the *Ghost*."

"And when they have learned to run it themselves, what? What they did to that man this morning would have been a mercy compared to what would happen if they turned me over to those creatures, as surely they would have done, to keep them *docil*. You saw how I was treated on the way to that devil's place." He flexed his shoulders, still raw from the cross.

"Are you up to this trip?"

"More so than you. You will never find your way to where we were taken following this road. In two miles it winds back into the mountain."

I unfolded the map from my pocket and showed it to him. He shook his head. "This will not get you to Cabo Falso, unless your bones are discovered and brought down the mountain. The Spaniards did not bother to explore this high, with gold so plentiful down below. A man could follow these trails for weeks and finish where he started. Did you forget the man DeBeauclair?"

"He was killed by Childress' men."

"Perhaps. There are creatures as dangerous, men and pumas, and then there are the mountains themselves. Do you think he cared whether he was slain by a bullet or slipped and fell a thousand feet onto his head? Do the men whose bones are piled at Childress' house care? No, *senor*; I did not drag you back from death to see you throw away your life because of a worthless piece of paper."

I put it away and rose. "There's no time to argue."

He ignored the hand I held out and pulled himself to his feet. "I think the captain must give up. Someone must look after the plantation."

"He's got twice as much reason now to keep going."

He did allow me to help him onto the mule's back. He took the lead then. After about a mile we heard hooves ringing on stone. I'd as soon have been proven wrong.

Just about then the grade to our left eased up and we left the road, dismounting to walk our animals through scrub and zigzag washes where the runoff from the rainy season carved treacherous ditches through earth and rock. He kept going as steadily as if he were following a flagstone path, detouring occasionally to go around a dense copse of pine or an enormous boulder, and always returning to his original course—I supposed. For all I made sense of our way we might have been traveling in circles; there were times even when I was sure we were going up instead of down, and I told him so.

"We are," he said, "for the moment. The Mother Mountains are not so kind as the Blessed Virgin."

"Will McCready be taking this route?"

"I think not. There are others easier on horses, but which take them farther out of the way."

I remembered that around noon, when the bay started favoring its left forehoof and with no knife handy I had to use my belt buckle to pry a mesquite thorn from the fetlock. Putting the cavalry farther behind us was a fair trade for the hazards of rough country.

We rested oftener than I liked, despite the advantage. Joseph never complained, but when I saw him list in his seat I reached over to touch his elbow and we dismounted so he could stretch out in the shade and gather strength. He'd started out pale under the brown of his race, and had taken on a yellowish tinge that disturbed me, and his skin glistened with more than just the sweat of effort. But in each case he recovered, or professed to have recovered, in less time than I would have in his condition, and what he knew of the fruits of his native land more than made up for the delay. The roots we ate were edible, however a St. Louis chef might scorn them for their bitter taste and toughness, and he had a botanist's knowledge of which plants flourished in the arid season because of the water they stored in their bulbous roots.

At dark we camped in a horseshoe-shaped depression gouged in passing by the heel of a glacier a million years before Solomon. He scraped the dirt off an albino hunk of twisted vegetation, broke it in two, and handed me half. We crunched and chewed and sat admiring a view New York millionaires shipped themselves first-class to Switzerland to see: thousands of acres of two-hundred-foot pines descending in rows like seats in an opera house to flat white sand—brief as a cuticle seen from that height—and beyond it the empty sky that hung over the blue Pacific.

He tipped back his head and spread his nostrils. They were as wide as shotgun bores. "I smell rain. At the first drop, we climb out of this hole fast as we can manage. I had a cousin who lay down in a dry riverbed to sleep off a bag of wine and woke up drowned to death."

"A puma would have got him sooner or later."

"One did. They are not always partial to live prey."

I laughed like an idiot. The joke wasn't that good, but it seemed I hadn't felt the urge since Helena. He stared at me for most of a minute, then dropped his jaw and let fly with the kind of hooting laughter you never saw in dime-novel Indians. I'd spent enough time with them to know they were gifted clowns, every last one, but it had been so long since I'd been in one's presence when he was in the mood I laughed harder yet, until I choked on my root and he slapped me on my back until I coughed it out.

If a man can love another man without inviting cruel whispers, I loved this one. I never knew what became of him. Three days later, spent crunching through scrub, picking our way across acres of rock, and trotting too briefly along stretches of level road, we came upon the *Ghost,* standing just as we'd left it, with the tree that had blocked it waiting to be removed, as calm as any great beast at rest, and after I traded my stolen gear for my good saddle and bridle from the stock car we parted company. Joseph assured me that my three-hundred-year-old map would get me to Cabo Falso–Cabo Infierno, Cape Hell, whatever you wanted to call it. I'd been there and back without ever seeing the place that sought the honor.

I patted the pocket containing Oscar Childress' last will and testament. It would be evidence enough for the United States to press the Mexican government to lay siege to the late major's plantation; with the usual contingent of U.S. troops serving in an "advisory capacity." That was how we'd taken the Southwestern states from Mexico in the first place.

"In Cabo Falso, where there is law to protect law, you may wire *Los Estados Unidos* and arrange your transportation back to the Montana Territory. Even Captain McCready would not attempt an action there that would place his dead master's grand plan at risk. They haven't everything yet in place; that much I overheard in my sickbed."

"You won't come with me?"

He shook his head. The sallowness was gone from his face, and it seemed to me it had started to take on flesh; although how those blasted roots could contribute to that I couldn't imagine. After forty years I wake from a dream of Mexico with that sharp taste on my tongue.

"I said I wish to be the first of my tribe to drive a train across the length of the Sierra Madre," he said. "What has happened since to make you think I would change my mind?"

"You haven't anything to defend it." I unshipped the Deane-Adams and held it out, butt-first.

One of his rare grins cracked his face, blinding white against the brown. "You will need it more than I, if you are to make your way back to your home. Have we not heard our pursuers, resolute even as of this morning? I have a weapon far more *efectivo*." He slapped the *Ghost*'s cowcatcher. It resonated like a great iron bell. At times I hear it still.

THE BOOK OF
MURDOCK

To Lydia Morgan Hopper:
God bless the child

For there is not a just man upon earth, that doeth good, and sinneth not.

—Ecclesiastes 7:20

The Seventh Angel

And the seventh angel sounded ... And the temple of God was opened in heaven, and there was seen in his temple the ark of his testament; and there were lightnings, and voices, and thunderings, and an earthquake, and great hail.

—REVELATION 11:15–19

On the last day of my life I went into Chicago Joe's Coliseum and ordered a cognac. The place had another name now, but those of us who remembered when the town was put together with canvas and tobacco spit still called it Chicago Joe's, or just the Coliseum if a lady was listening. It was fitted out more like a private parlor than a saloon, with brocade curtains covering the passage to the separate room where ladies sent their serving girls to have their pails filled with beer, but once you knew the place you could never look upon mahogany and flocked paper again without getting thirsty. The cuspidors were lined with blue porcelain and there was a brass call box on the wall at the end of the bar where the staff kept track of orders from upstairs. None of its pointers had been moved off level; it was late morning, with floaters drifting in shafts of sunlight, and all the hostesses were asleep.

The bartender was a hairy-fisted relic of tin-pan days, a veteran of bare-knuckle fights in the camp. Scar tissue blistered his face and his milky right eye moved independently of its mate, like a cue ball rolling aimlessly on a billiard table at sea. "What's the occasion? Old Gideon's more your taste." He poured a swallow of French into a cordial glass and restopped the bottle right away; evaporation cost dear.

"Today's my birthday."

"Which one?"

"The latest."

"Many happy returns."

He didn't try to sound sincere and I didn't pretend he was. I'd arrested him once for selling cigars without a federal license and shot a generous customer over some official matter I'd forgotten. The man had lived but lost the use of an arm, and after that he'd counted his change more closely. There was no guild for stove-up ranch hands, and consequently no pension.

But despite past differences the bartender was in decent humor when I slung back the drink and ordered another. I fancied there was even a twinkle in his blind eye. For the world had come round: A mail robber I'd chased into a ravine, shattering his mare's cannon, had been released by congressional intervention and was in town looking for redress for the loss of a favorite horse. The common wisdom was he was the better marksman and his reflexes were superior, he being younger. For once the common wisdom was right. I'd have been better off if I'd deprived him of a brother or a friendly banker, losses more easily forgotten; but pipe dreams ran higher than cognac.

I took more time with the second drink, pooling it on my tongue and letting it glide down, scraped a fifty-cent piece across the bar, and pocketed every penny that came back.

"And no more than justice it is," I heard the bartender mutter as I pushed out through the doors.

It was a clear crisp day—a regular Montana Particular—a little flinty with the wind skidding off the snowcaps on the Divide, setting my face tingling, flushed as it was from the good liquor. It wasn't cold enough to cover my best suit of clothes with bearskin or even heavy twill. The sky hurt to look at.

It depressed me beyond language. I'd buried my father on just such a day, and as I leaned on the shovel all I could think of was the splendor he'd missed. How much better to go into the ground with the clouds as black as weeds and weeping.

But no day is a good day to die. The Indians were as wrong about that as they were about everything else.

The local loafers were all out enjoying the first stretch of pleasant weather since the sodden thaw, smoking, yarning, scratching at the lively activity in their longhandles, and admiring the golden-brown arc their spittle made as it cleared the hitching rails and splashed into the muddy street. I knew a few of them to talk to, but they all withdrew inside or down the boardwalk as I approached, as nonchalant as spooked antelope. What I had was worse than smallpox. I tightened my left arm against my ribs just to feel the solid lump of the Deane-Adams in my armpit.

A water wagon passed, spilling its inevitable leakage from staves inadequately treated with pitch. I waited for it to clear, then stepped off the boards to cross Bridge Street. I'd just come out of the shade of the porch when the shock came.

I heard the crash and identified it even as I was falling. I hadn't counted on a carbine, or that it would be fired from a second-story window of the Bannack Hotel on the other side of Main. The echo growled in the mountains as I lay in the mud pedaling one leg for a purchase I couldn't find. A crowd gathered around. There's always a crowd to be had, no matter how empty the street at the start. You can't beat blood or free beer for civic interest.

I hoped they'd get the dates right on the stone. Hickok had made it only as far as thirty-nine, and mine is a competitive spirit.

I

Judge Blackthorne's
Epistle to the
Texicans

ONE

How much do you know about the Bible?"

"It's black, isn't it?"

Judge Harlan A. Blackthorne and I were seated in the library of the Helena Stockmen's Club on Fuller Street, drinking claret with a shard of rye, the Judge's own concoction, called Old Thunder's Gavel by the deputies who served him. The only book present was a hollowed-out copy of the *Montana Territorial Code* containing the pocket model Colt the Judge carried in response to the latest threat against his life. The club's reading material stood in presses in the dining room, clearing space for its much larger liquor supply inside oak cabinets in the room where we sat.

His expression betrayed a piety that didn't match his Satanic features and pitchfork beard. But as usual he shifted his annoyance to a less revealing subject. "Damn it, Deputy, I know your prejudice against displaying the badge of office, but you might pay me the respect of wearing it in my presence."

"Yes, Your Honor." I foraged it from a pocket and pinned it on. Blackthorne scowled whenever I addressed him by any title other than Judge. Anything else didn't quite fit my mouth, although I could get out a proper "sir" in times of admiration; and I did admire him, but I'd take a bullet through the star before I'd say it. He was a vain old rooster who never forgot an insult or a compliment.

He dismissed the shaft with a gesture that told me how deep I'd struck. I'd just returned from a messy errand in Oregon that had reflected badly on us both as well as on the federal court, and I hadn't scrupled to remind him I'd been against it from the start. That I was there at all when I should have been on leave while tempers cooled said he needed me for something unpleasant, and I was determined to let him twist until he got to the point.

"Do you seriously know nothing of Scripture?" he asked. "I'd expect someone of your frontier stock to have been brought up on sourdough and Jesus."

"Dugouts are designed for getting snowed in. There was always plenty of Jesus when the bread ran out. I caught a case of devotion, but it was like measles. You don't get it twice."

"Have you no faith apart from your oath to the Union?"

"I took it with my hand on a Bible. If I thought it was for more than show I'd have sworn on my pistol. I've seen good men die and bad men prosper, but never an angel to tip the scale. If I ever was going to, it would have been at Murfreesboro."

"Are you an atheist?"

"I never liked the ones who claimed to be. They all tried to convert me."

"An agnostic?"

"I don't know."

He frowned as if I'd made an inappropriate jest. The truth was I didn't know what the word meant. I learned later it was of recent coinage.

"But you can sham belief," he said.

I'd no idea where the conversation was headed, but already I didn't care for it by half. The Judge was a regular-attending Presbyterian; whether that was for community relations or because he thought as much of his immortal soul as he did of the bench wasn't something he shared with those of us who provided him with defendants, and I doubted he was any more forthcoming with his prosecutor or the local leaders he met with formally and at poker. I'd have suspected him of leading up to a dire announcement if I weren't certain he intended to live forever.

I said, "I can be an eagle or a duck. Which one depends on the job."

"I haven't said there is a job. You're on inactive duty."

"That's true. As long as we're just chewing the fat, where do you stand on Pharaoh's daughter finding baby Moses in the rushes? She spun a good yarn, but that was the last time anyone believed a story like it."

"That's blasphemous."

"You ought to know. You're using Holy Writ to recruit me for work."

"You're hopeless."

"If I didn't have hope I'd be dead in Oregon."

The forbidden subject jerked him back onto the rails. He rang for the steward, a bald, leathery Scot in a rusty tailcoat who'd navigated for Lewis and Clark and Noah, and asked him to fetch the big atlas from the dining room.

When he returned lugging a cloth-bound volume the size of a saddle blanket, Blackthorne opened it across the arms of his chair, made heretical marks on one of the watercolor maps with a gravity pen, and sat back. I rose and circled behind to study it over his shoulder. With a sinking heart I recognized the outline of Texas, my least favorite place after Dakota; which to be fair to Dakota had only been the place where I'd almost been slaughtered by the Cheyenne Nation. Even worse, the marks he'd made were in the panhandle, a spot that existed because the same incessant wind that blew it away daily blew in fresh dirt from Mexico. The panhandle would disappear when the sand ran out.

"I've marked the sites of five armed robberies that have taken place in the past six months," Blackthorne said. "Two banks, an Overland stage, two trains. The banks aren't our concern, but mail was stolen from the Overland and one of the trains, and that is."

"What's the matter with the federal court in Austin?"

"Its deputy marshals are spread thin over a jurisdiction the size of France. The Texas Rangers, who normally can be depended upon to fill the gap, are busy patrolling the border of Mexico for *bandidos*. Governor Ireland has asked us for our help, after Isaac Parker in Arkansas turned him down for obvious reasons."

Parker was the only U.S. jurist who was more put-upon than Blackthorne, with seventy-four thousand square miles of Indian Territory to tame by way of two hundred deputy marshals and a gallows in Fort Smith the size of a frigate. The two despised each other for reasons unknown to me, but they were united in their contempt for interferers from Washington.

"Still, five robberies. We can scrape up that many in parts of Montana most seasons. What's our end?"

"Method of operations was nearly identical in all five. That suggests the same band. At the pace they're going, they'll fish out their current waters in short order and relocate. I'd rather we fought them on Texas ground than ours. Innocent bystanders there are spread out more and less likely to take a stray round."

That was thin even for him, but I didn't press the point. If he were going to confide the truth to me, he wouldn't have bothered to put up even so transparent a lie. In any case we were interrupted by the antique steward, who'd returned to ask if we wanted more refreshment. To my surprise the Judge nodded, and the Scot took from a cabinet a cut-glass decanter and from another a bottle of Monongahela and mixed their contents in our empty glasses. Blackthorne was a one-drink, one-cigar man by order of his physician, who had seen him through a heart attack, and no one who answered to the Judge had ever asked for seconds in his presence.

Except me, of course; but this was the first time he'd joined me in the rebellion.

If the steward noticed that a valuable book from the club's collection had been defaced, his expression didn't show it, and he left without remark. Membership was restricted to owners of ranches exclusively, but although Blackthorne held no title to a single square inch of real property, an exception had been made in his case because he'd tried and convicted rustlers with such Old Testament fervor that not so much as a stolen pair of horns had crossed the territorial line in more than a year. It stood to reason that until one did, he could scribble dirty pictures all over the walls of the reception room on Ladies' Night without a mark appearing against his name in the register.

He closed the atlas and slid it over the arm of his chair until it leaned against the side. For a few moments I watched him shifting his weight on the cushions in search of a compromise between his bony angles and the arrangement of horsehair in the upholstery. The only seat that really suited him was the one behind the high bench in the courthouse. Just because he was physically restless, however, didn't mean he wasn't complacent in his mind. He knew I would raise the subject sooner or later.

I took a long draught of the Gavel and gave him his way. "The Bible."

"I take solace from it often. The beauty of the Song of Solomon stands out against its background of war, plague, and human sacrifice. I was reminded of it when 'Whispering Hope' swept through town last year; I was trying a case of rape, murder, and dismemberment, and the strains came through the window as an eyewitness was testifying. I was comforted by the reflection that ugliness and beauty—hell and redemption, if you will—have abided side by side on earth since the beginning. All the changes are superficial. I wonder if the Israelites gathered in the courtyard of the palace to predict Judgment Day the way our street philosophers do on Catholic Hill?"

"If so, and Solomon's father David was in charge, he'd have stuck them in the front lines and given them the first look."

"So some of the Word remained with you after all."

"Not enough to get me from the Kingdom of Israel to the panhandle of Texas."

He ran a finger around the top of his glass, drawing a dull hum from the crystal. He made some kind of decision and set it on his chairside table untouched. "Each of those robberies took place within three days' ride of Owen, a former buffalo-hunting center more lately concerned with sheepherding, with all the complications that represents with the local cattle interests.

Full-time brigand is passing out of fashion. Increased numbers of law enforcement officers and the Pinkertons' stranglehold has forced many road agents into the cover of legitimate employment. Jesse James and the Youngers scorned the life of the working ranch hand, but most of the later breed has come out of line shacks and the bunkhouse and fly back into them between raids. My theory is you're more likely to find these highwaymen rounding up strays in Palo Duro Canyon than hiding out in some cave planning their next outrage.

"The challenge, of course, is to penetrate that close society without raising the alarm—sending them into flight or open confrontation with their loyal friends at their side. A band of officers would bring about the former, and a single man poking about would almost certainly end up bleaching his bones somewhere on the Staked Plain. However, there is one profession that thrives on a healthy knowledge of the lives of the members of his community without arousing suspicion, and without prowling beyond his station and the various tables where he is invited to break bread."

I saw where he was heading then, and felt a nasty grin splitting my face. "I can stand for a cowhand because I've been one, and they took me for a saloon-keeper down in New Mexico because I know my way around a bar, but the first time I thump a pulpit, they'll smell brimstone clear to Chicago."

"You fail to appreciate the proposition. Men confide in their barbers, women in their dressmakers, but both sexes trust their ministers. In addition, the many social affairs that surround the church place the pastor in the best possible position to monitor gossip. No one knows his community better than the man who serves its spiritual needs."

"Get Ter Horst. His wife teaches Sunday school, and that sheep face of his belongs at the Last Supper."

"I considered him first, but he thought the plan profane. He threatened to resign."

"Whereas my soul's up for grabs. The star draws fire like a bottle on a fence rail, but I put it on when you ask. I won't reverse my collar for you. I never met a man struck by lightning who was decent company after we got past the obvious."

He smiled then, close-lipped without the teeth he wore only in the courtroom. "I felt certain once I scratched that infidel's hide I'd find a believer. You're too hard on yourself, Page. You have an ecclesiastical mien when you discuss a subject that arouses your passion. The rest is costuming."

That was when I knew I was beaten, although I argued my case a few more minutes just to make the conversation as disagreeable for him as it was for me. When Judge Blackthorne addressed me by my given name, there was no slack left in the leash.

TWO

I asked how long I'd be in seminary. He said I was leaving for Texas in two weeks.

I stared. "That's barely time to get through Genesis."

"Once again you undervalue your abilities, and you know I regard false modesty a mortal sin. I've seen you plow through a thick field report without pausing to lick your thumb. Genesis is only sixty-six pages in the standard King James edition, and the whole thing's shorter than *Ben-Hur* by two hundred sixty. But then Lew Wallace always was prone to wander."

"How did you know that?"

"Every schoolboy knows he got lost on the way to Shiloh, leading to huge Union losses. It was a great victory for the army when he turned toward literature."

"I mean how did you know the number of pages in King James? I've met men who can recite it front to back who couldn't tell you that."

"As can I. As can a magpie, with as much comprehension of the spirit behind the words. Annex to that in my case a talent for figures." He tugged out his fine platinum watch, engraved with his name by President Polk for distinguished service during the war with Mexico; I assume a medal had come with it, but the watch and the bullet-chewed tricolor flag that hung on the wall of his chambers were the only souvenirs he displayed from that episode. "I know, for example, that of this moment you have eleven thousand, three hundred and forty-four minutes to make yourself intimate with the Book of Books before your train leaves. I caution you to use them all. There are Texans who can barely write their names but who will drag you through cactus if you overlook a comma in Ezekiel; again, a feat of exhibition rather than of faith. That panhandle country is undiverting and made to order for scholarly study."

"There's more to being a minister than reading and regurgitating verses. You haven't even told me my denomination."

"The vacancy you're filling was left by a Unitarian, which is the nearest thing established doctrine offers to religion à la carte. We'll go one step further from popery and make you an evangelist. That way there will be no truck with arcane ceremony and personal strictures. You're free to take strong drink and fornicate, although I advise more than usual discretion in both pursuits. You're aware of *el ley del fugo*?"

"*La ley de la fuga*. The law of flight applies only to fleeing suspects. It's a license to slaughter."

"I sense error in both constructions, but I keep forgetting your season in New Mexico. It's been many years since I laid siege to Montezuma." The ends of his moustache turned down steeply. He hated to be caught in a mistake in the midst of a dissertation, and had found more than one attorney in contempt for correcting him in court. "The interpretation of the law becomes broader the farther one travels west or south of the more populous settlements. Your discovery alighting from the back porch of a married rancher upon his return home would not overstretch its spirit. Letter is another matter, but by the time a judgment was reached it would be unlikely to do you any material good."

"I can be killed for that here, and spend my last night in my own bed."

"Not yours, to be technical, but the point is moot in any case, since you're making the journey. Texas is the only state that retains the privilege of secession, and some of the natives behave as if it's exercised it already. They're savages in silk hats."

"I know Texas, or most of it. That's why I came back to Montana."

"Riding herd, no doubt, upon its indigenous unchewable bovines." He tapped the arm of his chair with the edge of the watch as if it were his gavel. "A pulpit is not a saddle. You'll require a tutor for the public parts, as well as in the niceties of the rectory and parlor."

"I'm fresh out of suggestions. I don't know any of

the ministers in town, and I'm not sure they'd take kindly to a stranger asking them how to defraud a flock of the faithful."

"I know an Episcopalian who'd shoot you as like as not with the pistol he uses to protect the sacramental wine. But I'd not send you out cold even in Helena on so delicate a mission. You'll want Eldred Griffin; *Father* Griffin, though I'd sound him out before I employed the title. I'm not certain if the custom of addressing ex officios as 'President' and 'Governor' extends to the clergy, and this fellow may take it amiss whatever the protocol." He rang for the steward and asked for envelopes and writing paper. The man withdrew, taking with him the big atlas, which he'd retrieved without asking—a veiled reference, I thought, to the Judge's desecration of its contents.

"A Catholic priest?" I asked.

"Defrocked. Distasteful term. One pictures a bishop tearing off the man's vestments in the churchyard and stomping his chalice flat."

"I hope he's not a colorful old character. I draw them like flies."

"You'll have no difficulty on that account. He's not many years older than you, and according to the Reverend Clay of the Presbyterian church, he suffers from chronic melancholia. Mr. Webster defines black as the absence of color."

The steward returned with a sheaf of foolscap and some envelopes. Blackthorne took two of each, sent him away with the rest, and shook ink into the business end of his pen. Using the table at his elbow, he spent some minutes writing, signed both pages in his elaborate hand, waved them dry, folded them into envelopes, and addressed each. He tucked in the flaps and held them out.

"The first will introduce you to Griffin. Don't lose the second; it's for the captain of the Texas Rangers in Wichita Falls, who will prepare you for what to expect in Owen. I know I can trust you not to steal a look at them."

I opened each of the envelopes in turn and read the letters while he seethed. They were headed by the name of the Helena Stockmen's Association in halftone letters and a steel-point engraving of the club's brick headquarters. I refolded them and put them back, tapping the Texas-bound envelope with a finger. "Judge Blackthorne's Epistle to the Texicans?"

"You try my patience, Deputy. Did you think they contained instructions to assassinate you?"

"Anytime someone says he can trust me it means I can't trust him. What are the odds the thought never crossed your mind?"

"It's crossing it now."

"Am I really one of the most reliable officers in the federal system?"

"That depends on the area in which one relies upon you. Captain Jordan has slain sixteen men in the line of duty, whereas I'm told former Father Griffin is drawn to straight talk with no embroidery. For those reasons you may get along with both. Then again, you may not for the very same reasons. I still receive letters from the White House in response to calls for your extradition to Canada on behalf of the North West Mounted Police."

"It doesn't sound like this Captain Jordan wastes much time writing letters." I slid the envelopes into my inside breast pocket next to the underarm rig I wore in town.

"Were I you, I would cosset him at every opportunity. The Rangers are known for recruiting their officers on the basis of results rather than strict conformity to the rule of law."

"Cosset Jordan, talk turkey with Griffin. So long as I don't mix them up I can't go wrong."

Blackthorne smiled. I preferred it when he wore his teeth. I asked where I could find Griffin.

"In the Catholic cemetery."

Every time I returned to Helena, it seemed, more brick buildings had been erected to replace frame structures built on the same sites. This was because the city burned down every few years, and fireproofing is more effective than reeducating residents in the proper use of flame. One day the whole place would be brick, like Chicago, and it would be time for me to move on, because there's no room in civilization for a fellow with bark left on him.

The Cathedral of the Sacred Hearts of Jesus and Mary was one of the oldest local landmarks constructed of that sturdy material, and had sheltered many refugees from blazes under its spiky-crowned bell tower. I climbed Catholic Hill and discovered something new since I was there last: a large structure—brick, of course—risen in place of the wooden boarding school of Saint Vincent's Academy, where the nuns of the order taught children their letters as well as Numbers. It had burned or been torn down and replaced. But Sacred Hearts still dominated the hill.

I swore they'd done the work during my brief visit to Oregon, but then a lot more time had passed since I'd been near that church or any other. I didn't even know for sure what faith I'd fallen out of; my father never told me just Who he prayed to when he set his trap line in Blackfoot country, and my mother had kept her old gods to herself. I would be a challenge to instruct. My knuckles hurt just thinking about it.

Farther down the street, inside a grille fence topped with iron fleurs-de-lis, slumber the Catholic settlers of Last Chance Gulch, along with others of the same persuasion, under crosses and tablets and the odd bugling angel. But cemetery populations are continually expanding without attrition, and a larger lot had been purchased on the edge of town to accommodate later arrivals and marble vaults for the well-heeled.

Even old graves need tending, however, and vandals and thieves with spades need to be discouraged. A dwelling had been built for caretakers and their families on the last plot of unturned earth — some said atop the bones of forgotten pioneers whose wooden markers had burned or been carried away. It was a doll's house really, designed along the lines of the stately mansions of the suddenly rich on Benton Avenue and Lawrence Street, but scaled down to proportions more appropriate to its humble tenants. It was the same mansard roof, the same mullioned panes in Roman arches, the same gracious wraparound porch; but twelve paces would take you from the front door into the backyard, and even from the outside you could tell that a man not much taller than myself would have to duck when he climbed the stairs to the second story. And I am not tall.

I worked the bell pull and took off my hat when the door opened, as I would have upon entering a place of worship. The man who opened it was in his middle forties, my height (I wondered if he'd been hired for his slight stature, to preserve the plaster ceilings), and to my observation the owner of the only other shaven male chin and upper lip west of Pennsylvania. His cheeks were high ovals, his hair cut short and black without gray, and his eyes were that pale shade of blue that photographers have to touch up on the glass plate to keep them from reproducing dead white. He wore neither coat nor collar, but with his black waistcoat buttoned and white shirt fastened to the throat he appeared fitted out to preach the gospel in any church I'd ever entered.

"Father Griffin?"

"Eldred Griffin." He had a low, even voice that never strayed above or below a straight line—or so I thought then. It had the quality of a chant. "You're Page Murdock." He touched a pocket in his waistcoat. I'd sent him Judge Blackthorne's letter by way of a messenger, with a note of my own, but I hadn't expected him to keep either on his person. The way he touched it made me think of an amulet to ward off—well, me.

I showed him the simple six-pointed star. "Am I interrupting anything?"

"Only my retirement."

I pocketed the star and took out his response. "You invited me here."

He glanced at it without interest. "It isn't my hand."

"Eldred, you know very well it's mine." This was a new voice.

He half turned from the doorway, giving me a straight shot across the shallow entryway at a small woman standing framed in an arch leading to the rest of the house. Her hair, brown with streamers of gray, was skinned back and fastened behind her head, and her face was round, without a single feature that called attention to itself. She wore a dark brown dress, nearly black, and plain to the point of pride; a placket concealed the buttons. An egg-shaped stone the color of slate in an old-fashioned setting showed on the index finger of her right hand, folded over its mate at her waist. It was her only ornament.

Griffin didn't forget his manners. "My wife, Esther. Page Murdock."

My hat was already off, so all I could do was incline my head. I had the impression she was older than her husband. Her gaze acknowledged my gesture, then went to him. "How often have you said you wanted to pass on what you know?" she asked. "I thought it an opportunity to learn whether you have the gift."

"You might have discussed it with me before you acted."

"Oh, Eldred. When have you ever discussed anything with anyone? If I hadn't acted, you would still be clipping weeds ten years from now."

"It's honest labor."

"Not if it's not what God intended."

"He speaks to you, whereas with me He is silent."

"Mr. Murdock did not come here to listen to us quarrel. Invite him in."

"You know what he wants. To pose as a man of the cloth in order to catch a rogue. Sin for sin, and I am to be his accomplice. 'Speak not in the ears of a fool: for he will despise the wisdom of thy words.'"

"'The integrity of the upright shall guide them,'" she said.

"'. . . but the perverseness of transgressors shall destroy them.'"

"Should I be taking notes?" I asked.

THREE

In which faith were you raised?" Griffin asked.

"Christianity," I said. "I'm pretty sure."

"I meant which church."

"I was born six thousand feet up in the Bitterroots. I never saw a church until I was almost grown."

His pale eyes clouded. "Your parents were savages?"

"Only my father. My mother was some part Indian."

"Which tribe?"

"Nez Perce, I think."

"You don't know?"

"I wasn't encouraged to ask questions."

"And so with those qualifications you chose to enter law enforcement."

"No one chooses that. I just sort of drifted into it after the buffalo ran out. In between I punched cows and shot wolves in the winter for the bounty, but I made too thorough a job of it. When wolves got scarce I became a drunk for a while and got to know a few jails. In one of them the sheriff turned out to be an old bunkmate. He told me the U.S. marshal was hiring here in Helena. It was the only work I could get where my recent history didn't count against me."

"And how long have you been about it?"

"Ten years last April. Felons don't seem to run dry like buffalo and wolves and whiskey."

"A fortunate turn for the citizenry. Road agentry is the only calling you haven't answered."

"I disagree. The frontier keeps changing. There's always a paying position that didn't exist last week. What did you do before you became a priest?"

"I was an altar boy."

We were seated in a pair of split-bottom chairs in a room he called his study, a dim cell at the top of a flight of stairs you practically had to crawl up on hands and knees to keep from cracking your skull on the square timber across the top. One wall slanted with the roof and the rest were a jumble of books stuck in at every angle between two-inch-thick pine shelves. More books and loose papers climbed corners to the low papered ceiling. A lamp with a blackened chimney smoked on a small writing table near his chair, stinging my eyes while illuminating little but itself. The room smelled of coal oil and moldy bindings.

One queer thing I'd noticed: None of the rooms I'd passed through on the way there contained a visible religious symbol of any kind. The study was no exception. I'd never been in a Catholic household that didn't display a large crucifix or a picture of Jesus somewhere prominent.

He returned to my origins. He would be one of those biblical scholars who cut Methusaleh in half to count the rings. "The Nez Perce are an intelligent people. Large cranial capacity. I taught them at the Saint Ignatius Mission when I was in seminary. You favor them in the jaw. In the forehead, not so much."

"My father came from Aberdeen. He used to smash stoneware jugs with his head to win bets."

"You must have been proud."

"Grateful for the inheritance. I've stopped more than my share of pistol butts and I can still walk a straight line."

"You and I are not of the same flesh," he said. "I cannot think of any other circumstances that would place us both in one room." He leaned forward as if to rise. "I'm not going to help you. The only reason I didn't turn you away at the door is I'd never be quit of it as long as Esther is around to remind me."

As if in response to her name, his wife knocked and entered, carrying a brass lamp and a silver tea set on a tray. She was the only one of us who didn't have to lower her head to clear the doorway. She set the tray on a squat square footstool stacked with volumes—there wasn't a bare horizontal space in the room, but this one at least was level—traded lamps, and blew out the one that had been fouling the air. The room brightened immediately. I don't know that it had entirely to do with a clear chimney and a well-trimmed wick.

She poured for us both. I don't like tea, but when she'd mentioned brewing it I'd assented, because I wanted her present for what I did then. I fished a leather poke from my side pocket and placed it on the tray where the pot had stood. It clanked.

"I'm authorized by the United States District Court for the Territory of Montana to offer you a hundred dollars in gold for divinity lessons," I said. "Judge Blackthorne advised me to pay half in advance and the rest upon completion. I'm putting it all on the table. The risk of flight in your case seems small."

"It used to be thirty pieces of silver. The treasury must be in good condition."

"Eldred, the man is our guest."

I said, "It's more than twice what I earn in a month, but we're asking for a season's instruction in two weeks. The object of betrayal is a gang of highwaymen, not Jesus."

"You're overlooking the rest of the congregation, who will come to you in search of guidance. 'Have ye not spoken a lying divination—'" He broke off with a sidelong glance at his wife. It occurred to me that her knowledge of the Bible ran deeper than his. I seemed to have stumbled into an old argument.

"It won't be a lie if you teach him the proper words."

"A profane man profanes holy words merely by speaking them."

"The sword of God is not so brittle," she said. "And Mr. Matthews has refused to extend us any more credit at the meat market."

I'd gambled right. It was the men who were winning the West, but it was the women who kept the books.

Griffin sat back a fraction of an inch, fixing me with his pale eyes. "Were you baptized?"

"I've been up to my chin in the Canadian and all the way under in the Yellowstone. I almost drowned that time."

He looked at Esther. "Are you not yet convinced whom he represents? Must he sprout horns and hooves?"

"The Prince of Lies is not so clumsy or we would not fear him." She turned to me with the teapot in one hand and a full cup and saucer in the other. "Have you really never been christened in the faith?"

I shook my head.

"There's the end of it," Griffin said. "Tell Matthews I'll eat potatoes and miss Purgatory."

"Don't be theatrical. You hate potatoes. The solution is simple. Mr. Murdock will submit to be baptized, and we shall ask him to join us at supper tomorrow night after his lesson. Pork chops, I think." She handed me the cup and saucer, gave the other to her husband, and set down the pot, scooping the sack of coins from its path and putting it in the pocket of her plain apron, all in the same movement. Then she lifted the tray and left.

For a moment the only sound in the room was me

blowing on my tea. I looked across at him. "I don't suppose you'd care to do the honors."

"It wouldn't be sanctified. I'm no longer a priest."

"I'll ask Reverend Clay, then."

The crease between his brows deepened. It had looked like a scar to begin with. "The Presbyterian?"

"I'm posing as an evangelist. How good does it have to be?"

"Mother of God." He crossed himself. "Is there a sacred thing you don't hold in scorn?"

"I like the idea of the Good Samaritan. As for the rest, no one died for my sins. I wasn't born yet."

"By which I take you to mean you've invented some of your own."

"I'd be guilty of vanity if I said I had. I confess I've broken a Commandment or two in order to keep others."

"Do not use the word *confess* in my presence. The common belief is priests are unworldly and therefore unschooled in the wickedness of man. Those who subscribe to the theory have never sat in the darkness listening to a parishioner gloat over the details of unspeakable evil under the pretense of absolution. Nearing the end I became convinced that no number of Hail Marys would spare them the pit. Meanwhile I retired to the rectory each evening bearing their burden as well as my own."

"Is that why you left the priesthood?"

He sipped tea, drawing it in with a sucking noise like a horse drinking water, and set his cup in its saucer with a click. It seemed to place a full stop to the conversation. "No doubt you think that having chosen evangelism you've avoided the intolerable yoke of dogmatic principle. What the informed laity lacks in formal training it more than makes up for in passion. Have you ever attended a tent meeting?"

"No."

"There is always one about, every Sunday in mild weather. You and I will attend the next. What do you intend to wear on this southwestern sojourn?"

I ran a thumb under the left lapel of my coat. He shook his head slowly. I said, "Not black enough?"

"Not humble enough. A made-to-order suit on a minister's back means a hand in the collection plate."

"I can't find a fit in a ready-made that has room for this." I spread the coat to show him the Deane Adams in its suspender scabbard.

The skin of his face drew taut. "A righteous man arms himself with righteousness only."

"I consulted Samson and David on the matter. They came to a different conclusion."

"Do not seek to banter with me in Holy Writ. I will bury you, and we haven't time for it. You must not carry a pistol into a house of God."

"The last time I was in one I didn't see a gun check at the door. I'm going to Texas to break up a gang. If I save a soul, it's in the line of a collateral benefit. I've heard stories of pocket Bibles stopping bullets, but I don't credit them. Bandits carry heavy calibers as a rule."

He started to drink again, but his hand shook. He set cup and saucer on the writing table. "At least promise me you won't brandish it in church."

"I could, but it'd be a lie. They build churches and saloons from the same green wood and there are men who'd as soon bust a cap in a convent as in a brothel. I won't make a point of the business without good cause, I can swear to that much. That's why I need a coat that won't show a bulge."

"Pick one off the shelf a size too large. No, two sizes; the more shapeless the better. Bundle it in your bedroll, and when you reach your destination don't be too conscientious about brushing and pressing. You can't preach convincingly about a camel passing through the eye of a needle if you look as if you'd get stuck yourself."

"Should I let out my whiskers and chew a plug?"

"Assuredly not. You must be clean in your habits and appearance. Does it not sting your professional pride when you encounter a slovenly peace officer?"

"I've trusted my life to a few. But I understand. A bad lawman paints us all. I'll pack a razor and look to my nails."

"Clean them, don't pare them. And under no circumstances allow a barber to shave you. Fifteen cents for a haircut is as much as most ministers can afford, and they will forego a meal to avoid becoming shaggy. Fortunately, sustenance will not be a problem. Most parishioners consider having even a mediocre minister to their homes for dinner the same as purchasing an indulgence." He touched his flat belly. "Mind you, don't be taken in by the conventional belief that all country wives are superb cooks. You'd be wise to carry a sack of peppermints in your pocket to settle your stomach."

"I didn't realize the work was so dangerous."

Nothing like a smile crossed his features. "Many men—out here in particular—make the mistake of confusing a cassock with a skirt. They have no concept of the level of courage required to walk the path of the lamb in a den of lions. Any fool can muster the strength to face a mortal enemy. Only one man in a thousand can find it within him to turn his back on one. Are you that man?"

I hesitated for the first time in the discourse. "I don't know."

"An honest answer at last. Have you a Bible?"

"I own one. I didn't bring it. It seemed like carrying firewood to the forest."

"Bring it with you next time. It will save passing the text back and forth." He turned in his chair and lifted a volume the size of a traveling desk off the pile of books on his writing table—one-handed; his hands were slim and white, but as strong as a harvester's—opened it in his lap, and hooked on a pair of wire-rimmed spectacles from a waistcoat pocket.

And so began the catechism.

FOUR

I returned to my furnished room past midnight, limp as a bar rag. A hundred voices were shouting Bible passages in my head. Sunday school with Eldred Griffin was like digging postholes all day in the desert, and I'd done that too.

By gray dawn I was back in his study. He looked as fresh as I felt stale, wearing a clean collarless shirt with his waistcoat and trousers brushed and creased in the right places (he had no one to impress with his poverty) and a shine on his elastic-sided boots, round-heeled though they were.

That day began as did the next four, with the same question:

"Are you baptized yet?"

My answers varied:

"Not in the last six hours."

"I haven't had the chance."

"Reverend Clay went shooting."

"I'm catching a cold."

"I forgot."

On each occasion he made no comment, snapping open his leviathan Bible and directing me to turn to the passage before him in mine. He'd marked his place with a piece of razor strop scraped thin as flannel. My copy was bound in supple leather for traveling, with all the gold leaf worn off the outside lettering and its dog-eared pages rubbed nearly transparent at the edges, like a marked deck of cards. It had been left to me by Dad Miller, a deputy marshal who'd taught me two-thirds of what I knew about the hunting of men, including a posthumous lesson: Place the same faith in your friends as you do in your enemies. He'd had his throat cut while on watch by a member of his own posse.

Each day we interrupted our labors for breakfast, noon dinner, and supper. Esther Griffin was a good simple cook who skimped a bit on salt and pepper, but kept vinegar in a cruet on the table for my use; neither she nor her husband touched it. We ate meat on two evenings and crackles every morning, so I concluded that she had made peace with the butcher. We spread lard on slabs of coarse bread and washed everything down with chicory coffee and water, which she drew from a well uphill of the cemetery. She baked bread twice that first week and on Saturday a peach pie made from preserves sent to her by a sister in Michigan whom she hadn't seen in seven years. I gathered that although she belonged to a large family, this sister was the only member who stayed in touch. I assumed the break had something to do with Griffin's having quit the priesthood, but later I learned I was wrong. Anyway the pie was good, if the crust was a little doughy; she blamed the woodstove, which listed toward the corner where a stack of bricks had been inserted in place of a broken leg.

Conversation at table centered around food, and if it weren't for the preserves. I'd never have found out about the sister and Esther's estrangement from the rest of her people. Griffin never failed to thank her for cooking, and he always pronounced the grace. "Never defer this duty to anyone else when you're a guest," he told me the first time I joined them. "Your hosts will be too polite to refuse, but they'll resent you for it. The reason for having you over is to gain a place at God's table, and if you don't put in a good word, their chances are no better than even."

"Is there anything else I should know?"

"Eat with your fingers if they eat with theirs, but if they're too self-conscious to pick up a chicken leg in your presence, use a knife and fork. Don't let anyone see you pluck stray hairs from your food. And come prepared with plenty of fresh gossip."

"Isn't that violating some kind of oath?"

"The seal of the confessional doesn't extend to what you overhear in ordinary discourse, and doesn't exist at all outside the Roman Catholic Church. You must sing for your supper, especially if you want to hear what else is taking place among the congregation. The more garrulous the minister, the less laconic the host. That is the reason for this charade, is it not?"

"Still, it steers pretty close to bearing false witness."

He frowned at the bit of potato on his fork. It was the only vegetable I ever saw him eat, and he seldom did so without showing distaste. If it weren't for that I think he'd have come down with scurvy long before. "That raises another point. Never sermonize beneath another man's roof. He works six days a week only to be told on Sunday morning he is going to hell. He won't tolerate it in the afternoon."

"More cabbage?" Esther offered me the bowl.

I gained weight during that period, something I rarely did. Gluttony has never been one of my sins. I was used to bolting a steak in a saloon or a bowl of rabbit stew at a stage stop in order to keep from fainting and falling out of the saddle; sweets and savory seldom slowed me down when there was light out and miles to make. However, the ordeal upstairs made me ravenous. I think Esther Griffin enjoyed serving something other than bread and meat to someone other than herself, and took special care in the preparation. When she brought out the pie, she surprised Griffin by pouring a glass of cold milk for me from an earthenware pitcher.

"I traded Mrs. Nordström three eggs for a quart from her Maybelle," she said. She kept chickens in a little pen out back.

Griffin asked how she'd kept it cold.

"In the well, where else? You won't have an icebox in the house."

"Certainly not, with the market only three hundred yards away. The amount those pirates in the icehouse demand for water and cold, God's own bounty, will revisit them at end of days." He was as pinchpenny as any country preacher.

"It's very good." I have a weakness for cold milk.

Griffin said, "I suppose this means no eggs with our fatback tomorrow morning."

"It means hotcakes. I saved two."

His mood lightened then, and he spent several minutes in praise of Esther's hotcakes.

"Don't bore the man, Eldred. He'll find out tomorrow whether they taste like sunshine or black midnight."

He stopped talking and resumed eating. He touched on human whenever his wife was in the room. The rest of the time he was a slot machine that paid out in Scripture.

The sixth day of my training was Sunday. I came expecting a short lesson, as surely Griffin still attended morning services, and when he opened the door wearing a coat and hat I began to hope for a holiday. The coat was rusty and appropriately rumpled, and stove blacking had been applied to the kettle-shaped crown of his hat where the nap had worn off. He had on a stiff gutta-percha collar and a green cravat. When he asked about baptism, that's when I told him I'd forgotten.

"Come with me." He bustled me out the door and drew it shut behind him.

"Where are we going?"

"Where every nonheathen goes on Sunday."

"What about Mrs. Griffin?"

"She never attends church."

That surprised me more than when he'd told me there was no mention of apples in Genesis. I didn't even think to ask if it meant he'd married a heathen.

He'd hired a buggy and a shaggy gray. He left the whip in its socket and steered with the lines and short whistles. I'd suspected he avoided Sacred Hearts for reasons of his past, but when we left behind two Protestant churches, I got curious. Genuine wonder set in when we crossed the city limits and took the road that led to the Rockies.

In the foothills, where frost tipped the blades of grass like candle wax, we topped a low swelling rise— Griffin using the whip now to keep us from bogging down in mud from the spring runoff—and came within sight of a large gray tent pitched at the top of the next, looking like the offspring of the massive peak rising beyond it from a tarn of ground fog into streamers of cloud. A hundred yards away from the tent, the nearest stretch of level earth held a dense assemblage of carriages, buggies, and buckboards, and saddle horses browsing in the winterkill for tough new green shoots; it hardly seemed as if any form of transportation had been left in Helena, nor a dry hem or pair of boots among the men, women, and children who had picked their way up the hill. I heard a virile voice raised in song:

> There's a place above all others,
> where my spirit loves to be.
> 'Tis within the sacred shadow
> of the cross of Calvary.

It was as clear as newly minted silver but rang like iron on iron. From that day to this I've never heard one to approach it for depth or distance. I felt it in the soles of my feet, and they were eighteen inches above the ground. Then the chorus came in:

> In the shadow of the cross,
> in the shadow of the cross;
> there my spirit loves to be.
> In the shadow of the cross.

These voices were an inexact mix of male and female, full-throated and tentative, on key and off by a country mile; not all of them finished at the same time, and there was one bray in particular that shrank my gums from my teeth at the top of the scale. There's always one, and he never misses a service. But the best of them was a torn hinge compared to the soloist:

> *On the cross my Savior suffered,*
> *that He might atone for me.*
> *And I love the blessed shadow*
> *of the cross of Calvary.*

I asked Griffin who it was.

"Lawrence Lazarus Little; I have doubts about the second name. That's his outfit." He inclined his head toward a sheeted Studebaker wagon standing near the entrance to the tent, with DR. L. L. LITTLE'S TRAVELING TABERNACLE painted in Barnum letters on the canvas. A pair of Percherons stood hitched to it, eighteen hands high unshod, switching braided tails at flies buzzing around their great round haunches. "He styles himself a doctor of divinity. I can't contest it, but whatever his credentials, when he lifts his voice to God, our heavenly father must either listen or strike up the celestial choir to drown it out."

"Where do you know him from?"

"Denver. Cheyenne. Omaha. Wherever the church sent me, there he was. For years I thought he was an imp sent to bedevil me, but I knew nothing then of the tent-show circuit. I doubt he's overlooked a major population center or a tin-pan mining camp since he answered the Call. If he were Catholic he'd be a cardinal by now."

"What church is he with?"

"Southern Baptist."

That was the last answer I wanted, because I'd already suspected the worst, and the presence in a dale fifty feet beyond the tent of an acre of standing water did nothing to cheer me. It was an old buffalo wallow, from its size as ancient as the veins of gold that remained in the mountains, and worn into a perfect bowl by a thousand dead shaggies. Jagged panes of ice ringed the edge like painted glass.

I waited until we'd found a place among the other horses and vehicles and stepped down. "If you think I'm going in that frozen puddle," I said, "you've had too much traffic with miracles. I'll take my chances with the lake of fire."

He let the lines drop to the ground. It was a livery animal and wouldn't wander away from others of its kind. "It's just water. Don't tell me you've never crossed a river in colder weather than this."

"Then I had something worth getting to on the other side."

"Not like what's waiting for you this time."

"Just because you taught me to recite a few columns of verse doesn't mean you made me a believer."

He turned toward me. The shadow of his hat brim drew a mask around his washed-out blue eyes without concealing them; they seemed to glow like phosphor, but that's an old mesmerist's trick, and most spiritual counselors are students of the art. "Man is conceived in sin, and piles transgression upon transgression all the days of his life. The earth is nine parts water. Nine times nine would not begin to pale the stain of the first; not that brackish pond, and certainly not the paltry few drops the priests of my church sprinkle in a man's face, as if it came sixty dollars the barrel, and declare him cleansed. The Blood of the Lamb is a rare vintage and cannot be bought with Latin. The ceremony is a charming fraud, like confession, and like confession it fools none but fools. But it is the beginning of hope."

"Hope of what, salvation?"

"That's faith. Faith requires a higher power. Hope is

the belief that you can reverse the course of your own descent. It's the only mortal thing the devil fears, or he would not banish it at his gate. It involves free will, which will always be the enemy of him who would throw bad after bad. I will turn a faithless man out into the world to carry the Word, I am that corrupt, but I will spend eternity in limbo before I turn out a creature without hope to poison the hearts of my brothers."

"So religion is free will. I thought it was the opposite."

"You thought nothing until God placed you in my charge."

"Judge Blackthorne said I was hopeless. I said he was wrong."

"Prove it."

I looked from him to the wallow, which was easier to regard even with icicles bending the reeds in the center. Then I unshipped the Deane-Adams and gave it to him along with my wallet and the badge of office. Water does them no good, holy or no.

FIVE

From the chill mountain air we passed through the open flap into a Turkish bath. Barrel stoves glowed at both ends of the tent, and with the rows of folding chairs all occupied and standees pressed together like kernels of corn at the back, the air was close and sultry and stank heavily of unwashed wool. Just inside the entrance an articulated skeleton in new overalls and a homespun shirt handed us each a slim hymnal bound in dirty green cloth and a sheet of coarse paper printed with smudged black letters:

DR. L. L. LITTLE'S TRAVELING TABERNACLE
Lawrence Lazarus Little, D.D., officiating
"A little leaven leaventh the whole lump."
—GALATIANS 5:6

Beneath was a calendar scheduling Little's travels throughout the spring and summer of the Year of Our Lord 1884.

"He has a following," Griffin said. "Some of the devoted trail him from place to place to hear the same sermons again and again. The theory seems to be that the more you're preached at, the holier your glow in the eyes of God. Watch."

The man Little was short but disproportionately wide through the trunk, an oak barrel on squat legs with long arms furred from the backs of his hands to the insides of his elbows, where the roll of his striped shirtsleeves prevented me from seeing how far up the hair grew; the fact that it sprouted again from his spread collar and tangled with his beard suggested he'd resemble a baboon when stripped. As we watched, he made his way down the aisle between the rows of chairs and penetrated the rows themselves, snatching sweaty sheets of paper from hands thrust at him, marking them with a stump of orange pencil, and returning them. "Bless you, brother, bless you, sister, bless you, child." The rolling voice spread benediction like a honey wagon.

Griffin shouted into my ear; the din of voices calling for Little's attention was palpable. "He scratches his initials beside the present location on the programme, like a conductor punching tickets. All you need do to pass through the heavenly gate is present it with all the places marked off. That's the assumption, in any case. He's far too clever to suggest it himself."

I said nothing, sparing my throat. I'd seen Edwin Booth signing autographs for a similarly frantic mob outside a theater in St. Louis. The spectacle of a man of the cloth being treated the same as a celebrated actor was new in my experience.

Eventually—to mortal groans from those clamoring in the back rows—the minister broke off his pilgrimage and trotted back up the aisle to a low platform erected of green lumber at the front of the tent, illuminated by a pair of barn lanterns strung from poles. Gripping a hymnal in one thistled fist he bade the congregation turn to page forty-three. Griffin nudged me and we sang, "Father, We Come to Thee," with Little's massy bass soaring above all. When the last straggler finished, he exchanged the hymnal for a much larger book resting on a straightback chair missing a rung and held the object high above his head. It was a Montgomery Ward & Co. catalogue, bound in blue paper with an engraving of the firm's Chicago headquarters on the front.

Knowing laughter greeted this gesture, as at the appearance of a favorite comic act.

"Satan's wish book," Griffin said; "this is a masterpiece."

I glanced at his clean profile, dry as flax in the sodden heat. I couldn't tell if he was being ironic.

"I see by your reaction you're all familiar with this object," Little said, beginning quietly; for with hasty shushings the crowd had fallen silent but for the odd nervous cough. "It is a miracle of our century: three hundred pages of text and lifelike illustrations offering more than thirty thousand items of merchandise for sale at competitive prices, from a sterling silver button hook for ninety-eight cents to a parlor grand piano for ninety-eight dollars, not including shipping and handling." (Laughter.) "It is possible, thanks to the foresight and American-style enterprise of Mr. Aaron Montgomery Ward of Chicago, Illinois, to purchase a heavy three-seat full platform wagon, a suit of clothes, a Remington New Model double-barrel shotgun, and seventy-two dozen shirt buttons without stirring from the chair beside your hearth. A wish book, my dear late wife called it." (Sympathetic murmurs.) "In short, my friends, there is nothing worldly that a man or woman with the necessary wherewithal may not obtain without so much as changing from a pair of comfortable house slippers into street shoes." (Nods and glances.) "We are fortunate, you and I, to live in such a society."

WHAM! With a sudden arcing flash of his arm, he cast the heavy volume to the floorboards at his feet. Even those who obviously had been witness to the same action on previous occasions jumped in their seats; the stout middle-aged woman standing next to me grasped my upper arm, letting go with a hurried whisper of apology. I said something polite back. I was somewhat shaken myself.

"There is another kind of wish book, my friends; and I do not refer to competing sources issued by Mr. Ward's Johnny-come-lately colleagues back East, but to the temptations stocked by our Savior's rival down South." (Uneasy chuckles.) "Mind you, Satan's wish book is not comprised of paper and ink. The text and illustrations are written in fire and blood, and the prices are kept secret until the bill comes due. It is issued by the old established concern of Pride, Lust, Covetousness, Wrath, Gluttony, Envy, and Sloth, and it is available on any public street corner for the unwary to browse at leisure.

"The greedy man who would fill his purse with gold while his neighbor goes hungry shall, when the creditor calls, be fitted with a pack containing four hundred times four hundred troy ounces to bear upon his back four hundred times four hundred miles, and four hundred times four hundred more, until the end of all things;

"The vain woman whose waist cannot be made too small that she may corrupt weak men shall, when the creditor calls, don a corset fashioned from barbed wire, a strand wound round a wheel, and that wheel spun, constricting her middle and forcing her innards into her limbs through eternity;

"The lazy man who lingers abed, neglecting the Lord's honest labor, shall, when the creditor calls, be nailed to a cot of hard rock maple and grow running sores of everlasting agony;

"The satyr who defiles virgins shall, when the creditor calls, be flung among harpies and ravished with truncheons of iron heated red in the fires of the furnace;

"The child who covets his playmate's catapult, so that he would make away with it without asking leave, shall, when the creditor calls, be himself placed in a sling and shot into the devil's own dung heap, ever and anon;

"The wife of simple circumstances with a good and devoted husband, who looks with jealous eyes upon her neighbor's hired girl, shall, when the creditor calls, wait on torn hands and bleeding knees upon Beelzebub's slut, who spares not the scourge, until the oceans boil and the sun is like unto a lump of ice;

"Finally, the man who lays about his family with his fists when no fault is theirs shall, when the creditor calls, be made a bitten dog which is starved, and spat upon, and soils itself when kicked, and wallows in its unholy filth until Saint Peter whistles.

"These are the prices demanded for the wares advertised in Satan's wish book: everlasting misery, eternal pain, humiliation without end. Let it never be said that the old established concern of Pride, Lust, Covetousness, Wrath, Gluttony, Envy, and Sloth failed to provide full customer satisfaction.

"Turn now to page ninety-eight."

We were halfway through "Memories of Galilee" before anyone at ground level could direct enough attention to the lyrics to give them conviction, such was the effect of the sermon. Little himself, by going straight to the hymn without pausing, appeared to hold any sort of reaction in small regard. It was grand showmanship; he might have been preaching to none but himself. The impression was of a man who cared less for personal glory than for his responsibility to his master. Few actors would have taken the chance, and no politician.

I said something along those lines to Griffin after the song ended. He nodded without turning his head. "It's like needing perfect pitch to sing deliberately off-key. Only a man who's passionately in love with himself could manage to appear so humble."

He asked what I'd thought of the sermon. I said, "It's just about the crudest thing I ever heard, but I was sorry when it ended."

"It's requested more often than his 'Express Train to Hell.' He's in danger of wearing it out. I don't believe he's changed a word in six years."

"I doubt I can touch it, even if I took it for myself."

"Don't try. What works under canvas won't play under board-and-batten. These people come expecting a bonfire, not a hearth at which to warm their hands."

"Then why did you bring me, apart from the baptism? Or is that the only reason?"

"You could be baptized in any place of worship, although I concede that doing so under less than ideal conditions appealed to me as punishment for your procrastination. I wanted you to see at firsthand that it's possible for a man who has no faith to inspire belief in others. I hardly expect you to rise to Lawrence Little's station, but had you not seen him in full cry, your doubts might have condemned you to failure."

"Little's a charlatan?" We'd been conversing in murmurs; I dropped mine to a whisper. The stout woman next to me was sending scowls my way.

"He didn't start out a fraud or he'd never have been ordained. However, I know when bombast has taken the place of devotion. He's been making that substitution as long as I've been attending his circus."

"It seemed genuine to me."

"That's because you have not stood where he is standing, mouthing the words that come from your head and not your heart."

Just then the collection plate came around. It was a hammered copper bowl with wooden handles. When we finished contributing and passed it on, the set of Griffin's jaw told me that path of conversation was closed.

At length the services ended and the baptisms began. A flap of canvas had been stitched to either side of the tent at the ends of the platform to create makeshift dressing rooms for men and women, and I joined a line. Griffin touched my arm. "You needn't. There are more accommodating places."

"It's hot as hell anyway," I said.

"That's the intention."

When my turn came I changed into a loose gown of

unbleached muslin that reached to my ankles and gave my feet to a shapeless pair of shoes made from stiff uncured cowhide, with inner soles that felt like corrugated iron. I had my choice from a stack of gowns on a hewn bench and rows of footwear that looked uniformly uninviting, for the nippy weather outside had discouraged the less committed. I folded my clothes, put them and my boots in Griffin's hands for safekeeping, and went out to join one of two lines separated by gender marching toward the wallow. At first, the cold air felt good on my parboiled face, but as we shuffled along in half time to the congregation singing, "Jesus Wash Me," the sweat on my body seemed to form a jacket of ice. By the time we reached the edge of the water I was shivering and my feet felt like flagstones.

Brother Dismas, as I'd heard Little address the bald-headed beanpole who'd greeted us inside the tent, had shed his shirt and overalls for a gown and waded out to the middle without so much as a woof when the cold water came into contact with his testicles; his breath smoked in the air. Dr. Little meanwhile stood on dry land waving a brown-backed Bible and leading the chorus of hallelujahs that greeted each immersion. He was so enthusiastic, roaring in that voice so thoroughly cured in the barrel of his chest, that no one seemed to notice or mind that he never got his feet wet. I began to think that Griffin was right about him.

The water stung like needles when I went in, but as I pressed on, fighting to keep the gown from billowing and giving the parishioners more of a revelation than they'd come for, it clamped my legs in a vice that choked off all feeling. When I was crotch-deep, it pushed in with a surge that tore an oath from me, but if anyone heard it he must have thought I was overcome with rapture, because the reverend doctor went on encouraging the people still in line and didn't call down the lightning.

The good brother, who as far as I could tell was entirely hairless, with no sign that a razor had ever touched his bunched chin and sallow cheeks or had need to, laid a hand like a sashweight on my shoulder and asked me, in a high-pitched voice that twanged like a bullet off a rock, if I renounced Satan and all his works.

I said, "Sure, but—" and then I was under; he'd slid his hand down to the small of my back, placed his other palm against my chest, and folded me backward, plunging me in and out in less than a second. When I got loose, spluttering and wiping water from my eyes, he grinned at me with two lines of pink gum. "But what?"

"Don't put me all the way under. I can't swim."

"Nor can buffler. That's why they don't go in more'n hock deep." He turned to the woman who'd waded in behind me and asked her where she stood on Satan and his works.

I foundered back toward shore, where Griffin waited with my clothes. He knew better than to say anything. In the cobbled-up men's dressing room I tossed the gown onto the soaking heap on the ground, wiped myself down with a towel damp from other bodies, and put myself back together. When I left the tent, Griffin was standing with Dr. Little, who'd rolled down his sleeves and put on a fine black broadcloth Prince Albert with velvet facings on the lapels. The bathing party had broken up.

"Father Griffin tells me you seek redemption." His grip was as strong as Brother Dismas', but not as skeletal. "You could not have chosen a better guide."

I looked at the former priest and got nothing back. We hadn't discussed secrecy, but he'd spent too much time in the confessional not to know a confidence when he was told one.

I said, "He's opened my eyes. That was a stirring sermon."

He chuckled. It was as if a steam thresher were starting up in his throat. He had a bulging forehead that made him look as if he was balding, but at closer range a crop of black hair as thick and coarse as the one that covered his body grew up from a straight line and swept back in an arc to the nape of his neck. His eyes were brown, mottled like river stones, and small, even teeth flashed in his beard. "Inspiration struck in an outhouse in Creede, where a torn copy of Ward's spring catalogue furnished an essential service. God never knocks, nor waits without."

Griffin shook his hand and wished him luck on the remainder of his tour. We left as a middle-aged couple stepped up to the head of the reception line. "Amazing," said Griffin. "He took in more today than Sacred Hearts does in a month."

"Did you ask him if he needs a partner?"

He stopped walking and looked at me. "That is unkind."

Before I could respond he strode ahead. At the buggy he took my revolver and wallet and star from under the seat and gave them to me. We drove into town without a word. At the bottom of Catholic Hill he stopped to let me down and continued. There was no lesson that day.

SIX

Mrs. Blackthorne told me I'd find you here," I said. "I thought you didn't work on the Sabbath."

The Judge glared down at me. "I work every day. I'm not Pentecostal. It happens I report to chambers every other Sunday, when my parlor at home becomes the central headquarters of the Lewis and Clark County Book Club. Ostensibly they're discussing *The Adventures of Tom Sawyer,* but I doubt three of those esteemed ladies have read a line of Twain's. They gather to consume tea and thumping amounts of liverwurst and carve the ballocks off every married man in town."

Blackthorne stood on the top of a stepladder in the square, high-ceilinged room down the hall from his court where he retired to consider his rulings. He'd started with plenty of space, then crowded it with worktables, glazed book presses, books spread open to passages of current interest, leather portfolios stuffed with reports and depositions, and old numbers of the *Montana Post* and the *Congressional Register*, in which he kept track of freebooters locally and in the U.S. Capitol. The only vacant seat was his own embossed-leather chair behind the big American walnut desk. The strategy was to discourage lengthy digressions by requiring gouty defense lawyers with big bellies and bad backs to stand throughout meetings. It seemed to work; they rarely ran longer than fifteen minutes and his court disposed of more cases per month than any other in the federal system.

He was in his waistcoat and shirtsleeves, removing

dust from hefty legal volumes on his shelves with a deerskin rag. He never allowed the cleaners employed by the United States District Court to touch his personal library, which he'd assembled a piece at a time as he could afford it while clerking in a St. Louis firm and studying for the bar at night. They'd seen him through private practice, accompanied him to Washington during his lone term in the House of Representatives, and ridden in baggage cars, stagecoach luggage racks, the holds of steamboats, and on his own back when he'd crossed the prairie with his wife to take up his present post, and he wasn't about to trust them to any other hands.

He asked me how my education was progressing.

"You were right about Genesis," I said. "I made short work of it and have a dally around Exodus. Turns out the Bible's the easy part. Behaving as if I belonged in the same room with it's the part I'm having trouble with." I gave him an account of my morning.

Lawrence Little's chuckle and Blackthorne's shouldn't be referred to by the same term. The minister's was deep and plummy, the Judge's dry and sibilant, like a diamondback's buzz. "I wish I'd known. I'd have foregone the Reverend Clay's sermon on the destruction of Babylon and risked damnation just to see you tread water in a buffalo wallow in early spring."

"I'd respond to that, but I may need you to intercede for me with Griffin. If his door's not barred to me tomorrow I haven't got his measure."

"I doubt you have. No pleading on my part would improve your case. Griffin belongs to that stubborn cadre that's convinced I'm bound for hell. Every time I sentence a prisoner to hang I trespass upon the province of God."

"You might have let me know that before I went to

his house carrying a letter of introduction signed by you."

"I had nothing to lose by being straightforward, and with luck his cooperation to gain. He'd have known you came from me regardless. This way he's assured that no chicanery is involved."

"That won't help me now."

He twisted himself on the ladder, holding a tattered collection of Cicero's orations. The points of his brows were at their diabolical peak. "I honestly believe you're more self-obsessed than I. If he permitted you to cross his threshold on my behalf, condemned though I am, what makes you think he'll turn you away merely because you questioned his integrity?"

I saw there was no point in pursuing that line, so I chose another. "What made him break with the Church?"

"Ask him." He swept the rag across the untrimmed page edges and slid the book back into its slot.

"I did. He refused to answer."

"Then it's hardly my place to address the question."

"I didn't know you had a place."

He blew a dead bug off the top of *Principles Regarding the Division of Property in the State of Vermont, Vol. IX.* What system he used to categorize his library mystified me. "I keep an unruly pack of dogs to patrol a savage territory, Deputy," he said. "I hold the leash loose lest I break their spirit. Do not make the mistake of assuming I won't jerk it tight when one tries to urinate on me."

"I think you just did." I backed off. "He doesn't have a crucifix or a picture of Jesus anywhere in his house. If he's given up on faith, why do you suppose he's so concerned with how I represent it?"

"I wasn't aware he displayed no religious symbols

in his home. I've never been invited." He sounded thoughtful.

"I'm trying to understand the man. I'll make an unconvincing minister if I don't."

"You'll make one regardless. But Ter Horst won't budge from his pious stance and you're the only other man available who can string ten words together without a spitoon handy. You're in the way of being me." The Vermont volume had a snug berth; he rammed it home with the heel of his hand and climbed down. Abusing books seemed to be a privilege of ownership, denied all others. He extended the same philosophy to the officers of his court.

He got rid of the deerskin and spent a full minute brushing smears of dust from his waistcoat. "I daresay his complaint is not so much with belief as with the institution he served. No other concerns itself so completely with iconography. The absence of it from his own walls is a rebellion against Rome."

"What's his difference with the pope?"

"Chastity would be my guess. Celibacy. He opposes it."

"You're saying he threw the Church over for—"

"Hold your tongue on the Lord's day. As I understand the situation, it was a matter of romantic attraction, not lust."

"He fell in love with a woman? *Was* it a woman? I've heard stories."

"A woman was the reason, yes; but you've spent time with Griffin, and surely you've observed that whatever passion he has is reserved for the ethereal. The woman fell in love with him, and committed the blunder of confessing her temptations to her mother superior, who told the bishop, who cast her from the order. Griffin resigned in protest."

"She was a nun? What happened to her after that?"

"Her family disinherited her. Our society deals harshly with unmarried women of marked reputation with no one to support them and no skills with which to support themselves. A man like Eldred Griffin, having sacrificed his divine calling for the woman's sake, had no choice but to volunteer for the duty."

"Esther Griffin." I'd had it backwards, thinking she was the rock that kept him from collapsing under the weight of his own bitterness.

"Naturally, their betrothal lent credence to the rumors that her affections were requited, and that they had both sinned in the eyes of the Church. God spare us all from men who have the courage of their convictions."

He was one to talk. More than a few of his decisions had made enemies of powerful men he'd have been better served to pacify; letters to Congress had led to calls for impeachment. I said, "You know a lot about him for someone he hates."

"We've not met, and I doubt he'd confide in me if we had. A scandal limits itself to no particular denomination. The Reverend Clay is a gossip. If he weren't so useful as a source of intelligence, I might have converted to Lutheran years ago."

"It's no wonder he took it badly when I cast him in with Dr. Little. I'd have avoided it if you were half as forthcoming as Clay."

"You'd have found some other way to give offense. I suggest you make your peace. Your train pulls out in eight days."

Esther Griffin answered my knock Monday morning. She wore the same severe brown dress or one like it.

"Mr. Griffin is ill. You must come back tomorrow."
She started to close the door.

"Will it make a difference?"

She paused. "No."

"I didn't expect a lesson. I came to apologize."

"He said you would, after you spoke to your master. He won't accept."

"I want to do it anyway. If not to him, then to you."

She seemed to consider it. She had a kind face for all its lack of distinction. At length she moved aside to let me in.

The kitchen was her answer to her husband's study. In addition to the usual facilities for preparing meals and washing up after, it contained a bentwood rocker and a large sewing basket brimming over with spools of colored thread in a windowlit corner. A fancy bit of embroidery on white linen draped one arm of the chair. She went that way and twitched it so that the needlework didn't show, then moved a battered tea kettle from a trivet to the top of the wood range; apparently the silver set was for company, and I no longer qualified.

We sat at an oilcloth-covered table, where I pictured the couple sharing most meals, saving the simple dining room for guests. It wore a look of well-used comfort as opposed to the other, where even the hosts had seemed stiff and ill at ease; I was sure I'd been their first visitor in many a day.

She caught my glance straying toward the sewing corner. "I take in work sometimes. Eldred works hard, but there is only so much caretaking to be done in a small cemetery. We manage."

"I don't know when I've been in a place that felt so much like home."

"You're not married?"

I shook my head, and shook it again when she

asked if it was because of the nature of my work. "Most of the deputies have wives. Sometimes I think they fished out the stream. It means a lot of nights spent alone waiting for bad news."

"Men give up so easily. But then it's always easy making the decision you've wanted to all along."

I wondered what was keeping that pot from coming to a boil.

"You mentioned an apology."

"I spoke out of turn yesterday. My work doesn't put me in contact with many honest men. You're not at it long before you begin to think everyone has his hand out. At the time I wasn't in possession of all the facts, but I knew by his reaction I'd made a huge mistake."

"The facts in regard to what?"

Her eyes were the color of her dress, and faintly cowlike. That made what was behind them a concealed weapon. I braced my hands on the table and sat back. "In regard to how he came to leave the Church."

"Judge Blackthorne told you? How—no, never mind. The clergy is worse than a house filled with old women." She got up to tend to the pot, which had come to a boil. She spooned tea from a square tin into two cups, poured in the steaming water, stirred, and returned to the table carrying a cup and saucer in each hand. When she was seated she said, "It's been so many years, and still they're talking about it. You'd think nothing else has ever happened in the Church."

"You don't have to talk about it. I wasn't asking."

"Who else is there to talk to? All our closest neighbors are dead. The Sisters of Mercy from Sacred Hearts pick up their habits and hurry past this house and cross themselves after. They won't forgive us for leaving and the Protestants we meet won't forgive us for having been in."

"That's part of the reason I've gone this long without religion."

"No one is without religion; not the gambler who credits his winning streak to luck or the woman who blames her dark star because her husband beats her. Have you ever connected a good or bad experience with timing?"

"I have, but I assumed the responsibility."

"I'm sure that's what you told yourself, but let us say you're right, and for whatever reason you've chosen to live without God. That's not the same as saying that God has had no influence upon you. The steps you've taken to avoid Him have altered your journey."

I drank tea. I was beginning to aquire a taste for it, or at least for the way she brewed it. I'd had camp coffee that was less strong. "I can see why your husband doesn't encourage these discussions."

"My mother superior shared the aversion. I was naïve. A convent is no place for a lively exchange of ideas. I believe now that if I had not made the mistake of confiding my inner feelings to her, she would have found some other way to dispose of me."

"Then you have no regrets?"

She curled both hands around her cup and looked at her reflection on the surface. "I regret daily that I didn't hold my tongue and let nature find another course, one that did not destroy Eldred's life."

"Does he look at it that way?"

She picked up her ears, motioning for silence. The residents of that house seemed superhumanly attuned to the sound of their names. The stairs creaked and in a moment Griffin entered the kitchen. When he saw me he stopped, although of course he had to have known I was there. The place was small and voices traveled, even if words didn't."

"Did you return his money?" he asked his wife.

"I did not. We've spent some, and it would be weeks before we could save enough to return it. And you agreed to provide the instruction Mr. Murdock requested."

"I changed my mind."

I started my speech of apology, but she interrupted me. "You made a bargain; but we'll overlook that. A partial education in the ways of the Lord is worse than none at all. He might take what he's learned and not knowing the rest twist it to suit selfish purposes. I've heard you say that a hundred times about these traveling opportunists."

"He thinks I'm one of them."

"He's spent most of his visit telling me he doesn't. If you hadn't fled into your burrow when he knocked at the door, he'd have told you."

"There's been entirely too much telling going on. You've been doing most of the talking."

"Our story is known, but it's been poorly told. Should our enemies' version be the only one anyone hears?"

I scraped my chair back and stood. "I should leave."

"You should come upstairs," Griffin said. "A kitchen is for filling your belly, not your head."

SEVEN

The programme accelerated from that hour. Griffin seemed suddenly conscious of the time constraint and sped through the less illuminating biblical passages, questioning me sharply on certain points without warning, a bushwhacking maneuver that caught me unprepared the first time, but not again. His Church was founded on the New Testament, and lest the apostles be slighted for the sake of catching a train, we studied them between First and Second Kings. Infrequently he elaborated on the text, providing extraneous but revealing detail on the structure of the Roman legions and farming methods under the pharaohs of Egypt. His ragtag library was as heavy on history as it was light on theology; his massive Bible was the only religious authority in the room apart from himself. Arguments in print appeared to put him off as much as dissent from his wife, whom experience had taught him to defer to early and avoid a long and pointless discussion with the same result. He would not defer to rival philosophers.

One morning, near enough to date of departure to spoil my concentration with thoughts of linen and train changes, he marked his place in Deuteronomy with his bit of strop and shut the book with a thump. "How much experience have you had with speaking in public?"

"I've given manhunting parties their charges in town squares from here to California," I said.

"Bawling like a master sergeant and preaching to the faithful do not belong to the same world, particularly in a proper house of worship. You must speak as if you were alone with one parishioner, yet be heard as clearly in the rear pew as in the front. That last is important. People who sit in front are already disposed to pay close attention. It's the stragglers who perch near the door you must capture. They will fly at the first dry rustle."

"I'll try to get in some practice."

"What will you speak about?"

"I don't figure I can go wrong with 'Love thy Neighbor' and 'Stay Out of Hell.'"

He pulled his lips away from his teeth. I think they were false—no set ever grew so evenly or stayed so white—but the workmanship was superior to Judge Blackthorne's, which fit him so uncomfortably he wore them only on public occasions. He must have gone to a Catholic dentist while still a priest. "Why do you suppose most people go to church?"

The answer was too obvious for it to be anything but a trick question, but I've never learned anything by avoiding a trick. "To pray."

"They can do that at home. Some attend out of fear of damnation, or love of salvation, or because their friends and family expect them to, or to win public office, or to drum up business; back East, they would be the majority. Here on the frontier, most people surrender their one day of rest to be entertained. Be truthful. When you went in to hear Lawrence Little, did you expect to enjoy the experience?"

"No. I expected to be bored to my boots, then get frostbite in a buffalo wallow."

"I'd suspected there was truth in the compliment you paid him. Preposterous and blatant as it is, his Sunday-school-simpleton picture of hell is what puts them on their feet and brings back return customers who know the text by heart. Some of those who were baptized with you had already been in ponds and springs and swollen streams where the Traveling Tabernacle has stopped in the past. The blessing does not wear out or expire; renewal is not necessary. They wanted to be part of the show. Very few seriously believe they're in danger of being condemned perpetually. Those who do are not so simple as to accept Little's parable of the torturous corset as punishment for vanity. It's theater, and only a fool thinks Ophelia is going barking mad before his eyes. The rest do insist that the *performer* believes, or produces a reasonably convincing counterfeit, preferably with Roman candles or some substitute. If all they wanted was the Golden Rule, they would stay home and read Matthew."

"You're forgetting I'm going there to make arrests, not fill the collection plate."

"And when half your congregation stays home the second Sunday, who's to tell you whom to arrest? Barren soil yields dust."

I surrendered the point. "I'd planned to read straight from Scripture, but you've shot that down."

"You're supposed to interpret it, not parrot it. A casual familiarity with the statutes won't win a legal case or we'd not need lawyers who are themselves entertainers." He twisted to face his writing table and ransacked the heap of books and documents on top until he drew out a bundle of papers as thick as a brand book, bound lengthwise and sidewise with dirty cord. The edges were ragged and molting. They appeared to have been chewed by mice: *Church mice,* I thought, and surprised myself by feeling shame for thinking it. I wondered if piety was contagious.

I took the bundle, shedding paper flakes all over my lap. It was heavier than my own Bible and smelled like silage.

"My sermons," he said. "Call it 'The Gospel According to Griffin' if you like. You'll need to make them your own. I wrote them with a cadence in mind that was comfortable to me, but no two musicians play the same tune the same way. I expect them back. I'd almost sooner part with Esther."

Was there a flat note of insincerity in his *almost*? I asked myself if he didn't share his wife's regret. "Thank you. I doubt I'll be able to copy out many of them before I leave."

"I'm suggesting you take them with you. Yours is not a tent show. It may be months before you finish your mission. Your audience will expect something fresh each week."

"Are you sure you want to trust me with them? I've a habit of traveling light, with nothing I can't bring myself to abandon if the hunt goes the other way."

"I haven't decided to trust you with them yet. I'll reserve judgment until I've heard you read one in church. I've persuaded Father Medavoy to lend us the use of Sacred Hearts tomorrow morning. No services are scheduled that day. We'll have the place to ourselves and the odd sparrow."

"That's cutting it close. My train's Saturday. We're not halfway through the Bible."

"The seminaries are turning out graduates with a half knowledge of the Bible at best, and there are pastors who've forgotten more than that but continue to drift along on the same dogma they've been preaching for fifty years. As it stands, you know more than most of those who will come to you for spiritual aid, and it hasn't escaped my notice that you have the gift of blarney. My mother's people were Irish; I failed to inherit, but I have a healthy respect for it. I'm confident you'll find a way to fill the gap."

"I can't help but suspect you're giving me up as a lost cause."

"I resent the implication. I collect my pay for resodding sunken graves with my chin high, and if I thought I had shorted Judge Blackthorne in any way, I would return his gold if it meant working for Methodists to make up the difference."

I didn't know what to say to that, whether to ask why pulling weeds for the Methodist Church was more demanding than performing similar work for Sacred Hearts. Democrats vs. Republicans was enough of a closed door without pondering the politics of prayer. What I came up with was, "What if you don't like what you hear tomorrow morning? If I get a failing grade, do I get to stay home?"

"I've not met your employer, but based on what I've heard of his methods, he'll toss you into the furnace regardless of anything I might say. I seek merely to satisfy myself that I've done all I can in two weeks that can be expected of mortal man when faith is involved. If in my heart I cannot accept that I am doing other than releasing yet another profanity upon the land, I will beg your Judge on my knees to send me in your place."

"He'd never agree to that. It would be a death sentence."

"Just so."

A squeak from the floor below told me that Esther Griffin had opened the damper in the stovepipe to prepare noon dinner. I'd come to know the house like none I'd lived in since my father's dugout in the mountains, and the thought that I would soon leave it, with no good excuse to come back, put the cold lump of homesickness deep in my belly.

"I can't get the straight of you," I said. "How can you still be so devoted to God after He treated you as He has?"

He showed surprise for the first time since we'd met, and it was a testimony to how well I'd come to know him that I recognized it; the deep latitudinal lines that were so much a part of his forehead disappeared, the skin drawn taut by the movement of his scalp. It was a shape-shifting moment.

"God never deserted me," he said. "In return for my earthly disgrace He gave me Esther. It's a debt I can never repay. No other mortal in Creation has been permitted to take an angel unto himself."

"Have you said as much to Esther?"

"It would be superfluous. Angels know they're angels."

I didn't wander any deeper into country where I had no jurisdiction. He might have been able to address a churchful of people as if he were talking to one, but when it was just one he was wretched.

Our session ended and I went back to my room to look through the bundle. The undated pages were tanned and brittle and threatened to fall apart at the folds when I cut the cord. He'd filled them with a bold round hand with few crossouts and corrections and not a single blot. At first it seemed like poetry and I nearly gave up because I can't recite verse without sounding like a bored railroad conductor announcing the next stop, but when I tried one there in the privacy of my own quarters it came as easily as breathing. He'd found the difference between writing to be read and writing to be heard; what looked like broken pieces of sentences to the eye sounded like natural conversation when read aloud. Not surprisingly, because the Christian God is not the wrathful ogre of the Old Testament, there was little about flames that burned without consuming and much about forgiveness and mercy; but Eldred Griffin's Jesus was not the bearded lady I'd seen in picture books and in pasteboard frames on people's walls. Virile, decisive, and committed, his was the authority that hurled the money changers out of the temple and told the devil to go to hell with his kingdoms of gold. He reminded me of Griffin himself, who if he had not remade God in his own image had certainly placed his stamp upon Him.

I made my selection finally, and from sundown to well past midnight sat at the narrow drop-front desk that came with the room, transcribing the text onto a separate sheet, making small changes that suited my inferior breath control, and burning the phrases deep into my memory until my eyes gave out and I couldn't turn up the lamp any more without smudging the glass chimney. I retired then and spent the rest of the dark hours dreaming I stood naked at the pulpit before pews packed with my enemies. It made for a full house.

Griffin greeted me at the door of the Cathedral of the Sacred Hearts of Jesus and Mary and remarked that I hadn't slept well. I held up my pages of notes by way of answer.

"You're prepared, then. I expect much."

Thus pressed, I crossed the cavernous room up the center aisle, with the sensation that I was following the echo of my footsteps rather than the reverse. The morning sun leaning in through the tall stained-glass windows cast colored reflections on the oiled pews, and the sparrows Griffin had predicted fluttered between the rafters, looking for a place to perch and take in the performance. The place smelled of candle wax and varnish.

I mounted the steps to the pulpit. Father Medavoy, the pastor, was tall, and had directed a volunteer to raise it with planks for his comfort, bringing it to the top of my sternum. I felt like an altar boy serving out some kind of humiliating punishment. Griffin, no help, took a seat in the very back, nearly out of pistol range from where I stood arranging my pages on a slant-board with a pencil rail at the base.

I cleared my throat and began.

"Louder!"

I started again, raising my voice.

"Louder!"

I shouted.

"Not so loud! It's a sermon, not a roll call."

I made two more tries before he fell silent long enough for me to get to the body of the text. It was a parable of his own creation, about a boy whose brother had died before he was born, and who through a misunderstanding thought him an angel, to whom he prayed for an end to his parents' grief. It was guaranteed to wring tears from listeners, but acting upon some instinct I kept them from my own voice. It ended with the parents on their knees embracing their only child.

Silence struck like a bell. Even the light hiss of air stirring in the barnlike room had stopped. After a second (minute?) or two I began to hope I'd lost my hearing.

"Why did you pause before the last line?" Griffin asked then, and the air resumed stirring. Outside the nearest window a creaking carriage, which had halted in its tracks, started moving again.

"I thought it needed a running start."

"Leaps of faith don't. Why were you not moved by the tale?"

"I was, although I didn't expect to be when it started."

"I saw no tears and heard no sobs."

"I practiced to eliminate them. I heard somewhere that a humorous story sacrifices its effect when the speaker laughs. I gambled that the same holds true when the story's tragic."

"Indeed." Silence set back in. "Well, you won your gamble. You must let the listener draw from his own well. Why did you look up so seldom? Did you not commit your text to memory?"

"I did, but I got nervous."

"A display of fear is a confession of sin. You must speak as if each word has just occurred to you, and engage the eye of some random member of the audience. If he appears hostile, challenge him with your gaze to find fault with your point. If friendly, invite him into your exclusive tabernacle as One Who Understands. Leave the sheets at home and banish the temptation to steal a look."

I knew I could never do that, any more than I could go into a fight unarmed. "Am I as bad as all that?"

"I've heard worse right where you're standing. Do not interpret that to mean I consider you any better than scarcely adequate. However, only Our Father can grow wings on a frog in a fortnight. Step down."

I did, and started down the aisle, my knees wobbling like a broken spoke now that the ordeal was over. As I neared his pew he slid out and gave me a parcel wrapped in brown paper tied with string. It was bigger than the bundle of sermons but much lighter. "From Esther."

I unwrapped a folded shirt made of good simple gray linen. At first glance it looked like ordinary homespun, but the seams were double-stitched with uncommon skill. It was work more than worthy of a woman who took in sewing simply to help with the household accounts.

Such garments have attached collars generally, but a heavily starched white band had been fastened to it with studs. It was a preacher's clerical collar. I touched it. I'd never felt one.

"My last," Griffin said. "I thought I'd thrown them all out, but she said I overlooked this one, which happened to be my best. I suspect she squirreled it away."

The gift touched me. I thought I'd outgrown the emotion. "I'll try not to bring shame on it."

"It's blasphemous to promise miracles. I'll be satisfied if you don't get blood on it."

I thought of what he'd said the next day—my forty-third birthday—as I lay in a muck of dirt and dung waiting for a pair of my fellow pioneers to stir themselves to carry me to Dr. Alexander's office. I was saving my new shirt for the trip, and good job, because the one I had on was soaked through with blood.

At length I was collected and borne up the outside stairs to the little room above the hardware store, leaving behind the crowd that always gathers around medicine shows and shootings. Alexander, a wiry, excitable man of thirty, directed the volunteers to stretch me out on the cot and herded them outside. He locked the door, drew the window shade, and resumed his study of the *Herald* at his rolltop.

A moment later Judge Blackthorne came in from the private quarters in back. I was sitting now on the edge of the cot. He contemplated the stain on my shirt. "What did you use?"

"Calves' blood, from the meat shop. Matthews put it in a fish bladder. All I had to do was hang it around my neck under my shirt and give it a smack when I heard the shot."

"He'll keep silent?"

"He'd better. Half his business comes from the jail, and there are other markets in town. Where's Bullard?" Roy Bullard was the mail robber who was supposed to have been gunning for me.

"California, last I heard. That was Deputy Leffler behind the Winchester. He's a crack shot."

"He's too confident. The slug took a piece out of a porch post not two feet away. If he misjudged the wind, or I dove the wrong way, that's money wasted getting Griffin to make me a reformed character."

"It had to look convincing, and blank cartridges lack the authoritative report of a live round. We discussed all this. You need to be dead on the off chance someone recognizes you in Texas. The more witnesses the better, to make him doubt his own suspicions."

"If you wanted to make it credible you should have had ten men ambush me with shotguns."

"You've been reading dime novels about your exploits when you should have been studying Holy Writ." He unslung his watch and sprang the lid. "Ten minutes from now, the doctor will announce your demise to your admirers outside."

"Twenty," put in Alexander. "I have a reputation as well."

"Twenty it is. You will then be carried under cover of a sheet to Wilson's New Method Undertaking Parlor, where you will spend the next eighteen hours out of sight; the jail does business with Wilson as well, so his discretion is reasonably assured."

"*Where* out of sight?"

"The preparation room. I'm told there are no corpses there at present, but should the situation change, your natural stoic disposition will see you through any discomfort. I'm scheduling your services for tomorrow morning at nine: closed coffin, of course. By then you'll be in the baggage car of the eight-forty to Denver. After you change trains, you can ride to Amarillo with the rest of the human cargo, under the name Sebastian. Brother Bernard Sebastian of the Church of Evangelical Truth."

My lips twisted. I couldn't help it. "Saint Bernard?"

"Two saints, to be precise. Double the benediction."

"Your faith in numbers is misplaced. You've already dealt too many in on the hand."

"Death is a committee affair; but we must trust the cards. Rumors fuel the West. The deceased walk, the quick are dead. Last month Jesse James was seen coming out of an ice cream parlor in Chicago, and he's been worm fodder for two years. No one eats what's set before him without seasoning it heavily with irony. A bit of gaseous legend can only contribute to verisimilitude."

"I don't know that word, but if it means going off half-cocked, I agree with it."

He traded his watch for a thick wallet and held it out. I took it from habit; people had been giving me things for days. It was made of shoddy brown leather, fraying through at the fold. "Banknotes?"

"Personal effects: a letter from the fictitious Sebastian's dear dead mother, scribbled accounts of travel expenses, receipts for provisions, the usual mortal debris. They'll address questions about your identity. The devil is in the details." He smiled, lips tight.

II

The Parable of the Pilgrim

EIGHT

As it happened, Bucephalus Wilson, the undertaker, had a rush job, to improve the complexion of an old man who'd died of jaundice, and do it in time to ship him to Denver in the same baggage car Blackthorne had reserved for me. Since I had nothing better to do while waiting I helped out by handing things to Wilson, chiefly a pot of aluminum paste he applied as a sort of primer and a tin of pink powder to lend his customer the glow of health. It was interesting work, and the undertaker was good company, as might be expected since the Judge's deputies brought him so much business.

I won't dwell on that cold lonely ride across the High Plains, because it's as boring to tell as it was to experience. The old man's coffin gave me a seat, and I had a railroad lantern to warm my hands over until a porter came to tell me to put it out. A clerk had arranged to have my valise carried aboard, so I had my extra suit coat to keep me from freezing. I'd bought it, with black trousers to match, from a back room of the Drew Emporium where reclaimed and mended clothing sold for poverty prices. The coat was big enough to hide my revolver and shabby enough for a minister who survived on Christian charity.

As far as the train personnel were concerned I'd requested the windowless coach to flee an angry wife; boarding early under cover of darkness supported the story. I doubt they believed a word of it, but enough money had changed hands to keep their curiosity in check. In any case they didn't know where I was going after Denver, and they saw so much in the course of a working day to lower their opinion of the human race the odds were they forgot about me as soon as they finished unloading.

I didn't like the odds. A secret parsed more than two ways is like three men on one horse: You know it will collapse, but you're not sure when. But that was an inept comparison, because I was the only one in danger of falling. In Denver I went to the water closet three times to make sure I wasn't being followed. The other people waiting in the station looked at me sympathetically. It was obvious to them I had a medical problem.

It's a shuddery stretch from the Rockies to the desert Southwest, but the chair car felt like a private Pullman after the journey in baggage. I sank with a sigh of pleasure into horsehair stuffing that had shifted to accommodate backsides shaped very differently from mine and made myself intimate with the contents of Brother Bernard's wallet, and with the fabled Mr. Sebastian himself.

I sensed the Judge's devious hand behind the letter from Sebastian's mother, with perhaps Mrs. Blackthorne's gentler touch in the tender parts. I'd never seen a sample of her penmanship, but there was a womanly swoop in the tails and capitals, and I doubted anyone in the ruthlessly masculine organization of the

Helena federal court could have managed the endearing phrases it helped form. In between, a more calculating mind had leavened in information that provided the bearer with both a history and an iron-clad fence to prevent anyone from confirming or discounting it.

It was on the order of an expression of maternal gratitude and a helpful guide through the changeable landscape of a difficult world. Cleverly, Blackthorne had inserted pertinent details that explained how Sebastian had been thrust into it full-grown. Mother Sebastian, it seemed, had composed the letter to be discovered by her son among her personal effects, and read after her death. His father had been dead for many years. In his absence, young Sebastian had cared for his invalid mother in a house belonging to a Mrs. Brown in or near Denver. The father, a Church deacon, had tutored him in religion, so there was no reason to advise him about gentlemanly conduct once he was on his own, but the old lady took care to instruct her son on certain practical matters to ease his entry into the society of man. I learned from it how to save money, what to look for in a buggy horse, the importance of choosing friends cautiously, and the sort of woman to avoid. I'd have profited from knowing the first three twenty years ago, but I doubt I'd have paid much attention to the last even then. Perfidious women are an education all by themselves.

It was a remarkable document. I got lost in it, truth to tell, and found myself picturing an authentic Bernard Sebastian somewhere out there, born of an ailing mother rich in the wisdom of her years. It couldn't have been all fabrication. There was a rumor (which the Judge would have slashed to bits if it were ever mentioned in his presence) that the Blackthornes had lost a child in infancy years before they came to Montana Territory. Now I saw foundation in it. These were lessons intended for a youth who hadn't lived long enough to benefit from them. On the other hand, Mrs. Blackthorne was a great reader of novels, the chairwoman of a book club, and never missed the first night of a new production at the Ming Opera House, so I might have been wasting compassion on nothing more poignant than a lively sense of theater.

Purely as an instrument of my mission, it was expert craftsmanship. A place the size of Denver and its environs would be too thick in "Mrs. Browns" to encourage anyone to look up Sebastian's former landlady, and the name of the church where his father had served as a lay preacher wasn't mentioned; the city had dozens. A man of middle age seeking a pulpit in Texas could not have answered queries into his experience better than to claim he'd spent the last couple of decades nursing a bedridden patient and studying the Bible. Such exemplary sacrifice established him as a righteous man, and having a deacon for a sire entitled him to semiprofessional status at least. Mistakes made in front of the congregation would be assigned to his lack of an opportunity to practice what he'd learned in public.

So the old bastard was anticipating I'd fall on my face. As was I, but my pride was stung. All right, it's a sin, and so is wrath. I wanted to wring his neck.

I put back the letter and examined the rest. Someone familiar with my expense vouchers had come disturbingly close to duplicating my hand in the little writing block where Sebastian kept track of his travel budget. It, and what looked like a complete collection of receipts for possibles that he might need on the road, led me to believe that Brother Bernard was close with a buck, which befit a pilgrim of small means, but

it was overdone. Devotion is difficult enough to manufacture without having to try to be a prig as well. I
threw the receipts out the window.

I learned from a telegram, composed in Owen,
Texas, and sent through Wichita Falls by way of the
Overland, that Sebastian's request for a pastorship had
been accepted "on approval" by a director with the
First Unitarian Church who went by the intriguing
name of "R. Freemason." The lack of an outright commitment indicated there were concerns about my being an evangelist. Communication by telegraph meant
that a court contact in Denver had wired the original
petition, and sent the response to Helena.

Stuck in the fold of the wallet I found a stiff rectangle about the size of a penny stamp: an orange and
wrinkled tintype of a sheep-faced woman in her fifties, a son's only likeness of his sainted mother. I
wondered who she was really.

Blackthorne had thought of everything. He'd gone
to a deal of trouble to place me in the thick of a robbery investigation in someone else's jurisdiction. I
couldn't believe his only motive was to run the gang
to ground in Texas on the slim chance that if it were
left unfettered it might shift its activities to Montana
Territory.

Taking this assignment was like sitting in on a
poker game where the dealer made up all the rules.
I wouldn't mind losing so much as not knowing
why. But if I'd turned it down he'd have found something worse. That was the thing about the frontier:
There was always something worse.

Texas doesn't belong in the same sentence with the
place I considered home, or for that matter on the

same continent. As far as I was concerned it had broken off from southern Spain or northern Africa, blown about for a while to dry out some more like a dead cottonwood leaf, and come to rest a day's ride from the border of Colorado, where at least winter had the good manners to pause for conversation before heading north. To get there from where I'd started you had to cross the Cimmaron Strip: two hundred square miles of rugged land that was supposed to belong to the Indian Nations, but which had been overlooked when the territorial lines were drawn, leaving a slot-shaped hole in America where road agents scuttled like roaches when dawn broke. That was where mine would head if I put my foot wrong in Owen, and if I were reckless enough to follow them there, Brother Bernard would be dead before his first birthday. I'd taken the oath expecting to die in its honor, but dying twice in one season wasn't in it.

At Colorado Springs, our last stop in civilization, the greeters and loafers on the platform wore scarves and heavy pullovers and moved in close to warm themselves in the steam when the train braked. In Texas a couple of hours later, when we stopped to let off passengers and take on water, they wore loose cotton, sweat through under the arms, and stepped back to escape the moist heat. By then I'd shrugged out of my heavy preacher's weeds and pushed up the window against the furnace blast of wind scraping sand from Arizona Territory, which was the only place I'd spent time where you closed up the house to keep the heat out, and the only place that had somewhere to dump the heat it couldn't handle.

Somewhere being Texas.

Put that together with arid gusts that rocked the stationary cars like Confederate grapeshot, and you can begin to understand the conditions in panhandle country. No other spot on the map was better named, with the possible exception of the Dead Sea. You know that if you've ever tried to lift a heated skillet by its handle without first wrapping a rag around it. Sitting in that close coach, waiting for the train to pull out and fanning myself with Brother Bernard's wallet, I watched a stove-in galvanized bucket bounding across the prairie like a spooked antelope and wondered where it would stop this side of Arkansas, or if barring a fence or a corn rick or a sedentary hog, it would clatter through North Carolina, cross the Atlantic and the Gobi Desert, and make its way around the world back to that same patch of dead earth. That was one sophisticated bucket. I'd have gone out to intercept it, if for no other reason than that a rude receptacle of water shouldn't be more well-traveled than I, if I weren't afraid the train would leave me behind with the gilas and roadrunners.

That was my objection to Texas and its featureless landscape. I liked mountains on one side, waving grass on the other, and here and there a saloon or a brothel or even a bank or post office to interrupt the monotony, but the whole state was flat enough to duck under a fence. I'd ridden far for the court and had seen both extremes, cities of brick and stone decked out in coats of soot and spreading acres empty to the horizon. I wanted something in between, with an open window handy in case I changed my mind.

Then there were the Texans themselves; but more about them later.

I wasn't looking forward to crossing the same country again by horse. I'd overshot my destination for practical reasons and also for duty. There was as yet no rail line to Owen or anywhere within a full

canteen of it, and I had a Ranger station to report to
at end of track before I set out. Ever since he'd lost
two deputies in a misunderstanding in old Mexico,
Blackthorne had been a stickler about checking in
with local authority. The federales had taken the bigger hit, but he'd just escaped congressional censure
over the affair, and the Mexican major in charge had
been stood up against a wall in Mexico City.

As we resumed rolling, a man and woman entered
the car through the connecting door, balancing themselves against the sway with the support of the seats
and the weight of their bags. They were both dressed
for town, the woman in tightly woven tweeds as armor against cinders, and I thought they were together,
but after the man hoisted her portmanteau into the
overhead rack, she thanked him and they sat down
on opposite sides of the aisle, she to gaze out at the
scenery, such as it was, he to open a copy of *The Fort
Worth Gazette* and lose himself in the gray columns.

That was the payload, not counting freight, and it
didn't say much in favor of where we were heading. I
could only hope I could at least get drunk there.

I wished I'd bought a paper while we were stopped.
I didn't care what was going on in Fort Worth, and
there was never anything for me in the telegraph columns from New York and Washington, but I'd forgotten to bring a deck of cards and that last leg promised
even less in the way of diversion than all those that
had preceded it. I opened my Bible to Ecclesiastes. The
Preacher strummed the same three notes, time and op-
pression and no new thing under the sun; he must've
taken the same trip. I dozed, and woke, and saw nothing had changed outside, not even a shadow to tell
me how long I'd slept. The woman had given it up to

knit and the man was snoring with his *Gazette* spread over his face.

In due course we passed a pile of broken crates and empty lard cans that meant a settlement coming up. An ancient conductor with railroad-issue bad feet and a pair of moustaches the size of saddle pouches hobbled down the aisle shouting, "Wichita Falls," as if it were the first circle of hell.

Slowing, we slid through a neighborhood of chalk-gray houses and drew up alongside a station bright with fresh paint. I took my bones out of the seat and scooped my valise from the rack. "Where's the nearest place to get a steak and a bottle?"

The conductor's moustaches moved as he chewed. He parted them to squirt a muddy stream at the cuspidor at my feet. "Kansas City."

NINE

Lone Star lore, which is what the rest of the country calls a barefaced lie, says the first owner of the site on the Wichita River won it in a poker game. The other version is it was part of a legitimate purchase of land certificates, but he must not have thought much of them because he put them away and forgot they existed. When the trunk was opened almost forty years later, mice and squirrels had eaten all the better prospects and Wichita Falls was what was left.

The crook who platted the tract drafted a non-existent lake, cotton warehouses, and steamboats in quantity. None of those things ever materialized, and by the time the town had a church and a post office and a public school even the falls had vanished, pounded flat by the relentless water. After that it might have followed a hundred other Western towns into oblivion but for a land-concession deal with the Fort Worth & Denver Railway Company that amounted to property confiscation in return for a spur line. Behind the tracks came the station, a shingle and sorghum mill, a lumberyard, a general store, and promotion to county seat.

All this had happened in five years. When I first saw it, the place was built of loblolly pine shipped in from the East with no foundation between it and the natural limestone and smelled of sawdust and turpentine; when the wind shifted crossways the sting made your eyes water. All it took was a flake of hot ash from a pipe or a spark from a train wheel to wipe it out in four hours.

Except, of course, for the rails. The robber barons had stitched up the continent with steel thread that will still be there after the next great flood.

The station agent, a short twist of hickory with handlebars that extended past his shoulders, told me I could find Captain Jordan of the Texas Rangers in the back of the post office. I asked him if there was a hotel in town. He shook his head and gave me a ticket for my valise.

"How many bags have you got waiting to be reclaimed?" I asked.

"Just the one."

The regional Texas Rangers headquarters hung its shingle above a separate entrance to the post office, which was the only building in town flying the Stars and Stripes. I knocked, got a bark from inside, and opened the door on an office the size of a cloakroom. There was a plank floor without a rug, a barrel stove, a cot, the obligatory spitoon—pewter, with the initials of the Fort Worth & Denver Railway Company embossed on the flange around the top—a green-painted table, two chairs, a Windsor and a ladderback, and a male creature seated on the ladderback who might have been the twin of the station agent, left out in the weather. His handlebars were fair whereas the other's were brown and his hair had gone unbarbered long enough to curl back up toward the brim of his mottled pinch hat, but he had the same eyes like steel shot and hawk's-beak nose that looked as if it had been broken at birth.

He had a copy spread on the table of what looked like the same edition of *The Fort Worth Gazette* I'd seen aboard the train and was using a wooden yardstick and a clasp knife to cut a neat rectangle out of the lead column. He didn't glance up as I entered but told me to take a seat. He had a big voice for a small man; not as deep as Dr. Lawrence Lazarus Little's, but what it lacked in timbre it made up for in volume, with that burred edge that comes from shouting orders against the west Texas wind. I sat, and noticed that his yardstick was stenciled with the name of the Fort Worth & Denver Railway Company and that the knife he was using was the kind issued to porters to cut the tags off luggage and probably had the same legend printed on the handle. A panoramic photograph of two rows of Texas Rangers, one standing, one sitting cross-legged on the ground, all armed with pistols and carbines, hung crooked in a walnut frame on the wall behind his head. As far as I could tell, the railroad hadn't gotten around to slapping its brand on that.

He finished cutting, peeled up the rectangle, and spiked it on a spindle on a cast-iron base. Other cuttings, scraps of scribbled paper, and telegraph flimsies climbed halfway up the spindle.

I asked him if he'd been mentioned in the newspaper.

"Not me. The Rangers." He crumpled the rest and tossed it into an open crate in the corner by the Republic of Texas flag on a stand. "Every time we're in print I'm supposed to save it and send it on to San Antonio." He'd lowered his voice, but it still carried. I couldn't hear anything from the post office side, so the walls must have been stout. "That's what we do up here since we whipped the Comanches. All the men I need to keep the peace are down shooting greasers on the Rio Grande. Who the hell are you?"

"Are you Captain Jordan?"

"Would I be sitting in this shithouse if I wasn't?"

"Don't get your back up, Captain. The more people know I'm alive, the less chance I've got of staying that way." I showed him the star and the letter from Judge Blackthorne. His own star, which was nearly as plain as mine, hung on a pocket of his blue flannel shirt, with two inches of white union suit sticking out of the cuffs. He was one of those who believe in insulating themselves against the heat.

In his case it seemed to work. He wasn't sweating, and the room couldn't have been hotter if it had been built above a blacksmith's forge. He looked well past fifty, but taking into account the oven conditions in that country he might have been ten years younger. He didn't wear spectacles and held the letter at normal length while reading.

He laid it down, fingered through the stack of papers on the spindle starting at the base, and tore one

loose a third of the way up from the bottom, then
smoothed it out beside the letter. He wasn't compar-
ing the writing, because the second sheet was a telegram that had been taken down by a key operator in
Wichita Falls. It was a carefully whittled message
from Judge Blackthorne, who never spent a taxpayer's
penny on unnecessary verbiage, asking him to cooperate with a visitor bearing a letter from him. Learning
to read upside-down is useful in my work.

Jordan aimed a square-nailed thumb over his shoulder at the waste paper in the crate. "You're dead in
today's *Gazette*."

"In yesterday's *Independent,* too, up in Helena." I
tried not to preen. Vanity's a stubborn sin to lick when
you find out you're news so far outside your range.

"Anyone can write a letter. Got anything to prove
you're who you say?"

"I left my commission behind. Traveling with the
badge and letter was risky enough. I'll thank you to
burn the letter and I'm putting the badge in your
charge when I leave here."

He ruminated. Then he rolled onto one hip; to let
wind, I thought, and in that thick air I came closer to
panicking than I had since the Judge's sniper had
shaved things so thin back home. Instead he hauled
out a long-barreled converted Colt Paterson with a
worn brown finish from a scabbard that went down
into his back pocket, cocked it, and clunked it down
on the table. "I'll have that pistol under your arm."

I was wearing the coat I'd had tailored to cover it,
but he'd make it his business to know why I kept it
on in the heat. I lifted the Deane-Adams clear, holding the butt between thumb and forefinger like a dead
fish, and laid it inside his reach. He picked it up,
checked the cylinder, and gave it back.

"I heard you carried an English weapon. Those are harder to come by than this other gear."

I returned it to its scabbard and watched him take the Paterson off cock and put it away. "I heard the Rangers went to Peacemakers."

"Peacemaker didn't save my hide fourteen times in fifty-eight. What's your story?"

That put his age back into the fifties. "I've got a billet at the First Unitarian Church in Owen, where they think I'm a preacher named Sebastian, out of Denver. Governor Ireland asked us to lend a hand with a run of robberies in the panhandle."

"Why Owen?"

"So far it's the only place this bunch hasn't hit."

"Think it's next?"

"Only if they're foolish enough to tip their hand in their own parlor."

"Just because we carry our guns out in the open don't mean we're simple. We poked our heads into every attic, root cellar, and pigsty in town on the same suggestion. It didn't take long; you'll find out why when you see the place. We didn't turn up a cartwheel dollar unaccounted for nor a man who fit any of the descriptions close enough to sweat a confession out of him."

"Bet you sweated someone, though."

"San Antonio sends out a new Yellow Book every two or three years, to keep us current on who's got paper out on him. Some, when we know where they are, we leave for seed. The seed crop in Owen all had witnesses that put them home at the wrong times. Wrong for us, anyway. I'm satisfied."

"Some of the new breed have never been posted anywhere. They're in it for profit, not to settle old scores. They don't write letters to newspapers or do anything else to bring suspicion to them. You won't find them in your book."

"You want to know the first time I ever heard the words 'new breed'? December sixty-eight, when John Wesley Hardin bushwhacked and killed three Yankee troopers in Sumpter. I been here long enough to see a parcel of new breeds turn old, when they lived that long, and a bushel of new breeds pour in on their heels. You fixing to pray this bunch into turning themselves in?"

"I'm not fixing to do anything but keep my ears open. If the God-fearing folk there tell me something they didn't tell you, I'll report it and you can do what you want with it. We're not after glory."

"Glory, you think that's what this conversation is about?"

I'd pinked him where it hurt. I didn't know why Blackthorne saddled me with these jobs that required diplomacy. The last time I'd had to establish friendly relations with an elite law enforcement unit outside the U.S. marshals, I'd nearly started a war with Canada. "I wasn't born pinned to that star, Captain. I drove cattle between here and Mexico, and someone was always telling thumpers in the bunkhouse. A coroner's jury in San Antonio ruled 'death by suicide' in the case of five bandits mowed down by Texas Rangers because everyone knows what's in store for a desperado who sticks up a bank that close to Rangers headquarters. A reputation like that is worth a thousand extra men. It's in everyone's best interest not to claim outside credit, or glory, if you like that sort of language."

His steel-shot eyes regarded me from under brows that stuck out like spines. The resemblance to the man behind the counter in the train station was marked.

He tilted back his chair, scooped the wide framed photograph off its hook with one hand, banged the front legs back down, and laid the picture on my side of the table facing my way. A stone barracks stretched behind the two rows of armed men, with empty sky above and barren earth below. On the bottom, in brown ink in a neat copperplate hand, someone had written:

Ft. Sill, 10 June 1875

"That's me, Sergeant Andrew Jackson Jordan, aged none-of-your-goddamn business." His index finger banged the glass above a face that was all bone and a pair of eyes that photographed like blank whites, belonging to one of the Rangers seated on the ground. He'd worn chin whiskers then and the handlebars were smaller. Apart from that I didn't know how a man could have changed so much in nine years. I put him back down into his forties, and the veteran of 1858 around age eighteen.

"These here are Corporal T. J. McReady and Ranger James Poe. Mac and Jimmy. I never knew Mac's Christian name."

I looked at a young Irish roughneck and an Adam's apple with a head attached, seated on either side of the sergeant. He'd had several years on both.

He read my mind. "They called me Dad. They wasn't walking yet when I joined up."

"I guess there's a Dad in every outfit. Mine had one."

"A splay-footed mulatto name of Tilson took the picture about a week after the Comanches surrendered. It was white of the Yankees to let us sit for it, seeing as how they got the glory after we fought the bastards forty years, including the five we spent doing it alone while they was busy putting down rebels. Mac never had his likeness made before and kept asking when would it be ready. He never seen it. He was assassinated June twelfth. It was done from cover with a shotgun, from behind. We never did find who done it or why. Half his head was gone. His mother had to say good-bye to him through the coffin lid. Twenty-two he was."

"What about Poe?"

"Jimmy got tired of manhunting finally and shot himself behind the counter of a dry-goods store in Dallas. Later that day the city marshal found his wife shot dead in their house. Same caliber gun. They fell out over something and he got all the way to work before what he done caught up with him.

"Burial's free when you served with the Rangers. There's your glory."

"We've all got stories like that," I said. "I meant no disrespect."

He leaned back and rehung the picture, more crookedly than before. "We'll all of us be reunited in dust. I gave up on the other. Maybe I shouldn't talk like that in front of a padre."

"I'm not pretending to be a priest. And I'm not half sure you're wrong."

"We'll just leave that in the room, along with this here." He picked up the letter from Judge Blackthorne and set fire to it with a match from a twist of oilcloth he took from his flap pocket. When it had burned almost down to his fingers he let it fall to the floor and stamped out the flame.

I felt like taking off my hat. I'd missed my funeral.

TEN

"Two banks, the Overland, two trains, all in six months," I said. "Blackthorne said this gang leaves footprints, but he didn't say what they were."

"He always cut you loose this well informed?"

"He encourages independent action, outside his presence. To him that means traveling light on such things as too much preparation, which he says slows the brain and the hand. He's a son of a bitch is what he is."

"How's the pay?"

"I can't spend what I make, but that's only because I haven't had a week off since the last time I was shot."

"Sounds familiar. Why do you stick?"

"For the glory, same as you."

Jordan still had his matches out. He filled a short-barreled pipe from a pouch in his other flap pocket and started it, his cheeks caving in on the draw where the molars had rotted away. His front teeth—the lowers, anyway—were ground down to yellow-oak stumps. If he had uppers the handlebars covered them.

He shook out the match, dropped it on the floor, and pushed the pouch toward me. I shook my head.

"You're overplaying your part," he said. "I read the Bible cover to cover and back. San Antonio recommends it. It don't say a thing against smoking or chewing. The Reverend Wilcoxson up at the First Methodist orders cigars by the case from New Orleans."

"I never got the habit."

He puffed smoke out of the side opposite the pipe,

which as long as it was burning he never took out of his mouth. "I got a man who won't cuss and some who say they never touched a drop of the Creature, but when it comes to covering ground fast they'll all dump their coffee before their tobacco. I don't trust a man without a vice I can see or smell or taste. The one he's hiding might get me killed."

"I didn't say I didn't have any vices."

"I forgot to mention women, which can be worse than all the rest put together. I'm near certain it was another woman caused Jimmy Poe to shoot his wife and then himself."

"I approve of women in general, but I've been on friendly terms with the Creature most of my life."

"How friendly?"

"We were living in each other's pockets for a while. The commitment got to be too much. These days we just shake hands."

"Same here. It was Mrs. Jordan made me choose. She's dead, but it don't taste the same now that I don't have to hide it in the potato bin." He smoked. "I drink standing up. We got a nice little watering hole down the street with a cross draft from the river, though it's best to put it down fast before it boils."

"After we talk. Bartenders spill too much."

He scratched his congenitally broken nose. "How many know about this scheme apart from you, me, and the Judge?"

"Pretty much the entire territory of Montana, and I have my suspicions about the Santa Fe Railroad. As I see it I've got three weeks at the outside before everyone in the panhandle knows I'm still around and Brother Bernard never was."

"Who's he?"

"He's me. Sebastian's my other name."

"You had too many as it was. I wouldn't give it no three weeks. News travels faster by jackrabbit than Western Union."

"When's the next stage leave for Owen?"

"Eight in the morning."

"That's another day gone. We'd better get started. Has any of the gang been identified?"

"Not yet. They wear bandannas over their faces and only one does the talking."

"That describes half the men in your book. What is it about the robberies that ties them all to one bunch?"

"It's not so much the way they go about their business as how they look. Everyone that's ever read about Jesse James knows what to say and where to point his pistol and to get in and out fast; if I had my way I'd bring in every one of them dime novelists in leg irons for teaching folks how to break the law. But even they don't say Jesse and his guerrillas dressed alike even in the war."

"They wear uniforms?"

"Not so's you'd call 'em that, taken one at a time. When five men bust in all wearing white dusters, gray hats, and blue bandannas, that's the impression. That's how it's been all six times."

"Six? I counted five raids."

He plucked the piece he'd cut from the *Gazette* off his spindle and slapped it down in front of me. It was a sketchy description of a midnight run on a cattle ranch near a town called White Horse three days earlier. The thieves had shot the ranch hand on watch and turned five hundred head of Herefords north. Contact had been made with the Texas Rangers to investigate.

"What makes this our gang?" I asked.

"They gut-shot the man on watch, but he was still

talking when the man that came to fetch us took us to the line shack where they carried him. He didn't talk long. There was a little-bitty moon that night, what we call a rustler's moon, but it was enough to see what they was wearing."

"Dusters are common in dusty country. They could've had on brown hats and red bandannas. You can't see colors by moonlight."

"Nor did he, but different colors look different whatever the light. They was all the same. I say they was gray and blue."

"Too thin for court."

"It's a far piece out here between courts. They don't always make it."

"Five men?"

"Seven. I said it was five bust in on banks and such, but I didn't mention the one they left outside with a carbine and the one they left to hold the horses. At White Horse, the other hands had put together a P.C. and took out after them; we met them on their way back. They'd followed to the Canadian, where the bunch turned the herd into the river, but by then the moon was down and they couldn't see where they come out. The hands voted against making camp on account of the bushwhack risk."

"P.C." was Texas talk for *posse comitatus*. Guerrillas had brought the term west from Missouri; in many cases half a jump ahead of a posse. "Did you find where they came out?"

He nodded, puffing smoke. "It was sunup and the trail was cold. In the Nations it crossed some others left by legitimate outfits headed to market. We wired Fort Smith to alert the marshals, but them beeves are gone. Chicago's hungry."

"Where's White Horse?"

"Thirty miles southwest of where you're headed. Your Judge Blackthorne might be on the sunny side of right. Then again he might not."

"He might not. Rustling's hard work for cash bandits. They don't usually cross over."

"If it's the new breed, where'd they learn to ride if not a working ranch? I'm seeing a lot more buggies and buckboards than saddle horses these days."

"I notice you're not ready for a buggy yet. If you rode out there and up into the Nations and back in three days, you ought to be lathered up as bad as your mount."

"That ugly little mustang needs more'n a short trot like that to break a sweat. I wish I could say the same for me. I just got back from the bathhouse when you knocked."

"When do you sleep?"

"When it hits. Some nights I don't make it as far as that cot."

"How many men do you have under you?"

"Fourteen. I came here with a company, but that was before the Frontier Batallion busted up. We done too good a job thinning out rebel scum, you see."

"You should've left a few more for seed."

"Wouldn't of done. Austin discovered Mexico and took all my best men. There's a powerful lot of ranch money down on the border and the governor's fixing to keep it in this country where he can draw on it come election time. That's what this bunch is counting on. It's a wonderment they took this long to test me."

"Why do they dress alike, you figure?"

"Keep from shooting each other."

"How much shooting takes place?"

"Less than you'd expect. They winged the shotgun

messenger on the Overland to make their point, but that was the worst of it till they killed that cowhand on watch. A bank manager got pistol-whipped when he forgot the combination to the safe, if you count that and if you count bankers. I won't say they go out of their way not to let blood, but they don't rattle. If that's the new way of robbing folks, I'm for it, and I'll shake their hands on the scaffold."

"I'd admire to have a talk with that shotgun messenger."

"Not the banker?"

"Him too, but shotgun men have good eyes and remember what they see."

"Just as well. The banker took his busted head home to Baltimore. The shotgun's staying with his sister in Owen till he heals, but I believe they're affiliated with the Church of Rome."

"I'll visit as a neighbor." I took out the sorry wallet and showed him the telegram from R. Freemason, director of the First Unitarian Church. "What can you tell me about him?"

"He ain't Catholic."

"I gathered that from the name."

"Dick Freemason runs sheep, not that you'd smell it on him. He's a gentleman rancher, lives in town with his wife in a big ugly house he had built, with a chandelier he had shipped from Italy and sent a special train down to fetch it. He sits on most of the town committees and had a big hand in banning whores from all the public areas before ten P.M. He pays exactly twice as many men as he needs to manage his spread. Ask me why."

"Because he runs sheep in cattle country."

He tried not to appear impressed. "You're quicker than you look."

"That's why I get these assignments. I suppose you asked his hired guns what they were doing at the time of the robberies."

"I did. I work this job. I'd of been suspicious if they all had stories, and I'm pretty sure at least two of them are in the Yellow Book under other names. But Freemason pays too much to make the risk worthwhile."

"No one pays that much."

"He comes close. Also he's a rough cob under the silk. Eleven jurors voted to send him to Huntsville after he had a bunkhouse thief horsewhipped to death. That was in Waco, before he came here. I don't know where he was before that. He don't talk like a Texan."

He took the pipe out of his mouth then to stifle a yawn. I was keeping him from his cot. I got up. "I'll pass on that drink. Brother Bernard shouldn't be seen in a saloon in broad daylight. Is there a place in town where I can put up my feet?"

"Corporal Thomson and his wife have a spare room and a baby on the way. They can use the money. White house with green shutters, two squares up and one over. Where's the rest of your gear?"

"I left it with the station agent. He looks enough like you to be kin."

"First cousin. I won't apologize for his manners. He was easier to live with before he hurt his back and had to leave the Rangers."

"Is he the reason you didn't volunteer for the border?"

"It meant promotion to major, but I turned it down when they offered. He can't ride and he can't sit up in a train. Since Elizabeth died the miserable bastard's all the family I got."

I shook his hand. "I'm Sebastian if Corporal Thomson asks."

"I recommend it. She's all right, but he likes to talk."

"Did the jury in Waco ever find out if Freemason wanted that man whipped to death?"

"I never heard."

"Maybe he's easier on the ministers who work for him."

He yawned openly. "Stick your fingers in the collection plate and find out."

ELEVEN

I never had the opportunity to board the gondola of a hot-air balloon, but I've ridden in Pullman parlor cars, and someone once said that apart from them no nineteenth-century invention accommodated itself to the comfort of passengers as well as the Concord coach: more than a ton of red-lacquered bentwood, suspended hammock fashion on a pair of leather thoroughbraces that rocked its human cargo gently over washes and rubble. But it was wasted on flat west Texas, so I didn't get one.

Wells, Fargo & Company, owner of the Overland, had sent all its Concords to more challenging country and stuck me in a square mud wagon on solid elmwood timbers that telegraphed every ridge and chuckhole directly to my spine. Dust caked the muslin side curtains, releasing gusts of ocher powder when the

cords were undone but forming no barrier whatso-
ever to fresh injections from outside. When they were
drawn and tied down, the hot wind battered at them
and whenever we turned crosswise to the blast the
coach wobbled and groaned and tried to heel over
like a ship. One of my fellow travelers, a barbed-wire
salesman from Indiana who carried a sample case
that opened in two halves to show his assortment of
Buckthorns, Champions, Spur Rowels, and Sawteeth
mounted on washboards, offered to bet me that at
times we were rolling on two wheels only, the others
lifted clear of the earth and spinning ineffectually.

I declined to take him up on the wager. Partly it was
because I wasn't half convinced he was wrong, but
mostly it was because I was in full preacher's kit, with
the Deane-Adams well concealed beneath the rusty
black sackcloth of my old coat and a badly used slouch
hat that ought to have had a couple of holes cut in the
brim for an ass to stick its ears through, and games of
chance were inappropriate. I smiled as I shook my
head, clinging to the valise on my lap and trying not to
cut my throat with Eldred Griffin's stiff clerical collar.

The first time I'd tried it on, in Corporal and Mrs.
Thomson's spare bedroom in Wichita Falls, I'd looked
at myself in the mirror above the wash basin and saw
a mean-faced, middle-aged gunman trying to pass as a
man of the cloth, but of course I was hobbled by
guilty knowledge. I'd known preachers who could
match a Kansas redleg for ruthless aspect and the
saintliest-looking one I'd ever seen, with white hands
and a gentle countenance, had hanged himself in a cell
in Billings after clubbing his wife to death with a boot
scraper during a heated discussion over some little
thing. I promised myself to shave more closely and
look to my nails and accept the rest with serenity.

The collar was another matter. I wasn't sure I'd ever get used to it in the Texas heat and there were plenty of sects that didn't require it, but having been seen with it on, I considered putting it away a risk to my mission. Griffin had outmaneuvered me at the last. The torturous gift was his vengeance for having been forced to compromise his principles. It was my hair shirt.

I kept the valise close because it contained his sermons. I'd given him my word I'd look after them, and I was rewarded for my vigilance when the driver turned abruptly to avoid striking some piece of wagon-road jetsam, overcorrected, and an iron-bound trunk toppled off the rack on the roof, broke its hasp when it struck the ground, and spilled out most of its contents. The driver drew rein and my only other companion, a careworn lawyer who dressed even more shabbily than I did, got out to scoop his linen and legal library back into the trunk. The mustard-colored volumes had been missent to Houston while following him from St. Louis; after they were rerouted by the railroad, he'd left his brand-new practice in Owen to go to Wichita Falls and bring them home personally.

I got that information from his anxious conversation with the driver while the trunk was being loaded, and he repeated it as he repacked. The heat and dust of the journey had not led to casual conversation except from the wire drummer, who seldom heard what was said in answer and failed to draw the obvious conclusion from silence.

The lawyer struck me as a worthier fellow. I respect a man who takes care of the tools of his trade; Blackthorne treated his soiled, mismatched texts as tenderly as a surgeon handles his saws and scalpels, and if I were on trial for my life I'd want no one else to sit in judgment.

Provided I was innocent.

The driver, who cursed the way other men breathed, bound the trunk with rope from the tackle in the boot to keep it from flying open again while his shotgun messenger stood by with the hammers eared back on his Stevens ten-gauge, dividing his attention equally between open country and the tattered attorney. He kept his counsel as to how the man might have rigged the mishap to lay the stage open to ambush. Guarding mail shipments is a suspicious profession.

There was no faulting his caution. There must have been something of value in the strongbox, because the passenger fares on that run wouldn't have fed the horses, much less paid for the wear and tear on the equipment.

The salesman and I stepped down to stretch our legs. It did nothing for my confidence in my disguise that the messenger watched me as closely as he did the others. His taut face and bunched chin beneath the black whiskers was the first evidence I'd seen that the recent bandit raids had the panhandle on the balls of its feet.

I asked the lawyer for his card.

He didn't hear me at first, concentrating as he was on the driver's skill with knots. Then he hoisted his bushy brows and smiled tragically at me from under muttonchops that had needed barbering a week ago. Gray tips and the general fall of his crest made him look ten years older than he probably was. He might have been on the green side of thirty-five.

"I thought you parsons pled your case with the Almighty Imponderable," he said. "I'm afraid I'm not licensed to practice before that bench."

I answered the smile with a humble one of my own,

or rather of Brother Bernard's. "I've no use for fence, but I took that gentleman's name." I tilted my head toward the third member of our party, who was relieving himself noisily into a clump of thorn scrub at the side of the road. I'd already forgotten what he called himself. "I see no reason not to make a running jump at getting to know my neighbors. Bernard Sebastian." I offered my hand.

"Father or Reverend?" He took it, stealing a look at my raiment. The treasures of the Vatican were not apparent.

"Brother. I'm merely a pilgrim on the path to righteousness."

"Well, Brother, you must have been walking it on your hands. I've shaken the paws of mule skinners with less muscle." He kneaded bruised fingers.

I apologized, stopping short of inventing an excuse. I would have to watch more than just my visual impression. The strength in my gun hand ill befit the meek.

He seemed to disregard it. "I haven't just had time to have cards printed. I've spent my first weeks in Texas tracking that trunk, which has scaled mountains and forded rivers and crossed the burning prairie, passing all manner of savages and baggage clerks, only to become a casualty twenty-five miles from its destination."

The driver hooked a heel on a corner of the item under discussion and heaved back on the rope to set the knot. "Better a busted trunk than a busted wheel. The Golden Rule don't hold up out here."

"You're hardly the resident expert," said the lawyer. To me: "I'm Luther Cherry. I expect delivery of my shingle any time, if that dullard of a sign painter ever gets it right. Why a man who can't spell should choose that line of work is a question only your immortal Client can answer."

"I'm sure He can, although I'd hesitate to approach Him with it. What kind of law do you practice?"

"Real property, chiefly land disputes; which makes me a colleague of sorts of Mr. Barbed Wire. I'd intended to open an office in Denver, but there's a glut there, as you might expect. Then I learned the legislature in Austin is debating a law to declare fence-cutting a felony. In Colorado Territory it's a misdemeanor punished by a fine, which Big Cattle pays routinely as part of the cost of running off their smaller competitors' stock."

"They'll never pass it," I said. "It would mean the end of the open range in this state."

"Cattle don't pay taxes. Landowners do, and entirely too much of it is going to waste on community grazing rights. In any case I anticipate a healthy demand for my counsel."

"I'm told ranchers here are accustomed to settling their disputes out in the open, with gunfire."

"I was told the same thing, and most of the inquiries I made confirmed it, when they received a response at all. The guard is changing, however, as change it must, before the relentless advance of civilization. The governor is in favor of the law, and he has the support of Mr. Richard Freemason of Owen, who wired me travel expenses in St. Louis as part of the retainer for my services."

The sheep baron seemed to cast a wide loop.

"We share a sponsor," I said. "Mr. Freemason is a director of the church where I am preparing to preach the gospel."

Some of the tragedy went out of Cherry's smile. "A

splendid sign! The sheep wars have been strangling the livestock industry, and Mr. Freemason means to have a hand in restoring peace. Was not the man whose wife bore the Prince of Peace a shepherd?"

"This one, at least, has made friends of two strangers."

"Will a Mrs. Sebastian be joining you later, or does your oath forbid the domestic custom?"

"It doesn't, but I have no wife."

His face fell. "That's a disappointment. Mrs. Cherry is closing the house in St. Louis and will board with her parents until I'm settled. It's lonely out here for a woman, they say."

"Mr. Freemason is married."

"I've not met him yet, though I've spoken with his wife, who told me he was away visiting the ranch until this week. She's gracious, but worldly—a bit out of Anna's set. She paints her face. The only other women I've seen are years older, except the ones who can't show themselves until the respectable citizens are home in bed." Abruptly he added, "Those who are not engaged until late setting their office in order, I mean."

He'd colored a shade, surprising me. None of the lawyers I'd known could have managed it.

"Yes," I said, acknowledging the problem of Original Sin. "Still, it's not exactly a mining camp."

"Did I hear you say you're bound for the camps?" The fence man joined us, buttoning his fly. He picked up only half of everything said within his earshot and folded it into a pitch. "Once I make my stake in Texas I'm off to the goldfields. There's nothing like six hundred yards of Glidden's Twist Oval to protect your claim from jumpers."

Cherry shook his head—not to contradict the other's impression of what we were talking about, but to address the new development. He'd do well in court. "I studied the crime for my bar examination. Claims are jumped in town, not in the field. It's a combination of bookkeeping and bribery."

The salesman considered what he'd taken from that, then lost interest. "They ain't come up with a barb for that yet." He climbed back aboard the coach.

The driver manhandled the trunk to the roof and lashed it to the rack. His messenger waited until we were all seated, then eased down his hammers and mounted to his place on top. As we jolted forward, Cherry watched the flat land rolling past. "It's this way clear to Owen. Does it ever change, do you think?"

I said, "I understand after you cross the Canadian it starts to level out."

He turned from his window, but I was careful not to intercept his look. The man sitting facing us was busy rearranging the samples in his case. I hoped—well, prayed—that if I learned to think before I spoke I might play my part as well as they played theirs.

TWELVE

Owen, Texas, was ten years old, older than Wichita Falls by five years and ancient by frontier standards, which had seen pick holes sprout into metropolises in six months, then blow away six weeks after the veins played out, and roaring end-of-track towns dismantle themselves and reassemble under different names farther down the ever-expanding line. Such places were as transient as Indian villages and left only piles of offal behind to mark their passage. Owen had kept the offal but refused to budge.

Increase Owen, scion of an old New England family and a putative former army major who had either resigned or been cashiered by Ranald MacKenzie at the end of the Red River Indian War in 1874, had built an adobe store on a tributary of the Canadian River called Wild Horse Creek, selling whiskey and provisions and ammunition to parties of buffalo hunters. On occasion he'd bartered for hides, and at the end of the first winter—and they were as cold in the panhandle as the summers were unbearably hot—when the stack of stiff green hides behind the building began to reek, he sold them to a tanner, who paid the market rate. This amounted to ten times what he'd taken in on all his other merchandise since opening his doors, wiping out cost of construction and stock. At that point he entered into a partnership with the tanner. With the Eastern demand for lap robes and doctors' coats and leather belts to drive the gears in Industrial Age manufactories at its peak, he might have retired in five years to a life of leisure and fine things if the buffalo had just held out.

They didn't. By then a little community had sprung up around the store, made up of gunsmiths, knife sharpeners, wheelwrights, crib girls, faro dealers, plank-bar saloons where busthead whiskey was sold and consumed by the jug, and all the other bluebottles that feed on a going concern. Owen had had the foresight to obtain a deed to a hundred acres on the creek and the knowledge to have it platted for town lots, but also the poor judgment to do it all on credit. When the great herds vanished and his debtors caught up with him, he shot himself with the Army Colt he'd carried in the Battle of Palo Duro Canyon; or had stolen from a sutler's after he'd been stripped of his weapons and rank, depending upon which story you preferred. Generally there's truth in everything that's said about a person, and if you took all the rogues out of the rotation the country would still belong to the Indians, who had rogues in plenty but not enough to check the press from the Atlantic coast.

Its founder's misfortune and death would have been the end of the city of Owen in the normal course of things, but the West was no normal place. The creek, which slowed to a trickle during droughts, never quite dried up, and the grazing was ideal for fattening herds of longhorns and Herefords being driven from the ranches down south to the Kansas railheads in Dodge City and Abilene. Tent saloons popped up like mushrooms, to be replaced quickly by frame buildings where brand whiskey was served in bottles on proper bars and brothels with parlors replaced the cribs. There were shootings, brawls, and the odd mysterious disappearance of a lucky poker player after he left the scene of his success, but nothing to compare with what was going on up north, where the cowhands were paid their full trail wages and had more to spend. Owen boasted the first hotel in the panhandle, and soon a Catholic church, attended mainly by Mexican masons and carpenters and their families. In 1878, a sheep rancher named Vallejo wedded the eldest daughter of one of them before its altar and was buried from there three months later after he was shot by an unknown assassin and his flock scattered. No one was ever brought to trial for his murder; just as well, as it was commonly accepted that no Texas jury would find against the cattle interests, which benefited most from discouraging the sheep trade in that state.

That was the beginning of Owen's ranching phase. By the time I arrived, relations between cattleman and shepherd had settled into a low simmer. Residents credited the uneasy truce to the appearance of Richard Freemason, whose eight-hundred-acre ranch on the other side of Wild Horse Creek was the largest in the region, and whose determination to raise sheep placed him on the side of one of the most oppressed groups on the prairie. He was the first rancher to encircle his spread with barbed wire. Three of his fence riders (who when questioned on the stand revealed a deeper knowledge of gun handling than posthole digging) were tried for the murder of a cowhand surprised in the act of cutting the wire to drive some strays across the spread instead of riding a mile out of his way to use the public gate, and convicted after forty minutes of jury deliberation. Freemason appealed the decision. It was upheld and the three were condemned to hang until Governor Ireland issued a full pardon, citing the right of a property owner and his trusties to defend it from trespassers and vandals. He made special note of the relative proximity of the gate and the minor nature of the inconvenience to the cowhand of obeying the law.

The precedent sent shockwaves from the Canadian to the Rio Grande. Prominent supporters of the cattle trade pronounced it a license to commit murder, but since that had been the effect of earlier decisions on the side of Big Cattle, few paid them any attention. Anyone who didn't believe the tide was changing took a ruder hit a few months later when a bill was introduced in the capital to make fence cutting a crime punishable by jail and a stiff fine. Freemason's single-minded crusade on his men's behalf was considered instrumental in this development, and as one public servant after another came forward in favor of the bill, it seemed likely to pass.

I got part of this history from the attendant who took my money and handed me a towel at the bathhouse and the rest from the clerk in the freight office, who took my valise for safekeeping and gave me a ticket to reclaim it. There is something about a clerical collar that brings out the tour guide in everyone. I was clean and close-shaven, but unbrushed. I'd played the impoverished preacher over whether to order the extra service at the launderer's where the bathhouse man had offered to take my clothes while I was soaking, then decided I'd make a better impression in a clean shirt and a white collar and a dusty suit than I would in a brushed one and yellow linen; for I'd chosen to pay a call upon my benefactor as soon as I was presentable. When the collar came back, the helpful launderer had put in enough starch to slice cheese with it.

Finding the house required no directions, although the clerk and the attendant, both proud citizens, had been eager to point it out. It stood on the only high ground in town, a conical hill erected with spades and dredges from level plain that brought the gables in line with the steeple of the Catholic church at the opposite end of the main street. The construction was a delirious arrangement of spires, grilles, turrets, and fretwork, with fishscale shingles and more shades of paint than a tart caught outside in daylight. A quartet of mature cottonwoods provided shade on all four sides at what must have been considerable expense; trees don't grow in such accommodating symmetry and so had to have been brought in after the house was built.

On my way there I passed the First Unitarian church,

a much simpler affair of whitewashed wood with a squat bell tower, common unstained windows, and its name painted in block letters on the lintel above the door. A squat woman with her hair in a bun quit sweeping the front steps to watch me pass in my working uniform. When I touched my hat, she stopped leaning on her broom and got back to business.

A long flight of steps cut from native limestone and sunk into the hill led to the front porch of the house. The porch was semicircular, with fluted Greek columns supporting a gothic roof and a shark's-mouth transom above the front door in the Queen Anne style. It was a crazy sort of house until you realized its architect had sought the effect of an ancient English castle that had acquired new additions in many styles over hundreds of years. Then you remembered you were in Texas and it went back to being a crazy sort of house.

The compass-and-square symbol of the Ancient and Honorable Fraternity of Free and Accepted Masons was carved in the center of the paneled mahogany door. I found a blue china bell pull and used it. The ringing on the other side was barely audible. Whoever had constructed the walls and door had built them to withstand a battering ram.

A fine-boned Mexican of around seventy, small as a boy, with white hair and dressed in a loose white cotton shirt and trousers, opened the door. His feet were brown and bare in woven-leather sandals and his face was the color of dark honey and every bit as smooth. Mine had more wrinkles.

I took off my hat and gave him Sebastian's name. "I think Mr. Freemason is expecting me."

"Please come in." No accent accompanied the words.

He closed the door behind me, took my hat, and left me standing in a baronial foyer with a fourteen-foot ceiling, wainscoted with polished walnut six feet up, and furnished on either side with a bench and a chair with high straight backs that looked as inviting as iron maidens. The windows were equipped with wooden shutters that could be swung shut and bolted from inside, with gun ports that would assume the shape of the Swiss cross when the shutters were closed. Either the owner of the house was a fiend on the subject of security or he'd come prudently prepared to defend himself during sheep wars.

In a little while the old man returned, his sandals making no sound at all on the parquet floor, and led me past a cantilevered staircase and down a hall hung with English hunting prints to another paneled door and swung it wide. He held it while I went through the opening and pressed it shut behind me with a faint gasp of a click. The room was an office large enough to contain two of Texas Rangers Captain Jordan's and the post office next door. There were panels on the walls, dark and ancient, a row of oaken file cabinets, several tables scattered with newspapers and Eastern periodicals, and a gargantuan desk six feet tall that opened out into rows of compartments and drawers for letters, stationery, rolls of paper, and ledgers, with a hinged writing surface and scrolled architectural features that probably doubled as secret niches revealed only by hidden mechanisms known only to the cabinetmaker and the owner. When closed, the fixture would assume the appearance of a chiffo-robe built to shelter a foppish collection of gentlemen's suits of clothes. It was made of cherrywood, deep red and glistening, with burled-walnut insets; an office in itself, redundantly contained within an office.

It impressed me more than anything else I'd seen since I'd spotted the house on my way into town. This marvel of nineteenth-century business machinery was only the third one I'd seen; the others had stood in the private office of the president of the biggest bank in Louisiana and a brokerage firm in Chicago, and they had not been as ornate, the median model geared for less extravagant budgets. I'd heard J. Pierpont Morgan had one in his New York City mansion, but this was my first personal experience of one in a private house.

The man seated in front of it, in a padded leather chair swiveled to face me, was somewhat less impressive physically, but then the dimensions of the house and his reputation had prepared me for a large man on the order of Grover Cleveland or Jumbo the elephant; one of those notorious trenchermen who ate a bucket of oysters for breakfast, sides of pork for dinner, and blew their noses into silk handkerchiefs the size of bedsheets. Richard Freemason was not a small man in comparison to his Mexican manservant, but compact, with slender hands adorned only with a Masonic ingot on the left little finger and a narrow torso in a snug waistcoat of figured silk, small feet in calfskin shoes that gleamed like polished mahogany, and a sandy Vandyke beard trimmed by a barber who ought to have been making violins or miniature portraits in enamel. The only thing large about him was his forehead, which bulged out from the bridge of his nose like Lawrence Lazarus Little's, but with a lower hairline and a sharp widow's peak that made him appear more lupine than leonine. A dedicated phrenologist would have coveted that head, shaved and pickled and marked out in ink like a butcher's chart, the choice cuts labeled Reason, Aggression, Strategy, and

Logic. Humor and Fear would occupy the tiniest compartments, like the ones reserved for wire brads in the Brobdingnagian desk.

Tightly packaged men are restrained as a rule, preferring to let the other fellow make the first gesture. Richard Freemason appeared to exist outside the rules. The moment the door snicked shut, he sprang from the chair and strode the distance between us in half the time of a long-legged man, seizing my hand in a grip that was not so much ironclad as electric; when we broke contact, I still felt the tingle to my fingertips.

"Damned glad to see you!" His tenor voice was clipped, telegraphic, with a British edge that might have been affected, but was too narrow to expose as outright fraud. "I hope you'll pardon the blasphemy, but between the kneelers and the Scotchmen and the poured-in-the-mold Dutch Reformed I've been on the defensive longer than the Jews. Do you know the Baptists say that both my blessed parents and nine-tenths of the world are in hell merely because they didn't embrace Christ as their savior? Surely the devil's ship is sunk to the gunnels."

It was the most succinct description of the Catholic, Presbyterian, and Calvinist faiths I'd heard, including Eldred Griffin's. The Baptists always summed up quickly.

"All paths lead to God," was all I could think of to say.

"A most Christian sentiment."

"Actually it's Buddhist. I studied the world's religions for purposes of comparison." Which was true of Eldred Griffin, whose apostasy had sent him in various directions searching for a substitute.

The sheepman didn't seem to disregard this statement so much as file it away for future review. Unlike Judge Blackthorne, he would be a difficult man to annoy. He waved me into a Morris chair in a reading corner beside a barrister case lined with sets bound in morocco and returned to his swivel. I noticed his back never touched the back of the chair. "How was your journey from Denver?"

"Educational. This is the farthest I've ever been from home. I was engaged for many years caring for my poor mother."

"Have you lived in Colorado Territory your entire life?"

I allowed myself—him, too—a small smile. "Only until eight years ago, when it became a state."

"That was clumsy of me. You must understand I have enemies who think they can benefit by surrounding me with spies. May I ask for some documentation? Costumes are easily come by."

"Certainly." I drew out the shabby wallet and gave him the telegram I'd received from him by way of Denver. He glanced at it and returned it. I had the impression he was inventorying the rest of the wallet's contents as I slid the flimsy back inside.

"Your predecessor, the Reverend Rose, retired last month to live with his daughter and son-in-law in California. He was a holy man but a trial at the pulpit, and the lay fellows who have been filling in read directly from the Bible. If you can manage not to put half the congregation to sleep, you'll be a success."

"I haven't had much practice in public, but I've come with a collection of original sermons."

"Did you write them yourself?"

"I dictated them to an acquaintance. I think best while pacing." It was plagiarism, but any reference to my mentor might inspire questions whose answers wouldn't hold up to scrutiny. If he got hold of Griffin's sermons and compared the writing to mine, the differences would be explained.

"I think you'll find the accommodations behind the church comfortable. Sunday is the day after tomorrow. Do you think you'll be settled enough to preside?"

"I'm looking forward to it."

The door opened and a woman leaned in. She hesitated when she saw me. The look she gave me was long and cool. "I'm sorry, Richard. I thought you were alone."

I gripped the arms of my chair hard enough to leave nail marks in the leather and rose behind my host.

"Quite all right, dear. I wanted you to meet Brother Bernard Sebastian, our new minister. My wife."

She closed the door and rustled her skirts across the floor to offer her hand. It was as cool as her eyes, which were blue in the porcelain pallor of her face. She was some years younger than her husband. "Welcome to Owen, sir." Her voice was a contralto, sandy at the edges, thrilling. Before I could thank her she turned toward Freemason. "You asked me to remind you of your committee meeting."

"Is it so late?" He confirmed the time by a gold watch no thicker than a coin and returned it to his waistcoat. "Please forgive me, Brother. Some scoundrel wants to build a saloon on the site we've set aside for a school, and there are one or two fools on the committee whose priorities are suspect." As he spoke he removed a Prince Albert lined in white silk from a hall tree and shrugged into it.

"I'll pray you triumph," I managed to say.

"Dear, the brother has come many miles, the last several in that torture trap of a stage from Wichita Falls. Please offer him refreshment."

"Of course."

He grasped my hand again and left. Mrs. Freemason swung her gaze back to me. "He means tea."

"I was afraid of that."

She wore a pale green satin dress with a square neckline that exposed her collarbone, a fine one that shone like polished marble. She unclasped a thin gold chain from around her neck with the air of one undressing and used the tiny key attached to unlock a cabinet behind a wall panel. "Fielo is a wonderful servant, but he has a problem. Richard carries his key on his watch chain." From the recess she drew a bottle of Hermitage and two cut-crystal glasses, which she filled to the rims on the writing surface of the great desk.

"You won't get anywhere with that dog collar, Page." She handed me a glass. "The devil isn't a fool."

THIRTEEN

I smiled, ill feeling it. "How long has it been, Colleen? Three years. It was Mrs. Baronet then. You were in widow's weeds."

"I was Mrs. Bower again when I met Richard, but don't take any courage from that. You've nothing to gain from threatening to expose me. I told him my story."

"Even Poker Annie?"

"Especially Poker Annie. Other names I went by, too, that even you don't know. He'd have found out about all of them in time. Many people owe him favors. One of them is letting them live. But you're aware of that."

"I heard about the horsewhipping in Waco."

She made a face, not that it lessened her attraction. Her hair was still startlingly black, without assistance, and when she wore it piled on her head as today she looked like a Spanish princess painted by a Renaissance artist who wanted to keep his job. Except for the blue eyes, of course. They were as Irish as her name. Luther Cherry, the lawyer, had said she painted her face, but he must've been sensitive about such things. She knew how to apply it so that it called attention to her best features rather than to itself.

"Richard put a fool in charge and nearly paid for his poor judgment with his life," she said. "It was ironic that the one thing that tripped him up was someone else's fault."

I pretended disinterest. She obviously thought I'd come to spy on Freemason, as he'd suspected himself, and setting her straight wouldn't teach me anything about my supposed employer, who'd begun to interest me. We were seated, I in the Morris chair, she in her husband's business throne before the desk. She filled it better. She was slender, but her skirts and petticoats just fit between the arms and although she wasn't tall, the way she held herself, with her back straight and her chin lifted, gave that impression. Her narrow feet were encased in green satin slippers that matched the dress, her trim ankles in black stockings.

I'd seen her without all those things, or anything else, and she had been just as much of a pleasure to look at, treacherous as she was. Colleen Bower and I went back five years and a thousand miles.

I took a drink and sighed. Hermitage is good sipping whiskey, and I'd been dry since the day of my untimely death. "I suppose it'd be a waste of time to try to convince you I've put aside my wicked past to carry the Word to the heathen."

"Why not as Brother Page? Bernard Sebastian is just the kind of name Harlan Blackthorne would invent. How is the old bastard; ailing, I trust? I heard his heart was stricken, but I didn't credit it. He hasn't one."

"It didn't mellow him. Can a man who's heard the Call not change his name and wipe the slate?"

"I read newspapers. I confess I felt a twinge of regret when I read of your assassination."

I gave it up as a bad investment. She'd been a professional cardsharp for years and was impossible to bluff. "That was the Judge's idea, too, in case someone recognized me. People believe what they read in print, God knows why." I felt my face twisting at the blasphemy. The clothes had begun to wear the wearer.

"I won't, from now on. This is about what happened in Montana Territory, isn't it? That ogre in Helena never forgets a slight."

"It was a little more than a slight." I said it without thought, not wanting to hesitate and tip my hand. I'd been sure from the start Judge Blackthorne hadn't sent me to Texas as a favor to Austin.

"An injury, then; and to his reputation, which is the only place he can be stung. What's the statute of limitations on a wound to a man's pride?"

"None, where he's concerned. I wasn't aware you'd met." I was still trying to draw her out.

"We haven't. But friends of mine have, and they came to regret it. That was neither here nor there to me until just now, when I found out he still has his sights set on Richard."

"I'd forgotten you're always loyal to your husbands."

She drew healthily from her glass and set it on the desk. She looked thoughtful; but then her expressions operated independently of her honest emotions, if indeed anything about her was honest. "Like Judge, like deputy, I see," she said. You're still holding me responsible for what happened in San Sábado."

"Breen, too. Don't forget Breen."

"Everyone else has. The place doesn't even exist anymore. In the meantime I've heard rumors about your time in Canada and San Francisco. You're growing notorious."

"You do read newspapers."

"Not only that. You've become a staple of the ten-cent press. I can't wait to see what they'll write about your time in Owen."

"*The Man Who Died Twice*," I said, "if this conversation is allowed to leave this room."

"At long last you've learned fear. Are you begging for my silence?"

"I'm asking for it. It won't have to be for long, just until I've finished what I haven't started yet."

"I cannot believe you expect me to conspire in a plot against my husband."

There was nothing for it. There never had been, but I'd been bound to make the attempt. "I'm not here for Freemason, whatever he's done. I never came across his name until I read it in a telegram to Brother Bernard on my way here. He sent it himself, inviting me to replace the Reverend Rose, whoever he may have been."

"You always were an accomplished liar. I'm glad we never played poker in earnest."

"I give you my word if the job has anything to do with Freemason I wasn't told."

"Then what is the job?"

"I won't tell you that."

She nodded. "At least you didn't say you can't. That's one lie even you couldn't bring off."

The subject needed changing. It wasn't as if we'd forget to come back to it. "How did you hook up with Freemason?"

"In Waco. I was dealing faro in a place called the Hispaniola, in a district known as the Reservation, where vice was licensed and taxed. The owner had an arrangement with the local collector, but he neglected to tell me. Five minutes after the dirty little man tapped out, I was in jail on some trumped-up ordinance prohibiting women from playing games of chance in the public room. Richard saw the arrest, figured out what had happened, and had me out on bail in a half hour; it was Friday night, and otherwise I'd have been stuck in that cell until the arraignment Monday morning. Somehow my court date never was set. That was before the infamous horsewhipping, which gave his enemies in the cattle trade an opportunity to remove him as an inconvenience. By then we were married."

"He wouldn't accept a simple thank you?"

She picked up her glass and drank. "I'd throw this in your face if it didn't mean I'd have to pour another. I don't want to give him the impression I share Fielo's problem. Naturally I can't tell him I joined his new minister in a drinking bout."

"Does that mean you won't peach?"

"'Peach.' You did visit San Francisco." She rattled her nails on the glass. She used a clear polish or else one of palest coral; Colleen was not self-effacing, but nor was she vulgar. "I've been sitting here thinking I'd be foolish not to keep you where I can watch you for the time being. Next time, Blackthorne might send someone I won't be able to spot so easily."

"I'll take that with thanks."

"I'm not doing it for you. If it comes down to you or Richard—well, you cannot make me believe you ever expected to die in bed."

"What happened in Montana Territory?"

"Why are you in Texas?"

We'd come around in a circle. She knew now that by mentioning the place at all she'd given me more information than I'd come with, but the only victory I could take from that was partial acceptance of my pledge that Freemason wasn't my target. She'd be dealing no more lucky hands.

I cradled my drink in my palms. "What do you do all day, besides make sure Fielo stays out of the liquor?"

"I keep the books for the ranch, sign the draughts for payroll and expenditures, threaten suppliers with legal action when they short us. With what's left I maintain the household accounts. It's not that much different from operating a card concession."

"This house alone would be more challenging. I heard about the chandelier from Italy."

"Venice," she said. "We hung it in the upstairs ballroom. Actually it sat in a crate on a dock in New Orleans for fourteen months before Richard bought it from a cotton merchant in St. Louis for less than the cost of shipping. The man managed to go broke while it was crossing the Atlantic. Everything in this house was acquired for a fraction of its value, including the building materials, scavenged from the failure of others, and we've borrowed against all of it, every penny. I'll bet you the price of this hideous desk you have more cash available than Richard and I."

"I wouldn't know what to do with the desk. All the paperwork I've ever done would be lost in the top row of pigeonholes. What keeps you from going under with the others?"

"The future of the sheep market. Sheep are cheaper to graze than cattle, because they don't have to be fat to produce wool, and the wool is less expensive to ship. We invest little in breeding, because the same flock continues to produce without replacement; shearing isn't fatal, like skinning and butchering. When we've gotten all the coats and mufflers and mittens we can from a ewe or a ram, we sell it for the hide and meat. Anyone with half a head for figures can see there's less maintenance and more profit in sheep. I'm not saying the cattle will go the way of the buffalo, but in a generation the worst enemies of the trade will have to run sheep just to subsidize the cost of maintaining a meat herd. Richard's associates know that, and are willing to let their investments ride for a few years until the sheep wars come to an end. You've heard what's happening in Austin?"

"I heard he had a hand in it. How many more gunmen will he have to snatch from the gallows before you're in the black?"

She leaned forward slightly in her seat, a maneuver I remembered from sitting across a table from her. It was a rare male player who could divide his concentration between the shadows inside her bodice and the suits he was holding. "We've begun to hear the same argument from the beef barons," she said. "In nearly the same words sheepmen used back when the horse was in the other stall. It's a cry for mercy. By now you've read enough of the Old Testament to know the traditional answer to that."

"I didn't know *you'd* read it."

"My father was a choirmaster. I won't tell you where or with which church; I play close and don't allow anyone to stand behind me. He expected his children to be theosophical prodigies—encouraged it with the flat of his belt, and sometimes the buckle. You've seen the scars."

I had. I'd thought it ungentlemanly to inquire.

"God entered into a wager with Satan that His most faithful servant could not be shaken from his faith. It cost Job everything: property, wife, children, sanity. He cried, 'Why has Thou forsaken me?' God could not answer because of the terms of the bet. Even then, Job refused to forsake God, Who once He'd collected His winnings rewarded his loyalty with property, a new wife, and a litter of children to replace what he'd lost. He thought by that stroke to have compensated Job in full for his dead wife and slain children, incidentally ignoring what *they'd* lost. The story had a great influence on me. When I ran away from home I pledged always to be the one who placed the bet, not the one who was bet upon." She sat back smiling. "That's why I'm with Richard. In Waco I saw his wager and raised him me."

"It's not a bet in the Bible," I said. "There wasn't a pot for God to scoop into His hat."

"Ask Job's wife and children if there's a distinction."

I shook my head and put aside my glass. "I'm an evangelical. My message is one of redemption and forgiveness."

"That's the New Testament. First came the slaughter."

FOURTEEN

She asked me when I was taking up my duties.

"Right away, provided you give me a recommendation."

"It's a partnership, not a matriarchy. That system always fails. I've promised you my silence and given you my conditions. I've no reservations about your ability. I've seen you turn a lynch mob into a hospitality committee without even drawing your pistol. Are you wearing it, by the way? There must be a reason for that dreadful sack you have on."

"I left it in my valise at the freight office. I didn't seem to need it to get past a seventy-year-old Mexican."

"You thought you'd be searched."

"The man went to the trouble and expense of constructing a hill so he could look down and see who's coming. I spotted that even before I found out the place was built like a fort. An ordinary preacher might be able to explain why he was armed. I can't afford it."

"That won't always be the case, will it?"

"I didn't bring it all this way to leave it with Wells, Fargo."

"Richard took precautions that were wise when he built the house. Once that fence-cutting bill becomes law, I'll have the shutters taken down and plant roses. There won't be any invading armies to use them for cover."

"In your place I'd wait until someone cuts a fence and see what happens. There's a new lawyer in town with a trunk full of laws and less than half of them with teeth."

She lifted her brows; she didn't pluck them close and they made strong apostrophes above her already expressive eyes. "You've met young Mr. Cherry. You don't waste time."

"I haven't it to waste."

"He doesn't approve of me, but then he's his wife's creature. She's one of those mouse-faced tyrants men wear in lockets around their necks in place of a leash."

"We met on the stage from Wichita Falls, where he went to retrieve his trunk. He didn't show me a like-ness."

"Nor me. I spotted it, from as far away as you spot-ted this house. Depend upon it, he wears one, and he wouldn't part with it any more than a broke horse would stray far from a loose bridle. I expect that in a horse but I despise it in a man."

"I always wondered what attracted you to me."

"You're too arrogant for the ministry, Page, but that will change. You just haven't met a woman who will stay as long as it takes." Her lips twitched at the corners; her Irish puck was up. "Thank you for the advice about the law. With whose welfare are you concerned, Richard's or mine?"

I picked up my drink and finished it. "He has good taste in whiskey, and the panhandle's ugly enough even with you around for distraction. If something happened to you both I couldn't stand the place."

"It has its virtues. When you find the time to spare you must ride out to Palo Duro Canyon and spend the day. Such country is the real reason Adam left Eden."

"Your father had more influence than you think.

You know Scripture better than I do, and I've had a steady diet of it for three weeks."

"I had it for sixteen years. I've had opportunity to go back to the table. Someday you must ask me about Memphis."

"I will," I said. "When I find the time."

She emptied her glass and said nothing, which I interpreted as a dismissal. I stood. "Freemason says I'll be comfortable behind the church. Does that mean no snakes?"

"Mrs. McIlvaine won't have them. She wouldn't have *me* if I weren't Richard's choice. Women don't approve of me any more than house-trained men. They see in me what they gave up when they set out to train them."

"I think we almost met." I described the woman I'd seen sweeping the church steps.

"I don't suppose she was cordial. She saves the energy she might spend on the social graces to assault the dust in the church and parsonage. She seems to tolerate it outdoors, but only because she's life-size and Texas is so big. Texas avoids direct confrontation, however. You'll find less sand in your sheets than anywhere else this side of the gulf."

I turned the glass knob on the door but didn't pull on it. "You said Freemason knows everything about you. What does he know about me? I don't mean Brother Bernard. If he suspected who I was, he wouldn't have left me alone in the house with you."

"He knows I'm no tame blossom." From her loose right sleeve she drew a trim American Arms pistol hardly bigger than my thumb, then slid it back. It was secured by a rubberized strap to her wrist; a quick flick would have placed it in her palm ready to fire.

It's not a comfortable thing to carry around the house, so I guessed she'd taken it from the cabinet with the whiskey. "As for my past, I didn't bore him with details," she said. "I look forward to hearing your sermon Sunday."

"I'll select it with you in mind."

"No Magdalens or Jezebels, I hope. I've always given you credit for being an original thinker."

In the hallway, the old Mexican appeared from the woodwork with my hat and led me to the door. A bolt shot behind me.

I went from there to the freight office for my valise. The friendly clerk asked what I'd thought of the Freemason mansion, as he called it.

"I found it grand, but I'm a man of simple tastes."

"Did you meet Mrs. Freemason?"

"She was quite gracious."

"The wife thinks she's stuck up. I say she's shy. A lot of folks who don't talk much in society are just nervous about saying the wrong thing."

"That's a very Christian thing to say."

He beamed, as if he'd just been baptized. He had a face designed for beaming, red and round between black side-whiskers. He didn't seem eager for me to leave, so I took a chance and asked about the shotgun messenger who'd been shot trying to guard a stage from bandits.

"That's Sweeney," he said. "Charlie Sweet, and he's right named. They all take the work seriously, but I don't think I ever saw him without a smile on his face. He was smiling when they pulled out the slug, I heard. He's helping out in his sister's restaurant, dishing out soup and washing crockery, till he can sit a coach, on account of his back. The Pan Handle, she calls it: two words."

"A clever woman. I thought I might be able to bring him cheer, but from what you say it may be the reverse."

"He'd welcome a visit just the same. He and Jane are papists, but I don't suppose she'd object to Charlie sitting down with any man of the cloth. Between you and me, she works him like a horse. It's a chore to call her Miss Sweet, so most of us just tip our hats or take them off when we visit her establishment, not that it improves her disposition. Good biscuits," he added.

"I'll look in on them first chance I get." I offered him a nickel for looking after the bag, but he shook his head and smiled.

The door to the First Unitarian church was unlocked. I went inside. The place was clean and unremarkable, with a flight of open steps to the bell tower, bare planks between two rows of polished-pine pews, and a plain pulpit on a platform with two steps leading up to it. A parlor stove was placed just where it needed to be to dry out the coats and hats that would hang from a row of pegs when it rained or snowed; apart from that it was out of place in that simple room, with filigree and mica through which the flame would glow whenever the mercury dipped below broiling. It stood on three elegantly curved legs like a Chippendale chest.

"It was a gift from Mr. Freemason. A common barrel stove would've heated the place just as well."

It was a woman's voice barely, deeper even than Colleen Freemason's, with a burr that might have been smuggled from Scotland and kept in storage to preserve it until that moment. She'd come in through a door that opened onto the raised platform and stood holding her broom bristles up, like a rake. All these many years later, Mrs. McIlvaine remains one of my strongest memories of Owen, although we never exchanged more than a hundred words in all. I still see her with that broom. I never saw her without it.

She took me through that side door and across a patch of burned-out grass behind the church to a salt-box that stood on the same lot, an afterthought assembled from lumber left over after the church was finished and generously referred to as the parsonage. The sitting room held a rocking chair, a straightback with a caned seat that rocked more predictably on its short leg, and a small laundry stove that could warm a bowl of soup or brew a pot of coffee but not both at the same time, in a space about the size of Eldred Griffin's grim study in the caretaker's shack in Helena. A single partition separated it decently from the pastor's sleeping quarters, where I could lie on the iron-framed bed with a pencil in each hand and write my name on both opposing walls. In ugly weather a white enamel chamber pot under the bed spared the necessity to visit the gaunt little outhouse in the corner of the lot.

The place was spotless, and no wonder. There was little in it to impede the progress of Mrs. McIlvaine's ruthless broom. The Reverend Rose, it developed, had taken his small personal library with him when he went west, leaving me with nothing to occupy my time that first night except the Bible and a brown page of advertising from a newspaper of unknown vintage someone had used to line the drawer in the spavined nightstand. When I tired of the Book of books I learned that at some point in history, gentlemen's English worsted suits of clothes had been available at J. Pearson's General Merchandise for eight dollars.

FIFTEEN

I awoke at dawn for the twelfth time since retiring, famished and stiff. I hadn't eaten since noon yesterday, at a station stop where boiled beef and tinned peas made up the bill of fare, but I'd been too tired from the trip to venture out from the parsonage once I'd established residence. I was in possession of a new set of aches on top of those I'd acquired from the Overland. The bed needed slats and a mattress whose horsehair stuffing hadn't migrated to the outer edges. Someone—I learned later it was the fourteen-year-old son of one of the lay readers who had taken up the slack between pastors—had stocked the woodbox beside the stove; I built a fire, warmed a kettle I filled from the pump outside, and used it to freshen up and shave over an enamel dishpan that served as a basin, then finished dressing and went out to greet my first full day in Owen.

It greeted me back with a sixty-mile-an-hour gust, the first of many that had me chasing my old slouch hat across the Staked Plain all day long. You have to train a hat. I was sorry I'd left my regular one behind, even if the quality was too good for a penniless preacher. I wondered if a stampede string would look out of place on a pedestrian headpiece, but in the end I decided that the sight of a scarecrow leaning into the wind holding down the crown with one hand was humble enough to help the disguise.

I put my hunger to dual advantage and stepped into the Pan Handle, where the freight office clerk had told me I'd find Charlie Sweet helping out his sister while he recovered from his bullet wound. As I leaned the door shut against the gale from outside, the smell of hot grease scraped at my empty stomach. Six tables covered with oilcloth took up most of the space in the small room, leaving only a narrow crooked path for the server to pass carrying his steaming tray. Fortunately he was rail thin, and fresh-looking hollows in his cheeks suggested that the ordeal of recuperation had swindled him out of pounds he could ill spare. He walked with the stiff gait of a man with a bad back; that was where the bullet had entered, but from experience I gathered he was less concerned with pain than with preserving stitches. A pair of rugged boots stuck out beneath the hem of his long apron.

It was early, and only two tables were occupied. When he finished setting out plates of food on one, he turned my way with the empty tray under one arm. "Sit anyplace, Parson. You got your choice of sausage and eggs or eggs and sausage. Flapjacks if you like, but I wouldn't today: weevils in the batter."

"Sausage and eggs, then, please, and black coffee. Scrambled," I added. That was the easiest way to prepare eggs and Brother Bernard wasn't a man to create inconvenience.

He nodded curtly and pushed through a door that swung on a pivot into the sizzling chamber of the kitchen. I selected a table in a corner by a window to cut down on eavesdroppers. In less than five minutes, he returned bearing my order on the tray and a two-gallon coffeepot in the other hand. He put the plate in front of me, its contents still cooking furiously, and filled a thick stoneware mug with the densest, blackest brew I'd seen in more than a week. His face, which had lost much of what appeared to have been a lifelong burn, flushed deep copper in appreciation when I expressed pleasure at the sight.

"Mud's my department," he said. "Janey's Wild Bill with a skillet, but she never made coffee the same way twice in a row and always weak as a drownded kitten."

"I understand you're more accustomed to sitting on top of a stagecoach than waiting on tables."

"I am for a fact, and I'll be back up there soon. This ceiling's commencing to come down on me."

"Not too soon, I hope. I'm told a bullet wound is not a thing to rush healing."

He regarded me through eyesockets brambled with creases. Three inches of fair whiskers circled his lower face in the Mormon manner, but the tiny crucifix he wore at his throat supported the reports that he was a Roman Catholic. I'd begun to take note of such things. "You come educated. You the new fellow over at the Unitarian?"

"I got in yesterday. People have been most helpful in acquainting me with the community. I hope I didn't upset you with what I heard."

"There's no shame in getting shot. I intend to turn the shame on them that done it, soon as I'm in a position to. I reckon you'd say that's taking the Lord's own vengeance unto myself."

"'Judge not lest ye be judged.'" I took a bite of sausage. It was spicier than I like it, but when I swallowed, the acids in my belly pounced on it like sitting prey. I wasn't looking at him. "Would you like to talk about it?"

"Well, Parson, I'm not just your denomination."

"You may think of me as a sympathetic stranger, and disregard the collar. I'm here to make friends, not poach on my neighbor's property."

He stroked the underside of the fringe on his chin. "You best tie in. That lard sets up like tar when it gets cold. I'll go see what's keeping them biscuits." He returned to the kitchen, stopping on the way to make sure the other diners were contented.

I ate my eggs, which were just right, and drenched my self-recrimination in the strong coffee. I'd come on just as strong and chased away my first best source of direct information on the Blue Bandannas, as I'd come to think of them.

Shortly after the door swung shut on him I heard raised voices, a man's and a woman's. They were hushed quickly and he came back out carrying three steaming bowls covered with checked cloths, one in his right hand, the other two lined up along his left arm from the crook of his elbow to the base of his palm. He set one on each of the other occupied tables, placed the third before me, drew out the chair facing me, and sat down.

"Janey's more of a chore to work for than Wells, Fargo," he said, taking a biscuit for himself, "but if blessed Mary had an oven, she couldn't bake better."

I took one and broke it apart. It was as light as a banknote and piping hot. I'd noticed there was no butter on any of the tables, but when I bit into it I realized why. It melted on my tongue. "The next time I encounter an atheist I'll send him here. He'll not question miracles again."

He winked, chewing. "We're powerful close to blaspheming here, Reverend. They're better than most, but they won't smuggle a sinner past Saint Peter."

"That was my hunger speaking, from its impiety. I missed supper." I had been ladling it out with a shovel; the mark was dangerous to fall short of, but just as bad to overshoot. I wiped my hands with my napkin and held one out, introducing myself. "Brother, not Reverend. I have no claim to any title not granted by the fraternity of man."

He took it in a palm ridged with calluses from the lines. "Circuit rider. Well, Father Cress may not approve, but he's a thorny old bush. Charlie Sweet. Sweeney to friends and such."

"I hope to earn that honor. Are you much in pain since your ordeal?"

"It hurt worse coming out than it did going in. I'd be back in the traces by now if it wasn't for the risk I'd start bleeding again. Then it's three more weeks on my belly and Janey changing the dressing two times a day and calling me all kinds of a damn fool while she's about it. Pardon my language, Reverend— Brother. I ain't in gentle company so frequent." He crossed himself and popped the rest of his biscuit into his mouth.

"Have those men been captured?" I used mine to swab grease off my plate, putting concentration into it.

"They ain't, and it's thanks to the governor that's so. Now that the sheep trouble's let up, all he and the Rangers care about is what Pablo and Jose are up to down on the border. I say let 'em snatch a few head and stick up riders fool enough to carry more'n a cartwheel dollar that close to old Mexico. They'll just spend what they get in Texas, because there ain't a thing worth buying where they come from. Sow it around."

"One might say the same about the men who waylaid you."

"No, sir, that's false. This bunch buries its money, or goes up to Denver or somesuch other place that needs it like a hen needs a pecker. Pardon my coarse language." He crossed himself again. "If I had a five-cent

piece for every double eagle that showed up on a
bar or a store counter anywhere in a hundred miles,
I'd have a dime. I can abide a thief, though I'm pledged
to lay down my hide to stop them in their taking
ways and by God I will, but a miser's bad for business." He pardoned himself and made the sign a third
time.

"What makes you think they're not still in Denver
or someplace like that?"

"That fellow that told Randy to throw down the
box had West Texas all through his speech. I heard
that even laying on the ground with a slug in my back.
You can't put that on, not when a West Texan's on the
other end of it. You ever meet anyone from West
Texas?"

"Not until I got here. I've led a sheltered life."

"Not the reason. You didn't on account of no West
Texas boy ever leaves it for long. It gets in you like a
tapeworm; you can't stay away even if you was
wanted here for topping a nun." His theme had him
so worked up he forgot to ask forgiveness from me or
the pope. "He's here, count on it, and so's his crew.
They rustled a thousand head of Herefords outside
White Horse just last week."

Captain Jordan had said it was five hundred. Rumors seemed to grow faster in that arid soil than
other places, but I wasn't supposed to know anything
about the rustling so I didn't correct him. His was the
first statement I'd heard that corroborated Judge
Blackthorne's conviction that the gang operated close
to home. "Did you tell the authorities the man was
local?"

"I told everyone that bothered to listen, but it skidded off 'em like spit. Bad hats come from Missuri and

Kansas and from down below the Rio Grande. Nobody wants to hear we're growing our own."

I doubted that was the reason. As far as I could tell he'd spoken of this to Texans exclusively, who might be expected to regard one of their own as less than sensitive to differences in dialect; but shotgun messengers crossed state and territorial lines and guarded passengers from all over the country. They might not be connoisseurs of geographical speech patterns, but they would know domestic from imported. "Why West? Don't all the natives of this state sound the same?"

"To you, maybe, but you're green. Much east of San Saba they could pass for Virginia, though not to a Virginian, like as not. I don't claim special powers, just good hearing."

"What about the driver; Randy, was that his name? Didn't he back you up?"

"Randy's from Connecticut originally. He thinks everyone talks funny once you get past New Haven."

"Does he live here in town?"

"His wife got spooked after the robbery and made him move to Louisiana and clerk in a freight office. You ask a lot of questions for a preaching man."

I could have played that two ways: emphasize my willingness to bring comfort to the stricken or fall back on Brother Bernard's past. I chose the one less holy. "I'm sorry to pry. This is the first time I've been more than five miles from where I was born. I'm overcome with the strangeness of it all. I never realized this country was so big."

He laughed then, and helped himself to another biscuit. I'd scored with his provincial pride. "Oh, well, Brother, if the panhandle's as big as you think it gets, wait till you take the train to El Paso. You can hide all of New England and most of Michigan between there and where we're sitting."

Other diners had begun to file in. The kitchen door opened and a woman nearly as thin as Sweet leaned in, wiping her hands on her apron. She stared at the back of his head until he turned her way, started, and rose. "Thanks for the palaver, Brother. It saved me scrubbing pots."

I stood and shook his hand again. "I can see you're both busy. I'd like to come by sometime and meet your sister."

"You wouldn't like it long. She lumps in Protestants with pagans and Chinamen."

I took out my wallet, but he stopped me with a palm. "Put it in the poor box on me," he said. "I'm not so certain as Janey. I like to back the other fellow's hand just in case."

I thanked him and left. I was in the right place, I was sure of that now. I just didn't know what for.

SIXTEEN

The First Unitarian Church of Owen was filled nearly to capacity that first Sunday, but having made few contacts during my brief time in town, I put it down less to personal impression than to plain curiosity. A medicine show or a company of dwarves would have filled the place as efficiently.

I'd committed a professional blunder early, when Mrs. McIlvaine hastened in at my first pull on the bell rope, flung down her broom, and seized the rope from my hands. No one had told me bell ringing was one of her duties, and from the alien serenity in her expression while she tugged away I concluded it was her favorite. She said not a word to me the rest of the day; which when you factored in how few she measured out all told made for a profound silence.

Almost all the pews were filled when Richard and Colleen Freemason arrived and walked all the way up the aisle without stopping to a space in front that had been conspicuously left vacant. He wore a black morning coat with piped lapels over a gray double-breasted waistcoat and gray trousers without a crease to indicate that it had ever spent time on a shelf with the ready-mades, she an unadorned velour dress with her hair gathered beneath a tricorne hat angled slightly with a small feather. The dress looked black until she crossed through a sunbeam slanting in through a window, when it proved to be a very dark maroon. Freemason shook the odd hand, scarcely slowing his pace. Standing at the pulpit, I took mental note of the hands he didn't shake because they weren't offered, and the faces that went with them; they were stony as a rule and turned straight ahead as he passed. In this way I managed to catalogue those acquaintances connected with or sympathetic to the cattle trade. Colleen kept her gaze forward. I remembered what the clerk in the Wells, Fargo office had said about her aloof reputation. That friendly fellow sat near the center of a pew halfway down, next to a woman close to his age whose expression was as grim as those of Freemason's enemies. I'd seen that same look on many female faces over the years when Colleen was present. The women were always respectable in appearance and nearly always less attractive.

When the couple was seated, Freemason with his banker's tile in his lap, I ventured a look from my notes and met Colleen's eyes, blue and cool and casually friendly, fully in keeping with the wife of a church director who wished the new pastor well on his first day. To this day she remains the best poker player I ever met, and I've played with Luke Short and Arnold Rothstein.

I broke contact to put my pages in order. I was as nervous as a cat. Everything Eldred Griffin had told me about when and where to pause, how often to look up, and where to look fled from memory. Speaking in an empty church to a stern taskmaster of a tutor had been unsettling; pretending wisdom of things spiritual before a packed house put bats in my stomach, and the certain knowledge that at least one of my listeners knew me for a fraud made my throat dry as Texas. I took too hearty a drink from the tumbler of water Mrs. McIlvaine had set out for me on the shelf beneath the lectern and had to fight back an explosive cough, which I covered by clearing my throat noisily into a fist. This was worse than facing a pistol in a hostile hand, because I knew what to do if mine misfired. There was nothing to duck behind that would spare me from scorn and only ignominious retreat through the side door for escape. I thought of Judge Blackthorne in his pew in the Presbyterian Church in Helena and wondered if he paused in his devotions to consider my situation and allow himself a smile with his cumbersome teeth.

I was wearing the fine shirt Esther Griffin had stitched for me with her husband's cutthroat collar, and had spent the previous evening brushing my coat and trousers and blacking my town shoes, which pinched and made me yearn for my good broken-in boots, but which at least distracted my attention from the terror of the moment. With unsteady fingers I opened my hymnal, as worn and grubby as any that had been placed in the racks, held it flat atop my notes, took a deep breath, and led the parishioners in a hymn. I've a strong voice and had been told I could sing without embarrassing myself unduly, but I was grateful for the baritones in the gallery that drowned out the wobble.

The hymn had a calming influence, as of course it was intended to; by the time the last stanza finished in the rafters I felt a little less like bolting. Someone coughed in the silence. I took that as my downstroke and began my sermon.

I'd moved the hymnal to the shelf beside the tumbler and brought up the Bible I'd carried from Montana Territory, opening it to the passage I'd marked with a strip I'd torn from the old newspaper lining the drawer in the parsonage. I wet my throat again—a small sip this time—and read:

"'Now there was a day when the sons of God came to present themselves before the Lord, and Satan came also among them.

"'And the Lord said unto Satan, Whence comest thou? Then Satan answered the Lord, and said, From going to and fro in the earth, and from walking up and down in it.

"'And the Lord said unto Satan, Hast thou considered my servant Job, that there is none like him in the earth, a perfect and an upright man, one that feareth God, and escheweth evil?

"'Then Satan answered the Lord, and said, Doth Job fear God for nought?

"'Hast not thou made an hedge about him, and about his house, and about all that he hath on every side? Thou hast blessed the work of his hands, and his substance is increased in the land.

"'But put forth thine hand now, and touch all that he hath, and he will curse thee to thy face.

"'And the Lord said unto Satan, Behold, all that he hath is in thy power; only upon himself put not forth thine hand.'"

Hereupon I closed the book with as much reverberation as I could muster, wishing it were as substantial as the one in Griffin's study, which boomed like a rebel four-pounder when he slammed it shut. I was, however, aware of a sudden awakening in my audience; I'd been correct in guessing that the succession of lay readers who'd been putting them to sleep with rote had not deigned to depart from the text, and from the reaction I made bold to ponder whether the Reverend Rose had been in the practice of delivering sermons from his own hand. What I did wasn't heresy, not yet, but I felt an edge of uncertainty in the air, heavily tinged as it was with furniture oil and Sunday-suit mothballs, and uncertainty was something I knew a thing or two about.

"My friends," I said, "you know this story: In his desperation to turn Job against God and prove his point, Satan rustled his sheep and oxen, dropped a house on his seven sons and three daughters, and afflicted him with boils. Job was no more than mortal, complaining bitterly of his losses and his miseries, which he professed he had done nothing to bring upon him. But he maintained his faith in his Lord even when his wife counseled him to curse God and die, and so the Lord restored his chattel twofold, granted him seven new sons and three new daughters, and gave him twice his threescore and ten in years as a reward for his unshakeable faith while Satan crept away beaten, with his forked tail tucked between his legs."

To illustrate this image, which does not appear in the Book of Job, I walked two fingers across the top of the pulpit, staggering a little. Amusement rippled through the crowd. I let it die down, then continued.

"Some would say that God was flattering Himself when He declared that justice had been rendered unto His servant, that seven new sons and three new daughters did not replace the lives of the first seven sons and three daughters, and that doubling the span of Job's days denied him reunion with those he had lost at the end of his threescore and ten. They're right, of course."

That drew a gasp and a murmur, but I was concentrating on Colleen, who met my gaze with polite interest, nothing more. It was as if we hadn't discussed the subject only the day before yesterday.

I said, "One sheep looks pretty much like another, and an ox is just a steer broken to harness. Even Charles Goodnight would be hard pressed to distinguish between two longhorns standing side by side." More chuckles. Goodnight had brought prosperity to the region when he established his ranch near Palo Duro Canyon, and was a popular subject locally. "Children are another matter. Nothing but the resurrection of Job's original sons and daughters would serve as adequate compensation for his sufferings.

"God knew this. He wept for Job's great loss, and rendered unto him the only justice available; for there can be but one mortal resurrection in the Holy Book, and that must be performed by His son."

I rearranged my pages, pretending to read them. I'd committed the text solidly to memory. I looked up and smiled. "Owen has been kind to this pilgrim, cleansing him and giving him bread and protecting his small heap of belongings, refusing to accept anything in return. Nowhere have I seen greater evidence of faith in God. I'm told that before I came, this country had been afflicted with range wars and highwaymen, stricken by murderers and forsaken by those who were pledged to keep it from evil. Yet you welcomed a stranger not with suspicion or malice, but with love. And so Satan has lost again, and must go to and fro in the earth in search of some other victim to prove his false theory; for the Book of Owen is a work still in progress."

There was no applause, naturally, but when I called for another hymn, the house responded with energy, basses booming, sopranos trilling, and the inevitable tone-deaf howls enthusiastic. It wasn't exactly the equivalent of a standing ovation, but I had the impression I'd passed my first test. I added points by bringing the services to a close after reading the community announcements I'd been given and reciting the forty-first psalm.

I took my place beside the door to the street as the parishioners filed out, shaking hands with the men and bowing to the women. My notices were mostly positive, although one red-faced fellow who'd slept through most of the morning, stirring just long enough to hear me refer to myself as a pilgrim, expressed the opinion that I should have withheld Plymouth Rock until Thanksgiving. An old woman in rusty weeds told me she wished her husband had lived to hear me speak, and spent five minutes cataloguing his trials while others grew impatient and left the line behind her.

Richard Freemason took my hand in his iron grip; either he was accustomed to dealing with politicians or Captain Jordan had been mistaken when he'd called him a gentleman rancher. Poking letters into pigeonholes is poor exercise for the hands.

"I felt I'd made a good choice in you when we met," he said. "It's a pleasure to have that feeling confirmed."

"Thank you, sir. I had misgivings about the references to sheep and cattle."

"Those wars are finished, and subtlety is lost on Texas. You should publish."

"I wouldn't presume."

"Nonsense. I have some acquaintances in publishing, who may have some contacts with the ecclesiastical press. I'll give you a recommendation."

I thanked him, and found his wife's gloved hand in mine. "Wherever did you find your inspiration?" Her smile carried no trace of mockery.

"I found it in a charming new acquaintance, Mrs. Freemason," I said. If she wanted to broach the subject in the presence of her husband, I wouldn't back away. "I came with a bundle of sermons, but none was appropriate to our discussion. I promised you a sermon in return for your gracious hospitality, you may remember."

Freemason said, "The story of Job is one of Colleen's bugbears. I'd no idea you two had dissected theology at the house."

"Brother Bernard is very approachable, dear. I won't say he's converted me to the God of the Old Testament, but he makes an excellent case for the defense. One might think he knew his way around the halls of justice." She'd made a bargain not to expose me. Nothing had been said about torture.

I put a smile on my face I hoped was modest. "My father was a deacon. One of his happiest entertainments was to engage me in religious discourse from the time I was old enough to read scripture."

"My father was a butcher in Manchester," Freemason said. "I can't recall a single intelligent conversation I ever had with him. Tell me, Brother, with which church was your father affiliated?"

I'd made a mistake in volunteering a detail from Sebastian's manufactured past. Now I hesitated to provide specific information that could be exploded by a simple inquiry.

Colleen, of all people, came to my rescue. She placed a hand on his arm. "Dear, we mustn't monopolize the brother. Others are waiting to speak with him."

"Of course. Mrs. Freemason and I would be honored to have you in for dinner. Will you be free this afternoon?"

"I'm honored to accept." There was nothing for it but to open myself to further inquisition. Inventing an excuse wasn't an option. I've always found it difficult to tell a white lie while I was living a direct falsehood.

"Splendid! Two o'clock."

Colleen's smile was angelic. That was when she was at her most diabolical. She gave me a nod and left on her husband's arm.

By the time the church doors closed I had three more invitations to dine that week. Returning to the parsonage, I locked the door, opened my valise, took out the bottle of Old Forester I'd brought from Helena, and helped myself to a secular swig.

SEVENTEEN

M y mother was American," Richard Freemason said. "Still is, I suspect, although we haven't spoken in ten years. She's never forgiven me for deserting her for the frontier, but since she always cashes the bank draughts I send her in Boston, she hasn't wasted away from a broken heart. I'm a man, and therefore unworthy of her trust. I have my father to thank for that. He proposed to her in London while she was taking the Grand Tour with her parents, representing himself as the owner of a chain of meatpacking plants that exported abroad, but after a wedding trip to Brighton she learned he had only the one shop and his most distant customer lived six squares away. She divorced him when I was five and brought me with her back to the States. Evidently, having made one disastrous decision on the spur of the moment, she was determined to take her time arriving at the second."

"And was that disastrous as well?" I sat back to give Fielo, the venerable Mexican manservant, room to ladle chowder into my shallow china bowl. Ocean fish was an almost nonexistent delicacy in West Texas.

"Eventually, but I had a hand in how it turned out. My grandparents furnished her with an annuity to help rear me until age eighteen. I leapt the fence at fifteen, and when they found out they cut her off without a penny. She made me aware of that fact in her response to a letter I sent months later, bringing her up to date on my experiences since quitting the maternal nest. That was our last exchange. She's never sent me so much as an acknowledgment for the money I send regularly—have done, since I got my first job stocking shelves in a dry goods in St. Louis. Her bank takes care of that by providing the canceled draughts with her signature on the back."

"Still," I said, "you have kept the Fifth Commandment. That speaks well of you."

"It speaks better of Colleen, who insisted I continue after I expressed the opinion that I had paid the old lady sufficient rent for the time I spent in her womb."

Colleen shook her head when the old man arrived at her place with his tureen. He served Freemason and returned to the kitchen. "As with bold entrepreneurs the world over," she said, "odious rumors follow Richard everywhere he goes. The monthly emolument is a small price to pay to avoid accusations of abandoning his own mother."

That was vanity and a sin, but I forebore to point it out. Griffin had drilled into me the importance of not preaching to one's hosts. Furthermore it was a lie. Colleen had climbed to a precarious level where her past balanced delicately against her current claim to respectability. Whispers that she'd bewitched her husband into maintaining her in luxury while his mother starved would make her an expensive liability if he intended to increase his grip on the panhandle (if that was his aim; I hadn't gotten his measure yet). To an extent, her true motives exonerated her. The Bible says nothing against taking action in one's own defense.

The dining room was small by the standards of that type of house, but seemed spacious by way of its lack of fussy detail. It contained none of the porcelain bric-a-brac and lace and velvet drapery that turned large Eastern salons into crowded airless warehouses where you had to plan your entrances and exits beforehand to avoid knocking over some favorite piece of gimcrack. The rectory table was less than ten feet long and stood on four handsomely turned legs atop a rug of Old World manufacture with both halves of the globe embroidered in its center, with five of the full set of shieldback chairs placed against the walls and a massive sideboard carved from fruitwood where additional courses could be placed to keep the serving apparatus operating smoothly during larger affairs than ours. Good landscapes hung in gilt frames and a crystal chandelier built on the modest scale of the room were the only ornaments in sight. I sensed the hand of the lady of the house in the decoration. She would march resolutely in the opposite direction of the gold-etched mirrors, glistening mahogany, and dripping bronze barbarity of the saloons where she'd made her living before she found an easier way.

The food was excellent, and in keeping with the room's quiet taste. After the chowder we ate roasted breast of duckling in a light cream sauce, asparagus in butter, sweet potatoes, warm moist bread (in my experience second only to Jane Sweet's biscuits at the Pan Handle restaurant), and finished with mincemeat pie and coffee poured from an oriental silver decanter. The cook, Freemason said, had come from Belgium to open a tearoom with her husband in New York City, only to lose him to fever during the voyage. The sheepman had discovered her slinging delicately seasoned stew in a bunkhouse full of ranch hands who wouldn't know fennel from feather grass and appropriated her to serve as his personal chef. The coffee was as good as Charlie Sweet's, refined probably with eggshells without recourse to the mythical properties so many amateur brewers assign to chicory.

I was relaxed, but on my guard. That medicinal jolt of whiskey had flattened my nerves and I had a story ready in case Freemason pressed the point of my fictional father's church: The fires that had plagued Denver until an ordinance was passed requiring all new construction to be made of brick had claimed any number of such institutions, an excuse I hoped would retard the process of confirmation long enough for me to finish my work in Owen. He didn't ask, however. He seemed more concerned with how much part the First Unitarian church might play in the progress of civilization in the region. Primarily he sought assurance that the railroad would come to town instead of bypassing it for White Horse or some other point, leaving Owen to dry up and blow away before the incessant wind from Arizona.

"Please don't be offended when I tell you there was resistance to appointing an evangelist to the pastorship," he said, stirring sugar into his cup. "Some members of the board of directors opposed the, er, rootlessness of your particular denomination. I reminded them that solid Unitarianism had done nothing to slow the erosion every time the Reverend Rose served up one of his tasteless homilies from Numbers. Surely there is no other book that so thoroughly replicates the effect of reading a shopkeeper's inventory."

I smiled. "Fifty and three thousand and four hundred of the children of Naphtali, six hundred thousand and three thousand and five hundred and fifty of the children of Israel, threescore and two thousand and seven hundred of the children of Dan. I confess that I could never satisfy myself as to the correct total of my mother's household accounts until I arrived at the same sum three times. I must own that my reason

for trying to put life in my sermons is not entirely self-
lessness. It's important for a minister to set a good
example by staying awake at the pulpit."

"And so you did. And so did the congregation,
mostly." He'd been seated in front of the red-faced
parishioner who'd snored his way through most of
the service from the first hymn to the last "Amen." "I
daresay you bought me some credibility with the rest
of the board this morning. The true test will come
next Sunday, when we learn the amount of attrition
now that native curiosity is satisfied."

"You may concern yourself with other things, Richard. Brother Bernard is no flash in the pan."

I looked at the lady of the house, sipping her coffee
black from a cup so thin I could see the contrast
between the contents and its surface. I wasn't looking for any sign of dissembling, because I knew they
wouldn't show. After the journey through the bleak
landscape of the Cimmaron Strip and what lay south
of it, I owed myself the pleasure of the sight. It was
no wonder Freemason had disregarded the disadvan-
tages of her life story in order to place her at the head
of his table.

Not precisely the head; the couple observed the
egalitarian practice of sitting not at opposite ends of
the refectory piece, but side by side in the middle, facing their guest. Butcher's son that he was (and whatever else he may have been, robber baron or murderer
or festering thorn in Judge Blackthorne's thick hide),
he had a gift for politics. That was as important a trait
in a ranching pioneer as rough justice and vision.

"Other concerns indeed," said he, and when I turned
my attention back to him there was no indication on
his face that the conversation had been light until
then. "The sheep wars are finished, barring the odd

inevitable flare-up, but these bandits must be addressed. Railroad builders think nothing of blasting their way through miles of granite, but a series of disconnected raids can force them to change their course by a hundred miles. I know you've heard about our late troubles in that area. You had breakfast yesterday with Charlie Sweet."

I was careful there. The palmists may have been right: Give a man or a thing a moment's thought in some company and it's the same as saying the name aloud. "I didn't see you there."

"I wasn't; Madame Lemonnier's ducklings and pastries have spoiled me for the beans and bacon in the Pan Handle. It's a small town still, and that collar stands out. By now, half the population's convinced you've converted Sweeney from Roman idolatry, if not his formidable sister."

It was as much a question as a statement, and I took my time chewing and swallowing a mouthful of pie before I answered. "I'd heard about the stagecoach robbery when I stopped in Wichita Falls. The clerk in the freight office here gave me more details. When I found out Mr. Sweet was the man serving me breakfast, I inquired about his health. I've learned that talking about such things brings comfort."

"Taking action against them brings surcease. Sometimes I think the raids are not disconnected after all, and that these brigands have set themselves to drive me to ruin."

"You're being melodramatic," Colleen said. "You suffered direct losses in three of the raids, but not all. Considering the amount of business you do, and how dependent it is upon the railroads, you make a broad target."

"In a way I'm connected to them all. When they hit

their first train they made off with my payroll. The second was carrying securities I'd borrowed from my bank in Chicago to repair the loss. The cattle they rustled at White Horse were purchased from Goodnight to trade in Colorado for breeding stock to improve my wool yield. I've suffered more than anyone from these raids, and if the railroad bypasses Owen because of them, I'll be a pauper. I confess, Brother, to envying Job at one point during your sermon. My faith is not so stalwart."

I resisted reminding him that Sweet and the cowhand slain at White Horse may have suffered as much. "If Job's convictions were less rare, I'd have no work."

Colleen said, "You might chide him for the sin of pride. Not every misfortune takes place with him in mind."

"I wouldn't presume, in his own house. I trust pains were taken to keep secret the details of how the valuables were being transported."

Freemason's bulbous forehead gathered in bunches. "They were known to no one but my representatives, myself, and the people I do business with. Are you suggesting a Judas?"

"I'm unqualified to suggest it. I'm unschooled in the ways of the world, and too curious for comfort. Please accept my apologies."

He lifted his cup to his lips. "Sometimes innocent eyes see clearest. Lord knows my garden is crawling with serpents."

Colleen said, "Perhaps the Brother suspects Eve."

I made so bold as to intercept her gaze, but it lingered less than an instant before turning to her husband, who made a dry sound in his throat and patted her hand. "My dear, I'd sooner suspect the Brother of an indiscretion." He returned to his reflections. "If I find this serpent and sever its head, another will take its place. I've beseeched the governor to send us a company of Rangers, but it appears I exhausted all my goodwill in Austin when he agreed to support the fence-cutting law." He set down his cup for refilling by Fielo, who'd appeared behind his left shoulder. "I admit I hadn't considered the possibility of a breach in my wall. That suggests a single enemy. I wonder which one."

Colleen said, "Find the breach and trace it to its source."

"But where to start?"

"Coffee, Señor?" The old Mexican hovered over me with the decanter.

III

The Book of Judas

EIGHTEEN

Colleen reminded Freemason he had work waiting and insisted on seeing me to the door. He shook my hand and withdrew to his study as she looped her arm inside mine. It felt pleasant, even if the last time she'd done that was just before someone had tried yet again to kill me.

"You came all this way to break up a gang of common bandits?" She spoke low. People who keep servants do as a rule.

"I didn't say that."

"You didn't have to. Richard is the second person in town you've spoken to about the robberies. You have no outside interests, Page. You're quite dull when you come down to it."

"We can't all be as inspirational as Brother Bernard."

"I'm not your spy. I've more to gain by being loyal to my husband than by robbing him."

"You said yourself he's gone bust."

"I've seen busted from both sides. His kind has a different definition. When he hasn't ten cents for a shave he can raise a million dollars on his reputation.

There ought to be another word for that kind of busted."

"There is. It's called running a bluff. All the more reason to hit him for the hard cold cash he gets up that way."

"I'm not like that anymore."

I laughed. "I don't believe it. No one ever accused you of being dull."

"I'm serious. You get awfully tired dealing from the bottom of the deck. You start to wonder if the suckers are right and the game's more fun if you play it according to Hoyle."

"You wouldn't know Hoyle if he bet his watch and chain against the pot."

We'd reached the door. She looked up at me. Her eyes were as clear as flakes of sky. How they stayed that way when they were attached to Colleen Bower's brain stumped me worse than the Infinite. "I'd suspect you of personal motives if I thought you ever had human qualities," she said. "Did I break your heart?"

"You as much as said I don't have one."

"Someone broke mine long before we met, and you know something? You can still feel the pain in a leg after it's been cut off and buried."

"What about the houseboy? He's old enough to start thinking about a pension."

"Fielo belongs to an old aristocratic family wiped out by Juaristas in the revolution. He fought for his country in the Mexican War, only to lose everything, including a son, after Maximilian fell twenty years later. He came here with nothing but the rags on his back and a ferocious hatred for all *bandidos*. He wouldn't lift a finger to help out the Yankee variety. Anyway, he's frail, his duties aren't physically demanding, and Richard pays him nearly as much as his top hand on the ranch. I asked him to. I doubt the old fellow would take the risk."

"I'd like to visit the ranch. Can you arrange it?"

"So it's the gang you're after."

"Yes. Are you happy now that you got me to say it?"

"The word is relieved. I wanted to make sure you weren't acting as Blackthorne's avenging angel."

"What happened between Freemason and the Judge?"

"Ask the Judge." She opened the door and held it.

"What about the ranch?"

"Shall I say you're eager to bring the godless hands into the fold?"

"Tell him Brother Bernard wishes to know more of the world."

"And if he responds that he wishes to know more of Brother Bernard?"

"He won't. I accepted this invitation to give his people time to search the parsonage. I hid my traveling bottle in the outhouse and left a letter from Bernard's sweet dead mother where they wouldn't have to look too hard to find it."

Her face drew taut over its very good bones. "Only a deeply corrupt man would suspect such corruption of a man he'd met only twice."

"Avenging angels don't get haloes. The man who taught me my gospel made that clear."

He hadn't trusted the job to someone clumsy from the bunkhouse. If I hadn't purposely left the drawer in the nightstand slightly ajar and done some other things to provide tells that someone had been through the place, I'd have thought no one had entered it from the time I left until the time I returned. Mrs. McIlvaine had Sunday afternoon off, to do whatever it was she did when she stood her broom in its shallow closet in the church, so I was fairly certain she hadn't been in to clean. The counterfeit letter containing Sebastian's brief biography was where I'd placed it, folded under the brass lamp on the nightstand with his mother's tintype leaning against its base, but the lamp was turned slightly. That pointed to a literate intruder who'd taken down the information to report to his employer.

It being Sunday, I was sure a communication would be going out to Denver by tomorrow's Overland, seeking to confirm the letter's sparse details. Blackthorne never confided the nature of his intelligence organization to subordinates; I had to assume that whoever had handled Sebastian's telegraph exchange with Freemason was in charge of such follow-ups, but I didn't trust him, or for that matter anyone else who held my fate in his hands. I had only the hope that the vague wording of the letter on the nightstand would slow down the inevitable long enough for me to get what I needed and make away. Since that involved pumping the Judge for the details of his past relationship with Freemason, I propped myself up in the iron bed with a writing block on my knees and drafted the following message:

Dear Mr. Smith,

    I've been in Owen days only and everyone I've met has gone to great lengths to make me feel important. Although I confess to homesickness, it is, I'm convinced, God's will that I am in a place where I know

my work is useful and wanted. Already I flatter myself
that I have brought comfort to the afflicted. Mr.
Freemason's confidence in my humble gifts is reas-
suring and gives me strength to believe that nothing
I did in the past is a tenth part of the good that my
service to the Lord will accomplish here. All that
came before is prelude to the hard work and sleep-
less nights put to the purpose of bringing light to
Texas.

Please accept my sincere thanks for your kindness
to a stranger.

Yours in faith,
Bernard Sebastian

I smudged up several sheets, counting words, striking
some out, and adding others, before I had a draft I
could transcribe in proper penmanship and put aside
to mail by way of the Overland to Mr. J. Smith in care
of General Delivery in Wichita Falls. Captain Jordan,
who'd assured me there were upwards of two dozen
"J. Smiths" in town and among the ranches and settlements within plausible riding distance, had a standing
agreement with the postmaster to hold all missives
thus addressed for his scrutiny. Together we'd worked
out a code that would enable me to write what appeared to be a harmless communication to some random brief friendly acquaintance while putting the
Texas Rangers to service to the federal court. It was a
simple enough cypher, but with sufficient room provided for to drench it in homely verbiage: After the
greeting, every twentieth word conveyed the actual
message. If it was urgent and assistance was required
immediately and in force, I would begin with "My
dear Mr. Smith"; otherwise, I was asking Jordan to

forward the actual text by Western Union to Blackthorne. I had written:

important know Freemason's past before Texas

After placing the letter in the nightstand drawer
where I didn't care who found it if I happened to become separated from it, I got up and fed the scribbled
sheets to the fire in the laundry stove. I'd taken all
the precautions I could, without feeling one bit more
secure than I had before I'd written it. I don't place
much trust in encryptions, on the theory that what
one or two men could create, one or two others could
dismantle. Carrier pigeons had at least the advantage
of passing through no human hands between dispatch
and delivery, but the thought that my life depended on
a creature that spent most of its time from one mission to the next picking lice from its feathers was
worse than knowing that the number of people who
were in on my masquerade would fill out the regimen-
tal band at Fort Custer, with the last person I'd trust
with either my wallet or my hide sharing a bed and
who knew how many secrets with the man whose
measure I was trying to take.

It was enough to drive a God-fearing man to drink.
I was weighing the relative risk of retrieving the whiskey bottle from the outhouse when someone knocked
on the door of the parsonage. I reached for my collar,
then decided to leave it off and went through the
sitting room with my sleeves rolled up and a towel
from the dishpan–wash basin over my arm, the
Deane-Adams concealed inside its folds.

At first glance I thought the man on my front step
was Freemason, but then I saw the frock coat was too
large for the visitor's slight frame and the silk hat

rested too low on his forehead, bending down his ears, and knew him for Fielo, the aged houseboy, wearing his master's castoff. He removed the hat, cradling it with a forearm, and held out an envelope with the Masonic compass-and-square embossed on the flap.

I laid the towel with the revolver rolled inside it on the rocking chair and took the envelope. The note was an invitation from Richard Freemason to accompany him to his ranch Tuesday at dawn. I asked the old man to take my acceptance to him with thanks. He bowed, turned, replaced the hat, and applied himself to the long walk back down the street and the steep climb up the limestone steps to the castle on the hill. He wasn't as frail as Colleen made out.

NINETEEN

Unexpectedly, I found my suspicions confirmed—or at least supported—the next morning, when the door to the freight office opened away from my hand and I was face to face once again with Fielo, who hesitated, raised and lowered his hand-me-down silk hat, and stepped past me onto the boardwalk. There were any number of reasons why the manservant of a busy ranch owner would have business with a stagecoach line, but I was satisfied that he'd just posted a letter to Denver on Freemason's behalf to test Brother Bernard's story.

It was Monday and a coach stood ready before the door. That meant a waiting line inside and I joined it.

Luther Cherry, looking every bit the scarecrow I'd met during the trip from Wichita Falls, in a morning coat plastered with lint and stray hairs, stood at the head of the line, arguing with the friendly clerk behind the counter.

"Four-fifty just to carry a letter to St. Louis? I might as well pay a little more and deliver it in person."

"I'm sorry, sir; that's the special delivery rate. Undoubtedly it will come down after they string a telegraph line from Wichita Falls. It always does—competition, you understand. But that won't happen until after the railroad comes through."

"Until which time, Wells, Fargo will behave as arrogantly as any of the Eastern trusts. My God, I could buy a decent suit of clothes and pocket fifty cents!"

Clearly this invited a suggestion, but being affable by nature the clerk made another. "Regular delivery is two dollars, if you don't mind it taking an extra day or so."

"That won't do." Muttering to himself, the lawyer produced four banknotes from a lank wallet and laid them on the counter, then snapped open a Scotchman's coin purse and placed a twenty-five-cent piece, two dimes, and a nickel on top of them. The man behind the counter transferred them to a cash box, stamped a postmark on a long envelope in front of him, and poked it into a pigeonhole at his elbow.

On his way to the door, Cherry, grumbling still, nearly passed me without looking up.

"Life in the wilderness is not as reasonably priced as it was centuries ago, Mr. Cherry," I said.

"Indeed it is not, friend." He recognized me then and halted. "Good morning, Brother. I worked late Saturday night and overslept the next day, missing your sermon. I heard it brought down the house."

"Hardly that, but the reception was most kind."

"I'm sorry you overheard that altercation. I miss my wife, but if I continue to communicate with her at these rates I won't be able to afford her fare." He glanced down at the envelope in my hand. "I hope your people are patient. The Overland is no place for a man sworn to poverty."

"Fortunately, I made a new friend in Wichita Falls. The collection plate won't suffer mortally."

He was only half listening, preoccupied with the hands of his nicked watch. Presently he apologized for the demands of his workload, said good-bye, and took his leave.

When my turn came I handed the clerk my letter to Mr. J. Smith and paid its freight from the loose change in my pocket. He bent my ear over the excellence of the Sunday services until the people behind me began to clear their throats and shuffle their feet. A man tipped his hat and a woman dipped her chin as I walked past. I touched my brim to both. I understood then, a little, about the seductive nature of the Call. Edwin Booth was no more celebrated a figure on the streets of Chicago and San Francisco than a minister in a desert settlement.

Dawn comes early in flat country. I'd just entered the church Tuesday, carrying my second cup of cowboy coffee (paint stirrer required) when the creak of a harness drew me to the door. A Brewster-green Stanhope stood on red wheels beside the boardwalk, hitched to a round-bottomed sorrel with the shoulders of a Percheron; and good job, because it was pulling two passengers already.

Freemason, in a duster and flat-brimmed Stetson,

sat holding the lines behind Luther Cherry. Today the sad-faced lawyer wore a straw hat and sturdy tweeds, out at the elbows but a happier union than his town coat. He clutched a battered leather briefcase on his lap and held down his flapping hat with his other hand against a mild forty-mile-an-hour wind. As I climbed aboard, he pressed in close to the driver to make room on a seat properly built for two.

"Another good morning to you, Brother," he said. "I apologize for the close quarters. I had a question about the boundaries, and Mr. Freemason was gracious enough to invite me to the ranch to see them for myself. No doubt you're growing tired of me by now."

He was a drab companion, and I've never warmed to skinflints, but I protested the opposite. Surreptitiously I wedged my arm between us to keep him from pressing against the revolver in its scabbard. I didn't want to take the chance of Mrs. McIlvaine finding it in the parsonage, and in any case I wasn't about to venture into open country unarmed.

Freemason measured out a smile of contrition. "I yielded to an impulse. The cabriolet is at the ranch, and all the two-seaters are out on hire from the livery. I had this rig built to my order, so it's sound, and Bess is accustomed to hauling furniture in tandem, but by the time we cross the river I fear we'll be on rather more intimate terms with one another than we bargained for."

I said, "I don't mind. Mr. Cherry's presence shortened my journey here."

"A fine piece of fortune," said the sheepman. "I engaged both of you sight unseen, on the strength of my judge of character. Cherry clerked in the St. Louis firm that handled most of my transactions. When he passed the bar with applied study in real property, I retained him immediately. The man's knowledge is worth ten miles of fence."

The lawyer laughed. "If I may speak for Brother Bernard as well as for myself, it's handy there's just the one seat. You might otherwise have been tempted to bring along our friend the wire drummer, and expose us all to an exhaustive lecture on the relative merits of Glidden versus Reynolds, and whether Sunderland's Kink is as effective a deterrent as the Brink Twist."

"I've had my life's portion of those fellows." Our host released the brake and gave the lines a flip; Bess rolled her haunches and we were in motion. "They make no distinction between the walrus hide of a bull and the tender membrane of a ewe. Great patches of scar tissue are as devastating to the harvest of wool as blight to corn. Barbs are designed to contain cattle, dumb brutes that wander away from sure feed to graze on dead thistle in the desert. A week-old lamb knows better than that. No doubt Bo Peep abused her flock." No hint of a smile cracked his countenance.

I changed hands on my hat and shouted across the wind. "If you don't mind my asking, why, then, did you lobby so hard to strengthen the fence-cutting law?"

"Not to keep sheep in, you can be sure of that. I fought for it in order to keep the damn cattlemen out."

At length we crossed Wild Horse Creek at a point where deep ruts left by other vehicles marked the ford. The waters had just begun to recede from the spring runoff, and lapped at our hubs. When we rolled up the bank on the other side, the big mare shrugged, sprinkling us all. "A second baptism," offered Cherry.

For a mile or so we rode alongside four strands

of wire strung between crazy crooked scrubwood posts that any rancher in good timberland would have scorned in favor of straight pine or cedar, while the tough short stubble of buffalo grass gradually gave ground to a lush expanse of bluestem nearly three feet high, ideal for grazing. Freemason had chosen his location well. The relentless wind combed the tops in hypnotic waves, like the pattern on the surface of an inland ocean. I directed my gaze away from it toward the level horizon to keep from becoming drunk on the sight. The grasses of the High Plains are proof that you can get seasick on dry land.

I spotted the horse and man in the road first, just ahead of the rancher, who stiffened at the sight. The man was out of the saddle and kneeling near the fence in the attitude of cutting the wire. Freemason leaned forward and drew a brass-receiver Winchester from the footboards at the base of the seat onto his lap. This alerted Cherry.

"What a place to come bang up," he said. "It's lucky for him we happened along."

Trust a lawyer to size up a situation at one glance. I could see then that the man was too far from the fence to threaten it. At first I thought his horse had thrown a shoe, but as we drew near I saw that the man down on one knee with his back turned toward us was scraping at its right forefoot with a knife, paring the hoof or prying at a stone or some other object that had gotten wedged inside the iron. Our host relaxed, loosening his grip on the pistol stock of the repeater.

"Need help, friend?" he called out.

The man spun on his knee without rising, cocking and leveling a long-barreled Colt at Freemason across the crook of his right arm. He wore a gray hat, range flannels, and a blue bandanna that covered the lower half of his face.

My reflexes were a split second faster than the rancher's; my hand made an entirely involuntary move toward the revolver under my coat, but I stopped it through sheer force of will before it had covered a half inch. The masked man was concentrating on Freemason, who snatched at the carbine across his lap. The Colt flamed and something struck a post holding up the Stanhope's canvas roof. Freemason abandoned the Winchester to seize the lines and calm Bess.

The report seemed to serve double duty as a signal. From the fence and road, the grass-covered ground sloped gently toward the river, forming a shaggy apron some thirty feet wide between hardpack and water. In one smooth motion, a handful of horses scrambled to their feet, seeming to rise from the earth itself as if on hinges and levitating riders into their saddles.

I was more impressed than frightened. It takes more than just good horsemanship to keep eight hundred pounds of nervous animal down on its side without snorting or tossing a head or a tail; two hands are hardly enough to keep it calm and its nostrils covered and man and horse hidden in grass not much more than knee high, and simple athletic ability alone won't let him rise with it, slipping one foot into the stirrup and swinging the other leg over its back in the same movement, man and beast uniting as one. It was like something out of Revelation:

The first beast was like a lion, and the second beast like a calf, and the third beast had a face as a man, and the fourth beast was like a flying eagle.

And the four beasts had each of them six wings
about him; and they were full of eyes within . . .

Only there were five beasts, clad in pale dusters,
gray hats, and blue bandannas, and when the man in
the road swung aboard his horse, the muzzle of his
revolver remaining on point like the needle of a compass, we faced six armed men, the others kneeing their
mounts forward until they formed a half circle about
us with weapons in hand.

A sharp double-clack rang out across the wind, and
I turned my head as a seventh rider cantered our way
from Freemason's property on the other side of the
fence with a fresh round levered into a Spencer rifle.
He wore the uniform of the pack, a strip of tanned
and weathered face showing between the top of his
bandanna and the brim of his hat.

"What does the Good Book say about seven angels?" Cherry asked me in a low voice.

"These aren't angels."

Ten yards from the fence, the newcomer shouted
and smacked his reins across his horse's withers,
breaking it into gallop. It closed the distance in seconds
and left the earth with no more apparent effort than a
balloon rising, clearing the top strand of wire with
inches to spare and braking to a halt short of the road,
forelegs stiff and its rider leaning back on the reins, the
repeater cradled along his right forearm.

Cherry did a foolish thing. Startled by the feat of
athletic horsemanship and the thud of the landing, he
shifted on the seat and his briefcase slid from his lap.
He lunged to catch it. The Spencer bellowed and there
was one less lawyer in Texas.

TWENTY

Something hot and wet splashed the back of my left hand; it was Luther Cherry's blood as he arched his back upon impact, then sagged against me with all his weight. He was breathing, but the nasty sucking sound meant a shot lung and a short life.

For me, there was no harnessing my instincts. Bess tried to rear between the traces, occupying both of Freemason's hands and all of his concentration. The Deane-Adams was in my right hand pointed at the man with the Spencer before I could give any thought to the action.

Six hammers and the lever of the repeater crackled across the wind. Facing seven muzzles, I let the revolver fall to the floorboards and raised my palms to my shoulders.

I was conscious of Freemason's eyes on me, leveled across Cherry's bent frame.

For five minutes—it was more likely seconds—only the wind stirred. Then the man with the Spencer jerked his head at the rider nearest me, who nudged his mount alongside the buggy, leaned over to slide the Winchester off Freemason's lap, and tossed it to another rider nearby, who caught it one-handed. He scooped up the Deane-Adams and examined it, then flipped it toward the man with the Spencer. The Helena baseball team could have used that bunch in the infield.

"Check out the satchel."

The lawyer's briefcase was opened and its contents dumped out. Papers fluttered in every direction like bats flushed from a cave. The rider shook his head and dropped it in the road.

"Nice iron for a plug-hat preacher." The man with the Spencer raised my weapon and sighted down the barrel at a point between my eyes. His voice carried above the wind with the ease of someone accustomed to raising it, with a West Texas accent as flat as the panhandle. I was convinced he was the man Charlie Sweet had heard giving the orders during the Overland robbery. "Too good anyway for potting snakes and such."

"He's right handy with it, too." The man who'd picked it up had marbles in his mouth, or more practically a cud in his cheek.

I said nothing. I could feel the muzzle on me as if it were pressing against the bridge of my nose.

At length the Spencer man lowered it, shook the shells out of the cylinder, and flipped the revolver back my way. That was a surprise, but I kept my hands where they were while it dropped at my feet with a clunk; it might have been a trick to make me grab for it and claim self-defense, with Freemason to furnish eyewitness testimony. Frontier courts didn't always mess with complications like an unloaded firearm.

"What do you want?" asked the rancher, speaking up for the first time. "I don't have much cash on me, and you can't break up my watch seven ways."

"We don't want your money, sheepman. We thought you was a payroll wagon."

"You know me?"

"I can smell you." He nodded to the man who'd disarmed us, who jacked all the shells out of the Winchester and slid it across the buggy's floorboards.

"Why so generous?" Freemason asked.

"Can't use the weight. Comes a choice betwixt gold and iron, I choose gold." He socked the Spencer into a scabbard slung from his saddle horn and gathered his reins. "You best get help for your friend, for what good it does. He was green or he'd know better than to jump like a jackrabbit when there's guns about."

He backed his horse off the road, then wheeled, followed closely by the others, in the direction we'd been headed. They bent low, raking their spurs for speed, billows of dust erupting from their horses' heels. We could see them a long time before they turned south away from the road and shrank from sight. Then a moan from Cherry brought us back to more urgent matter.

"He'll never make it to town," Freemason said.

"He won't make it anyway."

"We have to do what we can. There's a line shack in a mile." He snatched the whip from its socket, wrapped the lines snugly around one wrist, and slashed at the mare's hindquarters.

Bess was lathered and broken-winded when we reached the nearest gate, and by the time Freemason drew rein before a swaybacked building constructed of local stone with a patchwork roof of mud and straw, she was used up for the week, and possibly for life. A pair of smudge-bearded line riders came out to greet us with rifles, and when they recognized their employer, laid them down and helped us carry the lawyer inside. The interior was a mulch of soot and grease and tobacco and the stench of burning dung from the pit at the base of the chimney where a two-gallon coffeepot simmered on its hook, with a heavy overlay of man.

Line shacks are self-contained extensions of ranch headquarters. Because of their remoteness during heavy weather, they're as well stocked as any center of civilization. One of the riders produced medical supplies from an oilcloth pouch, cut away Cherry's blood-drenched shirt with scissors, cleaned the bubbling wound in his chest with alcohol, plucking away threads and pieces of lint with forceps, and discarded several yards of sopping red bandage in the tar bucket he and his partner used for a trash receptacle before the bleeding slowed enough to apply a patch. It was all to comfort the wounded man, like the jug whiskey they gave him from a tin cup, supporting his head with a hand while he drank; for his lungs were filling with blood and there was nothing else for it but to prop him up with pillows to slow the process and watch as he drowned on dry land.

Soon he lapsed into unconsciousness, and at a signal from the rancher I accompanied him outside while the man who'd attended to Cherry kept an eye on him and his partner substituted a kettle for the coffeepot in the chimney and coaxed gravy from fatty chunks of mutton with a ladle. I wondered if one or both of them had been among the three hands the governor had pardoned for the murder of a fence cutter from cattle country. They'd looked more comfortable holding those rifles than they did looking after the domestic chores.

Bess had been unhitched and stood motionless in the corral apart from the linemen's mounts, head down and blowing. Freemason, athletic as slight men often are, swung himself over the top rail, seized an empty gunnysack off a nail next to the back door of the shack, and used it to rub the mare down. "I suppose we can console ourselves those road agents' informants misled them for once," he said. "I've made no new arrangements for a payroll delivery."

I said, "I see no reason to assume the virtue of truth on their behalf. Perhaps you were their target after all."

"For what purpose? They didn't rob me."

"Maybe shooting Mr. Cherry unsettled them."

"Shooting that shotgun messenger didn't dissuade them from going ahead and robbing the Overland."

"Maybe they wanted to shoot Cherry."

"Ludicrous. Granted there's an open season on lawyers, especially with that fence-cutting bill out of committee, but they couldn't have known he'd be with me. I didn't know myself until I invited him last night."

"Who else knew?"

"Apart from whomever Cherry might have spoken to? Only my wife."

I watched him, down on one knee scrubbing rivulets of lather from a foreleg. He stopped and looked up at me through the rails. "They made a good point about that weapon you carry. I suppose English revolvers are easier to obtain in Denver."

"I wouldn't know. It's the first revolver I've ever bought. The man who sold it to me said I'd need it for protection from wolves and red Indians."

"He must have shown you how to use it. I don't believe any of the men I pay to protect my property could have produced it more quickly."

"My father told me it isn't enough just to read Scripture. One must understand it as well. It occurred to me the same would hold true for a weapon. I practiced quite a bit."

"I'm surprised you had time left to contemplate the words of our Lord. Can you hit anything with it?"

"Tins and bottles."

He rose, flicking dust from the knee of his trousers. "These bandits haven't a history of making mistakes. Perhaps I was the target, but when they shot Cherry they decided it would carry the message as well. Killing me would accomplish nothing; Colleen would appoint someone to manage the ranch in my place, because the alternative would be bankruptcy. If they frighten me off, the fence bill would lose support in Austin, and Big Cattle will continue to dominate Texas. These are not garden-variety highwaymen. Goodnight and his cronies are paying them to harass me and clear the way to claim all the grazing land for themselves."

"It seems underhanded. They've never been shy about doing battle out in the open."

"That was when they were winning, and no one in authority would oppose them. I should flatter myself that I've at least driven them to cover."

"It does help to explain why you've suffered from these robberies more than anyone," I said. "What did you make of the brand on their horses?"

"I saw no brand. I was too busy looking at their weapons."

"I got a close look when the one who disarmed us came alongside." I looked around for a stick, but good luck finding one in that country. Instead I used the toe of my shoe to trace the following symbol in the dust at my feet:

Freemason draped the sweat-soaked gunnysack over the top fence rail and leaned on it as he studied the mark, which disintegrated before our eyes in the incessant wind; in a moment, it was as if it had never existed.

"A Star of David," he said. "Do you think they're Jews?"

"If so, they'd be foolish to advertise it during robberies, given their history. I think it's more likely whoever owns the brand calls it the Double Triangle or something like that. Have you never seen it?"

"Never. I know some people with the Stock-Raisers Association; they won't let me in, but a band like this is bad business for everyone. If the brand is registered, we'll trace them."

The man we'd left with Luther Cherry opened the back door. Freemason looked a question at him, but he turned my way. "He's awake, preacher, but not for long. He wants you."

I found the lawyer propped into a half-sitting position. He'd bled through his bandages again, draining his face of all color. His lips were moving, but no sound came out. I took off my hat and bent close enough to feel his moist breath on my ear. Freemason and the man who'd come to fetch me stood at the foot of the bed. The other hand continued stirring the kettle over the fire.

"My mother was Catholic." It took Cherry twice as long to say the words as it takes to write them. "My father wouldn't have it, but she smuggled it in to me. Will you hear my confession?"

I said, "I haven't the authority to forgive you on behalf of God."

"That's all right. I don't believe a priest does either. I have some things that need saying. I don't care if you pass them on, though I'd take it a kindness if you'd spare my wife."

"I can promise that."

He spoke for several moments, drawing whistling breaths between words. The men at the foot of the bed leaned forward, but I could barely hear him with his lips nearly touching my ear. His breath seemed to be cooling as I listened, like embers fading in a hearth. At length he stopped talking in mid-sentence. I turned my head to face him. His eyes grew soft, softer; a cloud passed between them and what lay behind. I lifted my hand and kneaded them shut.

My Bible rode in the side pocket of my coat. I took it out, but I didn't open it.

"'The Lord is my shepherd,'" I said; "'I shall not want. . . .'"

TWENTY-ONE

I fail to see why you won't tell me what he told you," Freemason said. "You said yourself he didn't care so long as you kept it from his wife."

I said, "Because I can doesn't mean I should."

"But you're not a priest."

"I avoid discussions of the relative merits and deficiencies of other denominations. However, I hold the seal of the confessional to be the mainstay of the Roman Catholic Church."

"I think you're forgetting I belong to the board that employs you."

"If you want to put it on that basis, it's my Christian duty to spare you the ordeal of dismissing me. I'll submit my resignation."

"Let's not go off half-cocked, Brother. You must understand my concerns are professional as well as personal. If you know something about Cherry's behavior during the time he was representing me, it's only natural I'd press you for details."

We were in the sheepman's paneled study, where we'd retired after delivering Luther Cherry's body to the undertaking parlor that held the contract with the town council in cases of death by misadventure. Freemason had sent one of the line riders to ranch headquarters for a wagon to carry the remains. At the same time he'd sent the other man to Wichita Falls to report the incident to Captain Jordan at Texas Rangers headquarters. That day's Overland stage had come and gone, but a good man on a horse would overtake and pass it. Thought of the Overland reminded me of something I'd forgotten.

"Your interests are no more personal than Cherry's," I said. "I can tell you of a thing I saw yesterday morning at the freight office." I recounted the lawyer's argument with the clerk over the rate required to send a special delivery letter to St. Louis.

"Unpleasant, but hardly unusual," Freemason said. "The rates are outrageous, but they're the price of free enterprise. Still, everyone has the right to complain."

"Nevertheless, he paid the amount, refusing the lower rate for regular delivery because it would take a few days longer. He made change from a pocketbook."

"That's what it's for. It's also called a change purse."

"Perhaps things are different in Texas, but where I come from, a man who goes to that length to corral every penny is considered parsimonious."

"They're not different. I don't use one myself, lest the men I do business with get the impression I'm hard up for cash. Cherry was cheese-paring; I admire that in someone I appoint to help handle my affairs. I fail to see why he should be condemned for it."

I looked humble, or made the effort. "It's not my place to save or condemn. I merely mentioned the episode because he was so quick to decide in favor of paying more for the sake of expediency. He said the letter was for his wife. Surely there was nothing in it so urgent it couldn't wait a few more days."

"I begin to understand you." He frowned, drumming his slim, well-kept fingers on a leaf of his towering desk. "It strikes me someone should ask the clerk in the freight office about the address on the envelope."

"He'd be violating the law if he disclosed it."

He didn't appear to be listening. "You raise the suggestion that Cherry was the squirrel chewing holes in my wall, providing details of my business arrangements to some factotum in St. Louis, who forwarded them on to that gang of pirates."

"I wouldn't bear false witness."

"With good reason. Cherry was new to Owen. My problem predates his arrival by months."

"You told me he'd been active in the firm that represents you a long time before you retained him personally. That would put him in possession of a great deal of privileged information."

Fielo, the aged manservant, knocked and entered, carrying a tea set on a tray. His master asked him if Mrs. Freemason had returned from her errands.

"Not yet, sir. Shall I pour?"

"No. Set it down and return to your other duties. Let me know when she's back."

When the door drew shut, Freemason looked at me.

"This isn't a discussion to be conducted over tea. Where do you stand on spirits?"

"I wouldn't presume. I'm told they're an ecclesiastical invention."

"Good man." He stood and used a key attached to his watch chain to unlock the hidden wall cabinet. I pretended curiosity, as if I hadn't seen it before. "Colleen thinks the old man is a drinker on the sly," he said. "I haven't seen any evidence myself, but she's far more attuned to the domestic arrangements than I, and her attention to detail is impressive. She has a man's brain. I think that's what attracted me to her. She maintains all the books on the ranch. If something were to happen to me, I'm quite certain she could manage the place quite well on her own."

"You must trust her very much."

"A wise man told me you can trust no one or trust everyone and take the same chances. I prefer to err on the side of conservatism." He poured from the bottle of Hermitage. "I was instrumental in preventing Colleen from serving a jail sentence in Waco. She dealt cards there, which is a profession admirably suited to accounting. Between the morning she was freed and the day I proposed marriage, I had her thoroughly investigated by the Pinkertons, who confirmed everything she'd disclosed to me about her past and a number of things she neglected to mention. I'm a businessman, Brother, not a gambler. I never enter into a proposition until I've studied it from all sides and isolated the risk."

Turning from the cabinet, he held out one of the cut-crystal glasses. When I reached for it, his free hand lashed out and enclosed my wrist in his iron grip. It was my gun hand.

"That's a pistoleer's weapon you carry," he said. "It's been well kept. In order to complete the performance, if you armed yourself at all you'd lug around some ancient cap-and-ball cannon with rust on the cylinder; but that wouldn't do if you were forced to use it. That's the flaw in any masquerade: To put it over properly one must become what one appears, rendering the exercise useless." He smiled in his neat beard. "Wouldn't you agree, Marshal?"

TWENTY-TWO

Deputy," I corrected. "I'm not political enough for a presidential appointment. Where'd I tip my hand?"

"Where didn't you? Your choice of weapons, that history you concocted for yourself, your deportment in general. If I let go of your wrist, will you agree to keep that hand in plain sight?"

I nodded. I'd considered throwing my drink in his face to distract him while I went for the scabbard, but I hated to waste good sipping whiskey. He released his grip, poured for himself, and sat down.

"A careful way of speaking and a veil of humility can't obscure the habits of a lifetime," he said. "This morning when you came to the church door, you glanced up and down the street and scanned the rooftops before you stepped outside. I doubt you were even aware you did it. A man who's spent most of his life shut in with his mother feels no reason to take such precautions. Mind you, I suspected you before that. You have a whiff of brimstone about you. They haven't developed a soap pious enough to scrub it off."

I drank. "I was pretty certain you'd had someone go through my things. I never said I'd been shut in with my mother or even that I had one. That was all in a letter I brought with me when I came."

"It never left the parsonage, only the salient details. I told you I don't invest without investigation. My wife won't remember, but she once made reference to a former acquaintance in law enforcement who had the look of a starved wolf. That's the first impression I had of you, after disregarding the sackcloth and ashes and that collar. Excellent suggestion, that. Few people look beyond a thing so obvious."

"Thank you. It almost makes up for the heat rash."

"None of this was sufficient to leap to any conclusions, of course. Then I remembered reading of the conspicuous death of a deputy U.S. marshal of some reputation up in Montana Territory. Your choice of firearms settled the matter. Legends don't overlook such crumbs. You really ought to have left it behind."

"I hadn't time to break in a new one and keep up with my Bible studies."

"At least you're not the kind that clings to a lie in the face of all evidence. It's refreshing."

"I don't ride a horse back into a burning stable."

"I wish we'd had this conversation Sunday. It would have saved me postage to Denver. Poor Cherry was right: The rates are confiscatory."

"I ran into Fielo at the freight office. I'd guessed he was there to track down Brother Bernard."

Freemason rolled liquor on his tongue and swallowed. "Really, I thought what happened between your Judge Blackthorne and me went to rest with the

Grant administration. I wouldn't have expected him to carry a grudge."

"Grudges aren't like mule packs. The bigger they are, the longer you can carry them."

"Still, he's an old political infighter. He knows when it's time to cut your losses and get back to business."

"A lot of lawyers lost their case because they thought they could predict him." My mouth was dry, but I resisted raising my glass because my hand might shake. I was close to an explanation of why I was in Texas.

"Just what is he after? In ten years I've done nothing that would place me in his power. Or is it your mission to adjust that situation? I believe you said something a few moments ago about bearing false witness."

I shot from the hip. "Nothing like that. The law's his lasso. He'll take a couple of dallies on it, but he won't break it. Some new evidence has come to light to make that old grudge a little easier to carry."

Fielo knocked, came in at his master's invitation, and reported that Mrs. Freemason had returned. Freemason nodded and dismissed him. When we were alone again, the rancher sat back for the first time and steepled his hands. I knew then I'd misfired.

"No new evidence can reverse a presidential pardon," he said. "Blackthorne didn't tell you anything about our history. I'd thought you were remarkably circumspect for a man of action. What's your real purpose? I can have you locked up as an impostor, on suspicion of your intentions. With all this banditry about, and when information comes back from Denver casting doubt on the existence of a preacher named Sebastian, no one will question your incarceration for weeks."

"I've been in jail before." I was making time to think. Whatever was in the Judge's mind, it would collapse under its own weight while I was behind bars, and with no way to get in touch with him, I'd be stuck counting stones in the walls while the Blue Bandannas were free to hare around shooting cowhands and shotgun messengers and generally breaking the peace. I drank, no tremors, and set aside my glass. "Until I came here, I didn't even know you and Blackthorne had a history. The first time I saw your name was when I read it on your telegram inviting Brother Bernard to serve as pastor. I was sent to investigate the panhandle robberies."

"That's a tale. Every one of them took place outside his jurisdiction."

"Strictly speaking, his jurisdiction covers all crimes against the United States. Two of the robberies involved the mail. Also he's concerned that left to its own devices this band will eventually expand their depredations to Montana Territory. He'd rather fight them on the High Plains than in Virginia City."

"He said that?"

"He did."

"Did you believe him?"

"I wasn't required to."

"I don't believe you."

"Let's talk about something else, then. For what crime were you pardoned by President Grant?"

He checked that without blinking. "You said you knew nothing about my connection with Blackthorne until you came here. Who told you?"

I was busy saying nothing when Colleen Freemason entered without knocking. Clearly she'd been listening outside the door. "I told him, Richard."

She was dressed fetchingly in a straw hat with a

curled brim and feathers, a trim tweed suit over a plain shirtwaist, black-and-ivory patent-leather pumps, and black felt gloves with ivory buttons. Her cheeks were flushed from the wind. As she was naturally high-colored, she might have stepped out of a Renaissance painting and come there by way of a Victorian dress shop. She was staring at me; accusingly or not, I could never tell.

"Indeed," Freemason said. "The past becomes the present. That wasn't our arrangement."

"Nothing's changed. I made the same error you did. I assumed he was here to try to snare you in some way. From what I just overheard, you told him more than I did."

I turned my attention from her, which was always a chore. "Since you did, you might as well tell me the rest. I've been floundering in the dark since before I left Helena."

Freemason frowned, then pulled his hands apart and placed them on the arms of his chair. His mouth opened; Colleen stepped close and placed a gloved hand on his shoulder.

"The past is not the present." She was still looking at me. "We've made our home here. We've obeyed the law, and Richard has assisted it. You're the one who's sailing under false colors. We owe you nothing."

"A pretty speech," said her husband. "I'd be more impressed if you'd *told* me his colors were false. Have you taken up where you left off?"

She snatched away her hand as if he'd bitten it.

I anted in. "She made it clear the last time we spoke in this room there'd be none of that. I swore my business here had nothing to do with you and Blackthorne and asked her to keep the secret. Too many people knew already, and there was no telling what someone else might guess if your attitude toward me was any different from what was expected between a church director and his parson. Not wanting to see a man murdered in the course of his work and having serious feelings for him aren't the same thing."

"We both have secrets, Richard. We agreed we weren't each other's confessor."

"A fine match." He swirled the contents of his glass, then tossed them back like any hand fresh off the trail. Then he got up to refill.

"Pour me one as well." Colleen stripped off her gloves and drew the pin from her hat.

"I keep coming back to why those bandits were waiting for us," I said when we were all seated. "Until now, they've made no mistakes. Their sources have been too good."

Freemason still looked sour, and it had only a little to do with what had happened near his ranch. "Everyone puts a foot wrong sometimes. I married a woman I can't trust."

"I don't care. You're forgetting I'm not really a minister. One mistake is possible, but this was also the first time they've struck this close to Owen. Their avoiding it is what brought me here in the first place. They must have had a compelling reason to break that cardinal rule. Whenever something like that happens, I ask myself what recent change might have brought it about."

"That would be you." Colleen, informed of the day's events, sat upright in a chintz-covered chair, the only remotely feminine object in the room and obviously kept for her use. She held her glass at bodice level with the surface of the liquid as flat as a sheltered pond. "You're Owen's newest resident."

"Just barely. Luther Cherry arrived just before me."

"You keep harping on Cherry," Freemason said. "He's dead."

"Another mistake. He made a grab for his briefcase when it slid off his lap. He was under the gun at the time, and when you have someone in that position the shooter's nerves are right up there on top. Shooting him was a natural reaction on the part of the man with the Spencer."

"Also disastrous, if you insist on believing that Cherry was their Trojan horse. That makes three mistakes. What are the odds of that happening, given their record so far?"

"Colleen's the cardplayer," I said.

She shook her head and sipped. "I'd fold rather than bet against them. It was no accident."

I said, "I think it was. Killing him, I mean. Everything else was planned. They weren't expecting a payroll wagon. That was just an excuse. Cherry was just settling in, and Freemason hadn't made it a secret he suspected he had a traitor in his employ. What better way to raise their man inside above suspicion than to shoot him during an attempted robbery, right in front of his employer?"

"By God." Freemason flushed deep copper, his glass hovering beneath his chin. "By God."

"The man I'll call Spencer meant to wing him," I went on, "but that's not an exact science when you're on horseback and your target's in motion. Either his aim was off or Cherry moved in the wrong direction. The bullet pierced a lung instead of just an arm."

The sheepman remembered his drink and took a

long draught. "Are frontier brigands capable of such Machiavellian measures?"

"The organized ones are," I said. "We're up against a bigger operation than any of us thought. If I'm right about that special delivery letter Cherry sent to St. Louis, it means he had a contact there who forwarded privileged information on to whoever the Blue Bandannas report to in this area. Someone's out to break you, and he's going to a hell of a lot of expense to do it."

"The cattle trade," he said. "That fence-cutting bill has them scared. If they manage to destroy me, no one will ever enforce it, and there will be no sheep rancher safe in the state of Texas."

I emptied my glass and set it down. "Cattlemen are too busy running their own spreads to act in concert. Maybe they've appointed someone, but whoever's behind the robberies has nothing else on his plate to distract him."

"I'll trace that letter Cherry made so much fuss about."

"You can do that. Chances are he sent it to someone at the legal firm you got him from, who can claim it was just some unfinished business; certainly he'll have destroyed the evidence, and all we'll have is Cherry's lie that he was writing his wife."

"Maybe his wife is the go-between."

Both of us looked at Colleen, whose chin elevated an inch in defense of her theory.

"She isn't," I said.

"How do you know?" she asked.

"Because when he confessed to conspiring against Freemason, he asked me to say nothing of it to her."

TWENTY-THREE

Freemason toyed with his glass. "Why didn't you tell me what he said the first time I asked? What was the point of pretending to speculate he died as a result of his own manipulations?"

"That part was speculation," I said. "He didn't live long enough to get around to it. As for the rest, I wasn't sure he was alone. I'm still not, but based on this conversation I'm reasonably satisfied it isn't your wife."

Colleen appeared unmoved; but so does the outside of a volcano. "What did I say to convince you I'm not?"

"Nothing. If you had, you'd still be under suspicion. It's never easy to tell when you're bluffing, but the higher the stakes, the harder you push a pair of deuces. You didn't say a word when your husband said he couldn't trust you. If ever there was a time for a traitor to prove herself loyal, that was it."

"God, but you're a bastard."

"I've worked for Blackthorne a long time. Some of it was bound to rub off." A clock outside the door chimed the hour; we'd been locked up most of the day. I looked at Freemason. "You'll see to Cherry's arrangements, I suppose. No doubt his wife will want to bury him in St. Louis."

"I ought to throw his carcass into the creek, but I've become a respectable man. I'll play the generous benefactor. The damage is done; nothing can be gained by blackening his memory. And what will you be about meanwhile?"

"Sunday is Easter. I've a sermon to prepare." I rose. Two pairs of eyes followed me.

Freemason said, "You intend to continue as Brother Bernard? Why? Without Cherry, the Bandannas have no hole card. The first time they act on their own they'll blunder into the hands of the Rangers as like as not."

"I said I'm not sure he was alone. In any case my orders are to break them up or bring them to justice. Also the church needs a pastor."

"Where will you start?" he asked.

"Matthew, twenty-six."

"You're trying my patience, Deputy."

"Brother," I said. "Let's not slip into any bad habits. I'm going to start by tracing that star brand. They've got as good an eye for horseflesh as any outlaw gang. The trader who sold seven premium mounts at a crack will remember who he sold them to."

He said, "The brand might not be registered. Smaller ranches crop up all the time. The ranchers are too busy getting established to bother right away, and the registrars can't keep up with the rest."

"You don't get animals like that from a start-up outfit. Someone had time to breed them. The brand has to be on file somewhere."

"Still, that's a lot of legwork for one man."

"If you're trying to find out how I operate, you're wasting my time as well as yours."

He flushed again. "You don't care who you insult, do you?"

Colleen said, "He has rules about which questions to answer honestly when he's playing a role, Richard. He likes to keep his lies in a separate pile, and he doesn't trust anyone."

I shook my head. "You can trust everyone and be

betrayed, or no one and betray yourself. My policy is to shoot straight down the middle."

"Even so," Freemason said. "Not trusting is a quality a man can do worse than to acquire."

The old Mexican came in after knocking, hesitated when he saw we were all standing, and spoke in a low tone to Freemason, who bent his head to listen. "Tell him to come in."

Fielo ghosted out, leaving the door open for the visitor. Captain Jordan of the Texas Rangers stood taller than he sat, despite bowed legs and a slight shoulder stoop. He wore what appeared to be the same faded blue flannel shirt, its pockets stuffed with smoking material, with leather-reinforced riding trousers stuffed into the tops of tall stovepipe boots, long-roweled Mexican spurs jingling behind the heels. He took off his pinch hat, revealing a bald crown cream-colored to the line where the hat ended and his tan began. He smelled of the sweat of horse and man. The steel-shot eyes looked tired and a stubble had sprouted on his chin, as white as his handlebars.

He introduced himself, grasped the sheepman's hand, and nodded to Colleen. When Freemason presented me, the Ranger showed no recognition. His grip would be the last thing about him to give out.

"What luck?" Freemason asked.

"Same as at White Horse," Jordan said. "Tracks turned into the creek and got lost in the tangle from the last herd that crossed. They know this country, all right. Can't figure out what made them steer so wide of it before this."

"Brother Bernard has a theory about that," began Freemason, only to abandon the rest at a look from me.

"I'm always open to spiritual guidance." Jordan nailed me with his gaze.

I smiled an apology. "That's the only kind I can offer. I just suggested that poor Mr. Cherry may have been the reason the gang singled us out."

"Any special reason, or does God speak just to you?"

It was an experience new to me, that moment: Two men working overtime to keep a third from knowing the full truth about one of them while the third pretended not to know it already. The frontier was no longer the simple place it used to be.

I told him of the lawyer's last words, and my thought that he'd engineered his own wounding in order to lift suspicion from himself. Jordan took it all in without comment. Colleen excused herself as a nonwitness and left us. The captain declined a drink, stuffed and lit his pipe, and gave us a detailed account of his quest beginning with the message Freemason had sent him in Wichita Falls by way of the rider from the ranch: He and his small command had traded their lathered mounts for fresh ones Freemason had made available for them at the line shack and followed the trail to extinction. He'd left his men to rest in town while he came to the house to report and gather information.

"What encouragement can you offer that I won't end up fighting this band over my last dollar?" asked the rancher.

"Not knowing how many you got, I can't answer. If the brother's right, a cockeyed scheme like that is a sign they're losing their smarts. However, I ain't what you might call a religious man. The evidence of things unseen don't hold up in San Antonio."

"What's the reward on these fellows' capture or death?"

"Five hundred a head."

"I'll add a hundred each, and see if I can get the Stock-Raisers Association to double it."

"That ought to make things right lively. If I had a blue bandanna I'd burn it." Jordan stood and offered his hand. "I'd like to ask the brother a couple of questions, just us. He's the one Cherry talked to. He might remember a thing or two more in a place where he's comfortable."

"You don't have to ask my permission, Captain. That's up to Brother Bernard."

"I'm afraid I can't tell you anything I haven't, Captain."

His lips parted to let something out, but I jigged my eyes right and left, hoping he wasn't an unsubtle man. He drew a breath and stirred his handlebars on the exhale. "Well, if you can't take a preacher at his word, who can you? It's getting late and I don't trust that stage trail. I'll spread my roll outside town and start back at first light. This trail won't get no warmer."

"I've got spare rooms gathering dust," Freemason said. "I'd consider it a favor if you'd put up here. Mrs. Freemason and I don't get many visitors. Pariahs, don't you know, under the veneer of respect."

"I'll remember you asked next time. Just now I got men getting set to stretch out on bare panhandle. It wouldn't set right with them to know I spent the night on feathers."

We left that house. At the bottom of the long flight of steps Jordan and I shook hands. "The parsonage behind the church," I said. "After dark. I'll leave the back door off the latch."

He didn't even nod, although I could feel the heat of curiosity glowing deep in those burnished eyes. We turned in opposite directions. As I did so I caught a glimpse of a curtain stirring in an upstairs window of the mansion. When she'd moved in, Colleen would have been sure to secure herself a room with the best view of the town.

The sun was long gone when someone tapped at the back door of the parsonage. I'd moved the lamp in the little sitting room to a spot where it wouldn't outline the opening and closed and latched the door behind him quickly. The sacking someone had put up to serve for curtains masked the windows.

"I don't see the need," Jordan said when we were seated. I'd given him the rocking chair, filled two tin cups from the bottle I'd brought from Helena, and drawn the straightback close so we could talk quietly. There didn't have to be professional spies; the Fielos and Mrs. McIlvaines of the world have soft soles and long ears. "I thought I did a fair job of explaining the palaver."

"I've got my reasons," I said. "They don't have to make sense to anyone but me."

He didn't pursue the point, and my respect for him went up another healthy notch. He tipped his hat as far back as only a Texan can without it falling off. "I'd as lief wrestle bobwire in the dark as have another meet like that one at Freemason's. Just who knows what?"

"His wife and I have a history. She kept her mouth shut, but he figured it out based on some things she'd told him in the past. Neither of them knows you and I have met before. I'd like to keep it that way for a while. People let down their guard when they think one man is all they have to worry about."

"I knowed something was in the wind when you gave me the evil eye there at the finish. First Cherry, now his boss? How big is this bunch?"

"I don't know, but Cherry wasn't in it."

He drank from his cup, his eyes fixed on mine above the rim. "Why would a man lie his way into hell with his last breath? And how do you know he did?"

"I don't. He confessed, but not to informing on Freemason's plans. He wanted me to know he'd strayed once from his marriage. It happened just the one time, he said, back in St. Louis, but he didn't want to die with it on his conscience. He asked me not to tell his wife. I think what happened had something to do with why he accepted Freemason's invitation to set up shop here in Texas.

"He was talking to the collar," I went on. "I'll probably draw another month in purgatory for it."

"That was the shebang? He jumped the traces?"

"If there was anything else he didn't last long enough to share it. In that situation you lead with the sin that's most on your mind."

"So why did you tell Freemason— Oh." The dawn appeared to break. He nodded. "That's why I came in the back way. How sure are you?"

"Not enough to take any sort of action. Subtracting Cherry, it's the only explanation for what happened out on the road, but I can't take that to Helena. Anyway, you can see why I didn't want anyone to think I had the chance to pass on what I knew to the Rangers. I have to be the lightning rod."

"A lightning rod can take a lot of hits. With a man, all it takes is one."

"I've been struck before."

He shook his leonine head. "I got to tell you, this is one game of poker where you're safer to share your cards."

"The deck's passed through too many hands as it is." I lifted my cup, but didn't drink. I tapped a finger on the rim and lowered it. "I've a strong hunch you can hold a secret till it sprouts leaves, but my hunches don't always turn out. It has to stop somewhere. I can't even trust my friends with what I plan to do next."

"Lone wolves are easier to kill. Just so you know."

"That doesn't mean it's easy. But if it happens, it means I figured right. The rest will be up to you."

He got out his pipe, leaving the makings in his pocket. He slid the stem along his lower lip, watching me through the thickets of creases that surrounded his eyes. "I don't mind dying while I'm moving forward. I'd sure as hell hate it while I'm going the other direction. They don't pay me enough to do it standing still. What do they pay you up there?"

"Free burial, same as you. Did you bring anything for me?"

"Thought you'd ask. Since I was fixing to be in the neighborhood I took it along." He gave me a thick fold of yellow paper from the flap pocket where he kept his tobacco pouch.

I unfolded it. It was a garble of unrelated words consuming several pages of Western Union scrip, signed HAB. Harlan A. Blackthorne's personal code was more complex than the one I'd worked out with Jordan, but it was a lot less chatty in appearance; anyone who saw it would know immediately it contained confidential information. I was relieved to see it was addressed to the Rangers station and not Bernard Sebastian.

"Anything for me?" Jordan asked.

"I don't know yet. It takes time to work out. I'll get word to you if there is."

"What you fixing to do now, fort up here and wait?"

"I'd just as soon post my plans on the church bulletin board. The biggest day in the Christian year is coming up; I expect a full house Sunday, and I have to get ready for it."

"I was you, I'd sling a skillet around my neck front and back. So far the Lord God Jesus is the only one ever clumb back up out of the grave come Easter."

"Well, I died up north and here I sit. Maybe He's got another miracle for me in His pocket."

TWENTY-FOUR

The lamp was guttering when I left off translating the Judge's response to my question about Freemason and turned in. I finished in the morning, but by then I'd already learned enough to piece together the rest. The old bastard behind the bench had been wise to wait until I was a thousand miles away before he opened Pandora's box.

I worked on my Easter sermon over coffee, ate noon dinner at the Pan Handle, where Charlie Sweet was too busy waiting tables to exchange more than a couple of friendly words, and made my first two missionary stops, to the Alamo and the Old Granada saloons, where the cowhands and the sheep hands did their respective drinking.

In the Alamo the bartender, a stove-up old waddie

with a rolling limp and a permanent squint, gave me a look intended for a natural enemy, and my collar made the customers nervous, anticipating a weekday sermon, but I put them all back on their heels by buying drinks for the men I stood with at the bar while ordering well water for myself. On the second round I moved my glass, leaving a wet ring on the glossy cherrywood, and traced a pair of intersecting triangles with my finger. I asked the men at my right and left if they'd seen a brand that looked like it. Each man looked closely, traded his position with the others to give them a view, and shook his head. The bartender finished drawing a beer, came over, and wiped away the symbol with his rag, muttering something that sounded like Hebrew. That threw me a little.

I drew the same blank at the Old Granada, where a pastoral engraving of a bearded shepherd and his flock hung above the bottles of busthead. Two of the sheep hands there saw the mark's resemblance to the Star of David, but no one had seen it in the flesh.

By then the local meeting place of the Texas Stock-Raisers Association, which occupied the second floor of the Elks Lodge, had opened its doors for dinner. The gatekeeper, a Prussian in a cutthroat collar with a straight back and military whiskers, sat me on a hard bench inside the entryway and kept me waiting for a half hour while he checked in diners, then as the flow ebbed sent a waiter to the little club library for a brand book. I spread it open on my knees, turned page after page of crudely drawn insignia, and found exactly what I'd expected: Nothing. For whatever reason—possibly one as harmless as its owner hadn't registered in time to make that year's record—the spread where the bandits' horses were raised didn't appear to exist in the eyes of the ranching establishment.

That left me as heavy as ever on suspicion but as light as usual on evidence.

The First Unitarian was packed for the second Sunday in a row, which I attributed more to the holiness of the day than to my skills as a spellbinder, although I flattered myself that I hadn't driven anyone into the arms of the Methodists. Richard and Colleen Freemason were in their customary pew up front; a brass plate on the end of the backrest bore witness to their contribution in its construction, as did the others celebrating other donors, but in their case the Masonic compass and square took the place of a name. I saw other familiar faces as well as some new ones among the worshippers standing in back. The lay volunteer circulating the collection plate had to dump his load in the old Wells, Fargo box on the platform behind the pulpit and go back for seconds. There was a new coat of paint there and roof repairs. I never was in a house of God that wasn't stumping for a new roof: Church shingles take a double beating, from rain above and prayers below.

I'd gone through the portfolio of sermons Eldred Griffin had placed in my charge and made a risky choice. The text rejected the common view of Judas' betrayal of Jesus as villainy, transforming him into a kind of flawed, tragic hero, who when he realized the enormity of his transgression had chosen to take his own life rather than to confess and repent, thus sentencing himself to an eternity in hell without parole. It fell short of expiating his guilt, but it hinted at personal redemption. As originally written, the sermon bordered on heresy; I was next to certain that Griffin had composed it after his own fall from grace, with no intention of ever reading it in public, and as such it required editing to avoid having myself nailed to the sorry crooked wooden sticks that West Texas had to offer in the way of a cross. I laid in the conventional condemnation of Iscariot and powdered it lightly with the defrocked priest's mercy, leavening out the sardonic quality with which it was drenched.

I don't know why I made the selection, except I was already out on a limb holding an anvil and an ounce this way or that didn't matter. Whatever happened, I'd presided over my last service in Owen.

There was a short silence after I finished, but no murmurs, and when I called for "Lead, Kindly Light," everyone in the congregation joined in.

"A bold piece." Freemason took my hand at the door. He looked puzzled. "Do you always fly this close to the flame?"

"The man who wrote it showed me how close is too close." There was now no reason to pretend authorship.

"You must tell me about him sometime."

"He wouldn't like it. He's bent on disappearance."

"Fugitive?"

"Yes, I think that describes him."

We were speaking low, but he leaned in close and dropped his voice almost to a whisper. "What luck tracing that brand?"

"It's not in the book, and none of the ranch hands I talked to remember seeing it."

"It must be a pirate outfit. They comb other spreads for mares with foals too young for branding, pare the mares' hooves to the quick so they can't wander far, and when the foals are ready to wean they rustle them and burn their own mark. It's as if the animals never existed. A fully grown unbranded horse invites investigation, but registering the brand involves answering too many questions. No one knows just how many such ranches exist. It's an impossible quest."

"Those are the ones I usually get."

"You're not dissuaded?"

I looked at him, but he was a hard man to read. "Do you want me to be?"

"I think it's too much for one man. Your death would weigh heavily on my conscience."

"Jordan and his Rangers are working on that brand, but they're spread thin themselves. I'm thinking of asking Judge Blackthorne to lean on the governor to put every available company on the job."

"That's wise, but why go so far around the barn? I'm sure I can persuade Ireland to see reason. That brand is the first thing we've found that can provide a link to the man responsible for these raids."

"With you applying pressure from below and Blackthorne applying it from above, I don't see how he can refuse the accommodation."

"At least let me send a rider to Wichita Falls with your message. The Overland proceeds at its own pace."

"I'll use both, in case one or the other is waylaid."

We regarded each other. It was the biggest time-waster anyone could imagine, even on a Sunday: Two men talking circles around the thing they both knew.

Colleen interrupted the game. In honor of the day she wore a purple velvet dress with a hat to match, trailing a broad yellow ribbon down her back to her waist. In one kid glove she clutched a closed parasol, yellow with purple trim. "Once again, Richard, you're holding up the line." She offered me her free hand. "Another intriguing sermon. A bit cosmopolitan for

Owen, don't you think? The people around here prefer their badmen painted in black with thick strokes."

I met her blue gaze, harder than Jordan's, more
opaque than Freemason's. "I like purple."

She smiled. "What a pretty compliment."

They moved on. The friendly freight office clerk
shook my hand, wrenching me from my reflections.
His face was troubled. "I was raised to love Jesus and
hate Judas. Now I don't know what to think."

"Hate is the devil's seed," I said. That seemed to lift
his spirits.

My reviews were mixed; I could tell by the silences
as well as by the remarks. The man who had snored
through most of my first services wrung my palm and
gave me high marks for preaching against sin; plainly
he'd awakened just in time to join the exodus for
the door. Some people who'd stopped to greet me
last Sunday swept on past the line without pausing. I
didn't expect them back even if I thought I'd be back
myself. I made mental note of everything to report to
Griffin, who might be interested to know the reaction,
even though I was sure it wouldn't surprise him.

I felt an indifference bordering on atheism. It had
been important that my debut was positive enough to
assure me some time in the community. Whether I left
it with a sour taste in its mouth signified nothing. One
way or the other, my time in Owen was growing short.

For a time after the last carriage creaked away, I
stood at the pulpit pretending to make corrections
in the margins of my notes while Mrs. McIlvaine's
broom swished relentlessly in the corners. My pencil
drew meaningless coils on the foolscap, unconsciously
imitating the patterns of dust turning in the shorten-
ing shafts of sunlight coming through the windows.
They circled patiently, killing time as they waited for

the bristles to stop moving so they could settle. It seemed God's plan that there should be dust, and that any attempt to banish it from His place on earth was doomed from the start; but housekeepers, too, have a patron saint, so their efforts carry some kind of endorsement. Everyone seemed to have one, except lawmen posing as ministers of the faith. I knew, because I'd looked it up. Nomads of the desert have one, so do nurses and the sick, innkeepers, storytellers, the desperate, fishermen, even thieves. Impostors alone are without representation. What did it matter what miracles you accomplished for the United States District Court if they condemned you in the court of heaven?

The assignment had gotten under my skin worse than all the others. I'd flogged whiskey and mucked out stalls for cover, been a Cheyenne slave and shared a cell with a matricide—rotten work, but you can scrub off the stink of sour mash, recover from prison food, and a good laundress can boil the manure stains out of your clothes. In time, exposure to other peoples and their ways can even restore your belief in the basic humanity of every race. Everything was reversible, except Moses and Ezekiel and Ruth and Solomon and Matthew. Once they burrowed under your skin they were there to stay, like the heads of chiggers. There wasn't a miserable deed or an act of charity in the Good Book that didn't resemble something I'd witnessed and had sometimes been part of. The words of those drifters and cobblers and drones and harlots and the odd bearded king were more accurate than *The Farmer's Almanack*.

At length the swishing stopped, a door thudded into its frame, and I was alone. Still I didn't stir from the pulpit, although I folded my pages and poked them into my breast pocket near the revolver in its rig. I stood gazing at the empty pews, feeling the reflected warmth from the squares of daylight creeping toward the east windows, smelling candle wax and walnut stain and the eternal dust, the dust of the Eternal, the presence of the Lord in every restless grain, searching for a place to lay His head and not finding it for more than a moment.

I brought up the Bible from its shelf beneath the lectern, rested it on its loose spine, and let go. It fell open to Second Kings, chapter twenty:

> In those days was Hezekiah sick unto death. And the prophet Isaiah the son of Amoz came to him, and said unto him, Thus saith the Lord, Set thine house in order; for thou shalt die, and not live.

I found that unsatisfactory. I was riffling through the pages for something more encouraging when a window flew apart and I fell over backward with what felt like the entire church resting on my chest.

TWENTY-FIVE

I'd had my fill of being shot at, whether I was part of the plan or not. When I realized I hadn't been hit, that when the bullet came through the window I'd gripped the edges of the pulpit from instinct and brought it down with me, landing on my chest and knocking out my wind, I got mad and shoved it off with strength I didn't have under ordinary circumstances.

The Deane-Adams was in my hand now and I made my way on knees and elbows to the broken pane, wheezing as I did so; I couldn't seem to take in enough air to satisfy my need. It was like swimming in deep water without having gulped in enough oxygen first.

I raised my head just high enough to see out, resting the barrel of the revolver on the sill, strewn with glass fragments and shards of molding. Out in the street the driver of a wagon loaded with furniture was straining at the lines, trying to keep his brace of wall-eyed, pawing grays from plunging, and townsmen were leaning out through doors and around the sides of porch posts, looking toward the church or turning their heads toward the rooftops across the street. That meant a rifle or carbine, discharging loudly enough in the open air to alert the town. When the gawkers ventured out from cover and started churchward, I knew the shooter was long gone. I stood.

Too fast. A swarm of bats flew off their perches inside my head, blocking out the light. I fell into the middle of them.

The crack in the plaster ceiling looked familiar. The first time I'd seen it I thought it looked like the bad map I'd followed into Murfreesboro with General Rosecrans. It was directly above the iron-framed bed in the parsonage.

Something tinkled. I thought of pieces of glass falling out of the window frame in the church and reached for my suspender scabbard, but I wasn't wearing it, or a shirt. I lay stripped to my waist on the top sheet. I took a tentative breath, then a deeper one. The air was as sweet as sugar. I gulped in a bellyful and let it out in a whoosh.

"It's amazing, is it not, how grateful one can be for the things he takes for granted, once he's been deprived of them? But then I shouldn't have to tell a minister that."

I recognized the voice without knowing why. I turned my head and watched a man with a spray of beard to the third button of his waistcoat returning instruments to his case. That was the tinkling I'd heard, and I knew him now for Dr. Littlejohn, one of the town's practitioners and a man who'd approved of both my sermons at the church door. He was sitting in the straightback from the sitting room, wearing a Masonic medal on his watch chain. He had the same insignia in brass on the latch of his black leather bag. I wondered if he was a creature of Freemason's or just a member of the brotherhood.

I used my tongue to clear the cobwebs from my mouth. "I had a horse squatting on my chest." My voice still sounded like cornhusks rustling.

"I thought at first you had a collapsed lung, but by the time I had your shirt off you'd begun to breathe normally, so it must have been temporary paralysis brought on by physical trauma. Pulpits are meant to stand behind, not used as counterpanes. You blacked out because you weren't taking in enough oxygen to feed your brain cells. I was afraid I'd have to crack your chest and insert a rubber tube to draw off the pressure."

"Have you ever done that?"

"No. I confess I was a little disappointed not to have the opportunity."

"Are you always this honest with your patients?"

"My practice would be more successful if I weren't. You're rather an unusual man in your profession yourself."

"Men of God have been shot at before."

"Not many react in kind or so quickly. That piece of furniture that fell on you is solid hickory. Most men would still be struggling to get out from under it when help arrived. You tossed it aside like a match and threw down on the enemy."

I turned my head the other way, and was relieved to see the Deane-Adams on the nightstand. "It's the second time in a week I had a bullet pass close to me. You get mad."

"Wrath isn't necessarily a sin. In this case it may have saved your life. You could have suffocated under the constriction."

"Who—?"

"Mrs. Freemason. She was on her way here for a visit when the shot rang out. She found you passed out on the floor and sent for me. By the time I got here, she'd recruited volunteers to carry you in here. I told her that was unwise; for all she knew, you had a broken back, and moving you might have been fatal. She said she knew a broken back when she saw one. How do you suppose she knew that?" He sat back with the bag on his lap, his hands resting on his thighs.

"She's a woman of many parts. Where is she?"

"In your sitting room. She's been waiting twenty minutes. I told her she should go home, but she demurred."

"Demurred."

He frowned in his impressive whiskers. "I agree the term seems inadequate. However, she has a way of slamming the door soundly on an argument with the air of someone declining an invitation to badminton."

"She's a well-bred jenny. What do I owe you?"

"I have my soul to consider. A day and a night in

that bed will suffice, for what my counsel is worth. I've an idea you're a mule from the same paddock."

"I always heard the Masons were honest men."

He fingered the engraving on his bag. "The clergy hasn't always been so charitable toward the order. When Father Cress sees me coming he crosses himself as if I were the Prince of Lies in person."

"Is it true your founders claimed to have removed the body of Christ from its tomb?"

"That's a canard," he said, reddening. "Catholic fanatics have been repeating it since before the Inquisition. We are a benevolent foundation, and as such represent competition with the Church. There's the source of these centuries of black blood."

The emotion in his voice assured me of his affiliation. I said I'd pray for him.

His color paled to normal. He rose, rested his bag on the chair, and drew the blanket up from the foot of the bed to cover me to the collarbone. "The proprieties, don't you know. I'll send her in now, but she can't stay long. I want to check your ribs while you're conscious to make sure they're not cracked and pinching. I'll bind them if they are. You bled a bit through the knees of your trousers, probably from lacerations when you were crawling through broken glass. They'll need cleaning and sticking plaster."

"I can see to that, and the ribs. This isn't the first spill I've taken."

"I didn't realize preaching the gospel was so dangerous."

I'd forgotten myself. The brain is slowest to recover when you've stepped back from the stony edge. "I was an awkward child."

"All the same," he said after a tense moment, "I'll stay and complete the examination. We can't have you surviving an attempt on your life only to pierce a lung with the end of a broken rib."

"You haven't asked why I was shot at."

"I assumed it was because of the subject of your sermon this morning. Judas is somewhat less popular in the State of Texas than General Santa Anna."

That was a bald lie, the assumption part, and he could see I knew it, but I didn't press the point. If there's a man who can keep a secret as well as a minister, he has *Doctor* in front of his name. Nevertheless, here was one more recruit to the side of the doubters. In a little while, that shot would be heard throughout the panhandle. My sheep's clothing was falling away in great bloody patches.

She came in with none of the hesitation of a respectable woman entering a man's bedroom, as if she were walking into her own. I'd seen her do that, with me following, but that wasn't going to happen ever again. She had on the velvet dress she'd worn to church, without the hat. The sunlight coming in through the front windows made a copper-colored aura around her pinned-up hair. Black as it comes, there is always red in it.

I gathered myself into a sitting position. I was careful about it, but a phantom blow struck my chest as if the pulpit had taken a second crack at me. I leaned back against the bedstead, breathing with my mouth open. No pinches, at least, so maybe no cracked ribs. I'd cracked my share, all right, falling off horses and grappling with unarmed fugitives, which made me something of an expert.

"Nasty bruise," she said, glancing at my chest.

"Call it divine retribution. It could've been worse. A Spencer packs a hell of a wallop inside its range."

"You saw it?"

"I didn't have to. I was expecting it."

"Evidently."

I lifted a hand and let it drop to the blanket. "I thought it would happen out in the open. I fell into the sanctuary trap. That isn't a mistake I'd have made a few weeks ago. When the disguise assumes you, it's time to take it off and pin the badge back on."

"You never pin it on."

"That's what I was saying. That collar cuts off the blood flow to the brain. My instincts of self-preservation went with it."

She transferred the doctor's bag to the floor, inspected the seat of the chair for dust, and sat, resting her reticule in her lap. "I was certain you were dead."

"I disappoint a lot of people."

"I'm the one who sent for the doctor."

"There wasn't any reason not to, once you saw I hadn't been shot."

"I'm many things, Page, but a murderess isn't one of them."

I let that blow in the damn Texas wind. "What were you coming to see me about?"

"You're welcome. I should have known you wouldn't fall all over yourself with gratitude."

"Thanks. What were you coming to see me about?"

"I came to warn you."

"You came late."

"I was late finding out. You're behaving as if you wished it were anyone else."

"It wouldn't be the first time, when it was you."

"We weren't always enemies, you know."

I said nothing, watching her.

She shook her head infinitesimally. "Don't pretend. You never did know when I was bluffing."

The reticule was purple trimmed with yellow to match the rest of her kit. Colleen Bower was capable of letting her house burn down around her while she selected just the right ensemble for flight. She untied the bag and brought out a small rectangular envelope with the initials *C.B.* embossed in one corner; the *B* standing for either Bower or Baronet, her most recent married name but one. She wasn't the kind to let a powerful man like Freemason slap his brand on her.

The word *brand* echoed in my head, for any number of reasons. It turned a lingering trace of cold fire, like incendiaries on Independence Day. My mind was still moving at a dead walk.

I took the envelope from her gloved hand. "Your hole card?"

"A note. I couldn't be sure I'd find you in. God alone knows where a minister goes after the last 'Amen.'"

I lifted the flap, took out the matching letterhead, and snapped it open:

You're in greater danger than you know.

It was unsigned, but I knew her hand. I ran my thumb over the indentations the pen had made in the soft rag stock. There was a pale spot in the lower loop of the *d*, where the ink had run out and she'd paused to redip. She couldn't have manufactured it in my sitting room, and twenty minutes weren't enough to make the round trip to her house and back. A woman of her standing in the community couldn't afford to carry around a pot of ink and risk a stain on her handbag. A pencil and coarse paper were the only writing paraphernalia in the parsonage.

She was telling the truth. I waited for the earth to slip off its axis, but it went on creaking around, one miracle at a time.

I stuck the note back in its envelope and returned it. In that moment I knew my brain had been trying to tell me something. "I saw the brand on Freemason's buggy horse," I said.

"He puts it on everything. He doesn't belong, but he's obsessed with it because of his name. He wouldn't have the patience to go through initiation."

Her husband's brand was a stylized version of the Masonic compass and square:

"Hand me that bag." I pointed to the doctor's case on the floor.

She hesitated, then complied. I rooted among the brown bottles and wicked-looking instruments inside, found a grease pencil, and made alterations on the fraternal symbol etched on the latch, drawing two lines only:

TWENTY-SIX

A Star of David?" she said.

"Just a star. This one never had anything to do with religion."

"Is that the brand you saw on the bandits' horses?"

"One horse, but I've been all through that with Freemason. You can always tell when a string was raised under the same conditions. It only takes twenty seconds with a running iron to change two intersecting *V*'s into a star. Freemason was smart enough not to send the Blue Bandannas out marauding on horses wearing a mark from his spread, but he's a sheepman. He underestimated a cowboy's eye."

"Not by much, in this case."

"I haven't swung a lariat since you were in swaddles, but it's true I was tardy. Thinking like a minister and a lawman and a saddle tramp all at the same time is a challenge." I dropped the pencil back inside the bag and pushed it aside. "Where'd he tip his hand with you?"

"His foreman was careless about shutting the door to his study. Richard sent for him. I overheard just enough to find out where he was sending him from there."

"Tell me about the foreman."

"Jack Kolander, a rough character who thinks he's a devil with women. I've seen how he watches me when he thinks I'm not looking, but he's too smart to take it any further with the boss's wife. He'll never find a billet that pays as well. Richard could hire a full-time ranch manager for less."

"Did you ever ask him what Kolander does to earn it?"

"I just keep the books. Not asking questions I don't need to know the answers to is the trade I made for his not asking me the same."

"I thought you said there were no secrets between you."

"Plainly there are. I never knew how many until he accused me of betraying him by not telling him who you were."

"I can see why that would make you angry enough to come running here."

"I walked. I have a reputation to maintain. And you know me better than to think I'd throw over everything I have because my pride got stung."

I searched her eyes. I didn't know her at all. "You don't want to see me murdered. I'll take that as a compliment. Does this Kolander have a broad West Texas accent?"

"Who doesn't? When I first came here I had to learn a whole new language. For a long time I thought Bob Wire was one of Richard's hands. When I found out it was a kind of fence I sat down and listed the names of all the people I made a fool of myself with and who didn't bother to set me straight. That turned out to be a good thing. You can waste a lot of time learning who your enemies are."

"Who else is he overpaying?"

"Fielo, but that's a favor to me. It costs more to feed a breed ram than to staff a house with Mexicans, so what he makes doesn't scratch the budget. He's quiet, respectful, and he has only the one vice. Can you say the same?"

I let the wind take that one as well. "The others must be in it for a percentage. I'm betting they tent up at the ranch between raids. What buffalos me is why Captain Jordan and his Rangers couldn't tie any of them to descriptions of the Blue Bandannas when they visited."

"I remember that day. Kolander wasn't around. Someone cut the north fence and he took some men and followed a trail of slaughtered sheep as far as the Nations."

"How many men?"

"Five or six."

"Six. Freemason made sure the gang was absent when Jordan came to call. If the fence was cut, they cut it. If sheep were slaughtered, they slaughtered them. It was a small enough price to pay to keep them out of the hands of the law. It wasn't the first time he went out on a limb when his men were in trouble. You never know what the hired help might let slip when they think their boss has abandoned them."

"But why would Richard take such a risk? He was robbing himself."

"That's how he wanted it to look, and it's why he staged that robbery last week with me as a witness, to draw suspicion away from him. You said yourself he's almost bankrupt. He put his Blue Bandannas up to stealing his payroll, convinced outside investors to make it up, and had them steal that, too; he paid his handpicked bandits out of the first amount and probably cut them in for a piece of the rest and all of whatever they foraged on the side so it wouldn't look like he was the only victim. He pocketed the lion's share. Do you know the details of the trouble he got into up in Montana Territory?"

She watched me. "Is this another attempt to worm information out of me?"

"That time's past. Blackthorne came clean finally, when I pressed him. A dozen years ago Freemason was clerk of the U.S. District Court in Helena. That was shortly after Blackthorne took the bench and two years before I came to work for him. Your husband embezzled twenty thousand dollars from the operating budget and used it to start a sheep ranch near the Canadian border. He registered the land in the name of his assistant, and when an auditor from Washington turned up the shortfall, the assistant clerk was arrested, tried, and convicted of misappropriation of public funds."

Dr. Littlejohn rapped on the door. "That's long enough, Mrs. Freemason," he called. "The brother needs his rest."

She looked at me. We shook our heads simultaneously. She got up, recovered his instrument case, and went to the door. A moment of spirited conversation followed, ending when she passed the bag around the edge of the door, closed it, and turned the key in the lock. She returned to her seat.

I said, "I think you just cost me a parishioner."

"Does it matter?"

"Not to me, but I don't think I'll be named a saint of the Unitarian Church." I rubbed my chest. I was giving my bruised lungs a workout. "It fell apart in the end," I went on. "The assistant's wife hired investigators, who reviewed the records of the transaction at the county seat where the ranch was, and established that his signature was forged. It came too late for the assistant; a highwayman serving ten to fifteen years for stealing U.S. securities picked a fight with him in the federal penitentiary in Deer Lodge and let his brains out with a chunk of masonry."

"How much of this can you prove?"

"It's public record."

Her knuckles tightened on the reticule in her lap. "Richard said he was sentenced to seven years.

President Grant pardoned him after three months. Five of the twenty thousand went to the congressman who delivered the Republican vote in seventy-two. All this time I thought Blackthorne's complaint was political."

"The assistant clerk's name was Velasquez. His father was a prisoner of war during the fighting in Mexico; Blackthorne liked him, but Velasquez turned down his offer to sponsor him after the war. When his son came of age, he called in the marker. The Judge is vain and petty, but he believes in justice, the Presbyterian Church, and his personal obligations, in that order. He didn't say it—that damn code he uses takes too long on both ends, and he never explains himself anyway—but my guess is when he heard Freemason's name in connection with the robberies here, he wasn't sure enough of his suspicions to tell me and possibly send me off in the wrong direction. If his hunch was right, I'd stumble on it myself. In a way it was a vote of confidence from the son of a bitch."

"The son of a bitch," she agreed. "I might have gone on thinking I'd pulled myself out of the muck finally."

"Not you. You're too smart for Freemason. You'd have seen through him soon enough."

"Not as soon as you."

"I'm not married to him."

"You're smart enough to outsmart yourself," she said. "You knew when you told him Luther Cherry had confessed to being a spy for the Blue Bandannas he knew you were lying. If Cherry didn't set up that robbery on the road to clear himself, it had to have been Richard. You might as well have accused him straight out."

"If I did, he'd have thought I had enough information to arrest him. As long as he believed I was still building a case, he had a chance to prevent me from delivering it. That's why I turned Captain Jordan away when he said he wanted to ask Brother Bernard more questions in private. As long as Freemason thought I was the only one who suspected him, I could flush him out by drawing his fire. I did outsmart myself," I said, nodding. "I didn't think he'd mount a direct assault on me in the church, his church. He's more desperate than I thought."

She shook her head. "Less. He's beaten the system twice with pardons. Once you're out of the way he's convinced he's invincible."

"A common failing in men of influence. You ought to set your sights on a lowly road agent."

"Page, that's unkind even for you."

I looked at her, and the expression on her face surprised me more than the bullet through the window. Moisture glittered like bits of quartz in the corners of her eyes. If she'd brought that to a poker table I'd have cleaned her out.

A floorboard shifted outside the door; the squeak was sharp in the quiet of the room. She stood, rustling her skirts and muttering something about the damn doctor. Before she got to it, the door sprang open and struck the wall on our side. The man who'd kicked it lunged through the opening on the force of his own momentum, grabbed Colleen's shoulder, and spun her to face me with a forearm across her throat. He spun the Spencer rifle in his other hand by the lever, working a round into the chamber, and leveled it at me.

"Beg pardon, Reverend," he said, "it being the Lord's Own Day and all." His speech was as wide as West Texas, muffled a little by the blue bandanna that covered his face to the eyes.

TWENTY-SEVEN

M y hand twitched in the direction of the revolver on the nightstand, but I let it fall when he flexed his arm, drawing a strangled croak from Colleen.

"You're square with Jesus, Reverend, but maybe the lady ain't. Push that English pistol off the edge easy."

I did, using the tips of my fingers. The Deane-Adams struck the floor with a thud. The man with the rifle relaxed his grip a notch. Colleen sucked in air in a long draught.

"I'll have that strongbox from the morning," he said. "I heard you raked it in."

"Is that why you shot at me?"

"That was careless. By the time I got to the door the place was crawling. There's still a crowd got their snouts stuck to the windows. I figure if they see you lug that box out they won't think anything about it."

"They will if I'm with a masked man with a rifle."

"You won't be. The lady and me'll just make ourselves to home here till you get back."

"What if I just keep walking?"

"Well, now, that wouldn't set just right with the Almighty. When you get through them pearly gates she'll be waiting with a slug in her head. Same thing if you come back with anybody or anything but that box."

"Is it all right if I get dressed?"

"Sure. We can't have the parson slanching about half naked. Wouldn't be decent."

I slid out from under the sheet on the side opposite

where I'd dropped the revolver, retrieved my shirt, collar, and coat from the heap where the doctor had left them when he examined me, and drew them on slowly, my fingers fumbling with the collar button behind my neck. I knew the man and his weapon from the road to Freemason's ranch, and I didn't believe for a second that he'd come just for the church collection. He was Freemason's man; I wasn't to survive the transaction to bear witness against his employer. The box was extra incentive, and cover for my murder.

"Jack, I can make up the difference if you'll just leave. I—"

Jack Kolander, Richard Freemason's foreman, choked her off with his arm. In that instant I saw confusion in his eyes and satisfaction in Colleen's. If the plan was to leave her alive to back up the robbery theory, she'd just tipped it on its head. Plainly, he hadn't orders in case she identified him. The rancher had stopped short of condemning his wife.

I pressed in. "You weren't told some other things. The name's Murdock, not Sebastian. I'm a deputy U.S. marshal."

The confusion crystallized into something else. He'd made up his mind in favor of his own survival, and to hell with Freemason. "That makes things easier. I'd sooner slaughter a wolf than a lamb. Now fetch that box."

I pulled up my braces and turned toward the door, sliding one hand into a sleeve of my rusty black coat.

"I got men on roofs with repeaters," Kolander said, "in case she ain't reason enough to come back. When I hear shooting, I'll put one in her and clear out."

I turned back his way, still half in and half out of the coat. It put me a step closer. "You'll do it anyway, and you'll put one in me too as soon as I show up with the money. Why should I waste the time walking all the way to the church and back?"

"On account of every minute's one more you got, both of you." For emphasis he arched his back, tightening his grip and pulling Colleen off her feet.

That was a mistake.

She'd been preoccupied with keeping both feet on the floor to avoid strangling under her own weight. Now she scissored one leg and raked the heel of her pump down his right shin blade, probably drawing blood. He cursed in a high shrill voice. I whirled my coat underhand in a circle, caught the Spencer's muzzle with the hem, and jerked it toward the ceiling, which blew apart with a shower of plaster chunks and dust when the trigger jerked his finger. In the shock of the moment he relaxed his forearm. Colleen ducked out from under, grasping at the barrel of the rifle with both hands. She failed to gain a purchase, and as he swept it out of her reach he slammed the stock against the side of her head.

She collapsed—on top of me. I'd dived for the Deane-Adams on the floor, but got one foot tangled on the rung of the straightback chair beside the bed, and all three of us—me, Colleen, and the chair—wound up in a snarl of flesh and bone and pine. I groped for the revolver and found only plank floor.

Something clacked twice, the lever of a repeater jacking a shell into the barrel. A huge black bat flew across my vision; my coat, caught on the front sight of Kolander's Spencer. I wouldn't even see where the bullet was coming from.

A shot cracked; I flinched as if I were hit. Something heavy struck the floor hard enough to shake more plaster from the shattered ceiling. It spilled like salt onto the back of Jack Kolander's white duster, spread like angel's wings where he lay splayed out on his face, his arms flung out in the shape of a cross.

A needle of brimstone stung my nostrils, coming from the barrel of the small slim American Arms pistol in Colleen's kid leather palm. Her reticule lay open on the floor where it had fallen when I'd knocked over the chair.

Gunfire crackled outside. Hollow in the open and bent by the wind, it might have been a string of firecrackers going off; in the West every holiday is an occasion for fireworks. I found the Deane-Adams finally—it had skidded under the bed in the scramble—and got up. Colleen, athletic as ever, was already on her feet. I felt as if a dray had run over my chest, leaving deep ruts. I still feel it sometimes when I've lived wrong.

I nearly shot Captain Jordan coming in the door. Colleen came closer; I caught her elbow with an up-hand sweep just as she emptied her second barrel. The little slug dashed yellow splinters out of the door frame just above the Ranger's head. He had on the same clothes I'd seen him in last, riding gear, and carried a sawed-off Stevens ten-gauge shotgun in both hands crossways to his body, like a quarterstaff. His face was red beneath the deep bronze.

His eyes went straight from the distraction of the shot to the body on the floor.

"Dead," I said. "What about the rest?"

"One dead, one on his way. We winged another. One threw up his hands. Two more run off, but we know where they're headed. We followed 'em here from the ranch. I didn't exactly go back to Wichita Falls after I left here the other night," he said.

"I wish I'd known."

"I couldn't get word to you without scaring 'em back into cover." Belatedly, he took off his hat, watching Colleen. "We need to talk to your husband, Mrs. Freemason. You, too, maybe."

"She's out in the open," I said. "She's the one who shot Kolander."

He cradled the shotgun along a forearm, slid the hat off the back of the dead man's head, pulled it up by a fistful of hair, and tore loose the bandanna. It was a stubbled face with sandy moustaches and spider-traces of blood coming from the corners of his mouth. "Kolander, that's the name?" Jordan spoke to Colleen over his shoulder.

"That's him. Richard's at the house, or was when I left. I don't think he'll resist. It's past the time for gun-play. Now it's the lawyers' turn."

"We'll bring our guns along just the same."

I said, "You can't sneak up on him. His house overlooks the whole town."

"He built it to withstand cattle wars," Colleen said. "You can shoot at it all day and all night. All you'll do is break china."

Jordan chewed the ends of his handlebars. In his weathered face I saw faint traces of the fresh features of the young Ranger in the photograph in his office. It had been taken at Fort Sill, where the Comanche Nation had surrendered after breaking its back as-saulting a handful of buffalo hunters holed up at Adobe Walls.

"Man has to eat," he said finally. "We'll wait him out."

Colleen said, "I'll talk to him. I've always been able to make him listen to reason."

"No, ma'am. I'll not put a chip in his hands."

"I don't have to ask your permission. It's my house. You can place me under restraint, but I'll put up a fight. It will take three men. How many do you need to lay siege to a fortress?"

He looked at me. I shook my head. "I wouldn't argue with her. I still have scars."

She said, "He's no ordinary fugitive. He has resources. The chances are he's already put them to work. Why risk panicking him with an attack party?"

"Well, hell," he said; and that was the end of the resistance.

I unhooked my coat from the end of Kolander's Spencer and shrugged into it. The hole he'd blown through it had smoldered for a while, but it had stopped, leaving an evil smell. "You fixing to come with us?" Jordan asked.

"If you'll have me. This is the first time I've had the blinders off since Helena."

"Let's get to it, then, before our past life catches up with us."

I asked him for a moment and went to get my Bible. Colleen and Jordan watched in silence as I read over the dead man. When I finished I closed the book, put it in my side pocket, and took off the clerical collar. I put it on the bed and picked up the Deane-Adams.

TWENTY-EIGHT

Afternoon was well along; moving into position, our party threw saguaro-shaped shadows halfway across the street. The sun painted crimson stripes on the wrought-iron spikes that crowned the American castle on its manmade hill and reflected in flat sheets off the mullioned windows facing west, turning them into armor plate. There was nothing preposterous about the place now; it might have stood through the Crusades and expected to stand until the end of all things.

The businesses on both sides of the street were closed for the holy day, but Jordan had sent a man—it was Corporal Thomson, the young Ranger who'd put me up overnight in Wichita Falls, with a wife expecting a child—to roust out the shopkeepers stacking stock and recording inventory and persuade the residents of the houses to stay inside and away from the windows. It had taken him half an hour, but the captain hadn't wanted to alert Freemason by sending a party. He was being overcautious; all our quarry had to do was look out and see all the merchants locking up at the same time to know something was in the wind. In times past—Texas being Texas—the neighbors would have been recruited to serve in the assault, supplying their own weapons and ammunition, but the second generation of pioneers had moved into the protected category, like the people they'd left behind in the cities of the East. In twenty years, maybe less, citizens' posses would be a part of history, and professionals firmly in place to defend the peace unassisted. There would be a policeman on every corner, and no more deputy marshals required to ride circuit over an area the size of New Hampshire. It was progressive, inevitable, but I smelled in it the stink of my own grave.

As the light shifted, so did the demeanor of the gaunt house on its unnatural heap. It looked vulnerable—indecently so, as if by design. The heavy siege shutters I'd noticed on my first visit yawned wide, as if Freemason had declared open house. The thought chilled me there in the bright sun, in the hot wind. I felt suddenly as if we were the ones being hunted.

Jordan, directing operations from the deep doorway of the Catholic church, saw what I saw and reached a different conclusion. "Lit out, I expect. If he's forted up at the ranch, I'm going to have to send to San Antonio for more men. It'll take days."

I said nothing. When the Rangers were all in place, stationed at second-story windows and in narrow alleys, Colleen Bower emerged from the First Unitarian church. She'd put herself back together after the wrestling match in the parsonage, pinned her hat in place, and with her reticule wound around her wrist (without the pistol, which Jordan had taken charge of), the first lady of Owen might have been returning home from one of her regular errands. When she drew abreast of us, I stepped forward. The captain touched my arm.

"There's nothing for it if she gets hurt," he said. "The governor don't pay enough pension to look after my crippled cousin."

"It's the best way to take him alive. If he turns himself in through her, he'll go to his lawyers instead of his gunmen. Anyway, you've seen what happens when someone tries to hold her down."

I caught up with her and we walked like two strangers bound in the same direction, without speaking.

We climbed the long flight of steps to the front

door. She'd asked for five minutes alone with her husband; I'd determined to give her two. I hung back while she twisted the bell, waited, then twisted it again. It rang away back in a place of desertion.

She turned my way. "Fielo only leaves the house when Richard sends him. He can't think it's an ordinary day."

I didn't know whether she meant Freemason or the servant, but I wasn't sure of that either way. Those spread shutters haunted me. I didn't agree with Jordan that he'd flown to cover at the ranch. The situation was just the one the house had been planned and built for. I'd faced apparent traps before, but now I felt as if I were fighting the urge to walk right into one. The oath I'd taken had said nothing about battling my own nature.

I settled the point. When she untied her bag and fished out a key, I took it from her and moved her aside with a firm hand on her elbow. I drew the Deane-Adams and unlocked the door.

No one shot at me when I eased it open, using the thick door for a shield. The foyer was empty except of furniture. So were the adjoining rooms when I prowled through them, the baronial dining hall and a long kitchen with an enormous white-enamel Jewel stove and, suspended from the ceiling, clusters of copper and cast-iron pots and skillets. The air smelled of stale grease and dry herbs, as if no meal had been prepared there in months.

A tiny room off the kitchen contained a cot, a small chest of drawers, and a wash basin on a stand; the servant's quarters, abandoned also. A back door opened on a path worn through grass to a privy out back. I didn't check that. It was no place to hide with a fortress waiting.

There was one door I hadn't tried, but I didn't think it was for me to try it. I returned to the front step where Colleen, obedient for once, waited. She asked me if I'd looked in the study.

"No."

She read my face. I wished I knew what she saw there. I was behind it and I had no idea.

She said, "He feels safe there."

I nodded and stepped aside. She looked at me, not so much curious as inviting an explanation. "It's your house."

She came in and I followed her down the hallway, three steps behind with the revolver pointed toward the ceiling.

She knocked at the stout paneled door, spoke his name. No one answered. She tried the knob. "Locked. He has the only key."

She stepped away without being asked while I hammered on the door. My fist boomed like cannon practice; no strategic satisfaction. It was the quietest house I'd ever been in. Even a fallen-in shack on the prairie has something scuttling around inside.

I didn't try kicking. It was too much door and it had a heavy brass lock.

One of the sculptures that decorated the house was a bronze casting of a Knight Templar drawing his sword, the inescapable Masonic symbol emblazoned on his shield. It stood three feet high at the end of the hallway on a tall fluted pedestal with a marble base. I pocketed the Deane-Adams, hoisted the statue off its stand, and signaled Colleen to stand clear. I set myself and rammed the lock. It held, but on the second try I put a dent in the knight's helmet and got a splitting sound. A long shard of polished wood came away from the frame on the third. I laid the statue on the floor, fisted the revolver, and threw a heel at the lock. The door flew open with less resistance than expected and I caught the frame hard with my right shoulder to avoid falling headlong. It was the pulpit all over again; pain racked me from front to back, but the muzzle of the .45 found Richard Freemason in his embossed-leather chair as if I'd trained it.

He sat slumped in his shirtsleeves and a scarlet waistcoat, turned a quarter of the way on his swivel toward the tall massive desk. He hadn't moved even when the door exploded against the wall.

I saw why when I approached him and turned the chair my way by its back. He wasn't wearing a red waistcoat, or one of any other color. The knife that had nearly separated his head from his trunk had opened his jugular all down the front of his shirt. Only the whites of his eyes showed, and they were no more pale than his face.

I heard a high keening sound, but Colleen wasn't crying. It was my own breath straining to get in and out after another blow to the lungs and the strain of using a hunk of bronze the size of a newborn calf for a battering ram. I found out later the thing weighed a hundred and forty pounds. It took two men to put it back on its pedestal.

No, she wasn't crying, but her voice was tight. "He's taken his own life."

I didn't mention that there was no knife. For all I was aware, she knew where it was.

She didn't. The Rangers found him finally, in the little privy I hadn't bothered to look inside. In my defense I'll add that they only thought of it after they'd searched the house from the upstairs bedrooms, the ballroom with its fabulous chandelier, and water closet to the coal furnace in the basement.

He was propped primly with his back against the plank wall, sitting in his white linen uniform on the flipped-down seat, his long brown hands dangling between his thighs, the wrists sliced open almost neatly with what was probably the same knife he'd used to cut Freemason's throat, a butcher's tool with a curved blade still razor sharp after it had done its work; part of a set from the kitchen, it lay on the floor between his sandaled feet. A bottle of Hermitage with a teaspoonful of whiskey left in the bottom stood beside him on the seat. The liquor had thinned his blood, accelerating the process, but he was an old man and his heart had given out first. Colleen cried when she was told, as she hadn't for her husband. Her affection for the gentle old manservant was genuine.

I guessed what it was about, with intuition pumped up like my strength under pressure and pain, but I kept it to myself. It all came out when they searched him and found the note, in the same pocket where he'd placed the key he'd used to lock his master's body in the study. He'd wanted time to write it and see the thing through. He'd used a sheet of Colleen's notepaper, as if he refused to touch Freemason's Masonic stationery. It was written in a surprisingly fine hand, in Spanish; but the translation could wait. He'd signed it "Fielo Velasquez."

The Thirteenth Apostle

I have glorified thee on the earth: I have finished
the work which thou gavest me to do.

—John 17:4

Beyond some follow-up questions to my report,
Judge Blackthorne and I never discussed my time
in Texas again. He went to his grave without
another word on the subject. I can't make the same
claim, although mine lies open before me. I made mistakes that cost lives, souls too, and while I'm less certain
than ever about what's waiting, Owen is one burden
I'm determined to leave behind.

I have to include Eldred Griffin among the casualties. The doll's house in the Catholic cemetery was
shut up when I went there to return the shabby sheaf
of sermons, the shutters fastened and a padlock on the
front door. His death, punctuation to the gossip that
had hounded him for years, was still lively after two
weeks: His wife, Esther, had gone to his study to pour
him a second cup of tea and found him dead on the
floor, fallen in a heap from his chair, where he'd been
seated at his writing table sipping his first and reading
an Aramaic text from the third century. Grubs hin-
dered the growth of sod between the graves, arsenite

of lead was discovered in quantity on the premises, and one or two details about the condition of the corpse persuaded a coroner's jury to rule death by misadventure. No suspicion fell upon Esther. The rumor of suicide moved Father Medavoy of the Cathedral of the Sacred Hearts of Jesus and Mary to refuse interment in hallowed ground. Esther boxed up the remains and shipped them to her sister in Michigan, accompanying them in a day coach. I never found out if she sought or found reunion with her other relations. I wonder frequently if Griffin's part in my impostiture had deprived him of his last shred of faith, or if he kept it and like Judas in his Easter sermon chose eternal damnation to punish himself for questioning. Either way his fate lies heavily upon me.

Dr. Lawrence Lazarus Little, proprietor of the Traveling Tabernacle, settled in California, and forty years later at the age of eighty-two became one of the first ministers to preach over the ether. On certain nights when the air was clear, his five-hundred-watt "Electric Pulpit" came crackling over my set in Los Angeles. The booming voice had grown reedy with time, and I realized then that that astonishing baritone had provided ninety percent of his message, taking the place of conviction. Griffin had seen past it at its peak.

Richard Freemason's eight-hundred-acre sheep ranch was broken up by his widow and sold to satisfy his creditors, including the State of Texas, to which he owed property taxes in the thousands. The largest parcel went to the brother of a bishop in Dublin, who took pleasure in stripping away all the Masonic symbols, including the brand.

I never heard what became of Captain Andrew Jackson Jordan of the Texas Rangers. I assume he retired, because Governor Ireland transferred the rest

of the Wichita Falls office to San Antonio shortly after the last of the Blue Bandannas was captured and
sentenced to hang, and Jordan had made no secret of
his opposition to committing all the Rangers' best men
to the bandit problem on the border at the expense of
the panhandle. I picture him living out the rest of his
days smoking his pipe on the front porch on some
small spread where he looked after his cousin.

Its abandonment by the Rangers, together with the
bad reputation left by Freemason, took Owen out of
the running for a railroad spur from Wichita Falls. It
passed south to create Amarillo, which promptly
became the principal city in a region the size of many
states. That should have been the end of Owen, but it
had demonstrated its tenacity before. The sheep trade,
with a shot in the arm from the newly passed fence-
cutting law, kept the town alive, at the cost of the saloon business; for some reason sheep hands in those
days were more conservative carousers than cowboys.
Freemason's house, I'm told, still stands—converted,
appropriately, into a county home for the insane.

I'm living out my time in a comfortable bungalow
with a view of a swimming pool, the latest in a series
of enthusiasms to claim Southern California. I don't
swim—one immersion is enough for one lifetime,
even if it's a better prospect than a buffalo wallow—
but the improbably blue water is pleasant to look at,
a rare luxury for a "movie," which is a noxious class
restricted by many landlords. Movies are employees
of the picture business. I make my rent peddling my
experience to producers, who admire to include an
old frontier lawman in press releases promoting their
westerns. I'm freelancing now. I had a nice billet with
United Artists, Chaplin and Pickford's outfit, but they
let me go when a newspaper hack in the pay of a rival

studio wrote that Page Murdock had been gunned down in Helena in 1884, and that I was an impostor. It wasn't the first time Blackthorne's harebrained ruse cast doubt on my identity; but the place is rotten with frauds, and I manage to avoid eviction by the grace of UA's less discriminating competitors. How long it will last I can't say. I'll be clay soon enough, so I have no worries about corporeal matters. My spiritual condition is something else.

I'm writing down my confessions. They'd fill a good-size trunk, and I have to sit on the old Wells, Fargo strongbox I keep them in to lock it. It's bolted to the floor to discourage theft. It's a small town, word gets around, and scenarists are always pestering me for a look, which means they want to loot them for ideas. A safe deposit box would be more convenient—at least I wouldn't have to guard the pages at night with the venerable Deane-Adams—but I chased too many bandits in the old days to place much faith in banks. Anyway, I'm writing not to be read, but for the sake of my immortal soul. I search the Bible for comfort, with its pages falling out of the worn-out binding, and I say my prayers every night, mostly for the dead and partly for myself, because I sent more than a few of them to hell and maybe one or two to heaven. My soul isn't pure.

Fielo Velasquez left a stain. I didn't put that knife in his hand, but I might have prevented him from taking it up. He was the right age, the right nationality, and I should have seen something in the mysterious way he came to work for Richard Freemason, especially after I read that coded message about the son of Blackthorne's old friend who had died a death in prison that should have been Freemason's. I don't know why Fielo waited so long, or why he chose that day of all days to take a father's revenge, except perhaps that he might have sensed that time was running short and that he was about to be cheated out of it. Old men are prescient, I know now. And like Griffin he'd followed the example set by Judas.

I suppose that puts Freemason's fate on my head as well, but I don't spend as much time praying for him as I do most of the others.

Colleen buried the old man in the cemetery maintained by the First Unitarian church. I don't know who presided, because I'd left by then. Fielo was barred, of course, from the Catholic, but a number of mourners came out for the service in support of the first widow of Owen, whose bereavement under the circumstances seemed to have removed her at least temporarily from that order of women that is accepted because of position but not respected. She had a carriage packed with luggage and left town directly from the graveside. Her late husband's legal firm in St. Louis sent someone out to supervise the disposition of the ranch and the house in town.

Luther Cherry's widow experienced the same social promotion, but of a more permanent nature. After a respectable year she married a Missouri state senator who went on to serve two terms in Congress and may be our next vice president, or a member of a railroad board of directors, which is the logical alternative. She may have been worth the preposterous expense of writing her by special delivery from Texas, at that. I feel no guilt for what happened to Cherry, but I ask forgiveness for maligning him afterward, necessary as it was to flush Freemason from cover.

These days I spend a lot of time thinking about Colleen Bower. We met a few times after Owen, but I lost her trail after Blackthorne died and Washington sliced his jurisdiction into several easily corruptible pieces. Some years ago I thought I recognized a familiar figure in a *Saturday Evening Post* piece about an old *gringa,* name unknown, who organized arms shipments to Pancho Villa from El Paso and delivered provisions to revolutionists hiding in the caves of Chihuahua from General Pershing's punitive expedition following the raid on Columbus, New Mexico. The artist's rendition taken from an American poster offering a reward for her capture resembled Colleen around the eyes, but her hair had gone gray and the desert sun had cracked her fair complexion, so I wasn't sure. Villa's men called her *Nuestra Madre de la Orilla:* Our Lady of the Border. U.S. authorities called her an enemy of the state. That sums her up in my opinion.

AUTHOR'S NOTE

The Word Out West

The motif of the gun-toting preacher is nothing new in the literature and cinema of the American frontier. Oxymoronic though he may seem, the figure of the white-collared man in black with Scripture in hand and a revolver on his hip recurs frequently in the tapestry of the New World's answer to the mythos of Greece and Rome, and he has a historical foundation. The author is pleased to provide an incomplete checklist of those works that have celebrated him:

Barton, Barbara. *Pistol Packin' Preachers: Circuit Riders of Texas*. Lanham, Maryland: A Republic of Texas Press Book, Taylor Trade Publishing, 2005.

Barton's account, with a foreword by the great Western novelist Elmer Kelton, provides an eminently readable history of itinerant preaching in our most western state, with anecdotes both harrowing and rollicking about the struggle to bring Christianity to the wilderness. An entertaining piece of cocktail-party conversation appears wherever the book falls open.

Phares, Ross. *Bible in Pocket, Gun in Hand: The Story of Frontier Religion*. Lincoln, Nebraska: Bison Books, The University of Nebraska Press, 1971.

First published in 1964, Phares' volume roams over the broader territory of the frontier, with a strong emphasis on the raw humor of ecclesiastical doings on the border of civilization. This is a book to pick up and read at random whenever the reader needs a lift.

Five Card Stud. Directed by Henry Hathaway, starring Dean Martin, Robert Mitchum, Inger Stevens, Roddy McDowall, and Katherine Justice. 1968.

A good old oater of a Western movie, this old-fashioned whodunit set against a backdrop of desert and plain pits gambler Martin, in vintage Rat Pack persona, against Mitchum's quick-on-the-draw minister with a private agenda. Critic Leonard Maltin calls it "probably Hathaway's worst Western," but that hollowed-out Bible with a pocket pistol concealed inside is worth the price of the rental. Shallow, but enormously entertaining.

The Gun and the Pulpit. Starring Marjoe Gortner.

Production details on this 1970s made-for-TV movie are nearly nonexistent, but Gortner, famous for a short time as a child evangelist, made an impression in an even shorter acting career as a gunfighter posing as a preacher. The film resurfaces occasionally under the title *The Gun and the Bible*, a simplistic choice possibly predicated on the belief that most viewers don't know what a pulpit is.

Heaven with a Gun. Directed by Lee H. Katzin, starring Glenn Ford, Carolyn Jones, Barbara Hershey, John Anderson, and David Carradine. 1969.

Ford, who was never anything less than stalwart, puts in a solid performance in the *Shane*-like role of a former man of violence compelled by circumstances to strap on a gunbelt under his frock coat. One of those stirring movies in which a cowed community is shamed by its spiritual advisor into taking its fate in its own hands. (John Carradine, David's father, deserves honorable mention for playing clergy so often—most memorably as the tragic Jim Casy in *The Grapes of Wrath*—as to qualify for common-law ordination.)

Pale Rider. Directed by Clint Eastwood, starring Clint Eastwood, Michael Moriarty, Carrie Snodgress, Christopher Penn, and John Russell. 1985.

Eastwood's spooky savior wears a clerical collar and answers to "Preacher," but he spouts more bullets than gospel in a nearly scene-for-scene plagiarism of *Shane*, with a heavy overlay of his earlier *High Plains Drifter*. Former *Lawman* star Russell is hypnotic in his last role, but it's a dreary film and misses all the subtlety of its inspiration.